Two by Muriel Spark

The Ballad of Peckham Rye

The Bachelors

A Delta Book · 1964

A Delta Book
Published by
Dell Publishing Co., Inc.
750 Third Avenue
New York 17, New York
All Rights Reserved
Reprinted by arrangement with J. B. Lippincott Company
The Ballad of Peckham Rye   Copyright © 1960 by Muriel Spark
The Bachelors   Copyright © 1960 by Muriel Spark
Delta ® TM 755118
Library of Congress Catalog Card Number 64-13656
Manufactured in the United States of America
Cover Design by Jerome Martin
First printing March, 1964

Contents

The Ballad of Peckham Rye

For
ROBIN
with love

Chapter 1

"Get away from here, you dirty swine," she said.

"There's a dirty swine in every man," he said.

"Showing your face round here again," she said.

"Now, Mavis, now, Mavis," he said.

She was seen to slam the door in his face, and he to press the bell, and she to open the door again.

"I want a word with Dixie," he said. "Now, Mavis, be reasonable."

"My daughter," Mavis said, "is not in." She slammed the door in his face.

All the same, he appeared to consider the encounter so far satisfactory. He got back into the little Fiat and drove away along the Grove and up to the Common where he parked outside the Rye Hotel. Here he lit a cigarette, got out, and entered the saloon bar.

Three men of retired age at the far end turned from the television and regarded him. One of them nudged his friend. A woman put her hand to her chin and turned to her companion with a look.

His name was Humphrey Place. He was that fellow that walked out on his wedding a few weeks ago. He walked across to the White Horse and drank one bitter.

7

Next he visited the Morning Star and the Heaton Arms. He finished up at the Harbinger.

The pub door opened and Trevor Lomas walked in. Trevor was seen to approach Humphrey and hit him on the mouth. The barmaid said, "Outside, both of you."

"It wouldn't have happened if Dougal Douglas hadn't come here," a woman remarked.

He was standing at the altar with Trevor, the best man, behind him. Dixie came up the aisle on the arm of Arthur Crewe, her stepfather. There must have been thirty-odd guests in the church. Arthur Crewe was reported in the papers next day as having said: "I had a feeling the wedding wouldn't come off." At the time he stepped up the aisle with Dixie, tall in her flounces, her eyes dark and open, and with a very little trace round the nose of a cold.

She had said, "Keep away from me. You'll catch my cold, Humphrey. It's bad enough me having a cold for the wedding."

But he said, "I want to catch your cold. I like to think of the germs hopping from you to me."

"I know where you got all these disgusting ideas from. You got them from Dougal Douglas. Well, I'm glad he's gone and there won't be him at the wedding to worry about in case he starts showing off the lumps on his head or something."

"I liked Dougal," Humphrey said.

Here they were, kneeling at the altar. The vicar was reading from the prayer book. Dixie took a lacy handkerchief from her sleeve and gently patted her nose. Humphrey noticed the whiff of scent which came from the handkerchief.

8

The vicar said to Humphrey, "Wilt thou have this woman to thy wedded wife?"

"No," Humphrey said, "to be quite frank I won't."

He got to his feet and walked straight up the aisle. The guests in the pews rustled as if they were all women. Humphrey got to the door, into his Fiat, and drove off by himself to Folkestone. It was there they had planned to spend their honeymoon.

He drove past the Rye, down Rye Lane round-about to Lewisham, past the Dutch House and on to Swanley, past Wrotham Hill and along the A20 to Ditton, where he stopped for a drink. After Maidstone he got through the Ashford by-pass and stopped again at a pub. He drove on to Folkestone, turning left at the Motel Lympne, where yellow headlamps of the French cars began to appear on the road as they had done before. He stayed in the hotel on the front in the double room booked for the honeymoon, and paid double without supplying explanations to the peering, muttering management.

"Outside," said the barmaid. Humphrey rose, finished his drink with a flourish, regarded his handsome hit face in the mirror behind the barmaid, and followed Trevor Lomas out into the autumn evening, while a woman behind them in the pub remarked, "It wouldn't have happened if Dougal Douglas hadn't come here."

Trevor prepared for a fight, but Humphrey made no move to retaliate; he turned up towards the Rye where his car was parked and where, beside it, Trevor had left his motor-scooter.

Trevor Lomas caught him up. "And you can keep away from round here," he said.

Humphrey stopped. He said, "You after Dixie?"

"What's that to you?"

Humphrey hit him. Trevor hit back. There was a fight. Two courting couples returning from the dusky scope of the Rye's broad lyrical acres stepped to the opposite pavement, leant on the railings by the swimming baths, and watched. Eventually the fighters, each having suffered equal damage to different features of the face, were parted by onlookers to save the intervention of the police.

After Humphrey had been sent away from the door, and the matter had been discussed, Dixie Morse, aged seventeen, daughter of the first G.I. bride to have departed from Peckham and returned, stood in her little room on the upper floor of 12 Rye Grove and scrutinised her savings book. As she counted she exercised her pretty hips, jerking them from side to side to the rhythm of *Pickin' a Chicken,* which tune she hummed.

Her mother came up the stairs. Dixie closed the book and said to her mother through the closed door, "Quite definitely I'm not taking up with him again. I got my self-respect to think of."

"Quite right," Mavis replied from the other room.

"He wasn't ever the same after he took up with Dougal Douglas," Dixie said through the wall.

"I liked Dougal," Mavis replied.

"I didn't like him. Trevor didn't like him," Dixie said.

Hearing the front-door bell, Dixie stood attentively. Her mother went down and said something to her stepfather. They were arguing as to who should go and answer the door. Dixie went out on the landing and saw her stepbrother Leslie walking along the ground-floor passage in the wrong direction.

"Leslie, open that door," Dixie said.

The boy looked up at Dixie. The bell rang again. Dixie's mother burst out of the dim-lit sitting-room.

"If it's him again I'll give him something to remember me by," she said, and opened the door. "Oh, Trevor, it's you, Trevor," she said.

"Good evening, Mavis," Trevor said.

Dixie returned rapidly to her room to comb her black hair and put on lipstick. When she came down to the sitting-room, Trevor was seated under the standard lamp, between Mavis and her stepfather, waiting for the television play to come to an end. Trevor had a strip of plaster on his face, close to the mouth.

The play came to an end. Mavis rose in her quick way and switched on the central light. Her husband, Arthur Crewe, smiled at everyone, adjusted his coat and offered Trevor a cigarette. Dixie set one leg across the other, and watched the toe of her shoe, which she wriggled.

"You'll never guess who came to the door this evening."

"Humphrey Place," said Trevor.

"You've seen him?"

"Seen him—I've just knocked his head off."

Dixie's stepfather switched off the television altogether, and pulled round his chair to face Trevor.

"I suppose," he said, "you did right."

"*Did* right," said Dixie.

"I *said* did. I didn't say done. Keep your hair on, girl."

Mavis opened the door and called, "Leslie, put the kettle on." She returned with her quick little steps to her chair. "You could have knocked me over," she said. "I was just giving Dixie her tea; it was, I should say, twenty past five and there was a ring at the bell. I said to Dixie, 'Whoever can that be?' So I went to the door, and lo and behold there he was on the doorstep. He said, 'Hallo, Mavis,' he said. I said, 'You just hop it, you.' He said, 'Can I see Dixie?' I said, 'You certainly can't,' I said. I said, 'You're a dirty swine. You remove yourself,' I said, 'and don't show your face again,' I said. He said, 'Come on, Mavis.' I said, 'Mrs. Crewe to you,' and I shut the door in his face." She turned to Dixie and said, "What about making a cup of tea?"

Dixie said, "If he thinks I would talk to him again, he's making a great mistake. What did he say to you, Trevor?"

Mavis got up and left the room, saying, "If you want anything done in this house you've got to do it yourself."

"Help your mother," said Arthur Crewe absently to Dixie.

"Did he say whether he's gone back to the same job?" Dixie said to Trevor.

Trevor put a hand on each knee and gave a laugh.

Dixie looked from the broad-faced Trevor to the amiable bald head of her stepfather, and started to weep.

"Well, he's come back again," Arthur said. "What you crying for?"

"Don't cry, Dixie," Trevor said.

Dixie stopped crying. Mavis came in with the tea.

Dixie said, "He's common. You only have to look at his sister. Do you know what Elsie did at her first dance?"

"No," said Mavis.

"Well, a fellow came up to her and asked her for a dance. And Elsie said, 'No, I'm sweating.' "

"Well, you never told me that before," Mavis said.

"I only just heard it. Connie Weedin told me."

Trevor gave a short laugh. "We'll run him out of Peckham like we run Dougal Douglas."

"Dougal went of his own accord, to my hearing," Arthur said.

"With a black eye," Trevor said.

Round at the old-fashioned Harbinger various witnesses of the fight were putting the story together. The barmaid said: "It was only a few weeks ago. You saw it in the papers. That chap who left the girl at the altar, that's him. She lives up the Grove. Crewe by name."

One landlady out of a group of three said, "No, she's a Dixie Morse. Crewe's the stepfather. I know because she works at Meadows Meade in poor Miss Coverdale's pool that was. Miss Coverdale told me about her. The fellow had a good position as a refrigerator engineer."

"Who was the chap that hit him?"

"Some friend of the girl's, I daresay."

"Old Lomas's boy. Trevor by name. Electrician. He was best man at the wedding."

"There was I," sang out an old man who was visible with his old wife on the corner bench over in the public bar, "waiting at the church, waiting at the church."

His wife said nothing nor smiled.

"Now then, dad," the barmaid said.

The old man took a draught of his bitter with a tremble of the elbow and a turn of the wrist.

Before closing time the story had spread to the surrounding public bars, where it was established that Hum-

13

phrey had called at 12 Rye Grove earlier in the evening.

Even in one of the saloon bars, Miss Connie Weedin heard of the reappearance of Humphrey Place, and the subsequent fight; and she later discussed this at length with her father who was Personnel Manager of Meadows, Meade & Grindley, and at present recovering from a nervous breakdown.

"Dixie's boy has come back," she said.

"Has the Scotch man come back?" he said.

"No, he's gone."

Outside the pub at closing time Nelly Mahone, who had lapsed from her native religion on religious grounds, was at her post on the pavement with her long grey hair blown by the late summer wind. There she commented for all to hear, "Praise be to God who employs the weak to confound the strong and whose ancient miracles we see shining even in our times."

Humphrey and Dixie were widely discussed throughout the rest of the week. The reappearance of the bridegroom was told to Collie Gould, aged eighteen, unfit for National Service, who retold it to the gang at the Elephant; and lastly by mid-morning break at Meadows Meade the occurrence was known to all on the floor such as Dawn Waghorn, cone-winder, Annette Wren, trainee-seamer, Elaine Kent, process-controller, Odette Hill, uptwister, Raymond Lowther, packer, Lucille Potter, gummer; and it was revealed also to the checking department and many of the stackers, the sorters, and the Office.

Miss Merle Coverdale, lately head of the typing pool, did not hear of it. Mr. Druce, lately Managing Director, did not hear of it. Neither did Dougal Douglas, the former Arts man, nor his landlady Miss Belle Frierne who had known all Peckham in her youth.

But in any case, within a few weeks, everyone forgot the details. The affair is a legend referred to from time to time in the pubs when the conversation takes a matrimonial turn. Some say the bridegroom came back repentant and married the girl in the end. Some say, no, he married another girl, while the bride married the best man. It is wondered if the bride had been carrying on with the best man for some time past. It is sometimes told that the bride died of grief and the groom shot himself on the Rye. It is generally agreed that he answered "No" at his wedding, that he went away alone on his wedding day and turned up again later.

Chapter 2

Dixie had just become engaged to marry Humphrey when Dougal Douglas joined the firm of Meadows, Meade & Grindley, manufacturers of nylon textiles, a small but growing concern, as Mr. V. R. Druce described it.

At the interview Mr. Druce said to Dougal, "we feel the time has come to take on an Arts man. Industry and the Arts must walk hand in hand."

Mr. Druce had formerly been blond, he was of large build. Dougal, who in the University Dramatics had taken the part of Rizzio in a play about Mary, Queen of Scots, leaned forward and put all his energy into his own appearance; he dwelt with a dark glow on Mr. Druce, he raised his right shoulder, which was already highly crooked by nature, and leaned on his elbow with a becoming twist of the body. Dougal put Mr. Druce through the process of his smile, which was wide and full of white young teeth; he made movements with the alarming bones of his hands. Mr. Druce could not keep his eyes off Dougal, as Dougal perceived.

"I feel I'm your man," Dougal said. "Something told me so when I woke first thing this morning."

"Is that so?" Mr. Druce said. "Is that so?"

"Only a hunch," said Dougal. "I may be wrong."

"Now look," said Mr. Druce, "I must tell you that we feel we have to see other candidates and can't come to any decision straight away."

"Quite," said Dougal.

At the second interview Mr. Druce paced the floor, while Dougal sat like a monkey-puzzle tree, only moving his eyes to follow Mr. Druce. "You'll find the world of Industry a tough one," Mr. Druce said.

Dougal changed his shape and became a professor. He leaned one elbow over the back of his chair and reflected kindly upon Mr. Druce.

"We are creating this post," said Mr. Druce. "We already have a Personnel Manager, Mr. Weedin. He needs an assistant. We feel we need a man with vision. We feel you should come under Weedin. But you should largely work on your own and find your own level, we feel. Of course you will be under Mr. Weedin."

Dougal leaned forward and became a television interviewer. Mr. Druce stopped walking and looked at him in wonder.

"Tell me," coaxed Dougal, "can you give me some rough idea of my duties?"

"It's up to you, entirely up to you. We feel there's a place for an Arts man to bring vision into the lives of the workers. Wonderful people. But they need vision, we feel. Motion study did marvels in the factory. We had a man from Cambridge advising on motion study. It speeded up our output thirty per cent. Movements required to do any given task were studied in detail and he worked out the simplest pattern of movement involving the least loss of energy and time."

"The least loss of energy and time!" Dougal commented.

"The least loss of energy and time," said Mr. Druce. "All our workers' movements are now designed to conserve energy and time in feeding the line. You'll see it on the posters all over the factory, 'Conserve energy and time in feeding the line.' "

"In feeding the line!" Dougal said.

"In feeding the line," Mr. Druce said. "As I say, this expert came from Cambridge. But we felt that a Cambridge man in Personnel wouldn't do. What we feel about you is you'll be in touch with the workers, or rather, as we prefer to say, our staff; you'll be in the know, we feel. Of course you'll find the world of Industry a tough one."

Dougal turned sideways in his chair and gazed out of the window at the railway bridge; he was now a man of vision with a deformed shoulder. "The world of Industry," said Dougal, "throbs with human life. It will be my job to take the pulse of the people and plumb the industrial depths of Peckham."

Mr. Druce said: "Exactly. You have to bridge the gap and hold out a helping hand. Our absenteeism," he said, "is a problem."

"They must be bored with their jobs," said Dougal in a split second of absent-mindedness.

"I wouldn't say bored," said Mr. Druce. "Not bored. Meadows Meade are building up a sound reputation with regard to their worker-staff. We have a training scheme, a recreation scheme, and a bonus scheme. We haven't yet got a pension scheme, or a marriage scheme, or a burial scheme, but these will come. Comparatively speaking we are a small concern, I admit, but we are expanding."

"I shall have to do research," Dougal mused, "into their

inner lives. Research into the real Peckham. It will be necessary to discover the spiritual well-spring, the glorious history of the place, before I am able to offer some impetus."

Mr. Druce betrayed a little emotion. "But no lectures on Art," he said, pulling himself together. "We've tried them. They didn't quite come off. The workers, the staff, don't like coming back to the building after working hours. Too many outside attractions. Our aim is to be one happy family."

"Industry is by now," declared Dougal, "a great tradition. Is that not so? The staff must be made conscious of that tradition."

"A great tradition," said Mr. Druce. "That is so, Mr. Douglas. I wish you luck, and I want you to meet Mr. Weedin while you're here." He pressed a button on his desk and, speaking into an instrument, summoned Mr. Weedin.

"Mr. Weedin," he said to Dougal, "is not an Arts man. But he knows his job inside out. Wonderful people, Personnel staff. If you don't tread on his toes you'll be all right with Personnel. Then of course there's Welfare. You'll have some dealings with Welfare, bound to do. But we feel you must find your own level and the job is what you make it—— Come in, Mr. Weedin, and meet Mr. Douglas, M.A., who has just joined us. Mr. Douglas has come from Edinburgh to take charge of human research."

If you look inexperienced or young and go shopping for food in the by-streets of Peckham it is as different from shopping in the main streets as it is from shopping in

Kensington or the West End. In the little shops in the Peckham by-streets, the other customers take a deep interest in what you are buying. They concern themselves lest you are cheated. Sometimes they ask you questions of a civil nature, such as: Where do you work? Is it a good position? Where are you stopping? What rent do they take off you? And according to your answer they may comment that the money you get is good or the rent you have to pay is wicked, as the case may be. Dougal, who had gone to a small grocer on a Saturday morning, and asked for a piece of cheese, was aware of a young woman with a pram, a middle-aged woman and an old man accumulating behind him. The grocer came to weigh the cheese.

"Don't you give him that," said the young woman; "it's sweating."

"Don't let him give you that, son," said the old man.

The grocer removed the piece of cheese from the scales and took up another.

"You don't want as much as all that," said the older woman. "Is it just for yourself?"

"Only for me," Dougal said.

"Then you want to ask for two ounces," she said. "Give him two ounces," she said. "You just come from Ireland, son?"

"No, Scotland," said Dougal.

"Thought he was Irish from his voice," commented the old man.

"Me too," said the younger woman. "Irish sounds a bit like Scotch like, to hear it."

The older woman said, "You want to learn some experience, son. Where you stopping?"

"I've got temporary lodgings in Brixton. I'm looking for a place round here."

The grocer forgot his grievances and pointed a finger at Dougal.

"You want to go to a lady up on the Rye, name of Frierne. She's got nice rooms; just suit you. All gentlemen. No ladies, she won't have."

"Who's she?" said the young woman. "Don't know her."

"Don't know Miss Frierne?" said the old man.

The older woman said, "She's lived up there all her life. Her father left her the house. Big furniture removers they used to be."

"Give me the address," said Dougal, "and I'll be much obliged."

"I think she charges," said the older woman. "You got a good position, son?"

Dougal leaned on the counter so that his high shoulder heaved higher still. He turned his lean face to answer. "I've just started at Meadows, Meade & Grindley."

"I know them," said the younger woman. "A nice firm. The girl Waghorn works there."

"Miss Frierne's rooms go as high as thirty, thirty-five shillings," remarked the older woman to the grocer.

"Inclusive heat and light," said the grocer.

"Excuse me," said the older woman. "She had meters put in the rooms, that I do know. You can't do inclusive these days."

The grocer looked away from the woman with closed eyes and opened them again to address Dougal.

"If Miss Frierne has a vacancy you'll be a lucky chap," he said. "Mention my name."

"What department you in?" said the old man to Dougal.

"The Office," said Dougal.

"The Office don't get paid much," said the man.

"That depends," the grocer said.

"Good prospects?" said the older woman to Dougal.

"Yes, fine," Dougal said.

"Let him go up Miss Frierne's," said the old man.

"Just out of National Service?" said the older woman.

"No, they didn't pass me."

"That would be his deformity," commented the old man, pointing at Dougal's shoulder.

Dougal nodded and patted his shoulder.

"You was lucky," said the younger woman and laughed a good deal.

"Could I speak to Miss Fergusson?" Dougal said.

The voice at the other end of the line said, "Hold on. I'll see if she's in."

Dougal stood in Miss Frierne's wood-panelled entrance hall, holding on and looking around him.

At last she came. "Jinny," Dougal said.

"Oh, it's you."

"I've found a room in Peckham. I can come over and see you if you like. How——"

"Listen, I've left some milk boiling on the stove. I'll ring you back."

"Jinny, are you feeling all right? Maria Cheeseman wants me to write her autobiography."

"It will be boiling over. I'll ring you back."

"You don't know the number."

But she had rung off.

Dougal left fourpence on the telephone table and went

up to his new room at the very top of Miss Frierne's house.

He sat down among his belongings, which were partly in and partly out of his zipper bag. There was a handsome brass bedstead with a tall railed head along which was gathered a muslin curtain. It was the type of bed which was becoming fashionable again, but Miss Frierne did not know this. It was the only item of furniture in the room for which she had apologised; she had explained it was only temporary and would soon be replaced by a new single divan. Dougal detected in this little speech a good intention, repeated to each newcomer, which never came off. He assured her that he liked the brass bed with its railings and knobs. Could he remove, perhaps, the curtain? Miss Frierne said, no, it needed the bit of curtain, and before long would be replaced by a single divan. But no, Dougal said, I like the bed. Miss Frierne smiled to herself that she had found such an obliging tenant. "Really, I do like it," Dougal said, "more than anything else in the room."

The two windows in the room pleased him, looking out on a lot of sky and down to Miss Frierne's long lawn and those of her neighbours; beyond them lay the back gardens belonging to the opposite street of houses, but these were neglected, overgrown and packed with junk and sheds for motor-bicycles, not neat like Miss Frierne's and the row of gardens on the near side, with their borders and sometimes a trellis bower.

He saw a little door, four feet high, where the attic ceiling met the wall. He opened it, and found a deep long cupboard using up the remainder of the roof-slope. Having stooped to enter the cupboard, Dougal found he could almost walk in it. He came out, pleased with his fairly useless cave, and started putting away his shirts in the dark painted chest of drawers. He stroked the ceiling, that part of it which sloped down within reach. Some white powdery distemper came off on his fingers. He went downstairs to telephone to Jinny. Her number was engaged.

The linoleum in his room was imitation parquetry and shone with polish. Two small patterned mats and one larger one made islands on the wide floor. Dougal placed a pile of his clothes on each island, then hauled it over the polished floor to the wardrobe. He unlocked his typewriter and arranged his belongings, as all his student-life in Edinburgh Jinny used to do for him. One day in their final year, at Leith docks, watching the boats, she had said: "I must bend over the rails. I've got that indigestion." Already, at this first stage in her illness, he had shown no sympathy. "Jinny, everyone will think you're drunk. Stand up." In the course of her illness she stopped calling him a crooked fellow, and instead became bitter, calling him sometimes a callous swine or a worm. "I hate sickness, not you," he had said. Still, at that time he had forced himself to visit her sometimes in the Infirmary. He got his degree, and was thought of as frivolous in the pubs, not being a Nationalist. Jinny's degree was delayed a year, he meanwhile spending that year in France and finally London, where he lived in Earl's Court and got through his money waiting for Jinny.

For a few weeks he spent much of his time in the flat of the retired actress and singer, Maria Cheeseman, in Chelsea, who had once shared a stage with an aunt of Jinny's.

24

He went to meet Jinny at last at King's Cross. She had bright high cheek-bones and brown straight hair. They could surely be married in six months' time. "I've to go into hospital again," said Jinny. "I've to have an operation this time. I've a letter to a surgeon in the Middlesex Hospital.

"You'll come and visit me there?" she said.

"No, quite honestly, I won't," Dougal said. "You know how I feel about places of sickness. I'll write to you every day."

She got a room in Kensington, went into hospital two weeks later, was discharged on a Saturday and wrote to tell Dougal not to meet her at the hospital and she was glad he had got the job in Peckham, and was writing Miss Cheeseman's life, and she hoped he would do well in life.

"Jinny, I've found a room in Peckham. I can come over and see you if you like."

"I've left some milk on the stove. I'll ring you back."

Dougal tried on one of his new white shirts and tilted the mirror on the dressing-table to see himself better. Already it seemed that Peckham brought out something in him that Earl's Court had overlooked. He left the room and descended the stairs. Miss Frierne came out of her front room.

"Have you got everything you want, Mr. Douglas?"

"You and I," said Dougal, "are going to get on fine."

"You'll do well at Meadows Meade, Mr. Douglas. I've had fellows before from Meadows Meade."

"Just call me Dougal," said Dougal.

"Douglas," she said, pronouncing it "Dooglass."

"No, *Dougal*—Douglas is my surname."

"Oh, Dougal Douglas. Dougal's the first name."

"That's right, Miss Frierne. What buses do you take for Kensington?"

"It's my one secret weakness," he said to Jinny.

"I can't help it," he said. "Sickness kills me."

"Be big," he said, "be strong. Be a fine woman, Jinny."

"Understand me," he said, "try to understand my fatal flaw. Everybody has one."

"It's time I had my lie-down," she said. "I'll ring you when I'm stronger."

"Ring me tomorrow."

"All right, tomorrow."

"What time?"

"I don't know. Some time."

"You would think we had never been lovers, you speak so coldly," he said. "Ring me at eleven in the morning. Will you be awake by then?"

"All right, eleven." He leaned one elbow on the back of his chair. She was unmoved. He smiled intimately. She closed her eyes.

"You haven't asked for my number," he said.

"All right, leave your number."

He wrote it on a bit of paper and returned south of the river to Peckham. There, as Dougal entered the saloon bar of the Morning Star, Nelly Mahone crossed the road in her rags crying, "Praise be to the Lord, almighty and eternal, wonderful in the dispensation of all his works, the glory of the faithful and the life of the just." As Dougal bought his drink, Humphrey Place came up and spoke to him. Dougal recalled that Humphrey Place, refrigerator engineer of Freeze-eezy's, was living in the room below his and had been introduced to him by Miss Frierne that morning. Afterwards Miss Frierne had told Dougal, "He is clean and go-ahead."

Chapter 3

"What d'you mean by different?" Mavis said.

"I don't know. He's just different. Says funny things. You have to laugh," Dixie said.

"He's just an ordinary chap," Humphrey said. "Nice chap. Ordinary."

But Dixie could see that Humphrey did not mean it. Humphrey knew that Douglas was different. Humphrey had been talking a good deal about Douglas during the past fortnight and how they sat up talking late at Miss Frierne's.

"Better fetch him here to tea one night," said Dixie's stepfather. "Let's have a look at him."

"He's too high up in the Office," Mavis said.

"He's on research," Dixie said. "He's brainy, supposed to be. But he's friendly, I'll say that."

"He's no snob," said Humphrey.

"He hasn't got nothing to be a snob about," said Dixie.

"*Anything*, not *nothing*."

"Anything," said Dixie, "to be a snob about. He's no better than us just because he's twenty-three and got a good job."

"But he's got to do his overtime for nothing," Mavis said.

"He's the same as what we are," Dixie said.

"You said he was different."

"Well, but no better than us. I don't know why you sit up talking at nights with him."

Humphrey sat up late in Dougal's room.

"My father's in the same trade. He puts himself down as a fitter. Same job."

"It is right and proper," Dougal said, "that you should be called a refrigerator engineer. It brings lyricism to the concept."

"I don't trouble myself about that," Humphrey said. "But what you call a job makes a difference to the Unions. My dad doesn't see that."

"Do you like brass bedsteads?" Dougal said. "We had them at home. We used to unscrew the knobs and hide the fag ends inside."

"By common law," Humphrey said, "a trade union has no power to take disciplinary action against its members. By common law a trade union cannot fine, suspend, or expel its members. It can only do so contractually. That is, by its rules."

"Quite," said Dougal, who was lolling on his brass bed.

"You can use your imagination," Humphrey said. "If a member is expelled from a union that operates a closed shop. . . ."

"Ghastly," said Dougal, who was trying to unscrew one of the knobs.

"But all that won't concern you much," Humphrey said. "What you want to know about for your human research is arbitration in trade disputes. There's the Conciliation Act 1896 and the Industrial Courts Act 1919, but you

29

wouldn't need to go into those. You might study the Industrial Disputes Order 1951. But you aren't likely to have a dispute at Meadows, Meade & Grindley. You might have an issue, though."

"Is there a difference?"

"Oh, a vast difference. Sometimes they take it to law to decide whether an issue or a dispute has arisen. It's been as far as the Court of Appeal. I'll let you have the books. Issue is whether certain employers should observe certain terms of employment. Dispute is any dispute between employer and employee as to terms of employment or conditions of labour."

"Terrific," Dougal said. "You must have given your mind to it."

"I took a course. But you'll soon get to know what's what in Industrial Relations."

"Fascinating," Dougal said. "Everything is fascinating, to me, so far. Do you know what I came across the other day? An account of the fair up the road at Camberwell Green."

"Fair?"

"According to Colburn's Calendar of Amusements 1840," Dougal said. He reached for his notebook, leaned on his elbow, heaved his high shoulder and read:

There is here, and only here, to be seen what you can see nowhere else, the lately caught and highly accomplished young mermaid, about whom the continental journals have written so ably. She combs her hair in the manner practised in China, and admires herself in a glass in the manner practised everywhere. She has had the best instructors in every peculiarity of education, and can argue on any given subject, from the most popular way of preserving plums, down to the necessity of a change of Ministers. She plays the harp in the new effectual style prescribed by Mr. Bocha, of whom we wished her to take lessons, but, having some mermaiden scruples, she begged to be provided with a less popular master. Being so clever and accomplished, she can't bear to be contradicted, and lately leaped out of her tub and floored a distinguished fellow of the Royal Zoological Society, who was pleased to be more curious and cunning than she was pleased to think agreeable. She has composed various poems for the periodicals, and airs with variations for the harp and piano, all very popular and pleasing.

Dougal gracefully cast his book aside. "How I should like to meet a mermaid!" he said.

"Terrific," Humphrey said. "You make it up?" he asked.

"No, I copied it out of an old book in the library. My research. Mendelssohn wrote his *Spring Song* in Ruskin Park. Ruskin lived on Denmark Hill. Mrs. Fitzherbert lived in Camberwell Grove. Boadicea committed suicide on Peckham Rye probably where the bowling green is now, I should imagine. But, look here, how would you like to be engaged to marry a mermaid that writes poetry?"

"Fascinating," Humphrey said.

Dougal gazed at him like a succubus whose mouth is its eyes.

Humphrey's friend, Trevor Lomas, had said Dougal was probably pansy.

"I don't think so," Humphrey had replied. "He's got a girl somewhere."

"Might be versatile."

"Could be."

Dougal said, "The boss advised me to mix with everybody in the district, high and low. I should like to mix with that mermaid."

Dougal put a record on the gramophone he had borrowed from Elaine Kent in the textile factory. It was a Mozart quartet. He slid the rugs aside with his foot and danced to the music on the bare linoleum, with stricken movements of his hands. He stopped when the record stopped, replaced the rugs, and said, "I must get to know some of the youth clubs. Dixie will be a member of a youth club, I expect."

"She isn't," Humphrey said rather rapidly.

Dougal opened a bottle of Algerian wine. He took his time, and with a pair of long tweezers fished out a bit of cork that had dropped inside the bottle. He held up the pair of tweezers.

"I use these," he said, "to pluck out the hairs which grow inside my nostrils, and which are unsightly. Eventually, I lose the tweezers, then I buy another pair."

He placed the tweezers on the bed. Humphrey lifted them, examined them, then placed them on the dressing table.

"Dixie will know," Dougal said, "about the youth clubs."

"No, she won't. She doesn't have anything to do with youth clubs. There are classes within classes in Peckham."

"Dixie would be upper-working," said Dougal. He poured wine into two tumblers and handed one to Humphrey.

"Well, I'd say middle class. It's not a snob business, it's a question of your type."

"Or lower-middle," Dougal said.

Humphrey looked vaguely as if Dixie was being insulted. But then he looked pleased. His eyes went narrow, his head lolled on the back of the chair, copying one of Dougal's habitual poses.

"Dixie's saving up," he said. "It's all she can think of, saving up to get married. And now what does she say? We can't go out more than one night a week so that I can save up too."

"Avarice," Dougal said, "must be her fatal flaw. We all have a fatal flaw. If she took sick, how would you feel, would she repel you?"

Dougal had taken Miss Merle Coverdale for a walk across the great sunny common of the Rye on a Saturday afternoon. Merle Coverdale was head of the typing pool at Meadows, Meade & Grindley. She was thirty-seven.

Dougal said, "My lonely heart is deluged by melancholy and it feels quite nice."

"Someone might hear you talking like that."

"You are a terror and a treat," Dougal said. "You look to me like an okapi," he said.

"A what?"

"An okapi is a rare beast from the Congo. It looks a little like a deer, but it tries to be a giraffe. It has stripes and it stretches its neck as far as possible and its ears are like a donkey's. It is a little bit of everything. There are only a few in captivity. It is very shy."

"Why do you say I'm like it?"

"Because you're so shy."

"Me shy?"

"Yes. You haven't told me about your love affair with Mr. Druce. You're too shy."

"Oh, that's only a friendship. You've got it all wrong. What makes you think it's a love affair? Who told you that?"

"I've got second sight."

He brought her to the gate of the park and was leading her through it, when she said,

"This doesn't lead anywhere. We'll have to go back the same way."

"Yes, it does," Dougal said, "it leads to One Tree Hill and two cemeteries, the Old and the New. Which would you prefer?"

"I'm not going into any cemetery," she said, standing with legs apart in the gateway as if he might move her by force.

Dougal said, "There's a lovely walk through the New Cemetery. Lots of angels. Beautiful. I'm surprised at you. Are you a free woman or are you a slave?"

She let him take her through the cemetery, eventually, and even pointed out to him the tower of the crematorium when it came into sight. Dougal posed like an angel on a grave which had only an insignificant headstone. He posed like an angel-devil, with his hump shoulder and gleaming smile, and his fingers of each hand widespread against the sky. She looked startled. Then she laughed.

"Enjoying yourself?" she said.

On the way back along the pastoral streets of trees and across the Rye she told him about her six years as mistress of Mr. Druce, about Mr. Druce's wife who never came to the annual dinners and who was a wife in name only.

"How they bring themselves to go on living together I don't know," she said. "There's no feeling between them. It's immoral."

34

She told Dougal how she had fallen out of love with Mr. Druce yet could not discontinue the relationship, she didn't know why.

"You've got used to him," Dougal said.

"I suppose so."

"But you feel," Dougal said, "that you're living a lie."

"I do," she said. "You've put my very thoughts into words.

"And then," she said, "he's got some funny ways with him."

Dougal slid his eyes to regard her without moving his face. He caught her doing the same thing to him.

"What funny ways? Come on, tell me," Dougal said. "There's no good telling the half and then stopping."

"No," she said. "It wouldn't be right to discuss Mr. Druce with you. He's your boss and mine, after all."

"I haven't seen him," Dougal said, "since the day he engaged me. He must have forgotten about me."

"No, he talked a lot about you. And he sent for you the other day. You were out of the office."

"What day was that?"

"Tuesday. I said you were out on research."

"So I was," said Dougal. "I was out on research."

"Nobody gets forgotten at Meadows Meade," she said. "He'll want to know about your research in a few weeks' time."

Dougal put his long cold hand down the back of her coat. She was short enough for his hand to reach quite a long way. He tickled her.

She wriggled and said, "Not in broad daylight, Dougal."

"In dark midnight," Dougal said, "I wouldn't be able to find my way."

She laughed from her chest.

"Tell me," Dougal said, "what is the choicest of Mr. Druce's little ways?"

"He's childish," she said. "I don't know why I stick to him. I could have left Meadows Meade many a time. I could have got into a big firm. You don't think Meadows Meade's a big firm, do you, by any chance? Because, if you do, let me tell you, Meadows Meade is by comparison very small. Very small."

"It looks big to me," Dougal said. "But perhaps it's the effect of all that glass."

"We used to have open-plan," she said. "So that you could see everyone in the office without the glass, even Mr. Druce. But the bosses wanted their privacy back, so we had the glass partitions put up."

"I like those wee glass houses," Dougal said. "When I'm in the office I feel like a tomato, getting ripe."

"*When* you're in the office."

"Merle," he said, "Merle Coverdale, I'm a hard-working fellow. I've got to be out and about on my human research."

They were moving up to the Rye where the buses blazed in the sun. Their walk was nearly over.

"Oh, we're soon here," she said.

Dougal pointed to a house on the right. "There's a baby's pram," he said, "stuck out on a balcony which hasn't any railings."

She looked and sure enough there was a pram perched on an open ledge only big enough to hold it, outside a second-floor window. She said, "They ought to be prosecuted. There's a baby in that pram, too."

"No, it's only a doll," Dougal said.

36

"How do you know?"

"I've seen it before. The house is a baby-carriage works. The pram is only for show."

"Oh, it gave me a fright."

"How long have you lived in Peckham?" he said.

"Twelve and a half years."

"You've never noticed the pram before?"

"No, can't say I have. Must be new."

"From the style of the pram, it can't be new. In fact the pram has been there for twenty-five years. You see, you simply haven't noticed it."

"I don't hardly ever come across the Rye. Let's walk round a bit. Let's go into the Old English garden."

"Tell me more," Dougal said, "about Mr. Druce. Don't you see him on Saturdays?"

"Not during the day. I do in the evening."

"You'll be seeing him tonight?"

"Yes, he comes for supper."

Dougal said, "I suppose he's been doing his garden all day. Is that what he does on Saturdays?"

"No. As a matter of fact, believe it or not, on Saturday mornings he goes up to the West End to the big shops. He goes up and down in the lifts. He rests in the afternoons. Childish."

"He must get some sexual satisfaction out of it."

"Don't be silly," she said.

"A nice jerky lift," said Dougal. "Not one of the new smooth ones but the kind that go yee-oo at the bottom." And Dougal sprang in the air and dipped with bent knees to illustrate his point, so that two or three people in the Old English garden turned to look at him. "It gives me," Dougal said, "a sexual sensation just to think of it. I can quite see the attraction those old lifts have for Mr. Druce. Yee-oo."

She said, "For God's sake lower your voice." Then she laughed her laugh from the chest, and Dougal pulled that blond front lock of her otherwise brown hair, while she gave him a hefty push such as she had not done to a man for twenty years.

He walked down Nunhead Lane with her; their ways parted by the prefabs at Costa Road.

"I'm to go to tea at Dixie's house tonight," he said.

"I don't know what you want to do with that lot," she said.

"Of course, I realise you're head of the typing pool and Dixie's only a wee typist," he said.

"You're taking me up wrong."

"Let's go for another walk if it's nice on Monday morning," he said.

"I'll be at work on Monday morning. I'll be down to work, not like you."

"Take Monday off, my girl," Dougal said. "Just take Monday off."

"Hallo. Come in. Pleased to see you. There's your tea," Mavis said.

The family had all had theirs, and Dougal's tea was set on the table. Cold ham and tongue and potato salad with bread and butter, followed by fruit cake and tea. Dougal sat down and tucked in while Mavis, Dixie and Humphrey Place sat round the table. When he had finished eating, Mavis poured the tea and they all sat and drank it.

"That Miss Coverdale in the pool," said Mavis, "is

working Dixie to death. I think she's trying to get Dixie out. Ever since Dixie got engaged she's been horrible to Dixie, hasn't she, Dixie?"

"It was quarter to four," said Dixie, "and she came up with an estimate and said 'priority'—just like that—priority. I said, 'Excuse me, Miss Coverdale, but I've got two priorities already.' She said, 'Well, it's only quarter to four.' '*Only*,' I said, '*only* quarter to four. Do you realise how long these estimates take? I'm not going without my tea-break, if that's what you're thinking, Miss Coverdale.' She said, 'Oh, Dixie, you're impossible,' and turned away. I jumped up and I said, 'Repeat that,' I said. I said——"

"You should have reported her to Personnel," Humphrey said. "That was your correct procedure."

"A disappointed spinster," Mavis said, "that's what she is."

"She's immoral with Mr. Druce, a married man, that I know for a fact," Dixie said. "So she's covered. You can't touch her, there's no point in reporting her to Personnel. It gets you down."

"Take Monday off," said Dougal. "Take Tuesday off as well. Have a holiday."

"No, I don't agree to that," Humphrey said. "Absenteeism is downright immoral. Give a fair week's work for a fair week's pay."

Dixie's stepfather, who had been watching the television in the sitting-room and who suddenly felt lonely, put his head round the door.

"Want a cup of tea, Arthur?" said Mavis. "Meet Mr. Douglas. Mr. Douglas, Mr. Crewe."

"Where's Leslie?" said Arthur Crewe.

"Well, he ought to be in. I let him go out," Mavis said.

"Because there's something going on out the front," Arthur said.

They all trooped through to the sitting-room and peered into the falling dusk, where a group of young people in their teens were being questioned by an almost equal number of policemen.

"The youth club," Mavis said.

Dougal immediately went out to investigate. As he opened the street door, young Leslie slid in as if from some concealment; he was breathless.

Dougal returned presently to report that the tyres of a number of cars parked up at the Rye had been slashed. The police were rounding up the teenage suspects. Young Leslie was chewing bubble-gum. Every now and then he pulled a long strand out of his mouth and let it spring back into his mouth.

"But it seems to me the culprits may have been children," Dougal said, "as much as these older kids."

Leslie stopped chewing for an instant and stared back at Dougal in such disgust that he seemed to be looking at Dougal through his nostrils rather than his eyes. Then he resumed his chewing.

Dougal winked at him. The boy stared back.

"Take that muck out of your mouth, son," said his father.

"You can't stop him," said his mother. "He won't listen to you. Leslie, did you hear what your father said?"

Leslie shifted the gum to the other side of his cheek and left the room.

Dougal looked out of the window at the group who were still being questioned.

"Two girls there come from Meadows Meade," he said. "Odette Hill, uptwister, and Lucille Potter, gummer."

"Oh, the factory lot are always mixed up in the youth club trouble," Mavis said. "You don't want anything to do with that lot." As she spoke she moved her hand across her perm, nipping each brown wave in turn between her third and index fingers.

Dougal winked at her and smiled with all his teeth.

Mavis said to Dixie in a whisper, "Has *he* gone?"

"Yup," said Dixie, meaning, yes, her stepfather had gone out for his evening drink.

Mavis went to the sideboard and fetched out a large envelope.

"Here we are again," Dixie said.

"She always says that," Mavis said.

"Well, Mum, you keep on pulling them out; every new person that comes to the house, out they come."

Mavis had extracted three large press cuttings from the envelope and handed them to Dougal.

Dixie sighed, looking at Humphrey.

"Why you two not go on out? Go on out to the pictures," Mavis said.

"We went out last night."

"But you didn't go to the pictures, I bet. Saving and pinching to get married, you're losing the best time of your life."

"That's what I tell her," said Humphrey. "That's what I say."

"Where'd you go last night?" Mavis said.

Dixie looked at Humphrey. "A walk," she said.

"What you make of these?" Mavis said to Dougal.

The cuttings were dated June, 1942. Two of them bore

large photographs of Mavis boarding an ocean liner. All announced that she was the first of Peckham's G.I. brides to depart these shores.

"You don't look a day older," Dougal said.

"Oh, go on," Dixie said.

"Not a day," said Dougal. "Anyone can see your mother's had a romantic life."

Dixie took her nail file out of her bag, snapped the bag shut and started to grate at her nails.

Humphrey bent forward in his chair, one hand on each knee, as if, by affecting intense interest in Mavis's affair, to compensate for Dixie's mockery.

"Well, it was romantic," Mavis said, "and it wasn't. It was both. Glub—that was my first husband—Glub was wonderful at first." Her voice became progressively American. "Made you feel like a queen. He sure was gallant. *And* romantic, as you say. But then . . . Dixie came along . . . everything sorta wenna pieces. We were living a lie," Mavis said, "and it was becoming sorta immoral to live together, not loving each other." She sighed for a space. Then pulling herself together she said, "So I come home."

"*Came* home," Dixie said.

"And got a divorce. And then I met Arthur. Old Arthur's a good sort."

"Mum's had her moments," Dixie said. "She won't let you forget that."

"More than what you'll have, if you go on like you do, putting every penny in the bank. Why, at your age I was putting all my wages what I had left over after paying my keep on my back."

"My own American dad pays my keep," Dixie said.

"He thinks he do, but it don't go far."

"Does. Doesn't," Dixie said.

"I better put the kettle on," Mavis said.

Dougal said then to Dixie, "I didn't never have no money of my own at your age." He heaved his shoulder and glittered his eyes at her, and she did not dare to correct him. But when Humphrey laughed she turned to him and said, "What's the joke?"

"Dougal here," he said, "he's your match."

Mavis came back and switched on the television to a cabaret. Her husband returned to find Dougal keeping the cabaret company with a dance of his own in the middle of their carpet. Mavis was shrieking with joy. Humphrey was smiling with closed lips. Dixie sat also with closed lips, not smiling.

On Saturday mornings, as on Sundays, the gentlemen in Miss Frierne's establishment were desired to make their own beds. On his return at eleven o'clock on Saturday night Dougal found at note in his room.

To-day's bed was a landlady's delight. Full marks in your end-of-term report!

Dougal stuck it up on the mirror of his dressingtable and went downstairs to see if Miss Frierne was still up. He found her in the kitchen, sitting primly up to the table with half a bottle of stout.

"Any letters for me?"

"No, Dougal."

"There should have been a letter."

"Never mind. It might come on Monday."

43

"Tell me some of your stories."

"You've heard them all, I'm sure." He had heard about the footpads on the Rye in the old days; about the minstrels in the street, or rather carriageway as Miss Frierne said it was called then. She sipped her stout and told him once more of her escapade with a girl called Flo, how they had hired a cab at Camberwell Green and gone up to the Elephant for a drink and treated the cabby to two-penn'orth of gin, and returned without anyone at home being the wiser.

"You must have had some courting days," Dougal said.

But her narrow old face turned away in disdain at the suggestion, for these were early days in their friendship, and it was a full month before Miss Frierne, one evening when she had finished her nourishing stout with a sigh and got out the gin bottle, told Dougal how the Gordon Highlanders were stationed at Peckham during the First War; how it was a question among the young ladies whether the soldiers wore anything underneath their kilts; how Miss Frierne at the ripe age of twenty-seven went walking with one of the Highlanders up to One Tree Hill; how he turned to her and said, "My girl, I know you're all bloody curious as to what we have beneath the kilt, and I forth-with propose to satisfy your mind on the subject"; how he then took her hand and thrust it under his kilt; and how she then screamed so hard, she had a quinsy for a week.

But in the meantime when Dougal, at the end of his second week at Miss Frierne's, said, "You must have had some courting days," she turned her narrow pale face away from him and indicated by various slight movements of her bony body that he had gone too far.

Eventually she said, "Did Humphrey come in with you?"

"No, I left him round at Dixie's."

"I wanted to ask his private advice about something."

"Anything I can do? I give rare advice."

She was still offended. "No, thank you. I wish to ask Humphrey privately. Do I hear rain?"

Dougal went to bed and the rain danced on the roof above his head. A key clicked in the front door and Humphrey's footsteps, climbing carefully, rose to the first landing. Humphrey paused on the landing, a long pause, as if he were resting from some effort. Then Humphrey's steps fumbled up on the second flight. Either he was drunk or carrying a heavy weight, for he staggered at the top, just outside Dougal's door.

The long cupboard in Dougal's bedroom gave out a loud tom-tom as the rain beat on the low roof within, and together with this sound was discernible that of Humphrey staggering along the short passage to his own room.

Dougal woke again at the very moment, it seemed, that the rain stopped. And at this very moment a whisper and a giggle came from the direction of his cupboard. He switched on his light and got up. The cupboard was empty. Just as he was going to shut the small door again, there was a slight scuffle. He opened the door, put his head in, and found nothing. He returned to bed and slept.

On Monday morning Dougal got his letter. Jinny had finished with him. He went into the offices of Meadows, Meade & Grindley and typed out some of his notes. Then, at the morning tea-break, he walked over to the long, long factory canteen and asked especially for Odette Hill and Lucille Potter. He was told they were not at work that morning. "Taking the day off. Foreman's mad. Absenteeism makes him mad." He had a bun and a cup of tea, then another bun. A bell rang to mark the end of the tea-break. The men disappeared rapidly. A few girls loitered, as on principle, talking with three of the women who served the canteen. Dougal put his head on his arms in full view of these few girls, and wept.

"What's the matter with him?"

"What's the matter, son?" said a girl of about sixteen whom Dougal, on looking up, found to be Dawn Waghorn, one of the cone-winders whose movements when winding the cone, as laid down by the Cambridge expert, had seemed to Dougal, when he had been taken round the floors, very appealing. Dougal put down his head and resumed his weeping.

Dawn patted his poor shoulder. He slightly raised his head and shook it sadly from side to side. A woman came round from the canteen bar with a clean-folded oven cloth which she held out to him. "Here, dry your eyes before anyone sees you," she said.

"What's the matter, mate?" said another girl. She said, "Here's a hanky." She was Annette Wren who was in training for seaming. She was giggling most heartlessly.

"I've lost my girl," Dougal said, as he blew his nose on the oven cloth.

Elaine Kent, who was well on in her twenties, an experienced controller of process, turned on Annette Wren and told her to shut her mouth, what was there to laugh at?

The two other canteen women came round to Dougal, and he was now surrounded by women. Elaine Kent opened her bag and took out a comb. With it she combed

Dougal's hair as it moved with his head slowly from side to side.

"You'll get another girl," said one of the canteen women, Milly Lloyd by name.

Annette giggled again. Dawn slapped her face and said, "You're ignorant. Can't you see he's handicapped?"

Whereupon Annette burst into tears.

"Keep your head still," said Elaine. "How can I comb you if you keep moving your head?"

"It calms you down, a good comb," remarked one of the canteen.

Milly Lloyd was looking for a fresh handkerchief for Annette whose sobs were tending towards the hysterical.

"How did you lose your girl?" said Dawn.

"I've got a fatal flaw," Dougal said.

Dawn assumed this to be his deformed shoulder, which she now stroked. "It's a shame," she said. "Little no-good bitch I bet she is."

Suddenly Merle Coverdale appeared at the door in the long distance and started walking towards the group.

"Office," whispered Milly, "typing pool," and returned behind the canteen bar.

Merle shouted along the length of the canteen as she approached. "Tea for Mr. Druce, please. He was out. Now he's come in. He wants some tea." Then she saw the group round Dougal. "What the hell's going on?" she said.

"Migraine," Dougal said sadly. "A headache."

"You should all be back on the floor," Merle said to the girls. "There's going to be trouble."

"Who you to talk to us like that?"

"Who's she, coming it over us?"

And so Merle could do nothing with them. She said meaningfully to Dougal,

"I had a headache myself this morning. Came into work late. I went for a brisk walk on the Rye. All by myself."

"I dimly recall arranging to meet you there," Dougal said. "But I was prevented."

Merle gave him a hostile look and said to the canteen women, "What about that tea?"

Milly Lloyd put a cup of tea into Dougal's hand. Merle walked off, bearing Mr. Druce's tea, moving her neck slightly back and forth as she walked all the long length of the canteen. Annette took a cup of tea and, as she gulped it, tried also to express her rage against the girl who had slapped her. As Dougal sipped his tea, young Dawn stroked his high shoulder and said, never mind, it was a shame, while Elaine combed his hair. It was curly hair but cut quite short. Nevertheless she combed it as if it had been as long as the Laughing Cavalier's.

Dixie sat with Humphrey, Dougal and Elaine Kent in Costa's Café. Dixie yawned. Her eyes were sleepy. The only reason she had denied herself an early night was that Dougal was paying for the supper.

"I've felt tired all day," she said. She addressed the men, ignoring Elaine as she had done all evening, because Elaine was factory, even though Elaine was high up in process-control. After a trial period Elaine likewise confined her remarks to the men.

"Look what's just come in," Elaine said. Tall Trevor Lomas had just come in. He sat at the nearest table, with his head and shoulders turned away from Dougal's party, and stared out of the window. Trevor Lomas was at this time employed as an electrician by the Borough.

Trevor turned his head sleepily and permitted an eye to rest on Humphrey for a small second. Humphrey said "Hallo." Trevor did not reply.

Trevor's girl arrived presently, tall and copper-tinted, with a tight short black skirt and much green eye-shadow. "Hi, snake," said Trevor. "Hi," said the girl, and sat down beside him.

Dixie and Elaine stared at the girl as she slid out of her coat and let it fall on the back of her chair. They stared as if by duty, and watched every detail. The girl was aware of this, and seemed to expect it.

Then Trevor pushed back his chair, still seated, so that he half-faced Humphrey's party. He said to his girl in a loud voice: "Got your lace hanky on you, Beauty?"

Beauty did not reply. She was holding up a small mirror, putting on lipstick with care.

"Because," said Trevor, "I'm going to cry." He took his large white handkerchief out of his top pocket and flourished it before each eye in turn. "Going to cry my eyes out, I am," said Trevor, "because I've lost me girl. Hoo, I've lost me girl."

Beauty laughed a great deal. The more she laughed the more noisily did Trevor continue. He laid his head on the table and affected to sob. The girl rocked in her chair, her newly-painted lips open wide apart.

Then Dixie started to laugh.

Dougal shoved his chair back and stood up. Elaine jumped up and held his arm.

"Let be," she said.

Humphrey, whom the story of Dougal's weeping in the

canteen had not yet reached, said to Dixie, "What's up?"

Dixie could not tell him for laughing.

"Let be, mate," Elaine said to Dougal.

Dougal said to Trevor, "I'll see you up on the Rye outside the tennis court."

Elaine walked over to Trevor and gave him a push. "Can't you see he's deformed?" she said. "Making game of a chap like that, it's ignorant."

Dougal, whose deformed shoulder had actually endowed him with a curious speciality in the art of fighting, in that he was able to turn his right wrist at an extraordinary back-hand outward angle and to get a man by the throat as with a claw, did not at that moment boast of the fact.

"Cripple as I am," he merely said, "I'll knock his mean wee sex-starved conceited low and lying L.C.C. electrician's head off."

"Who's sex-starved?" Trevor said, standing up.

Two youths who had been sitting by the window moved over the better to see. A Greek in an off-white coat appeared, and pointed to a telephone receiver which stuck out of the wall behind him in the passageway to the dim kitchen.

"I'll use that phone," he said.

Trevor gave him one of his long sleepy looks. Then he gave one of them to Dougal.

"Who's sex-starved?" he said.

"You are," Dougal said, while counting his money to pay the bill. "And I'll see you on the Rye within the quarter hour."

Trevor walked out of the café and Beauty hastily wriggled herself into her coat and tripped out after him. After them both went the Greek, but Trevor's motor-scooter had just moved off.

"Hasn't paid for coffee," said the Greek, returning. "What name and address he is, please?"

"No idea," Dougal said. "I don't mix with him."

The Greek turned to Humphrey. "I seen you here before with that fellow."

Humphrey threw half-a-crown on the table, and, as the four departed, the Greek slammed his glass doors behind them as hard as he judged the glass would stand up to.

The two girls got into Humphrey's car, but he at first refused to drive them up to the Rye. Dougal stood and argued on the pavement.

Humphrey said, "No, not at all. Don't go. Don't be a fool, Dougal. Let it pass. He's ignorant."

"All right, I'll walk," Dougal said.

"I'm going to send Trevor Lomas home," Humphrey said. He left Dougal and started up the car and drove off with the girls, Dixie in front and Elaine behind agitating, too late, to be let out.

Dougal arrived at the tennis courts six minutes later. Some seconds before he arrived he had heard a sound as of women screaming.

Between two distant lamp-posts, in their vague oblique light, a group was gathered. Dougal discerned Humphrey and Trevor with a strange youth called Collie who was without a coat and whose shirt was unbuttoned, exposing his chest to the night air. These figures were apparently molesting three further figures who turned out to be Dixie, Elaine, and Beauty, who were screaming. Soon it appeared that the men were not molesting but restraining them. Dixie had a long-strapped shoulder bag with which she was attempting to lay about her, largely in the direction of Elaine. Elaine, who was at present in the grip of Trevor, managed to dig Beauty's leg with her steel stiletto heel. Beauty wailed and struggled in Humphrey's grip.

"What's going on?" Dougal said.

Nobody took any notice of him. He went and hit Trevor in the face. Trevor let go of Elaine so that she fell heavily against Beauty. Meanwhile Trevor hit out at Dougal, who staggered backwards into Humphrey. Beauty wailed louder, and struggled harder. Elaine recovered herself and used her freedom to kick with her stiletto heel at Trevor. Dixie, meanwhile, was attempting to release herself from the grasp of that strange youth, Collie, with the bared chest, by biting the arm that held her. The screams grew louder. Dougal's eyes were calculating his chance of coming to adequate terms with Trevor Lomas amidst the confusion when a curious thing happened.

The confusion stopped. Elaine started to sing in the same tone as her screaming, joylessly, and as if in continuation of it. The other girls, seeming to take a signal from her, sidled their wails into a song,

> Sad to say I'm on my way,
> I got a little girl in Kingston Town

meanwhile casting their eyes fitfully over the Rye beyond the trees.

The strange youth let go of Dixie and began to jive with Elaine. In a few seconds everyone except Dougal was singing, performing the twisting jive, merging the motions of the fight into those of the frantic dance. Dougal saw Humphrey's face as his neck swooped upwards. It was frightened. Dixie's expression was, with a decided effort, bright. So was Elaine's. A one-sided smile on the face of the strange boy, and the fact that, as he bent and twisted in the jive, he buttoned up his shirt, made Dougal look round outside the group for the cause of this effect. He saw it immediately. Two policemen were quite close to them now. They must have been observed at a distance of three minutes' police-pace when Elaine had started to sing and the signal had gone round.

"What you think this is—a dance hall?"

"No, constable. No, inspector. Just having a dance with the girls. Just going home, mate."

"Well, *go* home. Get a move on. Out of the park, the lot of you."

"It was Dixie," said Humphrey to Dougal on the way home, "that started the fight. She was over-tired and worked up. She said that tart of Trevor's was giving her looks. She went up to the girl and said, 'Who you looking at?' and then the girl *did* give her a look. Then Dixie let fly with her handbag. That's how it all began."

Rain started to fall as they turned up past the old Quaker cemetery. Nelly Mahone took a green-seeming scarf from a black bag and placed it over her long grey hair. She cried: "The meadows are open and the green herbs have appeared, and the hay is gathered out of the mountain. The wicked man fleeth when no man pursueth, but the just, bold as a lion, shall be without dread."

"Pleasant evening, though a bit wet," Dougal said.

Nelly looked round after him.

Up in his room Dougal poured Algerian wine and remarked as he passed a glass to Humphrey,

"The cupboards run the whole length of the attic floor."

Humphrey put the glass on the floor at his feet and looked up at Dougal.

"There was a noise in the cupboard," Dougal said, "the night before last. It went creak-oop, creak-oop. I thought it came from my cupboard here, but I think maybe it didn't. I think maybe it came from your cupboard through the wall. Creak-oop." Dougal bent his knees apart, then sprang up in the air. He repeated this several times. "Creak-oop," he said.

Humphrey said, "It's only on wet Saturday nights when we can't go up on the Rye."

"Isn't she heavy to carry upstairs?" Dougal said.

Humphrey looked alarmed. "Did it sound as if I was carrying her upstairs?"

"Yes. Better to let her walk up in her stocking feet."

"No, she did that once. The old woman came out and nearly caught us."

"Better to lie in the bed than in the creaky cupboard," Dougal said. "The chap in the room below will hear it."

"No, the old woman came up one night when we were in the bed. We were nearly caught. Dixie had to run and hide in the cupboard."

Humphrey lifted his glass of wine from the floor by his feet and drank it in one gulp.

"Don't worry yourself," Dougal said.

"It's a worry what to do. All right on fine Saturday nights; we can go up on the Rye and Dixie gets home about half-past eleven. But if it starts to rain we come back here. I don't see why not, I pay for the room. But there's the difficulty of getting her up, then down again in the morning while the old woman's at early church. Then she has to pay her brother Leslie five shillings a time to let her in quietly. And she worries about that, does Dixie. She's a great saver, is Dixie."

"It's a tiring occupation, is saving," Dougal said. "Dixie's looking tired."

"Yes, as a matter of fact she does lie awake worrying. And there's no need to worry. Terrible at seventeen. I said, 'What you think you'll be like in ten years' time?' "

"When are you getting married?" Dougal said.

"September. Could do before. But Dixie wants a certain sum. She has her mind set to a certain sum. It keeps her awake at night."

"I advised her to take Monday morning off," Dougal said. "Everyone should take Mondays off."

"Now I don't agree to that," Humphrey said. "It's immoral. Once you start absenting yourself you lose your self-respect. *And* you lose the support of your unions; they won't back you. Of course the typists haven't got a union. As yet."

"No?" said Dougal.

"No," Humphrey said, "but it's a question of principle."

Dougal bent his knees apart as before and leapt into the air. "Creak-oop, creak-oop," he said.

Humphrey laughed deeply with his head thrown back. He stopped when a series of knocks started up from the floor.

"Chap downstairs," Dougal said, "knocks on his ceiling with a broom handle. He doesn't like my wee dances." He performed his antic three times more, shouting, "Creakoop."

Humphrey cast his head back and laughed, so that Dougal could see the whole inside of his mouth.

"I have a dream at nights," Dougal said, pouring the

wine, "of girls in factories doing a dance with only the movements of their breasts, bottoms and arms as they sort, stack, pack, check, cone-wind, gum, uptwist, assemble, seam and set. I see the Devil in the guise of a chap from Cambridge who does motion-study, and he's the choreographer. He sings a song that goes, 'We study in detail the movements requisite for any given task and we work out the simplest pattern of movement involving the least loss of energy and time.' While he sings this song, the girls are waggling and winding, like this——" and Dougal waggled his body and wove his arms intricately. "Like Indian dancing, you know," he said.

"And," said Dougal, "of course this choreographer is a projection of me. I was at the University of Edinburgh myself, but in the dream I'm the Devil and Cambridge."

Humphrey smiled, looked wise, and said, "Inhuman"; which three things he sometimes did when slightly at a loss.

Chapter 4

Miss Merle Coverdale opened the door of her flat on Denmark Hill, and admitted Mr. Druce in the early evening of midsummer's day. He took off his hat and hung it on a peg in her entrance-hall which was the shape and size of a small kitchen table, and from the ceiling of which hung a crystal chandelier. Mr. Druce followed Merle into the sitting-room. So far he had not spoken, and still without a word, while Merle took up her knitting by the two-bar electric heater, he opened the door of a small sideboard and extracted a bottle of whisky which he lifted up to the light. Opening another compartment of the sideboard he took out a glass. He poured some whisky into it and from a syphon which stood on a tray on the sideboard splashed soda-water into his drink. Then, "Want some?" he said.

"No, thanks."

He sighed and brought his drink to a large chair opposite Merle's smaller one.

"No," she said, "I've changed my mind. I think I feel like a whisky and ginger."

He sighed and went to the sideboard, where, opening a drawer, he extracted a bottle-opener. He stooped to the cupboard and found a bottle of ginger ale.

"No, I'll have gin and tonic. I think I feel like a gin and tonic."

He turned, with the bottle-opener in his hand, and looked at her.

"Yes, I feel like a gin and tonic."

And so he prepared the mixture and brought it to her. Then, sitting down, he took off his shoes and put on a pair of slippers which lay beside the chair.

Presently he looked at his watch. At which Merle put down her knitting and switched on the television. A documentary travel film was in progress, and in accompaniment to this they talked.

"Drover Willis's," he said, "have started on their new extension."

"Yes, you told me the other day."

"I see," he said, "they are advertising for automatic weaver instructors and hands. They are going to do made-up goods as well. They are advertising for ten twin-needle flat-bed machinists, also flat-lock machinists and instructors. They must be expanding."

"Four, five, six," she said, "purl two, seven, eight."

"I see," he said, "they are advertising for an Arts man."

"Well, what do you expect? It was recommended at the Conference, wasn't it?"

"Yes, but remember, Merle, we were the first in the area to adopt that recommendation. Did he come into the office today?"

"No."

"Tell him I want to see him, it's time we had a report. I've only seen him three times since he started. Weedin wants a report."

"Remind me in the morning on the business premises,

Vincent," she said. "I don't bring the office into my home, as you know."

"Weedin hasn't seen him for a week. Neither Welfare nor Personnel can get word of him."

She went to clatter dishes in the scullery. Mr. Druce got up and began to lay the table with mats, knives and forks which he took out of the sideboard. Then he went out into the hall and from his coat pocket took a bottle of stomach tablets which he placed on the table together with the pepper and salt.

Merle brought in some bread. Mr. Druce took a bread-knife from the drawer and looked at her. Then he placed the knife beside the bread on the board.

"The Brussels are not quite ready," she said, and she sat in her chair and took up her knitting. He perched on the arm. She pushed him with her elbow in the same movement as she was using for her knitting. He tickled the back of her neck, which she put up with for a while. But suddenly he pinched the skin of her neck. She screamed.

"Sh-sh," he said.

"You hurt me," she said.

"No, I was only doing this." And he pinched her neck again.

She screamed and jumped from the chair.

"The Brussels are ready," she said.

He turned off the television when she brought in the meal. "Bad for the digestion while you're eating," he said.

They did not speak throughout the meal.

Afterwards he stood with her in the red-and-white scullery, and looked on while she washed up. She placed the dishes in a red drying-rack while he dried the knives and forks. These he carried into the living-room and put away in their separate compartments in the drawer of the side-board. As he put away the last fork he watched Merle bring in a tray with coffee cups.

Merle switched on the television and found a play far advanced. They watched the fragment of the play as they drank their coffee. Then they went into the bedroom and took off their clothes in a steady rhythm. Merle took off her cardigan and Mr. Druce took off his coat. Merle went to the wardrobe and brought out a green quilted silk dressing-gown. Mr. Druce went to the wardrobe and found his blue dressing-gown with white spots. Merle took off her blouse and Mr. Druce his waistcoat. Merle put the dressing-gown over her shoulders and, concealed by it, took off the rest of her clothes, with modest gestures. Mr. Druce slid his braces and emerged from his trousers. These he folded carefully and, padding across the room to the window, laid them on a chair. He made another trip bearing his waistcoat and jacket which he placed over the back of the chair.

They stayed in bed for an hour, in the course of which Merle twice screamed because Mr. Druce had once pinched and once bit her. "I'm covered with marks as it is," she said.

Mr. Druce rose first and put on his dressing-gown. He went to wash and returned very soon, putting a wet irritable hand round the bedroom door. Merle said, "Oh, isn't there a towel?" and taking a towel from a drawer, placed it in his hand.

When he returned she was dressed.

She went into the scullery and put on the kettle while he put on his trousers and went home to his wife.

A western breeze blew over the Rye and it was midsummer night, a Saturday. Humphrey carried the two tartan rugs from his car while Dixie walked by his side, looking to left and right and sometimes turning to see if the path was clear of policemen.

Dixie said, "I'm cold."

He said, "It's a warm night."

She said, "I'm cold."

He said, "We've got two rugs."

She walked on beside him until they came to their usual spot under a tree behind the hedge of the Old English garden.

Humphrey spread a rug and she sat down upon it. She lifted the fringe and started to pull at it, separating the matted threads.

He spread the other rug over her legs and lay leaning on his elbow beside her.

"My mum got suspicious the other night," she said. "Leslie told her I was stopping over Camberwell after the dance with Connie Weedin, but she got suspicious. And when I got in she asked me all sorts of questions about the dance. I had to make them up."

"Sure you can trust Leslie?"

"Well, I give him five shillings a week. I think it should be three shillings weeks when I don't stop out all night. But he's greedy, Leslie is."

Humphrey pulled her towards him, and started to unbutton her coat. She buttoned it up again. "I'm cold," she said.

"Oh, come on, Dixie," he said.

"Connie Weedin got an increment," she said. "I've got to wait for my increment till August. I only found out through the girl that does the copy die-stamp operation and had the staff salaries' balance sheet to do. Connie Weedin does the same job as what I do and she's only been there six months longer. It's only because her father's Personnel. I'm going to take it up with Miss Coverdale."

Humphrey pulled her down towards him again and kissed her face.

"What's the matter?" he said. "There's something the matter with you."

"I'm going to take Monday off," she said. "They appreciate you more if you stop away now and again."

"Well, frankly and personally," Humphrey said, "I think it's an immoral thing to do."

"Fifteen shilling rise, less tax, nine and six in Connie Weedin's packet," she said, "and I've got to wait to August. And they're all in it together. And if I don't get satisfaction from Miss Coverdale, who is there to go to? Only Personnel, and that's *Mr.* Weedin. Naturally he's going to cover up for his daughter. And if I go above him to Mr. Druce he'll only send me back to Miss Coverdale, because you know what's between *them*."

"When we're married you won't have to worry about any of them. We can get married Saturday week if you like."

"No, I don't like. What about the house? There's got to be money down for the house."

"There's money down for the house," he said.

"What about my spin-dryer?"

"Oh, to hell with your spin-dryer."

62

"That fifteen shillings less tax that's due to me," she said, "could have gone in the bank. If it's due to her it's due to me. Fair's fair."

He pulled the top rug up to her chin and under it started to unbutton her coat.

She sat up.

"There's something wrong with you," he said. "We should have gone dancing instead. It wouldn't have cost much."

"You're getting too sexy," she said. "It's through you having to do with Dougal Douglas. He's a sex maniac. I was told. He's immoral."

"He isn't," Humphrey said.

"Yes he is, he talks about sex quite open, any time of the day. Girls and sex."

"Why don't you relax like you used to do?" he said.

"Not unless you give up that man. He's putting ideas in your head."

"You've done plenty yourself to put ideas in my head," he said. "I didn't used to need to look far to get ideas, when you were around. Especially up in the cupboard."

"Repeat that, Humphrey."

"Lie down and relax."

"Not after what you said. It was an insult."

"I know what's the matter with you," he said. "You're losing all your sex. It's all this saving up to get married and looking to the lolly all the time, it takes the sex out of a girl. It stands to reason, it's only psychological."

"You must have been talking it over with Dougal Douglas," she said. "You wouldn't have thought of that by yourself."

She stood up and brushed down her coat. He folded up the rugs.

"I won't be talked about, it's a let-down," she said.

"Who's talked about you?" he said.

"Well, if you haven't talked about me, you've been listening to *him* talking."

"Let me tell you something," he said. "Dougal Douglas is an educated man."

"My mum's uncle's a teacher and he doesn't act like him. He doesn't cry his eyes out like Dougal did in our canteen." Dixie laughed. "He's a pansy."

"That's just his game. You don't know Dougal. I bet he wasn't crying really."

"Yes, he was. He only just lost his girl, and he cried like anything. Make you laugh."

"Then he can't be a pansy, or he wouldn't cry over a girl."

"He must be or he wouldn't cry at all."

On midsummer night Trevor Lomas walked with a somnambulistic sway into Findlater's Ballroom and looked round for Beauty. The floor was expertly laid and polished. The walls were pale rose, with concealed lighting. Beauty stood on the girls' side, talking to a group of very similar and lustrous girls. They had prepared themselves for this occasion with diligence, and as they spoke together, they did not smile much nor attend to each other's words. As an accepted thing, any of the girls might break off in the middle of a sentence, should a young man approach her, and, turning to him, might give him her entire and smiling regard.

Most of the men looked as if they had not properly

woken from deep sleep, but glided as if drugged, and with half-closed lids, towards their chosen partner. This approach found favour with the girls. The actual invitation to dance was mostly delivered by gesture; a scarcely noticeable flick of the man's head towards the dance floor. Whereupon the girl, with an outstretched movement of surrender, would swim into the hands of the summoning partner.

Trevor Lomas so far departed from the norm as to indicate to Beauty his wish by word of mouth, which he did not, however, open more than a sixteenth of an inch.

"Come and wriggle, snake," he said through this aperture.

Findlater's rooms were not given to rowdy rock but concentrated instead upon a more cultivated jive, cha-cha and variants. Beauty wriggled with excellence, and was particularly good at shrugging her shoulders and lifting forward her small stomach; while Trevor's knee-work was easy. Dougal, who had just entered with blond Elaine, looked round with approval.

During the next dance—forward half a step, one fall and a dip, back half a step, one fall and a dip—Beauty flicked her lashes towards the bandleader who was then facing the dancers, a young pale man with a thin neck which sprouted from a loose jacket of sky-blue. He acknowledged the gesture with one swift rise-and-drop of the eyebrows. Trevor looked round at the man who had now turned to his band and was flicking his limp wrists very slightly. Trevor's teeth said, "Who's your friend?"

"Whose friend?"

The crown of Trevor's head briefly indicated the bandleader.

Beauty shrugged in her jive and expressed her reply, both in the same movement.

Dougal was dancing with Elaine. He leapt into the air, he let go of her hands and dangled his arms in front of his hunched body. He placed his left hand on his hip and raised his right while his feet performed the rapid movements of the Highland Fling, heel to instep, then to knee. Elaine bowed her body and straightened it again and again in her laughter. The jiving couples slowed down like an unwound toy roundabout, and gathered beside Dougal. A tall stout man in evening dress walked over to the band; he said something to the band-leader who looked over his shoulder, observed the crowd round Dougal, and stopped the band.

"Hooch!" cried Dougal as the band stopped.

Everyone was talking or laughing. Those who were talking were all saying the same thing. They either said, "Tell him to take more water in it," or "Shouldn't be allowed," or "He's all right. Leave him alone." Some clapped their hands and said, " 'Core." The tall stout manager came over to Dougal and said with a beaming face, "It's all right, son, but no more, please."

"Don't you like Highland dancing?" Dougal said.

The manager beamed and walked away. The band started up. Dougal left the hall followed by Elaine. He reappeared shortly with Elaine tugging his arm in the opposite direction. However, he pressed into the midst of the dancers, bearing before him the lid of a dust-bin, which he had obtained from the back premises. Then he placed the lid upside down on the floor, sat cross-legged inside it, and was a man in a rocking boat rowing for his life. The band stopped, but nobody noticed the fact, owing to the many different sounds of mirth, protest, encouragement and rage. The dancers circled slowly around him while he performed a Zulu dance with the lid for a shield.

Two West Indians among the crowd started to object. "No, man."

"We don't take no insults, man."

But two other tall, black and shining dancers cheered him on, bending at the knees and clapping. These were supported by their woolly-cropped girls who laughed loud above the noise, rolling their bodies from the waist, rolling their shoulders, heads and eyes.

Dougal bowed to the black girls.

Next, Dougal sat on his haunches and banged a message out on a tom-tom. He sprang up and with the lid on his head was a Chinese coolie eating melancholy rice. He was an ardent cyclist, crouched over handlebars and pedalling uphill with the lid between his knees. He was an old woman with an umbrella; he stood on the upturned edges of the lid and speared fish from his rocking canoe; he was the man at the wheel of a racing car; he did many things with the lid before he finally propped the dust-bin lid up on his high shoulder, beating this cymbal rhythmically with his hand while with the other hand he limply conducted an invisible band, being, with long blank face, the band-leader.

The manager pushed through the crowd, still beaming. And, still beaming, he pointed out that the lid was scratching and spoiling the dance floor, and that Dougal had better leave the premises. He took Dougal, who still bore the dust-bin lid, by the elbow.

"Don't you get rough with him," Elaine shouted. "Can't you see he's deformed?"

Dougal disengaged his elbow from the manager's grasp and himself took the manager by the elbow.

"Tell me," Dougal said, as he propelled the manager through the door, "have you got a fatal flaw?"

"It's the best hall in South London and we don't want it mucked up, see? If we put on a cabaret we do it properly."

"Be kind enough," Dougal said, "to replace this lid on the dust-bin out yonder while I return to the scene within."

Elaine was standing behind him. "Come and leap, leopard," Dougal said, and soon they were moving with the rest.

They were passed by Trevor and Beauty. Trevor regarded Dougal from under his lids, letting the corners of his mouth droop meaningfully.

"Got a pain, panda?" Dougal said.

"Now, don't start," Elaine said.

Beauty laughed up and down the scale as she wriggled. When Trevor passed again he said to Dougal, "Got your lace hanky on you?"

Dougal put out his foot. Trevor stumbled. The band started playing the National Anthem. Trevor said, "You ought to get a surgical boot and lift your shoulder up to line."

"Have respect for the National Anthem," Beauty said. Her eyes were on the band-leader who, as he turned to face the floor, raised his eyebrows slightly in her direction.

"See you up on the Rye," Dougal said.

Elaine said, "Oh, no, you don't. You're seeing me home."

Trevor said, "You girls got to go home together. I've got a date with a rat on the Rye."

Several of the dancers, as they left the hall, called out to Dougal various words of gratitude, such as, "Thanks a lot for the show" and "You was swell, boy."

Dougal bowed.

Beauty, on her way to the girls' cloakroom, loitered a little behind the queue. The band-leader passed by her and moved his solemn lips very slightly. Trevor, close by, heard him say, "Come and frolic, lamb."

Beauty moved her eyes to indicate the presence of Trevor, who observed the gesture.

"She's going straight home," Trevor said through his nose, putting his face close to that of the band-leader. He gave Beauty a shove in the direction of the queue.

Beauty immediately turned back to the band-leader.

"No man," she said to Trevor, "lays hands on me."

The band-leader raised his eyebrows and dropped them sadly.

"You're coming home with me," Trevor told her.

"Thought you got a date on the Rye."

"He'll keep," Trevor said.

Beauty took a mirror from her bag and carefully applied her lipstick, turning her bronze head from side to side as she did so. Meanwhile her eyes traced the band-leader's departure from the hall.

"Elaine and I's going home together," she said.

"No, you don't," Trevor said. He peered out to the crowded entrance and there saw Elaine hanging on to Dougal. He caught her attention and beckoned to her by moving his forefinger twice very slowly. Elaine disengaged her arm from Dougal's, opened her bag, took out a cigarette, lit it, puffed slowly, then ambled over to Trevor.

"If you know what's good for your friend you'll take him home," Trevor said.

Elaine blew a puff of smoke in his face and turned away.

"The fight's off," she said to Dougal when she rejoined him. "He wants to keep an eye on his girl, he don't trust her. She got no morals."

As Trevor and Beauty emerged from the hall, Dougal, on the pavement, said to him, "Feeling frail, nightingale?"

Trevor shook off Beauty's arm and approached Dougal.

"Now don't start with him," Elaine shrieked at Dougal, "he's ignorant."

Beauty walked off on her own, with her high determined heels and her model-girl sway, placing her feet confidently and as on a chalk line.

Trevor looked round after her, then ran and caught her up.

Dougal walked with Elaine to Camberwell Green where, standing under the orange lights, he searched his pockets. When he had found a folded sheet of paper he opened it and read, " 'I walked with her to Camberwell Green, and we said goodbye rather sorrowfully at the corner of New Road; and that possibility of meek happiness vanished for ever.' This is John Ruskin and his girl Charlotte Wilkes," Dougal said, "my human research. But you and I will not say goodbye here and now. No. I'm taking you the rest of the way home in a taxi, because you're the nicest wee process-controller I've ever met."

"One thing about you I'll admit," she said, "you're different. If I didn't know you were Scotch I'd swear you were Irish. My mother's Irish."

She said they could not take a taxi up to her door because her mother didn't like her coming home with men in taxis. They dropped off at the Canal Head at Brixton.

"I'm leaving Meadows Meade," Elaine said, "Saturday week. Starting on the Monday at Drover Willis's. It's advancement."

"I saw they were advertising," Dougal said, "for staff at Drover Willis's."

They walked along by the Canal a little way, watching the quiet water.

Chapter 5

Mr. Druce said with embarrassment, "I feel I should just mention the fact that absenteeism has increased in the six weeks you've been with us. Eight per cent to be precise. Not that I'm complaining. I'm not complaining. Rome can't be built in a day. I'm just mentioning a factor that Personnel keep stressing. Weedin's a funny sort of fellow. How do you find Weedin?"

"Totally," Dougal said, "lacking in vision. It is his fatal flaw. Otherwise quite sane." He bore on his uneven shoulders all the learning and experience of the world as he said it. Mr. Druce looked away, looked again at Dougal, and looked away.

"Vision," said Mr. Druce.

"Vision," Dougal said, and he was a confessor in his box, leaning forward with his insidious advice through the grille, "is the first requisite of sanity."

"Sanity," Mr. Druce said.

Dougal closed his eyes and slowly smiled with his wide mouth. Dougal nodded his head twice and slowly, as one who understands all. Mr. Druce was moved to confess, "Sometimes I wonder if I'm sane myself, what with one thing and another." Then he laughed and said, "Fancy the Managing Director of Meadows, Meade & Grindley saying things like this."

Dougal opened his eyes. "Mr. Druce, you are not as happy as you might be."

"No," Mr. Druce said, "I am not. Mrs. Druce, if I may speak in confidence . . ."

"Certainly," Dougal said.

"Mrs. Druce is not a wife in any real sense of the word." Dougal nodded.

"Mrs. Druce and I have nothing in common. When we were first married thirty-two years ago I was a travelling salesman in rayon. Times were hard, then. But I got on." Mr. Druce looked pleadingly at Dougal. "I was a success. I got on."

Dougal tightened his lips prudishly, and nodded, and he was a divorce judge suspending judgment till the whole story was heard out.

"You can't get on in business," Mr. Druce pleaded, "unless you've got the fibre for it.

"You can't get on," Mr. Druce said, "unless you've got the moral fibre. *And* you don't have to be narrow-minded. That's one thing you don't have to be."

Dougal waited.

"You have to be broad-minded," Mr. Druce protested. "In this life." He laid his elbow on the desk and, for a moment, his forehead on his hand. Then he shifted his chin to his hand and continued, "Mrs. Druce is not broad-minded. Mrs. Druce is narrow-minded."

Dougal had an elbow on each arm-rest of his chair, and his hands were joined under his chin. "There is some question of incompatibility, I should say," Dougal said.

"I should say," he said, "you have a nature at once deep and sensitive, Mr. Druce."

"Would you really?" Druce enquired of the analyst.

"And a sensitive nature," Dougal said, "requires psychological understanding."

"My wife," Druce said, ". . . it's like living a lie. We don't even speak to each other. Haven't spoken for nearly five years. One day, it was a Sunday, we were having lunch. I was talking away quite normally; you know, just talking away. And suddenly she said, 'Quack, quack.' She said, 'Quack, quack.' She said, 'Quack, quack,' and her hand was opening and shutting like this——" Mr. Druce opened and shut his hand like a duck's bill. Dougal likewise raised his hand and made it open and shut. "Quack, quack," Dougal said. "Like that?"

Mr. Druce dropped his arm. "Yes, and she said, 'That's how *you* go on—quack, quack.' "

"Quack," Dougal said, still moving his hand, "quack."

"She said to me, my wife," said Mr. Druce, "she said, 'That's how *you* go quacking on.' Well, from that day to this I've never opened my mouth to her. I can't, Dougal, it's psychological, I just can't—you don't mind me calling you Dougal?"

"Not at all, Vincent," Dougal said. "I feel I understand you. How do you communicate with Mrs. Druce?"

"Write notes," said Mr. Druce. "Do you call that a marriage?" Mr. Druce bent to open a lower drawer of his desk and brought out a book with a bright yellow wrapper. Its title was *Marital Relational Psychology*. Druce flicked over the pages, then set the book aside. "It's no use to me," he said. "Interesting case histories but it doesn't cover my case. I've thought of seeing a psychiatrist, and

74

then I think, why should I? Let *her* see a psychiatrist."

"Take her a bunch of flowers," Dougal said, looking down at the back of his hand, the little finger of which was curling daintily. "Put your arms around her," he said, becoming a lady-columnist, "and start afresh. It frequently needs but one little gesture from one partner——"

"Dougal, I can't. I don't know why it is, but I can't." Mr. Druce placed a hand just above his stomach. "Something stops me."

"You two must separate," Dougal said, "if only for a while."

Mr. Druce's hand abruptly removed from his stomach. "No," he said, "oh, no, I can't leave her." He shifted in his chair into his business-like pose. "No, I can't do that. I've got to stay with her for old times' sake."

The telephone rang. "I'm engaged," he said sharply into it. He jerked down the receiver and looked up to find Dougal's forefinger pointing into his face. Dougal looked grave, lean and inquisitorial. "Mrs. Druce," Dougal said, "has got money."

"There are interests in vital concerns which we both share," Mr. Druce said with his gaze on Dougal's finger, "Mrs. Druce and I."

Dougal shook his outstretched finger a little. "She won't *let* you leave her," he said, "because of the money."

Mr. Druce looked frightened.

"And there is also the information which she holds," Dougal said, "against you."

"What are you talking about?"

"I'm fey. I've got Highland blood." Dougal dropped his hand. "You have my every sympathy, Vincent," he said.

Mr. Druce laid his head on his desk and wept.

Dougal sat back and lit a cigarette out of Mr. Druce's box. He heaved his high shoulder in a sigh. He sat back like an exhausted medium of the spiritualist persuasion. "Does you good," Dougal said, "a wee greet. A hundred years ago all chaps used to cry regardless."

Merle Coverdale came in with the letters to be signed. She clicked her heels together as she stopped at the sight.

"Thank you, Miss Coverdale," Dougal said, putting out a hand for the letters.

Meanwhile Mr. Druce sat up and blew his nose.

"Got a comb on you?" Dougal said, squeezing Merle's hand under the letters.

She said, "This place is becoming chaos."

"What was that, Miss Coverdale?" Mr. Druce said with as little moisture as possible.

"Mr. Druce has a bad head," Dougal said as he left the room with her.

"Come and tell me what happened," said Merle.

Dougal looked at his watch. "Sorry, can't stop. I've got an urgent appointment in connection with my human research."

Dougal sat in the cheerful waiting-room looking at the tulips in their earthy bowls.

"Mr. Douglas Dougal?"

Dougal did not correct her. On the contrary he said, "That's right."

"Come this way, please."

He followed her into the office of Mr. Willis, managing director of Drover Willis's, textile manufacturers of Peckham.

"Good afternoon, Mr. Dougal," said the man behind the desk. "Take a seat."

On hearing Mr. Willis's voice Dougal changed his manner, for he perceived that Mr. Willis was a Scot.

Mr. Willis was looking at Dougal's letter of application. "Graduate of Edinburgh?" said Mr. Willis.

"Yes, Mr. Willis."

Mr. Willis's blue eyes stared out of his brick-coloured small-featured face. They stared and stared at Dougal.

"Douglas Dougal," the man read out from Dougal's letter, and asked with a one-sided smile, "Any relation to Fergie Dougal the golfer?"

"No," Dougal said. "I'm afraid not."

Mr. Willis smiled by turning down the sides of his mouth.

"Why do you want to come into Industry, Mr. Dougal?"

"I think there's money in it," Dougal said.

Mr. Willis smiled again. "That's the correct answer. The last candidate answered, 'Industry and the Arts must walk hand in hand,' when I put that question to him. His answer was wrong. Tell me, Mr. Dougal, why do you want to come to us?"

"I saw your advertisement," Dougal said, "and I wanted a job. I saw your advertisements, too, for automatic weaver instructors and hands, and for twin-needle flat-bed machinists and flat-lock machinists and instructors. I gathered you're expanding."

"You know something about textiles?"

"I've seen over a factory. Meadows, Meade & Grindley."

"Meadows Meade are away behind us."

"Yes. So I gathered."

"Now I'll tell you what we're looking for, what we want. . . ."

Dougal sat upright and listened, only interrupting when Mr. Willis said, "The hours are nine to five-thirty."

"I would need time off for research."

"Research?"

"Industrial relations. The psychological factors behind the absenteeism, and so on, as you've been saying——"

"You could do an evening course in industrial psychology. And of course you'd have access to the factory."

"The research I have in mind," Dougal said, "would need the best part of the day for at least two months. Two months should do it. I want to look into the external environment. The home conditions. Peckham must have a moral character of its own."

Mr. Willis's blue eyes photographed every word. Dougal sat out these eyes, he went on talking, reasonably, like a solid steady Edinburgh boy, all the steadier for the hump on his shoulder.

"I'll have to speak to Davis. He is Personnel. We have to talk over the candidates and we may ask to see you again, Mr. Dougal. If we decide on you, don't fear you'll be hampered in your research."

The factory was opening its gates as Dougal came down the steps from the office into the leafy lanes of Nun Row. Some of the girls were being met by their husbands and boy friends in cars. Others rode off on motor-scooters. A number walked down to the station. "Hi, Dougal," called one of them, "what you doing here?"

It was Elaine, who had now been over a week at Drover Willis's.

"What you doing here, Dougal?"

78

"I'm after a job," he said. "I think I've got it."

"You leaving Meadows Meade too?"

"No," he said, "oh, no, not on your life."

"What's your game, Dougal?"

"Come and have a drink," he said, "and my Christian name is Douglas on this side of the Rye, mind that. Dougal Douglas at Meadows Meade and Douglas Dougal at Willis's, mind. Only a formality for the insurance cards and such."

"I better call you Doug, and be done with it."

Dixie sat at her desk in the typing pool and, without lifting her eyes from her shorthand book or interrupting the dance of her fingers on the keyboard, spoke out her reply to her neighbour.

"He's all one-sided at the shoulders. I don't know how any girl could go with him."

Connie Weedin, daughter of the Personnel Manager, typed on and said, "My dad says he's nuts. But I say he's got something. Definitely."

"Got something, all right. Got a good cheek. My young brother doesn't like him. My mum likes him. My dad likes him so-so. Humphrey likes him. I don't agree to that. The factory girls like him—what can you expect? I don't like him, he's got funny ideas." She stopped typing with her last word and took the papers out of her typewriter. She placed them neatly on a small stack of papers in a tray, put an envelope in her typewriter, typed an address, put more papers in her typewriter, turned over the page of her shorthand notes, and started typing again. "My dad doesn't mind him, but Leslie can't stand him. I tell you who else doesn't like him."

"Who?"

"Trevor Lomas. Trevor doesn't like him."

"I don't like Trevor, never did," Connie said. "Definitely ignorant. He goes with that girl from Celia Modes that's called Beauty. Some beauty!"

"He's a good dancer. He doesn't like Dougal Douglas and, boy, I'll say he's got something there," Dixie said.

"My dad says he's nuts. Supposed to be helping my dad to keep the factory sweet. But my dad says he don't do much with all his brains and his letters. But you can't help but like him. He's different."

"He goes out with the factory girls. He goes out with Elaine Kent that was process-controller. She's gone to Drover Willis's. He goes out with her ladyship too."

"You don't say?"

"I do say. He better watch out for Mr. Druce if it's her ladyship he's after."

"Watch out—her ladyship's looking this way."

Miss Merle Coverdale, at her supervisor's seat at the top of the room, called out, "Is there anything you want, Dixie?"

"No."

"If there's anything you want, come and ask. Is there anything you want, Connie?"

"No."

"If there's anything you want, come up here and ask for it."

Dougal came in just then, and walked with his springy step all up the long open-plan office, bobbing as he walked as if the plastic inlay flooring was a certain green and paradisal turf.

"Good morning, girls."

"You'd think he was somebody," Dixie said.

Connie opened a drawer in her small desk in which she kept a mirror, and looking down into it, tidied her hair.

Dougal sat down beside Merle Coverdale.

"There was a personal call for you," she said, handing him a slip of paper, "from a lady. Will you ring this number?"

He looked at it, put the paper in his pocket and said, "One of my employers."

Merle gave one of her laughs from the chest. "Employers—that's a good name for them. How many you got?"

"Two," Dougal said, "and a possible third. Is Mr. Weedin in?"

"Yes, he's been asking for you."

Dougal jumped up and went in to Mr. Weedin where he sat in one of the glass offices which extended from the typing pool.

"Mr. Douglas," said Mr. Weedin, "I want to ask you a personal question. What do you mean exactly by vision?"

"Vision?" Dougal said.

"Yes, vision, that's what I said."

"Do you speak literally as concerning optics, or figuratively, as it might be with regard to an enlargement of the total perceptive capacity?"

"Druce is complaining we haven't got vision in this department. I thought perhaps maybe you had been having one of your long chats with him."

"Mr. Weedin," Dougal said, "don't tremble like that. Just relax." He took from his pocket a small square silver vinaigrette which had two separate compartments. Dougal opened both lids. In one compartment lay some small white tablets. In the other were a number of yellow ones.

Dougal offered the case to Mr. Weedin. "For calming down you take two of the white ones and for revving up you take one of the yellow ones."

"I don't want your drugs. I just want to know——"

"The yellow ones make you feel sexy. The white ones, being of a relaxing nature, ensure the more successful expression of such feelings. But these, of course, are mere by-effects."

"Do you want my job? Is that what you're wanting?"

"No," Dougal said.

"Because if you want it you can have it. I'm tired of working for a firm where the boss listens to the advice of any young showpiece that takes his fancy. I've had this before. I had it with Merle Coverdale. She told Druce I was inefficient at relationship-maintenance. She told Druce that everything in the pool goes back to me through my girl Connie. She——"

"Miss Coverdale is a sensitive girl. Like an okapi, you know. You spell it O K A P I. A bit of all sorts of beast. Very rare, very nervy. You have to make allowances."

"And now you come along and you tell Druce we lack vision. And Druce calls me in and I see from the look on his face he's got a new idea. Vision, it is, this time. Try to take a tip or two, he says, from the Arts man. I said, he never hardly puts a foot inside the door does your Arts man. Nonsense, Weedin, he says, Mr. Douglas and I have many a long session. He says, watch his manner, he has a lovely manner with the workers. I said, yes, up on the Rye Saturday nights. That is unworthy of you, Weedin, he says. Is it coincidence, says I, that absenteeism has risen eight per cent since Mr. Douglas came here and is still rising? Things are bound to get worse, he says, before they get better. If you had the vision, Weedin, he says, you would comprehend my meaning. Study Douglas, he says, watch his methods."

"Funny thing I've just found out," Dougal said, "we have five cemeteries up here round the Rye within the space of a square mile. We have Camberwell New, Camberwell Old—that's full up. We have Nunhead, Deptford and Lewisham Green. Did you know that Nunhead reservoir holds twenty million gallons of water? The original title that Mendelssohn gave his *Spring Song* was *Camberwell Green*. It's a small world."

Mr. Weedin laid his head in his hand and burst into tears.

Dougal said, "You're a sick man, Mr. Weedin. I can't bear sickness. It's my fatal flaw. But I've brought a comb with me. Would you like me to comb your hair?"

"You're unnatural," said Mr. Weedin.

"All human beings who breathe are a bit unnatural," Dougal said. "If you try to be too natural, see where it gets you."

Mr. Weedin blew his nose, and shouted at Dougal: "It isn't possible to get another good position in another firm at my age. Personnel is a much-coveted position. If I had to leave here, Mr. Douglas, I would have to take a subordinate post elsewhere. I have my wife and family to think of. Druce is impossible to work for. It's impossible to leave this firm. Sometimes I think I'm going to have a breakdown."

"It would not be severe in your case," Dougal said. "It is at its worst when a man is a skyscraper. But you're only a nice wee bungalow."

"We live in a flat," Mr. Weedin managed to say.

"Do you know," Dougal said, "up at the police station they are excavating an underground tunnel which starts in the station yard and runs all the way to Nunhead. You should ponder sometimes about underground tunnels. Did you know Boadicea was broken and defeated on the Rye? She was a great beefy soldier. I think you should take Mr. Druce's advice and study my manner, Mr. Weedin. I could give you lessons at ten and six an hour."

Mr. Weedin rose to hit him, but since the walls of his office were made mostly of glass, he was prevented in the act by an overwhelming sense of being looked at from all sides.

Dougal sat in Miss Frierne's panelled hall on Saturday morning and telephoned to the Flaxman number on the little slip of paper which Merle Coverdale had handed to him the previous day.

"Miss Cheeseman, please," said Dougal.

"She isn't in," said the voice from across the water. "Who shall I say it was?"

"Mr. Dougal-Douglas," Dougal said, "spelt with a hyphen. Tell Miss Cheeseman I'll be at home all morning."

He next rang Jinny.

"Hallo, are you better?" he said.

"I've got soup on the stove. I'll ring you back."

Miss Frierne was ironing in the kitchen. She said to Dougal, "Humphrey is going to see to the roof this afternoon. It's creaking. It isn't a loose slate, it must be one of the beams loose in his cupboard."

"Funny thing," Dougal said, "it only creaks at night. It goes Creak-oop!" The dishes rattled in their rack as he leapt.

"It's the cold makes it creak, I daresay," she said.

The telephone rang. Dougal rushed out to the hall. It was not Jinny, however.

"Doug dear," said Miss Maria Cheeseman from across the river.

"Oh, it's you, Cheese."

"We really must get down to things," Miss Cheeseman said. "All this about my childhood in Peckham, it's all wrong, it was Streatham."

"There's the law of libel to be considered," Dougal said. "A lot of your early associates in Streatham are still alive. If you want to write the true story of your life you can't place it in Streatham."

"But Doug dear," she said, "that bit where you make me say I played with Harold Lloyd and Ford Sterling at the Golden Domes in Camberwell, it isn't true, dear. I *was* in a show with Fatty Arbuckle but it was South Shields."

"I thought it was a work of art you wanted to write," Dougal said, "now was that not so? If you only want to write a straight autobiography you should have got a straight ghost. I'm crooked."

"Well, Doug dear, I don't think this story about me and the Gordon Highlander is quite nice, do you? I mean to say, it isn't true. Of course it's funny about the kilt, but it's a little embarrassing——"

"Well, write your own autobiography," Dougal said.

"Oh, Doug dear, do come over to tea."

"No, you've hurt my feelings."

"Doug dear, I'm thrilled with my book. I'm sure it's going to be marvellous. I can't say I'm quite happy about all of chapter three but——"

"What's wrong with chapter three?"

"Well, it's only that last bit you wrote, it isn't *me*."

"I'll see you at four o'clock," he said, "but understand, Cheese, I don't like crossing the water when I'm in the middle of a work of art. I'm giving all my time to it."

Dougal said to Humphrey, "I was over the other side of the river on business this afternoon, and while I was over that way I called in to see my girl."

"Oh, you got a girl over there?"

"Used to have. She's got engaged to somebody else."

"Women have no moral sense," Humphrey said. "You see it in the Unions. They vote one way then go and act another way."

"She was nice, Jinny," Dougal said, "but she was too delicate in health. Do you believe in the Devil?"

"No."

"Do you know anyone that believes in the Devil?"

"I think some of those Irish——"

"Feel my head," Dougal said.

"What?"

"Feel these little bumps up here." Dougal guided Humphrey's hand among his curls at each side. "I had it done by a plastic surgeon," Dougal said.

"What?"

"He did an operation and took away the two horns. They had to shave my head in the nursing home before the operation. It took a long time for my hair to grow again."

Humphrey smiled and felt again among Dougal's curls.

"A couple of cysts," he said. "I've got one myself at the back of my head. Feel it."

86

Dougal touched the bump like a connoisseur.

"You supposed to be the Devil, then?" Humphrey asked.

"No, oh, no, I'm only supposed to be one of the wicked spirits that wander through the world for the ruin of souls. Have you mended those beams in the roof yet, that go Creak-oop?"

"I have," Humphrey said. "Dixie refuses to come any more."

Chapter 6

"What strikes me as remarkable," Dougal said, "is how he manages to get in so much outside his school hours."

Nelly Mahone nodded, trod out her cigarette-end, and looked at the packet of cigarettes which Dougal had placed on the table.

"Help yourself," Dougal said, and he lit the cigarette for her.

"Ta," said Nelly. She looked round her room. "It's all *clean* dirt," she said.

"You would think," Dougal said, "his parents would have some control over him."

Nelly inhaled gratefully. "Up the Elephant, that's where they all go. What was name?"

"Leslie Crewe. Thirteen years of age. The father's manager of Beverly Hills Outfitters at Brixton."

"Where they live?"

"Twelve Rye Grove."

Nelly nodded. "How much you paid him?"

"A pound the first time, thirty bob the second time. But now he's asking five quid a week flat."

Nelly whispered, "Then there's a gang behind him, surely. Can't you give up one of the jobs for a month or two?"

"I don't see why I should," Dougal said, "just to please a thirteen-year-old blackmailer."

Nelly made signs with her hands and moved her mouth soundlessly, and swung her eyes to the wall between her room and the next, to show that the walls had ears.

"A thirteen-year-old blackmailer," Dougal said, more softly. But Nelly did not like the word blackmailer at all; she placed her old fish-smelling hand over Dougal's mouth, and whispered in his ear—her grey long hair falling against his nose—"A lousy fellow next door," she said. "A slob that wouldn't do a day's work if you paid him gold. So guard your mouth." She released Dougal and started to draw the curtains.

"And here's me," Dougal said, "willing to do three, four, five men's jobs, and I get blackmailed on grounds of false pretences."

She ran with her long low dipping strides to his side and gave him a hard poke in the back. She returned to her window, which was as opaque as sackcloth and not really distinguishable from the curtain she pulled across it. On the floorboards were a few strips of very worn-out matting of a similar colour. The bed in the corner was much of the same hue, lumpy and lopsided. "But I'm charmed to see you, all the same," Nelly said for the third time, "and will you have a cup of tea?"

Dougal said, no thanks, for the third time.

Nelly scratched her head, and raising her voice, declared, "Praise be to God, who rewards those who meditate the truths he has proposed for their intelligence."

"It seems to me," Dougal said, "that my course in life has much support from the Scriptures."

"Never," Nelly said, shaking her thin body out of its

ecstasy and taking a cigarette out of Dougal's packet.

"Consider the story of Moses in the bullrushes. That was a crafty trick. The mother got her baby back and all expenses paid into the bargain. And consider the parable of the Unjust Steward. Do you know the parable of——"

"Stop," Nelly said, with her hand on her old blouse. "I get that excited by Holy Scripture I'm afraid to get my old lung trouble back."

"Were you born in Peckham?" Dougal said.

"No, Galway. I don't remember it though. I was a girl in Peckham."

"Where did you work?"

"Shoe factory I started life. Will you have a cup of tea?"

Dougal took out ten shillings.

"It's not enough," Nelly said.

Dougal made it a pound.

"If I got to follow them fellows round between here and the Elephant you just think of the fares alone," Nelly said. "I'll need more than that to go along with."

"Two quid, then," Dougal said. "And more next week."

"All right," she said.

"Otherwise it's going to be cheaper to pay Leslie."

"No it isn't," she said. "They go on and on wanting more and more. I hope you'll remember me nice if I get some way to stop their gobs."

"Ten quid," said Dougal.

"All right," she said. "But suppose one of your bosses finds out in the meantime? After all, rival firms is like to get nasty."

"Tell me," Dougal said, "how old are you?"

"I should say I was sixty-four. Have a cup of tea." She looked round the room. "It's all clean dirt."

"Tell me," Dougal said, "what it was like to work in the shoe factory."

She told him all of her life in the shoe factory till it was time for her to go out on her rounds proclaiming. Dougal followed her down the sour dark winding stairs of Lightbody Buildings, and they parted company in the passage, he going out before her.

"Good night, Nelly."

"Good night, Mr. Doubtless."

"Where's Mr. Douglas?" said Mr. Weedin.

"Haven't seen him for a week," Merle Coverdale replied. "Would you like me to ring him up at home and see if he's all right?"

"Yes, do that," Mr. Weedin said. "No, don't. Yes, I don't see why not. No, perhaps, though, we'd——"

Merle Coverdale stood tapping her pencil on her notebook, watching Mr. Weedin's hands shuffling among the papers on his desk.

"I'd better ask Mr. Druce," Mr. Weedin said. "He probably knows where Mr. Douglas is."

"He doesn't," Merle said.

"Doesn't he?"

"No, he doesn't."

"Wait till tomorrow. See if he comes in tomorrow."

"Are you feeling all right, Mr. Weedin?"

"Who? Me? I'm all right."

Merle went in to Mr. Druce. "Dougal hasn't been near the place for a week."

"Leave him alone. The boy's doing good work."

She returned to Mr. Weedin and stood in his open door

with an exaggerated simper. "We are to leave him alone. The boy's doing good work."

"Come in and shut the door," said Mr. Weedin.

She shut the door and approached his desk.

"I'm not much of a believer," Mr. Weedin said, quivering his hands across the papers before him. "But there's something Mr. Douglas told me that's on my mind." He craned upward to look through the glass panels on all sides of his room.

"They're all out at tea-break," Merle said.

Mr. Weedin dropped his head on his hands. "It may surprise you," he said, "coming from me. But it's my belief that Dougal Douglas is a diabolical agent, if not in fact the Devil."

"Mr. Weedin," said Miss Coverdale.

"Yes, I know what you're thinking. Yes, yes, you're thinking I'm going wrong up here." He pointed to his right temple and screwed it with his finger. "Do you know," he said, "that Douglas himself showed me bumps on his head where he had horns removed by plastic surgery?"

"Don't get excited, Mr. Weedin. Don't shout. The girls are coming up from the canteen."

"I felt those bumps with these very hands. Have you looked, have you ever properly looked at his eyes? That shoulder——"

"Keep calm, Mr. Weedin, you aren't getting yourself anywhere, you know."

Mr. Weedin pointed with a shaking arm in the direction of the managing director's office. "He's bewitched," he said.

Merle took tiny steps backward and got herself out of

the door. She went in to Mr. Druce again.

"Mr. Weedin will be wanting a holiday," she said.

Mr. Druce lifted his paper-knife, toyed with it in his hand, pointed it at Merle, and put it down. "What did you say?" he said.

Drover Willis's was humming with work when Dougal reported on Friday morning to the managing director.

"During my first week," Dougal told Mr. Willis, "I have been observing the morals of Peckham. It seemed to me that the moral element lay at the root of all industrial discontents which lead to absenteeism and the slackness at work which you described to me."

Mr. Willis looked with his blue eyes at his rational compatriot sitting before him with a shiny brief-case on his lap.

Mr. Willis said at last, "That would seem to be the correct approach, Mr. Dougal."

Dougal sat easily in his chair and continued his speech with half-closed, detached and scholarly eyes.

"There are four types of morality observable in Peckham," he said. "One, emotional. Two, functional. Three, puritanical. Four, Christian."

Mr. Willis opened the lid of a silver cigarette-box and passed it over to Dougal.

"No, thank you," Dougal said. "Take the first category, Emotional. Here, for example, it is considered immoral for a man to live with a wife who no longer appeals to him. Take the second, Functional, in which the principal factor is class solidarity such as, in some periods and places, has also existed amongst the aristocracy, and of which the main manifestation these days is the trade union movement. Three, Puritanical, of which there are several modern variants, monetary advancement being the most prevalent gauge of the moral life in this category. Four, Traditional, which accounts for about one per cent of the Peckham population, and which in its simplest form is Christian. All moral categories are of course intermingled. Sometimes all are to be found in the beliefs and behaviour of one individual."

"Where does this get us?"

"I can't say," Dougal said. "It is only a preliminary analysis."

"Please embody all this in a report for us, Mr. Dougal."

Dougal opened his brief-case and took out two sheets of paper. "I have elaborated on the question here. I have included case histories."

Mr. Willis smiled with one side of his mouth and said, "Which of these four moral codes would you say was most attractive, Mr. Dougal?"

"Attractive?" Dougal said with a trace of disapproval.

"Attractive to us. Useful, I mean, useful."

Dougal pondered seriously until Mr. Willis's little smile was forced, for dignity's sake, to fade. Then, "I could not decide until I had further studied the question."

"We'll expect another report next week?"

"No, I'll need a month," Dougal stated. "A month to work on my own. I can't come in here again for a month if you wish me to continue research on this line of industrial psychology."

"You must see round the factory," said Mr. Willis. "Peckham is a big place. We're concerned with our own works first of all."

"I've arranged to be shown round this afternoon," Dougal said. "And at the end of a month I hope to spend some time with the workers in the recreation halls and canteens."

Mr. Willis looked silently at Dougal who then permitted himself a slight display of enthusiasm. He leaned forward.

"Have you observed, Mr. Willis, the frequency with which your employees use the word 'immoral'? Have you noticed how equally often they use the word 'ignorant'? These words are significant," Dougal said, "psychologically and sociologically."

Mr. Willis smiled, as far as he was able, into Dougal's face. "Take a month and see what you can do," he said. "But bring us a good plan of action at the end of it. Drover, my partner, is anxious about absenteeism. We want some moral line that will be both commendable by us and acceptable to our staff. You've got some sound ideas, I can see that. And method. I like method."

Dougal nodded and took his long serious face out of the room.

Miss Frierne said, "That boy Leslie Crewe has been here. He was looking for you. Wants to go your errands and make a bob like a good kid. Perhaps his mother's a bit short."

"Anyone with him?"

"No. He came to the back door this time."

"Oh," Dougal said, "did you get rid of him quickly?"

"Well, he wouldn't go for a long time. He kept saying when would Mr. Douglas be home, and could he do anything for you. He was very polite, I will say that. Then he asked the time and then he said his Dad used to live up this road in number eight. So I took him in the kitchen.

I thought, well, he's only a boy, and gave him a doughnut. He said his sister was looking forward to marrying Humphrey in September. He said she saves all her wages and the father in America dresses her. He said——"

"He must have kept you talking a long time," Dougal said.

"Oh, I didn't mind. It was a nice break in the afternoon. A nice lad, he is. He goes out Sundays with the Rover Scouts. I'd just that minute come in and I was feeling a bit upset because of something that happened in the street, so——"

"Did he ask if he could go up and wait in my room?"

"No, not this time. I wouldn't have let him in your room, especially after you said nobody was to be let in there. Don't you worry about your room. Nobody wants to go into your room, I'm sure."

Dougal said, "You are too innocent for this wicked world."

"Innocent I always was," Miss Frierne said, "and that was why I was so taken aback that day by the Gordon Highlander up on One Tree Hill. Have a cup of tea."

"Thanks," Dougal said. "I'll just pop upstairs a minute first."

His room had, of course, been disturbed. He unlocked a drawer in his dressing-table and found that two notebooks were missing. His portable typewriter had been opened and clumsily shut. Ten five-pound notes were, however, untouched in another drawer by the person who had climbed to his room while Leslie had engaged Miss Frierne in talk.

He came down to the kitchen where Miss Frierne sighed into her tea.

"Next time that Leslie comes round to the back door have a look, will you, to see who he's left at the front door. His father's worried about his companions after school hours, I happen to know."

"He only wanted to know if you had any errands to run. I daresay to help his mother, like a good kid. I told him I thought you're short of bacon for your breakfast. He'll be back. There's no harm in that boy, I know it by instinct, and instinct always tells. Like what happened to me in the street to-day." She sipped her tea, and was silent.

Dougal sipped his. "Go on," he said, "you're dying to tell me what happened."

"As true as God is my judge," she said, "I saw my brother up at Camberwell Green that left home in nineteen-nineteen. We never heard a word from him all those years. He was coming out of Lyons."

"Didn't you go and speak to him?"

"No," she said, "I didn't. He was very shabby, he looked awful. Something stopped me. It was an instinct. I couldn't do it. He saw me, too."

She took a handkerchief out of her sleeve and patted beneath her glasses.

"You should have gone up to him," Dougal said. "You should have said, 'Are you . . .' —what was his name?"

"Harold," she said.

"You should have said, 'Are you Harold?', that's what you ought to have done. Instead of which you didn't. You came back here and gave a doughnut to that rotten little Leslie."

"Don't you point your finger at me, Dougal. Nobody does that in my house. You can find other accommodation

97

if you like, any *time* you like and when you like."

Dougal got up and shuffled round the kitchen with a slouch and an old ill look. "Is that what your old brother looked like?" he said.

She laughed in high-pitched ripples.

Dougal thrust his hands into his pockets and looked miserably at his toes.

She started to cry all over her spectacles.

"Perhaps it wasn't your brother at all," Dougal said.

"That's what I'm wondering, son."

"Just feel my head," Dougal said, "these two small bumps here."

"There are four types of morality in Peckman," Dougal said to Mr. Druce. "The first category is——"

"Dougal," he said, "are you doing anything tonight?"

"Well, I usually prepare my notes. You realise, don't you, that Oliver Goldsmith taught in a school in Peckham? He used to commit absenteeism and spent a lot of his time in a coffeehouse at the Temple instead of in Peckham. I wonder why?"

"I need your advice," Mr. Druce said. "There's a place in Soho——"

"I don't like crossing the river," Dougal said, "not without my broomstick."

Mr. Druce made double chins and looked lovingly at Dougal.

"There's a place in Soho——"

"I could spare a couple of hours," Dougal said. "I could see you up at Dulwich at the Dragon at nine."

"Well, I was thinking of making an evening of it, Dougal; some dinner at this place in Soho——"

"Nine at the Dragon," Dougal said.

"Mrs. Druce knows a lot of people in Dulwich."

"All the better," Dougal said.

Dougal arrived at the Dragon at nine sharp. He drank gin and peppermint while he waited. At half-past nine two girls from Drover Willis's came in. Dougal joined them. Mr. Druce did not come. At ten o'clock they went on a bus to the Rosemary Branch in Southampton Way. Here, Dougal expounded the idea that everyone should take every second Monday morning off their work. When they came out of the pub, at eleven, Nelly Mahone crossed the street towards them.

"Praise be to the Lord," she cried, "whose providence in all things never fails."

"Hi, Nelly," said one of the girls as she passed.

Nelly raised up her voice and in the same tone proclaimed, "Praise be to God who by sin is offended, Trevor Lomas, Collie Gould up the Elephant with young Leslie, and by penance appeased, the exaltation of the humble and the strength of the righteous."

"Ah, Nelly," Dougal said.

Chapter 7

"Yes, Cheese?" Dougal said.

"Look, Doug, I think I can't have this story about the Dragon at Dulwich, it's indecent. Besides, it isn't true. And I never went to Soho at that age. I never went out with any managing director——"

"It will help to sell the book," Dougal said. He breathed moistly on the oak panel of Miss Frierne's hall, and with his free hand drew a face on the misty surface where he had breathed.

"And Doug dear," said the voice from across the river, "how did you know I started life in a shoe factory? I mean to say, I didn't tell you that. How did you know?"

"I didn't know, Cheese," Dougal said.

"You must have known. You've got all the details right, except that it wasn't in Peckham, it was Streatham. It all came back to me as I read it. It's uncanny. You've been checking up on me, haven't you, Doug?"

"Aye," Dougal said. He breathed on the panel, wrote in a word, then rubbed it off.

"Doug, you mustn't do that. It makes me creepy to think that people can find out all about you," Miss Cheeseman said. "I mean, I don't want to put in about the shoe factory and all that. Besides, the period. It dates me."

"It only makes you sixty-eight, Cheese."

"Well, Doug, there must be a way of making me not even that. I want you to come over, Doug. I've been feeling off colour."

"I've got a fatal flaw," Dougal said, "to the effect that I can't bear anyone off colour. Moreover, Saturday's my day off and it's a beautiful summer day."

"Dear Doug, I promise to be well. Only come over. I'm *worried* about my book. It's rather . . . rather too . . ."

"Rambling," Dougal said.

"Yes, that's it."

"I'll see you at four," Dougal said.

At the back of Hollis's Hamburgers at Elephant and Castle was a room furnished with a fitted grey carpet, a red upholstered modern suite comprising a sofa and two cubic armchairs, a television receiver on a light wood stand, a low glass-topped coffee table, a table on which stood an electric portable gramophone and a tape recorder, a light wood bureau desk, a standard lamp and several ash-trays on stands. Two of the walls were papered with a wide grey stripe. The other two were covered with a pattern of gold stars on red. Fixed to the walls were a number of white brackets containing pots of indoor ivy. The curtains, which were striped red and white, were drawn. This cheerful interior was lit by a couple of red-shaded wall-lamps. In one chair sat Leslie Crewe, with his neck held rigidly and attentively. He was dressed in a navy-blue suit of normal cut, and a peach-coloured tie, and looked older than thirteen. In another chair lolled Collie Gould who was eighteen and had been found unfit for National Service; Collie suffered from lung trouble for which he was constantly under treatment and was at present on probation for motor stealing. He wore a dark-grey draped jacket with narrow black trousers. Trevor Lomas, dressed in blue-grey, lay between them on the sofa. All smoked American cigarettes. All looked miserable, not as an expression of their feelings, but as if by an instinctive pre-arrangement, to convey a decision on all affairs whatsoever.

Trevor held in his hand one of the two thin exercise books he had stolen from Dougal's drawer. The other lay on the carpet beside him.

"Listen to this," Trevor said. "It's called 'Phrases suitable for Cheese.'"

"Suitable for what?" said Collie.

"Cheese, it says. Code word, obvious. Listen to this what you make of it. There's a list.

"I thrilled to his touch

"I was too young at the time to understand why my mother was crying

"As he entered the room a shudder went through my frame

"In that moment of silent communion we renewed our shattered faith

"She was to play a vital role in my life

"Memory had not played me false

"He was always an incurable romantic

"I became the proud owner of a bicycle

"He spoke to me in desiccated tones

"Autumn again. Autumn. The burning of leaves in the park

"He spelt disaster to me
"I revelled in my first tragic part
"I had no eyes for any other man
"We were living a lie
"She proved a mine of information
"Once more fate intervened
"Munificence was his middle name
"I felt a grim satisfaction
"They were poles apart
"I dropped into a fitful doze."

"Read us it again, Trev," Leslie said. "It sounds like
English Dictation. Perhaps he's a teacher as well."

Trevor ignored him. He tapped the notebook and addressed Collie.

"Code," he said. "It's worth lolly."

An intensified expression of misery on Collie's face expressed his agreement.

"In with a gang, he is. It's bigger than I thought. Question now, to find out what his racket is."

"Sex," Leslie said.

"You don't say so?" Trevor said. "Well, that's helpful,
son. But we happen to have guessed all that. Question is,
what game of sex? Question is, national or international?"

Collie blew out his smoke as if it were slow poison.
"Got to work back from a clue," he said in his sick voice.
"Autumn's a clue. Wasn't there something about au-
tumn?"

"How dumb can you get?" Trevor enquired through
his nose. "It's a code. Autumn means something else.
Everything means something." He dropped the notebook
and painfully picked up the other. He read:

"Peckham. Modes of communication.

"Actions more effective than words. Enact everything. Depict.

"Morality. Functional. Emotional. Puritanical. Classical.

"Nelly Mahone. Lightbody Buildings.

"Tunnel. Meeting-house Lane Excavations police station yard. Order of St. Bridget. Nuns decamped in the night."

Trevor turned the pages.

Entry Parish Register 1658. May 5.
Rose, wife of Wm. Hathaway buried
Aged 103, who boare a sonn at the age
of 63.

Trevor said, "Definitely a code. Look how he spells 'son.' And this about bearing at the age of sixty-three."

Collie and Leslie came over to see the book.

"There's a clue here," Collie said, "that we could follow up."

"No," said Trevor, "you don't say so? Come on, kids, we got to look up Nelly Mahone."

"If we're going to have a row," Mavis said, "turn on the wireless loud."

"We're not going to have a row," said her husband, Arthur Crewe, in a voice trembling with patience. "I only ask a plain question, what you mean you can't ask him where he's going when he goes out?"

Mavis switched on the wireless to a roar. Then she herself shouted above it.

"If you want to know where he goes, ask him yourself."

"If you can't ask him how can I ask him?" Arthur said in competition with the revue on the wireless.

"What's it matter where he goes? You can't keep running about after him like he was a baby. He's thirteen now."

"You ought to a kept some control of him. Of course it's too late now——"

"Why didn't you keep some control——"

"How can I be at my work and control the kids same time? If you was——"

"There's no need to swear," Mavis said.

"I didn't swear. But I bloody well will, and there's no need to shout." He turned off the wireless and silence occurred, bringing a definite aural sensation.

"Turn on that wireless. If we're going to have a row I'm not letting the neighbours get to know," Mavis said.

"Leave it be," Arthur said, effortful with peace. "There's not going to be any row."

Dixie came downstairs. "What's all the row?" she said.

"Your step-dad's on about young Leslie. Expects me to ask him where he's going when he goes out. I say, why don't *he* ask if he wants to know. I haven't got eyes the back of my head, have I?"

"Sh-sh-sh. Don't raise your voice," Arthur said.

"He's afraid to say a word to Leslie," Dixie said.

"That's just about it," said her mother.

"Who's afraid?" Arthur shouted.

"You are," Mavis shouted.

"I'm not afraid. You're afraid. . . ."

"Keep time," said Trevor. "All keep in time. It's psychological."

And so they all three trod in time up the stone stairs of Lightbody Buildings. Twice, a door opened on a landing, a head looked out, and the door shut quickly again. Trevor and his followers stamped louder as they approached Nelly Mahone's. Trevor beat like a policeman thrice on her door, and placed his ear to the crack.

There was a shuffling sound, a light switch clicked, then silence.

Trevor beat again.

"Who is it?" Nelly said from immediately on the other side of the door.

"Police agents," Trevor said.

The light switch clicked again, and Nelly opened the door a fragment.

Trevor pushed it wide open and walked in, followed by Collie and Leslie.

Leslie said, "I'm not stopping in this dirty hole," and made to leave.

Trevor caught him by the coat and worked him to a standstill.

"It's all clean dirt," Nelly said.

"Sit over there," Trevor said to Nelly, pointing to a chair beside the table. She did so.

He sat himself on the edge of the table and pointed to the edge of the bed for Leslie and the lopsided armchair for Collie.

"We come to talk business," Trevor said, "concerning a Mr. Dougal Douglas."

"Never heard of him," Nelly said.

"No?" Trevor said, folding his arms.

"Supposed to be police agents, are you? Well, you can be moving off if you don't want trouble. There's a gentleman asleep next door. I only got to raise me voice and——"

Collie and Leslie looked at the wall towards which Nelly pointed.

"Nark it," Trevor said. "He's gone to football this afternoon. Now, about Mr. Dougal Douglas——"

"Never heard of him," Nelly said.

Trevor leaned forward slightly towards her and, taking a lock of her long hair in his hand, twitched it sharply.

"Help! Murder! Police!" Nelly said.

Trevor put his big hand over her mouth and spoke to her.

"Listen, Nelly, for your own good. We got money for you."

Nelly struggled, her yellow eyeballs were big.

"I get my boys to rough you up if you won't listen, Nelly. Won't we, boys?"

"That's right," Collie said.

"Won't we, boys?" Trevor said, looking at Leslie.

"Sure," said Leslie.

Trevor removed his hand, now wet, from Nelly's mouth, and wiped it on the side of his trousers. He took a large wallet from his pocket, and flicked through a pile of bank notes.

"He's at Miss Frierne's up the Rye," Nelly said.

Trevor laid his wallet on the table and folding his arms, looked hard at Nelly.

"He got a job at Meadows Meade," Nelly said.

Trevor waited.

"He got another job at Drover Willis's under different name. No harm in him, son."

Trevor waited.

"That's all, son," Nelly said.

"What's cheese?" Trevor said.

"What's what?"

Trevor pulled her hair, so that she toppled towards him from her chair.

"I'll find out more. I only seen him once," Nelly said.

"What he want with you?"

"Huh?"

"You heard me."

Nelly looked at the two others, then back at Trevor.

"The boys is under age," she remarked, and her eyes flicked a little to reveal that her brain was working.

"I ask you a question," Trevor said. "What Mr. Dougal Douglas come to you for?"

"About the girl," she said.

"What girl?"

"He's after Beauty," she said. "He want me to find out where she live and that. You better go and see what he's up to. Probable he's with her now."

"Who's his gang?" Trevor enquired, reaching for Nelly's hair.

She jumped away from him. Leslie's nerve gave way and he ran to Nelly and hit her on the face.

"Murder!" Nelly screamed.

Trevor put his hand over her mouth, and signalled with his eyes to Collie, who went to the door, opened it a little way, listened, then shut it again. Collie then struck Leslie, who backed on to the bed.

Trevor, with his big hand on Nelly's mouth, whispered softly in her ear,

"Who's his gang, Nelly? What's the code key? Ten quid to you, Nelly."

She squirmed and he took his moist hand from her mouth. "Who's his gang?"

"He goes with Miss Coverdale sometimes. He goes with that fair-haired lady controller that's gone to Drover Willis's. That's all I know of his company."

"Who are the fellows?"

"I'll find out," she said, "I'll find out, son. Have a heart."

"Who's Rose Hathaway?"

"Never heard of her."

Trevor took Dougal's rolled-up exercise book from an inside pocket and spreading it out at the page read out the bit about that Rose Hathaway who was buried at a hundred and three. "That mean anything to you?" Trevor said.

"It sounds all wrong. I'll ask him."

"You won't. You'll find out your own way. Not a word we been here, get that?"

"It's only his larks. He's off his nut, son."

"Did he by any chance bring Humphrey Place here with him?"

"Who?"

Trevor twisted her arm.

"Humphrey Place. Goes with Dixie Morse."

"No, never seen him but once at the Grapes."

"You'll be seeing *us* again," Trevor said.

He went down the dark stone stairs followed by Leslie and Collie.

"Killing herself," Merle said, "that's what she is, for money. Then she comes in to the pool dropping tired next day, not fit for the job. I said to her, 'Dixie,' I said, 'what time did you go to bed last night?' 'I consider that a personal question, Miss Coverdale,' she says. 'Oh,' I says, 'well, if it isn't a personal question will you kindly type these two reports over again? There's five mistakes on one and six on the other.' 'Oh!' she said, 'what mistakes?' Because she won't own up to her mistakes till you put them under her nose. I said, 'These mistakes as marked.' She said 'Oh!' I said, 'You've been doing nothing but yawn yawn yawn all week.' Well, at tea-break when Dixie was out Connie says to me, 'Miss Coverdale, it's Dixie's evening job making her tired.' 'Evening job?' I said. She said, 'Yes, she's an usherette at the Regal from six-thirty to ten-thirty, makes extra for her wedding savings.' 'Well,' I said, 'no wonder she can't do her job here!' "

Dougal flashed an invisible cinema-torch on to the sprightly summer turf of the Rye. "Mind the step, Madam. Three-and-sixes on the right."

Merle began to laugh from her chest. Suddenly she sat down on the Rye and began to cry. "God!" she said. "Dougal, I've had a rotten life."

"And it isn't over yet," Dougal said, sitting down beside her at a little distance. "There might be worse ahead."

"First my parents," she said. "Too possessive. They're full of themselves. They don't think anything of me myself. They like to be able to say 'Merle's head of the pool at Meadows Meade,' but that's about all there is to it. I broke away and of course like a fool took up with Mr. Druce. Now I can't get away from him, somehow. You've unsettled me, Dougal, since you came to Peckham. I shall have a nervous breakdown, I can see it coming."

"If you do," Dougal said, "I won't come near you. I can't bear sickness of any sort."

"Dougal," she said, "I was counting on you to help me to get away from Mr. Druce."

"Get another job," he said, "and refuse to see him any more. It's easy."

"Oh, everything's easy for you. You're free."

"Aren't you free?" Dougal said.

"Yes, as far as the law goes."

"Well, stop seeing Druce."

"After six years, going on seven, Dougal, I'm tied in a sort of way. And what sort of job would I get at thirty-eight?"

"You would have to come down," Dougal said.

"After being head of the pool," she said, "I couldn't. I've got to think of my pride. And there's the upkeep of my flat. Mr. Druce puts a bit towards it."

"People are looking at you crying," Dougal said, "and they think it's because of me."

"So it is in a way. I've had a rotten life."

"Goodness, look at that," Dougal said.

She looked upward to where he was pointing.

"What?" she said.

"Up there," Dougal said; "trees in the sky."

"What are you talking about? I don't see anything."

"Look properly," Dougal said, "up there. And don't look away because Mr. Druce is watching us from behind the pavilion."

She looked at Dougal.

"Keep looking up," he said, "at the trees with red tassels in the sky. Look, where I'm pointing."

Several people who were crossing the Rye stopped to

look up at where Dougal was pointing. Dougal said to them, "A new idea. Did you see it in the papers? Planting trees and shrubs in the sky. Look there—it's a tip of a pine."

"I think I *do* see something," said a girl.

Most of the crowd moved sceptically away, still glancing upward now and then. Dougal brought Merle to her feet and drifted along with the others.

"Is he still there?" Merle said.

"Yes. He must be getting tired of going up and down in lifts."

"Oh, he only does that on Saturday mornings. He usually stays at home in the afternoons. He comes to me in the evenings. I've got a rotten life. Sometimes I think I'll swallow a bottle of aspirins."

"That doesn't work," Dougal said. "It only makes you ill. And the very thought of illness is abhorrent to me."

"He's keen on you," Merle said.

"I know he is, but *he* doesn't."

"He must do if he's keen——"

"Not at all. I'm his first waking experience of an attractive man."

"You fancy yourself."

"No, Mr. Druce does that."

"With your crooked shoulder," she said, "you're not all that much cop."

"Advise Druce on those lines," he said.

"He doesn't take my advice any more."

"How long would you give him with the firm?"

"Well, since he's started to slip, I've debated that question a lot. The business is on the decline. It's a worry, I mean about my flat, if Mr. Druce loses his job."

"I'd give him three months," Dougal said.

Merle started to cry again, walking towards the streets with Dougal. "Is he still there?" she said. Dougal did a dancer's pirouette, round and round, and stopped once more by Merle's side.

"He's walking away in the other direction."

"Oh, I wonder where he's going?"

"Home to Dulwich, I expect."

"It's immoral," Merle said, "the way he goes back to that woman in that house. They never say a word to each other."

"Stop girning. You look awful with your red eyes. It detracts from the okapi look. But all the same, what a long neck you've got!"

She put her hand up to her throat and moved it up her long neck. "Mr. Druce squeezed it tight the other day," she said, "for fun, but I got a fright."

"It looks like a maniac's delight, your neck," Dougal said.

"Well, you've not got much of one, with your shoulder up round your ear."

"A short neck denotes a good mind," Dougal said. "You see, the messages go quicker to the brain because they've shorter to go." He bent and touched his toes. "Suppose the message starts down here. Well, it come up here——"

"Watch out, people are looking."

They were in the middle of Rye Lane, flowing with shopping women and prams. A pram bumped into Dougal as he stood upright, causing him to barge forward into two women who stood talking. Dougal embraced them with wide arms. "Darlings, watch where you're going," he said. They beamed at each other and at him.

"Charming, aren't you?" Merle said. "There's a man leaning out of that car parked outside Higgins and Jones, seems to be watching you."

Dougal looked across the road. "Mr. Willis is watching me," he said. "Come and meet Mr. Willis." He took her arm to cross the road.

"I'm not dressed for an introduction," Merle said.

"You are only an object of human research," Dougal said, guiding her obliquely through the traffic towards Mr. Willis.

"I'm just waiting for my wife. She's shopping in there," Mr. Willis explained. Now that Dougal had approached him he seemed rather embarrassed. "I wasn't sure it was you, Mr. Dougal," he explained. "I was just looking to see. A bit short-sighted."

"Miss Merle Coverdale, one of my unofficial helpers," Dougal said uppishly. "Interesting," he said, "to see what Peckham does on its Saturday afternoons."

"Yes, quite." Mr. Willis pinkly took Merle's hand and glanced towards the shop door.

Dougal gave a reserved nod and, as dismissing Mr. Willis from his thoughts, led Merle away.

"Why did he call you Mr. Dougal?" Merle said.

"Because he's my social inferior. Formerly a footman in our family."

"What's he now?"

"One of my secret agents."

"You'd send me mad if I let you. Look what you've done to Weedin. You're driving Mr. Druce up the wall."

"I have powers of exorcism," Dougal said, "that's all."

"What's that?"

"The ability to drive devils out of people."

"I thought you said you were a devil yourself."

"The two states are not incompatible. Come to the police station."

"Where are we going, Dougal?"

"The police station. I want to see the excavation."

He took her into the station yard where he had already made himself known as an interested archaeologist. By the coal-heap was a wooden construction above a cavity already some feet deep. Work had stopped for the week-end. They peered inside.

"The tunnel leads up to Nunhead," Dougal said, "the nuns used to use it. They packed up one night over a hundred years ago, and did a flit, and left a lot of debts behind them."

A policeman came up to them with quiet steps and, pointing to the coal-heap, said, "The penitential cell stood in that corner. Afternoon, sir."

"Goodness, you gave me a fright," Merle said.

"There's bodies of nuns down there, miss," the policeman said.

Merle had gone home to await Mr. Druce. Dougal walked up to Costa's Café in the cool of the evening. Eight people were inside, among them Humphrey and Dixie, seated at a separate table eating the remains of sausage and egg. Humphrey kicked out a chair at their table for Dougal to sit down upon. Dixie touched the corners of her mouth with a paper napkin, and carefully picking up her knife and fork, continued eating, turning her head a little obliquely to receive each small mouthful. Humphrey had just finished. He set down his knife and fork on the plate and pushed the plate away. He rubbed the palms of his hands together twice and said to Dougal, "How's life?"

"It exists," Dougal said, and looked about him.

"You had a distinguished visitor this afternoon. But you'd just gone out. The old lady was out and I answered to him. He wouldn't leave his name. But of course I knew it. Mr. Druce of Meadows Meade. Dixie pointed him out to me, once, didn't you, Dixie?"

"Yes," Dixie said.

"He followed me all over the Rye, so greatly did Mr. Druce wish to see me," Dougal said.

"If I was you," Humphrey said, "I'd keep to normal working hours. Then he wouldn't have any call on you Saturday afternoons—would he, Dixie?"

"I suppose not," Dixie said.

"Coffee for three," Dougal said to the waiter.

"You had another visitor, about four o'clock," Humphrey said. "I'll give you a clue. She had a pot of flowers and a big parcel."

"Elaine," Dougal said.

The waiter brought three cups of coffee, one in his right hand and two—one resting on the other—in his left. These he placed carefully on the table. Dixie's slopped over in her saucer. She looked at the saucer.

"Swap with me," Humphrey said.

"Have mine," Dougal said.

She allowed Humphrey to exchange his saucer with hers. He tipped the contents of the saucer into his coffee, sipped it, and set it down.

"Sugar," he said.

Dougal passed the sugar to Dixie.

She said, "Thank you." She took two lumps, dropped

them in her coffee, and stirred it, watching it intently.

Humphrey put three lumps in his coffee, stirred it rapidly, tasted it. He pushed the sugar bowl over to Dougal, who took a lump and put it in his mouth.

"I let her go up to your room," Humphrey said. "She said she wanted to put in some personal touches. There was the pot of flowers and some cretonne cushions. The old lady was out. I thought it nice of Elaine to do that—wasn't it nice, Dixie?"

"Wasn't what nice?"

"Elaine coming to introduce feminine touches in Dougal's room."

"I suppose so."

"Feeling all right?" Humphrey said to her.

"I suppose so."

"Do you want to go on somewhere else or do you want to stay here?"

"Anything you like."

"Have a cake."

"No, thank you."

"Why does your brother go hungry?" Dougal said to her.

"Whose brother goes hungry?"

"Yours. Leslie."

"What you mean, goes hungry?"

"He came round scrounging doughnuts off my landlady the other day," Dougal said.

Humphrey rubbed the palms of his hands together and smiled at Dougal. "Oh, kids, you know what they're like."

"I won't stand for him saying anything against Leslie," Dixie said, looking round to see if anyone at the other tables was listening. "Our Leslie isn't a scrounger. It's a lie."

"It is not a lie," Dougal said.

"I'll speak to my step-dad," Dixie said.

"I should," Dougal said.

"What's a doughnut to a kid?" Humphrey said to them both. "Don't make something out of nothing. Don't *start*."

"Who started?" Dixie said.

"You did, a matter of fact," Humphrey said, "with your bad manners. You could hardly say hallo to Dougal when he came in."

"That's right, take his part," she said. "Well, I'm not staying here to be insulted."

She rose and picked up her bag. Dougal pulled her down to her chair again.

"Take your hand off me," she said, and rose.

Humphrey pulled her down again.

She remained seated, looking ahead into the far distance.

"There's Beauty just come in," Dougal said.

Dixie turned her head to see Beauty. Then she resumed her fixed gaze.

Dougal whistled in Beauty's direction.

"I shouldn't do that," Humphrey said.

"My God, he's supposed to be a professional man," Dixie said, "and he opens his mouth and whistles at a girl."

Dougal whistled again.

Beauty raised her eyebrows.

"You'll have Trevor Lomas in after us," Humphrey said. The waiter and Costa himself came and hovered round their table.

"Come on up to the Harbinger," Dougal said, "and we'll take Beauty with us."

"Now look. I quite *like* Trevor," Humphrey said.

"He's to be best man at our wedding," Dixie said. "He's got a good job with prospects and sticks in to it."

Dougal whistled. Then he called across two tables to Beauty, "Waiting for somebody?"

Beauty dropped her lashes. "Not in particular," she said.

"Coming up to the Harbinger?"

"Don't mind."

Dixie said, "Well, *I* do. I'm fussy about my company."

"What she say?" Beauty said, jerking herself upright in support of the question.

"I said," said Dixie, "that I've got another appointment."

"Beauty and I will be getting along then," Dougal said. He went across to Beauty who was preparing to comb her hair.

Humphrey said, "After all, Dixie, we've got nothing else to do. It might look funny if we don't go with Dougal. If Trevor finds out he's been to a pub with his girl——"

"You're bored with me—*I* know," Dixie said. "My company isn't good enough for you as soon as Dougal comes on the scene."

"Such compliments as you pay me!" Dougal said across to her.

"I was not aware I was addressing you," Dixie said.

"All right, Dixie, we'll stop here," Humphrey said.

Dougal was holding up a small mirror while the girl combed her long copper-coloured hair over the table.

Dixie's eyes then switched over to Dougal. She gave a

long sigh. "I suppose we'd better go to the pub with them," she said, "or you'll say I spoiled your evening."

"No necessity," Beauty said as she put away her comb and patted her handbag.

"We might enjoy ourselves," Humphrey said.

Dixie got her things together rather excitedly. But she said, "Oh, it isn't my idea of a night out."

And so they followed Dougal and Beauty up Rye Lane to the Harbinger. Beauty was halfway through the door of the saloon bar, but Dougal had stopped to look into the darkness of the Rye beyond the swimming baths, from which came the sound of a drunken woman approaching; and yet as it came nearer, it turned out not to be a drunken woman, but Nelly proclaiming.

Humphrey and Dixie had reached the pub door. "It's only Nelly," Humphrey said, and he pushed Dougal towards the doorway in which Beauty stood waiting.

"I like listening to Nelly," Dougal said, "for my human research."

"Oh, get inside for goodness' sake," Dixie said as Nelly appeared in the street light.

"Six things," Nelly declaimed, "there are which the Lord hateth, and the seventh his soul detesteth. Haughty eyes, a lying tongue, hands that shed innocent blood. See me in the morning. A heart that deviseth wicked plots, feet that are swift to run into mischief. Ten at Paley's yard. A deceitful witness that uttereth lies. Meetinghouse Lane. And him that soweth discord among brethren."

"Nelly's had a few," Humphrey said as they pushed into the bar. "She's a bit shaky on the pins tonight."

A bright spiky chandelier and a row of glittering crystal

lamps set against a mirror behind the bar—though in fact these had been installed since the war—were designed to preserve in theory the pub's vintage fame in the old Camberwell Palace days. The chief barmaid had a tiny nose and a big chin; she was a middle-aged woman of twenty-five. The barman was small and lithe. He kept swinging to and fro on the balls of his feet.

Beauty wanted a martini. Dixie, at first under the impression that Humphrey was buying the round, asked for a ginger ale, but when she perceived that Dougal was to pay for the drinks, she said, "Gin and ginger ale." Humphrey and Dougal carried to a table the girls' drinks and their own half-pints of mild which glittered in knobbly-moulded glass mugs like versions of the chandelier. Round the wall were hung signed photographs of old-time variety actors with such names, meaningless to most but oddly suggestive, as Flora Finch and Ford Sterling, who were generally assumed to be Edwardian stars. An upright piano placed flat against a wall caused Tony the pianist to see little of the life of the house, except when he turned round for a rest between numbers. Tony's face was not merely pale, but quite bloodless. He wore a navy-blue coat over a very white shirt, the shirt buttoned up to the neck with no tie. His half-pint mug, constantly replenished by the customers, stood on an invariable spot on the right-hand side of the piano-top. As he played, he swung his shoulders from side to side and bent over the piano occasionally to stress his notes. He might, from this back view, have been in an enthusiastic mood, but when he turned round it was obvious he was not. It was Tony's lot to play tunes of the nineteen-tens and -twenties, to the accompaniment of slightly jeering comments from the customers, and as he stooped over to execute *Charmaine*, Beauty said to him, "Groove in, Tony." He ignored this as he had ignored all remarks for the past nineteen months. "Go, man, go," someone suggested. "Leave him alone," the barmaid said. "You just show up your ignorance. He's a beautiful player. It's period stuff. He got to play it like that." Tony finished his number, took down his beer and turned his melancholy front to the company.

"Got any rock and cha-cha on your list, Tony?"

"Rev up to it, son. Groove in."

Tony turned, replaced his beer on the top of the piano, and rippled his hands over *Ramona*.

"Go, man, go."

"Any more of that," said the barmaid, "and you go man go outside."

"Yes, that's what *I* say. Tony's the pops."

"Here's a pint, Tony. Cheer up, son, it may never happen."

At ten past nine Trevor Lomas entered the pub followed by Collie Gould. Trevor edged in to the bar and stood with his back to it, leaning on an elbow and surveying as it were the passing scene.

"Hallo, Trevor," Dixie said.

"Hi, Dixie," Trevor replied severely.

"Hi," Collie Gould said.

Beauty, who was on her fourth martini, bowed graciously, and had some difficulty in regaining her upright posture.

The barmaid said, "Are you ordering, sir?"

Trevor said over his shoulder, "Two pints bitter." He lit a cigarette and blew out the smoke very very slowly.

122

"Trev," Collie said in a low voice, "Trev, don't muck it up."

"I'm being patient," Trevor said through half-closed lips. "I'm being very very patient. But if——"

"Trev," Collie said, "Trev, think of the lolly. Them notebooks."

Trevor threw half-a-crown backwards on to the counter.

"Manners," the barmaid said as she rang the till. She banged his change on the counter, where Trevor let it lie.

Dougal and Humphrey approached the bar with four empty glasses. "Ginger ale only," Dixie called after them, since it was Humphrey's turn.

"One martini. Two half milds. One *gin* and ginger ale," Humphrey said to the barman. And he invited Trevor to join them by pointing to their table with his ear.

Trevor did not move. Collie was watching Trevor.

Dougal got out some money.

"My turn," Humphrey said, fishing out his money.

Dougal picked half-a-crown from his money and, leaning his back against the bar, tossed it over his shoulder to the counter. He then lit a cigarette and blew out the smoke very slowly, pulling his face to a grave length and batting his eyelashes.

Beauty shouted, "Doug, you're a boy! Dig Doug! He's got you, Trev. He does Trevor to a T." Tony was playing the *St. Louis Blues*.

"Trev," Collie said, "don't, Trev, don't."

Trevor raised his sparkling pint glass and smashed the top on the edge of the counter. In his hand remained the bottom half with six spikes of glass sticking up from it. He lunged it forward at Dougal's face. At the same swift moment Dougal leaned back, back, until the crown of his head touched the bar. The spikes of glass went full into one side of Humphrey's face which had been turned in profile. Dougal bent and caught Trevor's legs while another man pulled Trevor's collar until presently he lay pinned by a number of hands to the floor. Humphrey was being attended by another number of hands, and was taken to the back premises, the barmaid holding to his face a large thick towel which was becoming redder and redder.

The barman shouted above the din, "Outside, all."

Most of the people were leaving in any case lest they should be questioned. To those who lingered the barman shouted, "Outside, all, or I'll call the police."

Trevor found himself free to get to his feet and he left, followed by Collie and Beauty, who was seen to spit at Trevor before she clicked her way up Rye Lane.

Dixie remained behind with Dougal. She was saying to him, "It was meant for *you*. Dirty swine you were to duck."

"Outside or I call the police," the barman said, bouncing up and down on the balls of his feet.

"We were with the chap that's hurt," Dougal said, "and if we can't collect him *I'll* call the police."

"Follow me," said the barman.

Humphrey was holding his head over a bowl while cold water was being poured over his wounds by Tony, who seemed to take this as one of his boring evening duties.

"Goodness, you look terrible," Dougal said. "It must be my fatal flaw, but I doubt if I can bear to look."

"Dirty swine, he is," Dixie said, "letting another fellow have it instead of himself."

"Shut up, will you?" Humphrey seemed to say.

They got into Humphrey's car, speedily assisted by the

124

barman. Dougal drove, first taking Dixie home. She said to him, "I could spit at you," and slammed the car door. "Oh, shut up," Humphrey said, as well as he could.

Dougal next drove Humphrey to the outpatient department of St. George's Hospital. "Though it pains me to cross the river," Dougal said, "I think we'd better avoid the southern region for tonight."

He told a story about Humphrey's having tripped over a milk-bottle as he got out of his car, the milk-bottle having splintered and Humphrey fallen on his face among the splinters. Humphrey nodded agreement as the nurse dressed and plastered his wounds. Dougal gave Humphrey's name as Mr. Dougal-Douglas, care of Miss Cheeseman, 14 Chelsea Rise, S.W.3. Humphrey was told to return within a week. They then went home to Miss Frierne's.

"And I won't even see her again till next Saturday night on account of her doing week-nights as an usherette at the Regal," Humphrey said to Dougal at a quarter to twelve that night. He sat up in bed in striped pyjamas, talking as much as possible; but the strips of plaster on his cheek caused him to speak rather out of the opposite side of his mouth. "And she won't think of taking one day off on her holidays this year on account of the honeymoon in September. It's nothing but save, save, save. You'd think I wasn't earning good money the way she goes on. And result, she's losing her sex."

Dougal crouched over the gas-ring with a fork, pushing the bacon about in the frying-pan. He removed the bacon on to a plate, then broke two eggs into the pan.

"I wouldn't marry her," Dougal said, "if you paid me."

"My sister Elsie doesn't like her," Humphrey said out of the side of his mouth.

Dougal stood up and took the plate of bacon in his hand. He held this at some way from his body and looked at it, moving it slightly back and forth towards him, as if it were a book he was reading, and he short-sighted.

Dougal read from the book: "Wilt thou take this woman," he said with a deep ecclesiastical throb, "to be thai wedded waif?"

Then he put the plate aside and knelt; he was a sinister goggling bridegroom. "No," he declared to the ceiling, "I won't, quite frankly."

"Christ, don't make me laugh, it pulls the plaster."

Dougal dished out the eggs and bacon. He cut up the bacon small for Humphrey.

"You shouldn't have any scars if you're careful and get your face regularly dressed, they said."

Humphrey stroked his wounded cheek.

"Scars wouldn't worry me. Might worry Dixie."

"As a qualified refrigerator engineer and a union man you could have your pick of the girls."

"I know, but I want Dixie." He put the eggs and bacon slowly away into the side of his mouth.

The rain of a cold summer morning fell on Nelly Mahone as she sat on a heap of disused lorry tyres in the yard of Paley's, scrap merchants of Meeting-house Lane. She had been waiting since ten past nine although she did not expect Dougal to arrive until ten o'clock. He came at five past ten, bobbing up and down under an umbrella.

"They come to see me Saturday," she said at once.

"Trevor Lomas, Collie Gould, Leslie Crewe. They treated me bad."

"You've got wet," Dougal said. "Why didn't you take shelter?"

She looked round the yard. "Got to be careful where you go, son. Stand up in the open, they can only tell you to move on. But go inside a place, they can call the cops." Her nose thrust forward towards the police station at the corner of the lane.

Dougal looked round the yard for possible shelter. The bodies of two lorries, bashed in from bad accidents, stood lopsided in a corner. On a low wooden cradle stood a house-boat. "We'll go into the boat."

"Oh, I couldn't get up there."

Dougal kicked a wooden crate over and over till it stood beneath the door of the boat. He pulled the door-handle. Eventually it gave way. He climbed in, then out again, and took Nelly by the arm.

"Up you go, Nelly."

"What if the cops come?"

"I'm in with them," Dougal said.

"Jesus, that's not your game?"

"Up you go."

He heaved her up and settled in the boat beside her on a torn upholstered seat. Some sad cretonne curtains still drooped in the windows. Dougal drew them across the windows as far as was possible.

"I feel that ill," Nelly said.

"I'm not too keen on illness," Dougal said.

"Nor me. They come to ask after you," Nelly said. "They found out you was seeing me. They got your code. They want to know what's cheese. They want to know

127

what's your code key, they offer me ten quid. They want to know who's your gang."

"I'm in with the cops, tell them."

"That I would never believe. They want to know who's Rose Hathaway. They'll be back again. I got to tell them something."

"Tell them I'm paid by the police to investigate certain irregularities in the industrial life of Peckham in the first place. See, Nelly? I mean crime at the top in the wee factories. And secondly——"

Her yellowish eyes and wet grey hair turned towards him in a startled way.

"If I thought you was a nark——"

"Investigator," Dougal said. "It all comes under human research. And secondly my job covers various departments of youthful terrorism. So you can just tell me, Nelly, what they did to you on Saturday afternoon."

"Ah, they didn't do nothing out of the way."

"You said they treated you roughly."

"No, not so to get them in trouble."

Dougal took out an envelope. "Your ten pounds," he said.

"You can keep it," Nelly said. "I'm going on my way."

"Feel my head, Nelly." He guided her hand to the two small bumps among his curls.

"Cancer of the brain a-coming on," she said.

"Nelly, I had a pair of horns like a goat when I was born. I lost them in a fight at a later date."

"Holy Mary, let me out of here. I don't know whether I'm coming or going with you."

Dougal stood up and found that by standing astride in the middle of the boat he could make it rock. So he rocked it for a while and sang a sailor's song to Nelly.

Then he helped her to climb down from the boat, put up his umbrella and tried to catch up with her as she hurried out of the scrap yard. A policeman, coming out of the station, at the corner, nodded to Dougal.

"I'll be going into the station then, Nelly," Dougal said. "To see my chums."

She stared at him, then spat on the rainy pavement.

"And I don't mind," Dougal said, "if you tell Trevor Lomas what I'm doing. You can tell him if he returns my notebooks to me there will be nothing further said. We policemen have got to keep our records and our secret codes, you realise."

She moved sideways away from him, watching the traffic so that she could cross at the earliest moment.

"You and I," Dougal said, "won't be molested from that quarter for a week or two if you give them the tip-off."

He went into the station yard to see how the excavations were getting on. He discovered that the tunnel itself was now visible from the top of the shaft.

Dougal pointed out to his policemen friends the evidence of the Thames silt in the under-soil. "One time," he said, "the Thames was five miles wide, and it covered all Peckham."

So they understood, they said, from other archaeologists who were interested in the excavation.

"Hope I'm not troubling you if I pop in like this from time to time?" Dougal said.

"No, sir, you're welcome. We get people from the papers sometimes as well as students. Did you read of the finds?"

Towards evening a parcel was delivered at Miss Frierne's

addressed to Dougal. It contained his notebooks.

"I hope to remain with you," Dougal said to Miss Frierne, "for at least two months. For I see no call upon me to remove from Peckham as yet."

"If I'm still alive . . ." Miss Frierne said. "I saw that man again this morning. I could swear it was my brother."

"You didn't speak to him?"

"No. Something stopped me." She began to cry.

"Who put the pot of indoor creeping ivy in my room?" Dougal said. "Was it my little dog-toothed blond process-controller?"

"Yes, it was a scraggy little blonde. Looks as if she could do with a good feed. They all do."

Mr. Druce whispered, "I couldn't manage it the other night. Things were difficult."

"I sat at the Dragon in Dulwich from nine till closing time," Dougal said, "and you didn't come."

"I couldn't get away. Mrs. Druce was on the watch. If you'd come to that place in Soho——"

Dougal consulted his pocket diary. He shut it and put it away. "Next month it would have to be. This month my duties press." He rose and walked up and down Mr. Druce's office as with something on his mind.

"I called for you last Saturday," Mr. Druce said. "I thought you would care for a spin."

"So I understand," Dougal said absently. "I believe I was researching on Miss Coverdale that afternoon." Dougal smiled at Mr. Druce. "Interrogating her, you know."

"Oh, yes."

"Her devotion to you is quite remarkable," Dougal said. "She spoke of you continually."

"As a matter of interest, what did you say? Look, Dougal, you can't trust everyone——"

Dougal looked at his watch. "Goodness," he said, "the time. What I came to see you about—the question of my increase in salary."

"It's going through," Mr. Druce said. "I put it to the Board that, since Weedin's breakdown, a great deal of extra work falls on your shoulders."

Dougal massaged both his shoulders, first his high one, then his low one.

"Dougal," said Mr. Druce.

"Vincent," said Dougal, and departed.

Chapter 8

Joyce Willis said, "Quite frankly, the first time Richard invited you to dinner I knew we'd found the answer. Richard didn't see it at first, quite frankly, but I think he's beginning to see it now."

She crossed the room, moving her long hips, and looked out of the bow window into the August evening. "Richard should be in any moment," she said. She touched her throat with her fine fingers. She put to rights a cushion in the window-seat.

Still standing, she lifted her glass, and sipped, and put it down on a low table. She crossed the room and sat on a chair upholstered in deep pink brocade.

"I feel I can really *talk* to you now," she said. "I feel we've known each other for years."

She said, "The Drovers *were* getting the upper hand. Richard was, well, quite frankly, being pushed into the position of subordinate partner.

"The nephew, Mark Bewlay—that's *her* nephew, of course—came to the firm two—was it two?—no, it was three years ago, imagine it, in October. And he was supposed to go through the factory from A to Z. Well, quite frankly he was sitting on the Board within six months. Then the son John came straight down from Oxford last year, and same thing again. The Board's reeking with Drovers.

"One of Richard's great mistakes—I'm speaking to you quite frankly," she said, "was insisting on our *living* in Peckham. Well, the house is all right—but I mean, the environment. There are simply no people in the place. Our friends always get lost finding the way here; they drive round for hours. And there are blacks at the other end of the Avenue, you know. I mean, it's so silly.

"Richard's a Scot, of course," she said, "and in a way that's why I think you understand his position. He's so scrupulously industrious and pathologically honest. And it's rather sweet in a way. Yes, I must say that. He simply doesn't see that the Drovers living in Sussex in a Georgian rectory gives them a big advantage. A big advantage. It's psychological."

She said, "Yes, Richard insists on living near the job, as he says. And quite frankly, I have to put up with a good deal of condescension from Queenie Drover, although she's sweet in a way. She knows of course that Richard's a bit old-fashioned and prides himself on being a *real merchant,* they both know, the Drovers. They know it only too well."

She filled both glasses with sherry, turning the good bones of her wrists and holding the glasses at the ends of her long fingers with their lacquered nails and the bright emerald. She looked at herself, before she sat down, in the gilt-framed glass and turned back a wisp of her short dark-gold hair. Her face was oval; she posed it to one side; she said, "Of course it has been a disappointment that we had no children. If there had been a son to support Richard on the Board . . . Sometimes I feel, quite frankly, the firm should be called Drover, Drover, Drover Willis, not just Drover Willis.

"Richard was touched a few weeks ago," she said, "he told me so, when he met you one Saturday afternoon while he was waiting for me outside the shop, and he saw you working away on your Saturday afternoon, spending your Saturday afternoon with a Peckham girl, trying to get to know the types. Richard thinks you are brilliant, you know. A fine brain and a sound moral sense, he told me, quite frankly, and he thinks you're absolutely wasted in the personnel research job. The thing about you—and I saw it long before Richard and I'm not just saying it because you're here—you're so young and energetic, and yet so *steady*. I suppose it's being a Scot.

"Not many young fellows of your age," she said, "—I'm not flattering you—and of your qualifications and ability would be prepared to settle down as you have done in a place like Peckham where the scope for any kind of gaiety is so limited, there's nothing to do and there are no young people for you to meet. I'm speaking quite frankly, as I would to my own son if I had one.

"I feel towards you," she said, "as to a son. I hope—I would always hope—to count you as one of the family although, as you know, there are only Richard and me. I was so interested in your conversation the other night about so many things I didn't quite frankly know existed in this area. The Camberwell Art Gallery I knew of course; but the excavations of the tunnel—I had only read of its progress in the *South London Observer*—I didn't dream there was anything so serious and learned behind it."

She turned and plumped out the cushion behind her. She looked at her pointed toes. "You must sometimes come to town with us. We go to the theatre at least once a week," she said.

She said, "The idea that you should come on the Board with Richard in the autumn is an excellent one. It will almost be like having a Willis in the firm. Your way of speaking is so like Richard's—I mean, not just the accent, but well, quite frankly, I mean, you don't say *much,* but when you say something it's the right thing. Richard needs you and I think I'm right in saying it's an ideal prospect for a young man of your temperament, and it means serious responsibility and an established position within a matter of five or six years. You have this way of approaching life seriously, not just here to-day and gone to-morrow, and it appeals to Richard. Richard is a judge of character. One day the firm might be Drover, Willis & Dougal. Just a moment——"

She went over to the window, smoothing her waist, and glanced through the window as a car drew up in the small curved drive. "Here's Richard," she said. "He's been looking forward to having a serious chat with you this evening, and getting things settled before we go abroad."

"Is that you, Jinny?"
"Yes."
"Have you got any milk on the stove?"
"No."
"When can I come and see you?"
"I'm getting married next week."
"No, Jinny."
"I'm in love with him. He was sweet when I was ill."

"Just when I'm getting on my feet and drawing two pays for nothing," Dougal said, "you tell me——"

"It wouldn't have worked between us, Dougal. I'm not strong in health."

"Well, that's that," Dougal said.

"Miss Cheeseman's thrilled with her autobiography so far," Jinny said. "You'll do well, Dougal."

"You've changed. You are using words like 'sweet' and 'thrilled.' "

"Oh, get away. Miss Cheeseman said she was pleased."

"She doesn't tell me that."

"Well, she has some tiny reservations about the Peckham bits, but on the whole——"

"I'm coming over to see you, Jinny."

"No, Dougal, I mean it."

Dougal went in to Miss Frierne's kitchen and wept into his large pocket handkerchief.

"Are you feeling all right?" she said.

"No. My girl's getting married to another chap."

She filled the kettle and put it down on the draining board. She opened the back door and shut it again. She took up a duster and dusted a kitchen chair, back and legs.

"You're better off without her," she said.

"I'm not," Dougal said, "but I've got a fatal flaw."

"You're not drinking at nights, Dougal?"

"No more than usual."

She lifted the kettle and put it down again.

"Calm down," Dougal said.

"Well, it upsets me inside to see a man upset."

"Light the gas and put the kettle on it," he said.

She did this, then stood and looked at him. She took off her apron.

"Sit down," Dougal said.

She sat down.

"Stand up," he said, "and fetch me a tot of your gin."

She brought two glasses and the gin bottle. "It's only quarter-past five," she said. "It's early to start on gin. Here's to you, son. You'll soon get over it."

The front-door bell rang. Miss Frierne caused the bottle and glasses to disappear. The bell rang again. She went to answer it.

"Name of Frierne?" said a man's voice.

"Yes, what do you want?"

"Could I have a private word with you?"

Miss Frierne returned to the kitchen followed by a policeman.

"A man aged about seventy-nine was run over by a bus this morning on the Walworth Road. Sorry, madam, but he had the name Frierne in his pocket written on a bit of paper. He died an hour ago. Any relation you know of, madam?"

"No, I don't know of him. Must be a mistake. You can ask my neighbours if you like. I'm the only one left in the world."

"Very good," said the policeman, making notes. "Did he have any other papers on him?"

"No, nothing. A pauper, poor devil."

The policeman left.

"Well, there wasn't anything I could do if he's dead, was there?" Miss Frierne said to Dougal. She started crying. "Except pay for the funeral. And it's hard enough keeping going and that."

137

Dougal fetched out the gin again and poured two glasses. Presently he placed a kitchen chair to face the chair on which he sat. He put up his feet on it and said, "Ever seen a corpse?" He lolled his head back, closed his eyes and opened his mouth so that the bottom jaw was sunken and rigid.

"You're callous, that's what you are," Miss Frierne said. Then she screamed with hysterical mirth.

Humphrey sat with Mavis and Arthur Crewe in their sitting-room, touching, every now and then, two marks on his face.

"Well, if by any chance you don't have her, it's your luck," Mavis said. "I say it though she's my own daughter. When I was turned seventeen, eighteen, I was out with the boys every night, dancing and so forth. You wouldn't have caught me doing no evening work just for a bit of money. And there aren't so many boys willing to sit round waiting like you. She'll learn when it's too late."

"It isn't as if she parts with any of her money," Arthur Crewe said. "You don't get the smell of an oil-rag out of Dixie. The more she's got the meaner she gets."

"What's that got to do with it?" Dixie's mother said. "You don't want anything from her, do you?"

"I never said I did. I was only saying——"

"Dixie has her generous side," Mavis said. "You must hand it to her, she's good to Leslie. She's always slipping him five bob here and five bob there."

"Pity she does it," Arthur said. "The boy's ruined. He's money mad."

"What you know about kids? There's nothing wrong

138

with Leslie. He's no different from the rest. They all like money in their pockets."

"Where's Leslie now, anyway?"

"Gone out."

"Where?"

"How do I know? You ask him."

"He's with Trevor Lomas," Humphrey said. "Up at Costa's."

"There you are, Arthur. There's no harm in Trevor Lomas."

"He's a bit old company for Leslie."

"Grumble, grumble, grumble," Mavis said, and switched on the television.

Leslie came in at eleven. He looked round the sitting-room.

"Hallo, Les," Humphrey said.

Leslie did not speak. He went upstairs.

At half-past eleven Dixie came home. She kicked off her shoes in the sitting-room and flopped on to the sofa. "You been here long?" she said to Humphrey.

"An hour or two."

"Nice to be able to sit down of a summer evening," Dixie said.

"Yes, why don't you try it?"

"Trevor Lomas says there's plenty of overtime at Freeze-eezy if anyone wants it."

"Well, I don't want it," Humphrey said.

"Obvious."

"Who wants to do overtime all their lives?" Mavis said.

"I was just remarking," Dixie said, "what Trevor Lomas told me."

"Overtime should be avoided except in cases of necessity," Humphrey said, "because eventually it reduces the normal capacity of the worker and in the long run leads to under-production, resulting in further demands for overtime. A vicious circle. Where did you see Trevor Lomas?"

"It *is* a case of necessity," Dixie said, "because we need all the money we can get."

"That's how she goes on," Mavis said. "Why she can't be content to settle down with a man's good wages like other people I don't know. With a bungalow earmarked for October——"

"I want it to be a model bungalow," Dixie said.

"You'll have your model bungalow," Humphrey said.

"She wants a big splash wedding," Mavis said. "Well, Arthur and I will do what we can but *only* what we can."

"That's right," Arthur said.

"Dixie's entitled to the best," Mavis said. "She's got a model dress in view."

"Where did you see Trevor Lomas?" Humphrey said to Dixie.

"Up at Costa's. I went in for a Coke on the way home. Any objections?"

"No, dear, no," Humphrey said.

"Nice of you. Well, I'm going to bed, I'm tired out. You still got your scars."

"They'll go away in time."

"I don't mind. Trevor's got a scar."

"I better keep my eye on Trevor Lomas," Humphrey said.

"You better keep your eye on your friend Dougal Douglas. Trevor says he's a dick."

"I don't believe it," Mavis said.

"Nor do I," said Arthur.

140

"No more do I," said Humphrey.

"I know you think he's perfect," Dixie said. "He can do no wrong. But I'm just telling you what Trevor said. So don't say I didn't tell you."

"Trevor's having you on," Humphrey said. "He doesn't like Dougal."

"I like him," Arthur said.

"I like him," Mavis said. "Our Leslie don't like him. Dixie don't like him."

"I like him," Humphrey said. "My sister Elsie doesn't like him."

"Is Mr. Douglas at home?"

"Well, he's up in his room playing the typewriter at the moment," said Miss Frierne, "as you can hear."

"Can I go up?"

"No, I must enquire. Come inside, please. What name?"

"Miss Coverdale."

Miss Frierne left Miss Coverdale in that hall which was lined with wood like a coffin. The sound of the typewriter stopped. Dougal's voice called down from the second landing, "Come up." Miss Frierne frowned in the direction of his voice. "Top floor," she said to Merle.

"I'm miserable. I had to see you," Merle said to Dougal. "What a nice little room you've got here!"

"Why are you not at work?" Dougal said.

"I'm too upset to work. Mr. Druce is talking of leaving the country for good. What should I do?"

"What do you want to do?" Dougal said.

"I want to go with him but he won't take me."

"Why not?"

"He knows I don't like him."

Dougal stretched himself out on the top of his bed.

"Does Mr. Druce mention any date for his departure?"

"No, there's nothing settled. Perhaps it's only a threat. But I think he's frightened of something."

Dougal sat up and placed one hand within the other. He shortened his eyesight and peered at Merle with sublime appreciation. "Dougal," he said, "there is a little place in Soho, would you not come to spend the evening and have a chat? Mrs. Druce is just a bit difficult, she watches——"

"Oh, don't," Merle said. "It brings everything back to me. I can't tell you how I hate the man. I can't bear him to be near me. And now, after all these years, the best years of my life, the swine talks of leaving me."

Dougal lay back with his arms behind his head. "What's he frightened of?" he said.

"You," Merle said. "He's got hold of the idea that you're spying on him."

"In what capacity?"

"Oh, I couldn't say."

"Yes, you could."

"If you're working for the police, Dougal, please tell me. Think of my position. After all, I told you about Mr. Druce in all innocence and if I'm going to be dragged into anything——"

"I'm not working for the police," Dougal said.

"Well, of course, I knew you wouldn't admit it."

"What guilty wee consciences you've all got," Dougal said.

"Don't do anything about Mr. Druce, will you? The Board are just waiting for an excuse, and if they get to know about his deals and all that it will only come back on me. Where will I stand if he emigrates?"

"Who tipped Druce off? Was it Trevor Lomas?"

"No, it was Dixie, the little bitch. She's been going in and out to Mr. Druce a lot behind my back."

"Ah well. Take some shorthand dictation, will you, as you're here?" He got up and fetched her a notebook and a Biro pen.

"Dougal, I'm upset."

"There's nothing like work to calm your emotions. After all, you should be working at this moment. Are you ready? Tell me if I'm going too fast:

" 'Peckham was fun exclamation mark but the day inevitably dawned when I realised that I and my beloved pals at the factory were poles apart full stop The great throbbing heart of London across the river spelt fame comma success comma glamour to me full stop I was always an incurable romantic exclamation mark New para The poignant moment arrived when I bade farewell to my first love full stop Up till now I had had eyes for no others but fate—capital F—had intervened full stop We kissed dot dot dot a shudder went through my frame dot dot dot every fibre of my being spoke of gratitude and grief but the budding genius within me cried out for expression full stop And so we parted for ever full stop New para I felt a grim satisfaction as the cab which bore me and my few poor belongings bowled across Vauxhall Bridge and into the great world—capital G capital W— ahead full stop Yes comma Peckham had been fun exclamation mark' Now, leave a space, please, and——"

"What's all this about?" Merle said.

"Don't fuss, you're putting me off."

"God, if Mr. Druce thought I was working in with you, he'd kill me."

"Leave a space," Dougal said, "then a row of dots. That denotes a new section. Now continue. Throughout all the years of my success I have never forgotten those early comma joyful comma innocent days in Peckham full stop Only the other day I came across the following paragraph in the paper——' Hand me the paper," Dougal said, "till I find the bit."

She passed him the newspaper. "Dougal," she said, "I'm going."

"Surely not till you've typed it out for me?" he said. "There isn't much more to take down."

He found the paragraph and said, "Put this bit in quotation marks. Are you ready? 'The excavations on the underground tunnel leading from the police station yard at Peckham are now nearing completion full stop The tunnel comma formerly used by the nuns of the Order of St. Bridget comma stretches roughly six hundred yards from the police station bracket formerly the site of the priory unbracket to Gordon Road and not comma as formerly supposed comma to Nunhead. Archaeologists have reported some interesting finds and human remains all of which will be removed before the tunnel is open to the public quite shortly full stop end quotes.'"

"Is this a police report?" Merle said. "Because if so I don't want to do it, Dougal. Mr. Druce would——"

"Only a few more words," Dougal said. "Ready? New paragraph 'When I read the above tears started to my eyes full stop How well did I recall every detail of that station yard two exclamation marks The police in my day were far from——"

"I can't go on," Merle said. "This is putting me in a difficult position."

"All right, dear," Dougal said. He sat up and stroked her long neck till she started to cry.

"Type it out," Dougal said, "and forget your troubles. It's a nice typewriter. You'll find the paper on the table."

She sat up to the table and typed from her shorthand notes.

Dougal lay back on his bed. "There is no more beautiful sight," he said, "than to see a fine woman bashing away at a typewriter."

"Is Mr. Douglas in?"

"He's up in his room writing out his reports. He's busy."

"Can I go up?"

"I'll see if it's convenient. But he's busy. Come inside, please. What name?"

"Elaine Kent."

"Come up," Dougal called from the second landing.

"You may go up," Miss Frierne said. "Top floor." Miss Frierne stood and watched her climbing out of sight.

"You've been putting too much water in the plant," Elaine said, feeling the soil round the potted ivy. "You should water it once a week only."

"People come here to cry," Dougal said, "which accounts for an excess of moisture in this room."

She took a crumpled brown-paper bag from her shopping basket. They were Dougal's socks which had been washed and darned.

"There's talk going round about you," Elaine said.

"Makes me laugh. They say you're in the pay of the cops."

"What's funny about it?"

"Catch the Peckham police boys spending their money on you."

"Oh, I would make an excellent informer. I don't say plain-clothes policeman, exactly, but for gathering information and having no scruples in passing it on you could look farther than me and fare worse."

"There's a gang watching out for you," Elaine said. "So be careful where you go at nights. I shouldn't go out alone much."

"Terrifying, isn't it? I mean, say this is the street and there's Trevor over there. And say here's Collie Gould crossing the road. And young Leslie comes up to me and asks the time and I look at my watch. Then out jumps Trevor with a razor—rip, rip, rip. But Collie whistles loud on his three fingers. Leslie gives me a parting kick where I lie in the gutter and slinks after Trevor away into the black concealing night. Up comes the copper and finds me. The cop takes one look, turns away and pukes on the pavement. He then with trembling fingers places a whistle to his lips."

"Sit down and stop pushing the good furniture about," she said.

"I've gone and worked myself up with my blether," Dougal said. "I feel that frightened."

"Leslie was waiting for Mr. Willis at five o'clock the day before he went on his holidays. I saw him standing behind Mr. Willis's car. So I hung on just to see. And then Mr. Willis came out. And then Leslie came forward. And then Leslie said something and Mr. Willis said something. So I walked past. I heard Mr. Willis say, 'Have you left school?' and Leslie said, 'What's that to you?' and Mr. Willis said, 'I should want to know a good deal more about you before I took notice of what you say'— or it was something like that, Mr. Willis said. And then Mr. Willis drove away."

"Ah well," Dougal said, "I expect to be leaving here next month. Will you cry when I'm gone?"

"I'd watch it."

"Come on out to the pictures," Dougal said, "for fine evening though it is I am inclined for a bit of darkness." On the way out he picked up a letter postmarked from Grasse. He read it going down the street with Elaine.

Dear Douglas,

We arrived on Saturday night. The weather is perfect and this is quite a pleasant hotel with delightful view. The food is quite good. The people are very pleasant, at least so far! We have had one or two pleasant drives along the coast. Quite frankly, Richard needs a rest. You know yourself how he forces himself and is so conscientious.

Richard is very pleased with the arrangements we came to the other evening. It will be so much better to have someone to support him as there are so many Drovers in the firm now. (I almost think, quite frankly, the firm should be called Drover, Drover, Drover Willis instead of Drover Willis!) I hope you yourself are satisfied with the new arrangements. Richard instructed the accountant before he left about your increase and it will be back-dated from the date of your joining the firm as arranged.

I feel I ought to tell you of an incident which occurred just before we left, although, quite frankly, Richard decided not to mention it to you (in case it put you off!). A young boy in his teens waylaid Richard and told him you were a paid police informer employed apparently to look into the industries of Peckham in case of irregularities. Of course, Richard took no notice, and as I said to Richard, there would hardly be any reason for the police to suspect any criminal activities at Drover Willis's! Quite frankly, I thought I would tell you this to put you on your guard, as I feel I can talk to you, Douglas, as to a son. You have obviously made one or two enemies in the course of your research. That is always the trouble, they are so ungrateful. Before the war these boys used to be glad of a meal and a night's shelter, but now quite frankly . . .

Dougal put away the letter. "I am as melancholy a young man as you might meet on a summer's day," he said to Elaine, "and it feels quite nice."

They came out of the pictures at eight o'clock. Nelly Mahone was outside the pub opposite, declaiming, "The words of the double-tongued are as if they were harmless, but they reach even to the inner part of the bowels. Praise be to the Lord, who distinguishes our cause and delivers us from the unjust and deceitful man."

Dougal and Elaine crossed the road. As they passed, Nelly spat on the pavement.

Chapter 9

Merle Coverdale said to Trevor Lomas, "I've only been helping him out with a few private things. He's good company and he's different. I don't have much of a life."

"Only a few private things," Trevor said. "Only just helping him out."

"Well, what's wrong with that?"

"Typing out his nark information for him."

"Look," Merle said, "he isn't anything to do with the police. I don't know where that story started, but it isn't true."

"What's this private business you do for him?"

"No business of yours."

"We got to carve up that boy one of these days," Trevor said. "D'you want to get carved alongside of him?"

"Christ, I'm telling you the truth," Merle said. "It's only a story he's writing for someone he calls Cheese that had to do with Peckham in the old days. You don't understand Dougal. He's got no harm in him. He's just different."

"Cheese," Trevor said. "That's what you go there every Tuesday and every Friday night to work on."

"It's not real cheese," Merle said. "Cheese is a person, it isn't the real name."

"You don't say so," Trevor said. "And what's the real name?"

"I don't know, Mr. Lomas, truly."

"You won't go back there," Trevor stated.

"I'll have to explain to him, then. He's just a friend, Mr. Lomas."

"You don't see him again. Understand. We got plans for him."

"Mr. Lomas, you'd better go. Mr. Druce will be along soon. I don't want Mr. Druce to find you here."

"He knows I'm here."

"You never told him of me going to Dougal's, week-nights?"

"He knows, I said."

"It's you's the informer, not Dougal."

"Re-member. Any more work you do for him's going to go against you."

Trevor trod down the stairs from her flat with the same deliberate march as when he had arrived, and she watched him from her window taking Denmark Hill as if he owned it.

Mr. Druce arrived twelve minutes later. He took off his hat and hung it on the peg in her hall. He followed her into the sitting-room and opened the door of the side-board. He took out some whisky and poured himself a measure, squirting soda into it.

Merle took up her knitting.

"Want some?" he said.

"I'll have a glass of red wine. I feel I need something red, to buck me up."

He stooped to get the bottle of wine and, opening a drawer, took out the corkscrew.

"I just had a visitor," she said.

He turned to look at her with the corkscrew pointing from his fist.

"I daresay you know who it was," she said.

"Certainly I do. I sent him."

"My private life's my private life," she said. "I've never interfered with yours. I've never come near Mrs. Druce though many's the time I could have felt like telling her a thing or two."

He handed over her glass of wine. He looked at the label on the bottle. He sat down and took his shoes off. He put on his slippers. He looked at his watch. Merle switched on the television. Neither looked at it. "I've been greatly taken in by that Scotch fellow. He's in the pay of the police *and* of the board of Meadows Meade. He's been watching me for close on three months and putting in his reports."

"No, you're wrong there," Merle said.

"And you've been in with him this last month." He pointed his finger at her throat, nearly touching it.

"You're wrong there. I've only been typing out some stories for him."

"What stories?"

"About Peckham in the old days. It's about some old lady he knows. You've got no damn right to accuse me and send that big tough round here threatening me."

"Trevor Lomas," Mr. Druce said, "is in my pay. You'll do what Trevor suggests. We're going to run that Dougal Douglas, so-called, out of Peckham with something to remember us by."

"I thought you were going to emigrate."

"I am."

"When?"

"When it suits me."

He crossed his legs and attended to the television.

"I don't feel like any supper tonight," she said.

"Well, I do."

She went into the kitchen and made a clatter. She came back crying. "I've had a rotten life of it."

"Not since Dougal Douglas, so-called, joined the firm, from what I hear."

"He's only a friend. You don't understand him."

Mr. Druce breathed in deeply and looked up at the lampshade as if calling it to witness.

"You can have a chop with some potatoes and peas," she said. "I don't want any."

She sat down and took up her knitting, weeping upon it.

He leaned forward and tickled her neck. She drew away. He pinched the skin of her long neck, and she screamed.

"Sh-sh-sh," he said, and stroked her neck.

He went to pour himself some more whisky. He turned and looked at her. "What have you been up to with Dougal Douglas, so-called?" he said.

"Nothing. He's just a friend. A bit of company for me."

The corkscrew lay on the sideboard. He lifted an end, let it drop, lifted it, let it drop.

"I'd better turn the chop," she said and went into the kitchen.

He followed her. "You gave him information about me," he said.

"No, I've told you——"

"And you typed his reports to the Board."

She pushed past him, weeping noisily, to find her handkerchief on the chair.

"What else was between you and him?" he said, raising his voice above the roar of the television.

He came towards her with the corkscrew and stabbed it into her long neck nine times, and killed her. Then he took his hat and went home to his wife.

"Doug dear," said Miss Maria Cheeseman.

"I'm in a state," Dougal said, "so could you ring off?"

"Doug, I just wanted to say. You've re-written my early years so beautifully. Those new Peckham stories are absolutely sweet. I'm sure you feel, as I feel, that the extra effort was quite worth it. And now the whole book's perfect, and I'm thrilled."

"Thanks," said Dougal. "I doubt if the new bits were worth all the trouble, but——"

"Doug, come over and see me this afternoon."

"Sorry, Cheese, I'm in a state. I'm packing. I'm leaving here."

"Doug, I've got a little gift for you. Just an appreciation——"

"I'll ring you back," Dougal said. "I've just remembered I've left some milk on the stove."

"You'll let me have your new address, won't you?"

Dougal went into the kitchen. Miss Frierne was seated at the table, but she had slipped down in her chair. She seemed to be asleep. One side of her face was askew. Her eyelid fluttered.

Dougal looked round for the gin bottle to measure the extent of Miss Frierne's collapse. But there was no gin bottle, no bottle at all, no used glass. He took another look at Miss Frierne. Her eyelid fluttered and her lower lip moved on one side of her mouth.

Dougal telephoned to the police to send a doctor. Then he went upstairs and fetched down his luggage comprising his zipper-case, his shiny new brief-case and his type-writer. The doctor arrived presently and went in to Miss Frierne. "A stroke," he said.

"Well, I'll be off," Dougal said.

"Are you a relative?"

"No, a tenant. I'm leaving."

"Right away?"

"Yes," Dougal said. "I was leaving in any case, but I've got a definite flaw where illness is concerned."

"Has she got any relatives?"

"No."

"I'd better ring the ambulance," the doctor said. "She's pretty far gone."

Dougal walked with his luggage up Rye Lane. In the distance he saw a crowd outside the police station yard. He joined it, and pressed through with his bags into the yard.

"Going away?" said one of the policemen.

"I'm leaving the district. I thought, from the crowd, there might be some new find in the tunnel."

The policeman nodded towards the crowd. "We've just arrested a man in connection with the murder."

"Druce," Dougal said.

"That's right."

"Druce is the man," Dougal said.

"He's the chap all right. She might have been left there for days if it hadn't been for the food burning on the gas.

154

The neighbours thought there was a fire and broke in. The tunnel's open now, as you see; the steps are in. Official opening on Wednesday. Lights are being fixed now."

"Pity I won't be here. I should have liked to go along the tunnel."

"Go down if you like. It's only six hundred yards. Brings you out at Gordon Road. One of our men is on guard at that point. He'll know you. Pity not to see it as you've taken so much interest."

"I'll come," Dougal said.

"I can't take you," the policeman said. "But I'll get you a torch. It's just a straight run. All the coins and the old bronze have been taken away, so there's nothing there except some bones we haven't cleared away as yet. But you can say you've been through."

He went to fetch the torch. A young apprentice electrician emerged from the tunnel with two empty tea-mugs in his hand and went out through the crowd to a café across the road.

The policeman came back with a small torch. "Give this to the constable at the other end. Save you trouble of bringing it back. Well, goodbye. Glad to know you. I've got to go on duty now."

This tunnel had been newly supported in its eight-foot height by wooden props, between which Dougal wound his way. This tunnel—which in a few days' time was to be opened to the public, and in yet a few days more closed down owing to three scandals ensuing from its being frequented by the Secondary Modern Mixed School—was strewn with new gravel, trodden only, so far, by the workmen, and by Dougal as he proceeded with his bags.

About half-way through the tunnel Dougal put his bags

down and started to pick up some bones which were piled in a crevice ready to be taken away before the official opening. Then he held the torch between his teeth and juggled with some carefully chosen shin bones which were clotted with earth. He managed six at a time, throwing and catching, never missing, so that the earth fell away from them and scattered.

He picked up his bags and continued through the hot tunnel which smelt of its new disinfectant. He saw a strong lamp ahead and the figure of the electrician on a ladder cutting some wire in the wall.

The electrician turned. "You been quick, Bobby," he said.

Dougal switched out his torch and set down his bags on the gritty floor of the tunnel. He saw the electrician descend from the ladder with his knife and turn the big lamp towards him.

"Trevor Lomas, watch out for the old bones, they're haunted," Dougal said. He chucked what was once a hip at Trevor's head. Then with his left hand he grabbed the wrist that held the knife. Trevor kicked. Dougal employed that speciality of his with his right hand, clutching Trevor's throat back-handedly with his claw-like grip. Trevor went backward and stumbled over the bags, dropping the knife. Dougal picked it up, grabbed the bags and fled.

Near the end of the tunnel, where the light from the big lamp barely reached, Trevor caught up with him and delivered to Dougal a stab in the eye with a bone. Whereupon Dougal flashed his torch in Trevor's face and leapt at him with his high shoulder raised and elbow sticking out. He applied once more his deformed specialty. Holding Trevor's throat with this right-hand twist, he fetched him a left-hand blow on the corner of the jaw. Trevor sat down. Dougal picked up his bags, pointing his torch to the ground, and emerged from the tunnel at Gordon Road. There he reported to the policeman on duty that the electrician was sitting in a dazed condition among the old nuns' bones, having been overcome by the heat. "I can't stop to assist you," Dougal said, "for, as you see, I have to catch a train. Would you mind returning this torch with my thanks to the police station?"

"You hurt yourself?" the policeman said, looking at Dougal's eye.

"I bumped into something in the dark," Dougal said. "But it's only a bruise. Pity the lights weren't up."

He went into the Merry Widow for a drink. Then he took his bags up to Peckham High Street, got into a taxi and was driven across the river, where he entered a chemist's shop and got a dressing put on his wounded eye.

"I'm glad he's cleared off," Dixie said to her mother. "Humphrey's not glad but I'm glad. Now he won't be coming to the wedding. You never know what he might have done. He might have gone mad among the guests showing the bumps on his head. He might have made a speech. He might have jumped and done something rude. I didn't like him. Our Leslie didn't like him. Humphrey liked him. He was bad for Humphrey. Mr. Druce liked him and look what Mr. Druce has come to. Poor Miss Coverdale liked him. Trevor didn't like him. But I'm not worried now. I've got this bad cold, though."

Chapter 10

There was Dixie come up to the altar with her wide flouncy dress and her nose, a little red from her cold, tilted up towards the minister.

"Wilt thou have this woman to thy wedded wife?"

"No, to be quite frank," Humphrey said, "I won't."

Dougal never read of it in the newspapers. He was away off to Africa with the intention of selling tape-recorders to all the witch doctors. "No medicine man," Dougal said, "these days can afford to be without a portable tape-recorder. Without the aid of this modern device, which may be easily concealed in the undergrowth of the jungle, the old tribal authority will rapidly become undermined by the mounting influence of modern scepticism."

Much could be told of Dougal's subsequent life. He returned from Africa and became a novice in a Franciscan monastery. Before he was asked to leave, the Prior had endured a nervous breakdown and several of the monks had broken their vows of obedience in actuality, and their other vows by desire; Dougal pleaded his powers as an exorcist in vain. Thereafter, for economy's sake, he gathered together the scrap ends of his profligate experience—for he was a frugal man at heart—and turned them into a lot of cock-eyed books, and went far in the world. He never married.

The night after Humphrey arrived alone at the honeymoon hotel at Folkestone, Arthur Crewe walked into the bar.

"The girl's heart-broken," he said to Humphrey.

"Better soon than late," Humphrey said. "Tell her I'm coming back."

"She's blaming Dougal Douglas. Is he here with you?"

"Not so's you'd notice it," Humphrey said.

"I haven't come here to blame you. I reckon there must be some reason behind it. But it's hard on the girl, in her wedding dress. My Leslie's been put on probation for robbing a till."

Some said Humphrey came back and married the girl in the end. Some said, no, he married another girl. Others said, it was like this, Dixie died of a broken heart and he never looked at another girl again. Some thought he had returned, and she had slammed the door in his face and called him a dirty swine, which he was. One or two recalled there had been a fight between Humphrey and Trevor Lomas. But at all events everyone remembered how a man had answered "No" at his wedding.

In fact they got married two months later, and although few guests were invited, quite a lot of people came to the church to see if Humphrey would do it again.

Humphrey drove off with Dixie. She said, "I feel as if I've been twenty years married instead of two hours."

He thought this a pity for a girl of eighteen. But it was a sunny day for November, and, as he drove swiftly past the Rye, he saw the children playing there and the women coming home from work with their shopping-bags, the Rye for an instant looking like a cloud of green and gold, the people seeming to ride upon it, as you might say there was another world than this.

THE END

The Bachelors

For
Jerzy and Christine
with love

Chapter 1

DAYLIGHT was appearing over London, the great city of bachelors. Half-pint bottles of milk began to be stood on the doorsteps of houses containing single apartments from Hampstead Heath to Greenwich Park, and from Wanstead Flats to Putney Heath; but especially in Hampstead, especially in Kensington.

In Queen's Gate, Kensington, in Harrington Road, the Boltons, Holland Park, and in King's Road, Chelsea, and its backwaters, the bachelors stirred between their sheets, reached for their wound watches, and with waking intelligences noted the time; then, remembering it was Saturday morning, turned over on their pillows. But soon, since it was Saturday, most would be out on the streets, shopping for their bacon and eggs, their week's supplies of breakfasts and occasional suppers; and these bachelors would set out early, before a quarter past ten, in order to avoid being jostled by the women, the legitimate shoppers.

At a quarter past ten, Ronald Bridges, aged thirty-seven, who during the week was assistant curator at a small museum of handwriting in the City of London, stopped in the Old Brompton Road to speak to his friend Martin Bowles, a barrister of thirty-five.

9

Ronald moved his old plastic shopping bag up and down twice, to suggest to Martin that it was a greater weight than it really was, and that the whole business was a bore.

"Where," said Ronald, pointing to a package on the top of Martin's laden bag, "did you get your frozen peas?"

"Clayton's."

"How much?"

"One and six. That's for a small packet; does for two. A large is two and six; six helpings."

"Terrible price," said Ronald, agreeably.

"Your hand's never out of your pocket," said Martin.

"What else have you got there?" Ronald said.

"Cod. You bake it in yoghurt with a sprinkle of marjoram and it tastes like halibut. My old ma's away for a fortnight with the old housekeeper."

"Marjoram, where do you get marjoram?"

"Oh, Fortnum's. You get all the herbs there. I get a bag of stuff every month. I do nearly all the shopping and most of the cooking since my old ma's had her op. And old Carrie isn't up to it now—she never was much of a cook."

"You must have it in you," said Ronald, "going all the way to Piccadilly for herbs."

"I usually work it in with something else," Martin said. "We like our herbs, Ma and I. Come on in here."

He meant a coffee-bar. They sat beside their bags and sipped their espressos with contented languor.

"I've forgotten Tide," said Ronald. "I must remember to get Tide."

"Don't you make a list?" said Martin.

"No. I depend on my memory."

"I make a list," said Martin, "when my ma's away. I always do the shopping at the week-ends. When Ma's at home she makes the list. It's always unreadable, though."

"A waste of time," said Ronald, "if you've got a memory."

"Do you mind?" said a girl who had just come into the coffee shop. She was referring to Ronald's bag of shopping; it was taking up the seat which ran along the wall.

"Oh, sorry," said Ronald, removing his bag and dumping it on the floor.

The girl sat down, and when the waitress came to serve her she said, "I'm waiting for a friend."

She had black hair drawn back in a high style, dark eyes and an oval ballet-dancer's face. She returned the two bachelors' sleepy routine glance, then lit a cigarette and watched the door.

"New potatoes in the shops," Ronald said.

"They're always in the shops," said Martin, "these days. In season and out of season. It's the same with everything: you can get new potatoes and new carrots all the year round now, and peas and spinach any time, and tomatoes in the spring, even."

"At a price," said Ronald.

"At a price," Martin said. "What bacon do you get?"

"I make do with streaky. I grudge breakfasts," said Ronald.

"Same here."

"Your hand's never out of your pocket," Ronald said before Martin could say it.

A small narrow-built man came in the door and joined the girl, smiling at her with a sweet, spiritual expression.

He sat side by side with the girl on the wall-seat. He lifted the menu-card and spoke to her soundlessly from behind it.

"Good gracious me," murmured Martin.

Ronald looked towards the man, whose body was now hidden by the girl at his side. Ronald observed the head, unable to see at first whether his hair was fair or silver-white, but soon it was plainly a mixture. He was thin, with a very pointed, anxious face and nose, and a grey-white lined skin. He would be about fifty-five. He wore a dark blue suit.

"Don't stare," Martin said. "He's on a charge and I'm prosecuting him. He's coming up again before the magistrates next week. He has to report to the police every day."

"What for?"

"Fraudulent conversion and possibly other charges. Somebody in my chambers defended Seton ages ago. Not that it did either any good. Let's go."

Ronald put down the newspaper in his hand.

"Tide," said Ronald in the street. "I really must remember Tide."

"Which way are you going?"

"Across to Clayton's."

"I'm going there too. I haven't got a lot of groceries on the list, I'm dining out four times next week. Where do you go on Sundays?"

"Oh here and there," Ronald said, "there's always somebody."

"I go to Leighton Buzzard if anyone comes home to keep Ma company," said Martin. "It's rather fun and a change at Leighton Buzzard. But if Isobel stays in London I go to her in London." They had crossed the road.

"I've left my paper in the café," Ronald said inexpertly. "I'd better go back and fetch it. See you some time."

"Feeling all right?" Martin said, as Ronald turned on the curb to cross back over the road.

"Yes, oh, yes, it's only my paper."

"Sure?"—for Martin was touchily aware of Ronald's epilepsy.

" 'Bye." Ronald had crossed over.

He found the paper. He sat down again in a seat opposite the one he had recently occupied so that he could the more easily see the silver-yellow-haired man as he spoke in low tones effortful with convincingness, to the black-haired girl. Ronald ordered coffee and a cream cake. He opened his paper, from the side of which, from time to time, he watched the man who was deeply explaining himself to the girl. Ronald could not decide where he had seen the man before; he could not even be sure of having done so. "I'm becoming a prying old maid," he said to himself as he left, to explain his return to the café, preferring to call himself a prying old maid than to fully acknowledge his real reason: that he had been simply testing his memory; for he could not leave alone any opportunity to try himself on the question whether his epilepsy would one day affect his mental powers or not.

"No," the American specialist had said, irritable with the strain of putting a technical point into common speech, "there is no reason why your intellect should be impaired except, of course, that you cannot exercise it to the full extent that would be possible were you able to follow and rise to the top of a normal career. But you ought to retain and indeed expand your present mental capacity. The seizures will be intermittent; let me put it that your seizures concern the brain but not the mind. You will learn to prepare for them physically in some degree but not to control them. They won't affect the mind except in so far as the emotional psychological disturbances affect it. That's not my department."

Ronald had retained every one of these words importantly in his memory for the past fourteen years, aware that the specialist himself would possibly remember only the gist, and then only with the aid of his record cards. But Ronald held them tight, from time to time subjecting the words to every possible kind of interpretation. "Let me put it that your seizures concern the brain, not the mind." But he believes, Ronald argued with himself at times throughout the years, that the mind is part of the brain: then why did he say "Let me put it that . . ."? What was his intention? And anyhow, Ronald would think, I can manage. And anyhow, I might never have been able to follow and rise to the top of a normal career. What is a normal career? The law: closed to me;—but, his friends had said, you need not put in for Lord Chancellor, you could be a successful solicitor. Oh, could I? You haven't seen me in a fit. The civil service: closed to me. No, not at all, said his advisers. Medicine, teaching, get yourself into a college, try for a fellowship, you've got the academic ability—you know what some of the dons are like, there wouldn't be anything odd. . . .

"I could never be first-rate."

"Oh, first-rate . . ."

He had been twenty-three, a post-graduate, when the fits started, without warning, three months after he had turned his attention to theology. The priesthood: closed to me. Yes, said his friends, that's out; and, said his theological counsellors, it never would have been any good in any case, you never had a vocation.

"How do you know?"

"Because, in the event, you can't be a priest."

"That's the sort of retrospective logic that makes us Catholics distrusted."

"A vocation to the priesthood is the will of God. Nothing can change God's will. You are an epileptic. No epileptic can be a priest. *Ergo* you never had a vocation. But you can do something else."

"I could never be first-rate."

"That is sheer vanity"—it was an old priest speaking—"you were never meant to be a first-rate careerist."

"Only a first-rate epileptic?"

"Indeed yes. Quite seriously, yes," the old priest said.

It was at a time when he was having convulsions three times a week that he had allowed himself to be taken by an itinerant specialist to a research centre in California, with the purpose of submitting to a two years' clinical trial of a new drug. He was one of sixty volunteers from five to twenty-eight years old. Ronald lived in a huge sun-balconied hostel. Some of the other fifty-nine were mentally deficient. Most were neurotic. None was highly intelligent. Of the total sixty patients three failed to respond to the drug, and of these Ronald was one. Of these three, Ronald succumbed to the dreaded *status epilepticus,* enduring fit after fit, one after the other in rapid succession, only four days after the treatment had started.

"This is due to emotional apprehension," Dr. Fleischer told him when, after a week, he lay partially recovered, thin and exhausted, in a cool green and white room with the sun-blinds down. "You may withdraw from the experiment if you wish," Dr. Fleischer said. "Or you may continue with profit." Dr.

Fleischer's time and mind were largely occupied with the fifty-seven epileptics who had already begun to respond favourably to the new drug.

When Ronald was up and shakily walking about, drowsy from the effects of his usual drug, he weighed up for himself the price of his possible cure. The patients who were responding to Dr. Fleischer's treatment were all around him, they seemed even sleepier, drowsier than he—but, thought Ronald, this is not far from their normal condition, they were born half-awake.

"The new drug is successful," the smart fresh-lipsticked young research woman told him. "The drug has been found to have anti-convulsant and sedative effects on rats, and now it looks like being successful with the majority of patients here." She smiled through her rimless spectacles with eyes far away, on the job, efficient, creamy-complexioned, first-rate.

"Well, your drug makes me worse," Ronald said, feeling within himself, at that moment, the potentialities of a most unpleasant young man.

When he got the chance of another brief interview with Dr. Fleischer he said, "Do you understand what you are asking me to do when you urge me to persevere? I may have to undergo the repetitive fits again."

Fleischer said, "I am not urging you to persevere. I suggest your failure to respond to the drug is caused only by emotional resistance."

"Do you realise," said Ronald, "how long the few seconds of lucidity between the fits appear to be, and what goes on in one's mind in those few waking seconds?"

"No," said the doctor, "I don't realise what these lucid intervals are like. I recommend you to return to England. I recommend . . . I advise . . . No, there is no reason why your intellect should be impaired, except of course that you cannot exercise it to the full extent that would be possible were you able to follow and rise to the top of a normal career. . . ."

"Perhaps," Ronald said, "I'll be a first-rate epileptic and that will be my career."

Dr. Fleischer did not smile. He reached for Ronald's index card and wrote upon it.

Before he departed Ronald's brain was tested by a machine that was now familiar to him, and which recorded the electric currents generated by his convulsions and which was beginning to be used in the criminal courts of some American states to ascertain the truth of a suspect's statement, so that it was popularly called "the truth machine."

While he was awaiting the convenience of the man who was to escort him back to England, Ronald deliberately ignored the scene around him. His fellow-patients, week by week, busied themselves with tennis, bed-making, toy-making, and their jazz orchestra. It was only much later that these scenes, which he had made an effort not to notice, returned to Ronald again and again accompanied by Dr. Fleischer's words—long after the specialist must have forgotten them—and mostly at the moments when Ronald, bored by his self-preoccupation, most wished to forget himself, clinics, hospitals, doctors, and all the pompous trappings of his malady. It was at these moments of rejection that the obsessive images of his early epileptic years bore down upon him and he felt himself to be, not the amiable johnnie he had by then, for the sake of sheer good will and protection from the world, affected to be—but as one possessed by a demon, judged by the probing inquisitors of life, an unsatisfactory clinic-rat which failed to respond to the right drug. In the course of time this experience sharpened his wits, and privately looking round at his world of acquaintances, he became, at certain tense moments, a truth machine, under which his friends took on the aspect of demon-hypocrites. But being a reasonable man, he allowed these moods to pass over him, and in reality he rather liked his friends, and gave them his best advice when, in the following years, they began to ask him for it.

On his return from California he was surprised to find himself able in some measure to retain consciousness during his fits, although he could not control them, by a secret, inarticulate method which, whenever he tried to describe it to his doctors, began to fail him when next he practised it.

"I find it useful to induce within myself a sense," Ronald at first told his doctor, "—when I am going under—a sense that every action in the world is temporarily arrested for the duration of my fit—" .

"Seizure," said the doctor.

"My seizure," said Ronald, "and this curiously enables me to retain some sort of consciousness during even the worst part. I find it easier to endure this partial consciousness of my behaviour during the fits than to surrender my senses entirely, although it is a painful experience."

Immediately he had said it, he felt foolish, he knew his explanation was inadequate. The doctor remarked, "It's as I've said. There is always an improvement in the patient when he becomes used to his seizures. First he experiences the aura, and this enables him to take preliminary precautions as to his physical safety during the seizure. He learns to lie down on the floor in time. He learns . . ."

"No, that's not what I mean," Ronald said. "What I mean is something different. It is like being partly an onlooker during the fit, yet not quite. . . ."

"The seizure," said the doctor, meanwhile puzzling his brains with a frown.

"The seizure," said Ronald.

"Oh quite," said the doctor. "The patient might learn to exercise some control during the *petit-mal* stage to stand him in good stead during the *grand-mal* convulsions."

"That's right," Ronald said, and went home and, on the way, had a severe fit in the street; on which occasion his method would not work, so that he came to his senses in the casualty department of St. George's hospital, sick with inhalations which had been administered to him to arrest his frenzy.

Soon Ronald was obliged to earn his living. His father, a retired horticulturalist, still mourning the early death of his wife, took fright when he realised that Ronald was incurable. Ronald reassured him, advised him to buy an annuity and go to live at Kew; the father smiled and went.

Ronald got a job in a small museum of graphology in the City, to which people of various professions had recourse as well as curious members of the public. To Ronald's museum came criminologists from abroad, people wishing to identify the dates of manuscripts, or the handwriting attached to documents of doubt. Some came in the hope of obtaining "readings" by which they meant a pronouncement as to the character and future fortunes of the person responsible for a piece of handwriting, but these were sent empty away. Ronald gained a reputation in the detection of forgeries, and after about five years was occasionally consulted by lawyers and criminal authorities, and several times was called to court as witness for the defence or prosecution.

At the museum he had a room to himself, with an understanding that he could there have his fits in peace without anyone fussing along to his aid. He knew how to compose himself for a fit. He cultivated his secret method of retaining some self-awareness during his convulsions, and never mentioned this to his doctors again, lest he should lose the gift. He kept by him a wedge of cork which he stuck between his teeth as the first signs seized him. He knew how many seconds it took to turn off the gas fire in his small office, to take the correct dose of his pills, to lie flat on his back, turn his head to the side, biting his cork wedge, and to await the onslaught. It was arranged, at these times, that no one entering Ronald's office should touch him except in the event of blood issuing from his mouth. Blood was never seen at his mouth, only foam, for Ronald was careful with his cork wedge. His two old colleagues and the two young clerks got used to him, and the typist, a large religious woman, ceased to try to mother him.

After five years Ronald's fits occurred on an average of once a month. The drugs which he took regularly, and in extra strength at the first intimations of his fits, became gradually more effective

18

in controlling his movements, but less frequently could he ward off the violent stage of his attack until he found a convenient place in which to lie down. Twice within fourteen years he was arrested for drunkenness while staggering along the street towards a chemist's shop. Twice, he simply lay down on the pavement close in to the walls and allowed himself to be removed by ambulance. As often as possible he travelled by taxi or by a lift in a friend's car.

The porter of his flats had once found him, curled up and kicking violently, in the lift, and Ronald had subsequently gone over the usual explanations in patient parrot-like sequence. And, on these out-of-doors occasions, wherever they might take place, Ronald would go home to bed and sleep for twelve to fourteen hours at a stretch. But in latter years most of his fits occurred at home, in his room, in his one-roomed flat in the Old Brompton Road; so that his friends came to believe that he suffered less frequently than he actually did.

Ronald had settled down to be an amiable fellow with a gangling appearance, slightly hunched shoulders, slightly neglected-looking teeth and hair going prematurely grey.

"You could marry," said his doctor.

"I couldn't," Ronald said.

"You could have children. Direct inheritance is very rare. The risk is very slight. You could marry. In fact, you ought—"

"I couldn't," Ronald said.

"Wait till you meet the right girl. The right girl can be very wonderful, very understanding, when a fellow has a disability like yours. It's a question of meeting the right girl."

Ronald had met the right girl five years after his return from America. Her wonderful understanding of his fits terrified him as much as her beauty moved him. She was the English-born daughter of German refugees. She was brown, healthy, shining, still in her teens and splendidly built. For two years she washed his socks and darned them, counted his laundry, did his Saturday shopping, went abroad with him, slept with him, went to the theatre with him.

"I'm perfectly capable of getting the theatre tickets," he said.
"Don't worry, darling, I'll get them in the lunch hour," she
said.

"Look, Hildegarde, it isn't necessary for you to mother me.
I'm not an imbecile."

"I know darling. You're a genius."

But in any case the trouble between them had to do with
handwriting. Hildegarde had taken to studying the subject, the
better to understand the graphologist in her lover. Hildegarde
took a short course, amazingly soaking up, by sheer power of
memory, the sort of facts which Ronald had no ability to memorise and which in any case, if he was called upon to employ
them, he would have felt obliged to look up in reference books.

Thus equipped, Hildegarde frequently aired her facts, her
dates, her documentary references.

"You have a better memory than mine," Ronald said one
Sunday morning when they were slopping about in their bedroom slippers in Ronald's room.

"I shall be able to memorise for both of us," she said.

And that very afternoon she said, "Have you ever had ear
trouble?"

"Ear trouble?"

"Yes, trouble with your ears?"

"Only as a child," he said. "Earache."

She was by his desk, looking down at some handwritten notes
of his.

"The formation of your capital 'I's' denotes ear trouble," she
said. "There are signs, too, in the variations of the angles that
you like to have your own way, probably as the result of your
mother's early death and the insufficiency of your father's interest in you. The emotional rhythm is irregular, which means
that your behaviour is sometimes incomprehensible to those
around you." She laughed up at him. "And most of all, your
handwriting shows that you're a sort of *genius*."

"Where did you get all this?" Ronald said.

"I've read some text-books. There must be something in it—

it's a branch of graphology, after all."

"Have you practised interpreting various people's characters from their handwriting, and tested the results against experience?"

"No, not yet. I've only just read the books. I memorised everything."

"Your memory is better than mine," Ronald said.

"I'll be able to remember for us both."

And he thought, when we're married, she'll do everything for both of us. So that, when he remonstrated against her obtaining the theatre tickets, and told her he could perfectly well get them —"I'm not an imbecile"—and she replied, "I know darling, you're a genius"—he decided to end the affair with this admirable woman. For it was an indulgent and motherly tone of voice which told him he was a genius, and he saw himself being cooked for, bought for, thought for, provided for, and overwhelmed by her in the years to come. He saw, as in a vision, himself coming round from his animal frenzy, his limbs still jerking and the froth on his lips—and her shining brown eyes upon him, her well-formed lips repeating as he woke such loving patronising lies as: "You'll be all right, darling. It's just that you're a genius." Which would indicate, not her belief about his mental capacity but her secret belief in the superiority of her own.

After the affair had ended Ronald took to testing his memory lest it was failing him as a result of his disease. On the Saturday morning when the small thin man, Patrick Seton, had been pointed out to him in the café as one who was coming up for committal on Tuesday, Ronald, having faintly felt a passing sense of recognition, and left the café, and gone home, began once more to think of the man. But Ronald could not recall him or anything to do with him. He wished he had asked Martin Bowles the man's name. In a vexed way, Ronald sorted out his groceries, chucking them into their places in the cupboard. Then he went across to the pub.

There, drinking dark stout, were white-haired, dark-faced

Walter Prett, art critic, who was looking at a diet sheet, Matthew Finch, with his colourful smile and black curly hair, London correspondent of the *Irish Echo*, and Ewart Thornton, the dark, deep-voiced grammar-school master who was a spiritualist. These were bachelors of varying degrees of confirmation.

Ronald was actually forbidden alcohol, but he had found that the small quantity which he liked to drink made no difference to his epilepsy, and that the very act of ordering a drink gave him a liberated feeling.

He took his beer, sat down at his friends' table and soundlessly sipped. In nearly five minutes' time he said, "Nice to see you all here."

Matthew Finch ran a finger through his black curls. Sometimes a desire came over Ronald to run his fingers through Matthew's black curls, but he had given up wondering if he were a latent homosexual, merely on the evidence of this one urge. Once he had seen a married couple rumple Matthew's hair in a united spontaneous gesture.

"Nice to see you all together," Ronald said.

"Eggs, boiled or poached only," Walter Prett read out in a sad voice from his diet sheet. "Sour pickles but not sweet pickles. No barley, rice, macaroni—" he read quietly, then his voice became louder, and even Ronald who was used to Walter Prett's changing tones, was startled by this. "Fresh fruit of any kind, including bananas, also water-packed canned fruits," Walter remarked modestly. "No butter," he shrieked, "no fat or oil," he roared.

"I've got mounds of homework," said Ewart Thornton, "because the half-term tests have begun."

Matthew went over to the bar and brought back two pickled onions on a plate, and ate them.

Chapter 2

IT WAS six o'clock in the evening of that Saturday in a third-floor double room in Ebury Street. Patrick Seton sat in a meagre armchair which, since he was narrow at the shanks and shoulders, he did not fill as people usually did. Alice Dawes was propped in one of the divan beds, still half-dressed. Her friend Elsie Forrest sat on the other divan and folded Alice's skirt longwise.

"If only you would eat something you would see the thing in proportion," Elsie said.

"God, how can I eat? Why should I eat?" Alice said.

"You ought to build up your strength," Patrick Seton said in his voice which seemed to fade away at the end of each sentence.

"What's the use of her building up her strength if she's going to lose it that way?" Elsie said.

"It was only a suggestion," Patrick said, so that they could hardly hear the last syllable.

"Well, I'm not going to do it," Alice said. "You'll have to think of something else."

"There's this unfortunate occurrence next week. . . ."

"I don't see," said Elsie, "how they can bring you up on a charge if they haven't any grounds at all."

"Not the slightest grounds," Patrick said, more boldly than usual. "I'll be acquitted. It's a case of a jealous, frustrated woman trying to get her own back on me."

"You must have had to do with her," Elsie said.

"I never touched her, and I give you my word of honour," Patrick said. "It's all her imagination. She took a fancy to me at a séance, and I was sorry for her because she was lonely, and then I took rooms at her place and gave her advice. Of course, now, she's made up this utter entire fabrication. That's my defence. An utter, entire and absolute fabrication."

"Funny the police are taking it up if they've no proof," Elsie said.

Alice said from the bed, "I've got every faith in Patrick, Elsie. The police wouldn't allow him his freedom if they thought he was guilty. They would have him under arrest."

"Well if he's so sure he's going to get off, why did he bother to tell you? It's a shame upsetting you like this in your condition."

"I only," Patrick said softly, stroking his silver-yellow hair with his thin grey hand, and gazing at Alice with his pale juvenile eyes, "wanted to put it to Alice that after Tuesday and when this unfortunate occurrence is over we could make a fresh start if she would see the specialist and have something done before nature takes its course, and—"

"I won't have an abortion," Alice said. "I'd do anything else for you, Patrick, you know that. But I won't have it done. I'd be terrified."

"There's no danger," Patrick said. "Not these days."

"I would never risk it," Alice said. "Not with my disease."

"He may be unlucky on Tuesday," Elsie said.

"No question of it," Patrick said.

"Oh, Elsie, you don't know Patrick," Alice said.

Elsie said, "Why don't you both skip off abroad this week-end, while there's time?"

Alice looked at Patrick, clutching her throat, for she had once been to a school of drama, and though she was not an insincere girl, she sometimes remembered to express those emotions which she wished to reveal, by certain miming movements of the head, hands, shoulders, feet, eyes and eyelids. So she clutched her throat and looked at Patrick to convey a vulnerable anticipation of his reply.

His reply was so low-voiced that Elsie said "What?"

"Difficulty about passports if one is discovered. It would"—his voice rose to loud assertion—"look like an admission of guilt."

"Patrick is right." Alice's hand dropped from her throat and lay limp, palm-upward, on the divan-cover.

"You're going to leave Alice in a nice pickle if the case goes against you," Elsie said. "How long could you get at the outside?"

"Oh, Elsie," said Alice. "Don't."

Patrick looked at Elsie as if this remark were sufficient reply.

"And when," said Elsie, "does your divorce case come up?"

"In a couple of months," said Patrick, crossing his knees and looking down upon those knees.

"What date?"

"Twenty-fifth of November," Alice said. "I remember that date all right, because we'll be able to get married on the twenty-sixth."

Patrick's blue eyes dwelt upon her affectionately.

"On the twenty-sixth," he whispered and closed his eyes for a moment to savour his joy.

"I feel hungry," Alice said.

"Put your skirt on," Elsie said, "and we'll go and get something. Don't eat anything greasy, you'll only bring it up again."

Alice began wearily to get up.

"I'm starving," she said.

Elsie said, "Did you remember to take your injection this morning?"

"Of course," Alice said. "Don't be silly. Patrick gives me my injection every morning, regularly." She pointed to the jug with the syringe stuck into it.

"Well I only wondered, because you said you were so hungry. Don't diabetics always get hungry if they don't have their injections?"

"She's hungry because she brought up her lunch," said Patrick defensively.

Elsie looked at him suspiciously. "I hope you do give her the injection regularly," she said. "She needs taking care of."

It was then Patrick's mind turned a corner.

But he replied meekly: "Give her a good meal." He stroked Alice's cheek. "Don't work too hard tonight, darling."

"I doubt if I can go," said Alice who was standing shakily while zipping up her skirt. "Elsie will have to ring up."

"She'll have to get an easier job," Elsie said. "Coffee-bar work is too hard for a girl in her condition."

"What do you see in him?" Elsie said.

Alice took her mouthful of omelette at slow motion to denote reflectiveness, although she knew the answer.

"Well," she said, "I'm in love with him. He's *got* something. You don't know how wonderful he can be when we're alone. He's so good on the spiritual side. He recites poetry so beautifully. He's a sort of a real artist."

"I'll agree," Elsie said, "he's a first-rate medium. That I do admit."

"And he's got a soul."

"Yes," said Elsie, "I see that. But you know, he's a bit old for you."

"I like an older man. I think there's something special about an older man."

"Yes, but you wouldn't call him much of a man. I mean, if you didn't know him, if you just saw him in the street without knowing he was a medium, you'd think he was a little half-pint job."

"But I do know him. He means everything to me. He loves poetry and beauty."

"I'll tell you," Elsie said. "I've never really trusted him. He hasn't got a cheque book, you told me yourself. Now that's funny, for one thing."

"He's not mean with his money. I've never said—"

"No, but he hasn't got a cheque book, the fact remains."

"I think that's a materialistic way to judge. Patrick is not a materialist."

"No," said Elsie, "I don't say he is. But I think he gets carried away and makes up a lot of these stories he—"

"Oh, Elsie, a man like Patrick must have had a remarkable life. He's been through it. You can see that. And his wife must have been hell. Do you know, she—"

"Funny thing about that divorce," Elsie said, "he doesn't seem much worried about it."

"No, he's just waiting for it to come through, that's all."

"You'd think he'd have a bit more to do with the lawyers than he seems to have. And she might claim on him—"

"She hasn't a leg to stand on in the case. He's divorcing her, she's not divorcing him."

"What's her name?"

"I don't know. I wouldn't like to ask. It would be indelicate."

"Seen a photo?"

"No, Elsie. Patrick isn't that sort of man, Elsie."

"And about this at the Magistrate's Court on Tuesday," Elsie said, "well I don't know what to think."

Alice started to cry.

"You're only upsetting yourself," Elsie remarked, while she ate steadily on as one who proves, by eating on during another's distress, the unshakable sanity of their advice. Elsie also permitted herself to say, as she reached for another roll, "And you're kidding yourself where Patrick's concerned. I don't believe half a word he says. I think he's in trouble. You take my advice, you would clear off now, have the baby in a home, get it adopted, and start afresh."

Alice said, "I'll never do that, never. I trust him."

"He wanted you to get rid of the kid."

"Men are like that."

27

"Stop crying," Elsie said, "people are looking at you."

"I can't help it when you call him a liar. What about the message he got for you from Colin that night at the Wider Infinity. You didn't say that was lies. You said—"

"Oh, he's a good medium. But when Patrick's under the control I shouldn't think he could help saying what comes to him from the other side."

At eight o'clock Patrick Seton walked along the Bayswater Road, turned off it, then turned again into a cul-de-sac, at the end of which he mounted the steps of a house converted into flats where he pressed the top left-hand bell.

Presently the door was opened by a tall, skinny, young man of about twenty-three, with a cheerful smile.

"Oh Patrick!" he said, politely standing back to let Patrick pass into the passage.

"Well Tim," said Patrick as he climbed the stairs, "and how's the Central Office of Information?"

"The Central Office of Information," said Tim, "is all right, thank you." He cleaned his glasses with a white handkerchief as he followed Patrick upstairs to a modernly decorated flat. From the open door of a room came the sociable sound of voices. On the door of another room was hung a card on which was printed in blue Gothic letters the words

THE WIDER INFINITY
"In my Father's house are many mansions. . . ."
(John, 14, 2)

Tim passed by this room on a frivolous tip-toe to conceal whatever awe he might feel towards it, and led the way to the room where the company was assembled. Patrick stood a moment in the doorway, looking round swiftly to see who was present. At his entrance the chatter ceased for two seconds, then started again. Several people tentatively greeted Patrick while Tim, with the restrained gestures of one who is not above playing the well-trained footman, fetched Patrick a cup of China tea from a side table.

A distinguished-looking woman with white hair and a lined face, the features of which were absolutely symmetrical, appeared. Patrick respectfully put down his tea and took his hostess's hand in silence except for the word "Marlene."

"Patrick," she replied merely; and she rested her eyes on his, setting her head at a slight angle so that her long earrings swung as in a breeze.

Patrick's lower lip thinly began to tremble as he said in his almost inaudible voice, "I nearly didn't come in view of the unfortunate occurrence. But I felt it was my duty to do so."

"You were right, Patrick," Marlene said, still gazing at his eyes intensely. "There are naturally mixed feelings amongst us and she has been circulating rumours. But I have—and I know I can speak for the members of the Interior Spiral if not for the Wider Infinity at large—implicit faith in you. I'm only too grateful that we were guided to delay disclosing to her the existence of the Interior Spiral; that was fortunate. And had it not been for your powers as a great medium, and the warnings, we should most probably have issued the Communication to her last week. Oh—here she is."

A dumpy much-powdered woman of middle-age, wearing light-rimmed glasses, a grey felt hat and a blue coat and skirt had been ushered into the room by young Tim. She smiled brightly at her acquaintances by the door and even the lenses of her glasses seemed to glisten smilingly upon them. She had noticed Patrick, who had resumed his tea-cup into which he was gazing with dignity. Marlene glided up to the newcomer, took both her hands, bestowed upon her a customary soul-to-soul gaze, kissed her upon the cheek, and said, "Freda, you're just in time. I am about to proclaim the Commencement."

"Tea, Mrs. Flower?" Tim said to Freda, with the cup and saucer in his hand.

"The Commencement is about to start, Tim," said Marlene,

and as Tim hovered between handing the tea to Freda and not handing it to her, Marlene said "but of course you must have a little tea first, Freda, you must have your tea first."

Marlene noticed, without truly observing, a large man with pink and white cheeks whom she had not seen at previous meetings. He was standing massively half in, half out of the room, and he had apparently arrived at the same time as Freda. But Marlene did not take great notice of him, since there were few meetings at which a newcomer was not present, having been brought along by someone or other. The pink-and-white-cheeked man looked rather like, possibly, a friend of Tim's. Tim had yet to learn to be reliable.

Marlene said to Freda, "I shan't ring the bell till you've finished your tea. Don't hurry."

Freda gulped her tea, with her eyes wandering over the rim of the cup. Suddenly she started at the sight of Patrick.

"So *he's* here," Freda said.

"My dear Freda, mustn't we subordinate all our materialistic endeavours to those of the spirit?"

"It's most upsetting," Freda said, "and I'm surprised he has the nerve to show his face in here again. He's a fraud."

Tim gave out a gentle cultivated noise from the throat as if he really were clearing it, and shifted himself gracefully to another group.

Marlene's earrings swung as she moved her head distastefully from Freda's remarks. "The word fraud," she said, "is of the World. Freda, I don't think it should be voiced here. But I do see—I do understand—how a type of behaviour which is normal in our element, may appear, shall we say, mysterious in yours." She touched Mrs. Flower's hand in absolution from all her dumpy limitations. "I only hope," she said, "that nothing will happen to bring the Wider Infinity into disrepute. For myself, I don't care. I am thinking of—well, finish your tea, Freda dear, it is time for the Commencement."

She moved away, and dark Ewart Thornton who was one of the assembly, presently took her place, declaring deeply in her

30

ear, "I'm with you, Freda. A lot of us here tonight are with you. I meant to write to say so to you, but I've got such mounds of homework. The mid-term examinations. . . ."

Freda's spectacles shone with gratitude. "Does Marlene know your mind on the subject?" she said.

Ewart placed a finger to his lips while Marlene at the other end of the room proclaimed:

"The Circle will now enter the Sanctuary of Light."

Tea-cups were placed down and a hush fell on the assembly. Marlene Cooper led the way, as she had done regularly since the year after her husband died, and she had taken to thoughts of the spirit. For how, she felt, could it be that Harry Cooper, whom his worst business enemies admitted was sheer dynamite, could come to nought in the end? "No," she said, "Harry is as alive as ever he was. He is communicating with me and I am communicating with him." Certainly this was the case when he was alive, since they had then indulged in frequent noisy rows in different parts of the globe, she standing tensely clothed in her distinguished appearance, clasping and unclasping her long fingers, and shrieking; he sitting usually in an armchair answering her with short, loaded, meaningful words of power and contempt. He had been buried three months when, convinced of his dynamic survival, she had had him dug up and cremated, since this, it seemed vaguely to her, was more in keeping with the life beyond. To see his ashes scattered in the Garden of Remembrance was to conceive Harry more nearly as thin air, and since she had come to believe so ardently in Harry the spirit, she simply could not let him lie in the grave and rot.

Shortly after the cremation Marlene joined the Wider Infinity, an independent spiritualist group, proud of its independence from the great organised groups, and operating from a room in the region of Victoria. During the period of her initiation Marlene was impressed, the more and more especially when personal messages began to come through from Harry on the other side.

Patrick Seton was the first medium to get through to Harry.

"I have a message for our new sister, from Henry. Henry will not speak himself tonight but he will speak on another occasion when Carl is in control of Patrick," said Patrick. "But in the meantime Henry sends his affectionate regards and is thinking of you in his happy abode. He particularly wants to say you have been too generous and have stood by too long and let others take first place. You were born to be a leader but you have not yet fulfilled yourself. Now is the time to start living your true life." Patrick moaned. His mouth drooped, the lower lip disappearing into his chin. He looked very ill by the dim green light, and even when he had come round and the full lights were on, his complexion was more grey and the lines on his face deeper than before he had gone under. He was genuinely shaken.

"Amazing," Marlene whispered after the séance. For Henry was Harry's real name, and the Carl who was going to act as control in the promised future might very conceivably be that Carl, her boy friend that was, who had been killed in a motor-race in 1938; and indeed Marlene had been moved to wonder as far as she dared how Harry and Carl were making out together in the land of perpetual summer. And it had been summer-time when Harry had found out about Carl. But the possibility of Carl's acting as the spirit control between Harry and the medium seemed to make everything all right, and indeed there was an authentic rightness in the idea, for although Harry's had been the more dynamic personality, there was no use pretending that Carl's had not been the rarer.

And she thought it very like Harry to urge her to push herself to the fore. It was exactly what Harry would advise, being now incapacitated, or rather released from materialistic endeavours. It was almost as if Harry were urging her to take his place in life. It was so true that she had always let others take place before her.

Marlene, in order to be fair, went and attended a séance of another spiritualist group on an island near Richmond. But this was a disappointment, for the people were not quite the reasonable, respectable sort one expected to find in the spiritualist movement. One young man had hair waving down to his waist. One middle-aged woman with a huge blotchy face wore a tight cotton dress although it was early March. The place was not heated, and Marlene shivered. The woman in the tight cotton dress told Marlene she was going to give clairvoyance. She told Marlene nothing about Harry, only advised her to be careful of false friends, and not to despair, she wouldn't end her life alone.

"I'm not despairing," Marlene said.

The other members looked at Marlene with hushed hostile warnings, since she was interrupting the woman in her trance.

So Marlene remained with the Wider Infinity at Victoria. Soon, however, inspired by the dynamic spirit of Harry, she began to note this and that member who was perhaps unworthy of its high purpose. She led a purgative faction.

"We must," she said to Ewart Thornton, that big sane grammar-school master, "rid our Body of the cranks."

"I quite agree," Ewart said. "They lower the tone."

Two clergymen who were unembarrassed by wives or livings were retained; several women cashiers and bookkeepers who did not mind the journey from Wembley, Osterley and Camberwell on Monday and Thursday evenings; two middle-aged retired spinsters who were interested in art; one or two of Marlene's old friends who, however, were erratic in their attendance; a childless married couple in their early thirties; three widows; an Indian student who had been doing undefined research at the British Museum for fifteen years; a retired policeman whose wife, not a spiritualist, was a doctor's receptionist; Ewart Thornton, the schoolmaster; and Patrick Seton, who was, by common consent, the life and soul of the Circle.

"We must have a cross-section of the community," Marlene declared. "A sane cross-section. Why can't we have a labourer, for instance?"

No labourer who was worthy of his hire could be found. Ewart Thornton, however, was the means of introducing to the group a number of single schoolmasters and civil servants who, although interested in spiritualism, had never had sufficient courage to attend a séance. Some of these bachelors became regular members, others attended occasionally and compulsively when the desire to do so overwhelmed them. "My bachelors," Marlene called them.

"At least," she said, "we are all respectable now; we have no cranks."

"I hate cranks," Ewart said. "Insufferable people."

By the end of that year the Wider Infinity had moved its headquarters to Marlene's flat in Bayswater and Patrick and Ewart Thornton had so much become her closest intimates that very often this trio held private séances which were kept secret from the rest of the group. "Carl and Harry," Marlene said, "definitely understand my nature now better than they did in the flesh. Carl of course was always more evolved. Why does he call Harry by the name of Henry, I wonder?"

Patrick said, "I'm only the medium," and his voice died away on the last syllable.

"But you're a genius, Patrick—isn't he, Ewart?"

"Absolutely. That was excellent advice that came through from Guide Gabi about my headmaster. Had his character to a T. He expects me to do mounds of homework. Well I—"

"Señor Gabi is one of my best Guides," Patrick murmured. "But Henry is coming on. Through the influence of Carl, he—"

"Why doesn't Carl call him Harry?" Marlene said. "He never called him Henry while in the flesh, he always called him Harry."

"The name Henry represents his primary and more noble personality," Patrick said gently. "I'm sorry Marlene, I'm only the medium, I can't say Harry when I get Henry."

"Patrick, you're wonderful. It only proves your honesty."

She put a great deal of money into the training of mediums, Patrick Seton being the principal trainer; she liked most of all to have the more intelligent members, or those rare few with university degrees, trained as mediums. It gave her a thrill to see these knowledgeable novices going into and coming round from, their first and second feeble trances.

Eventually she recruited her young nephew, Tim, whom she had discovered to have no religion at all. Tim had not enjoined, but she, perceiving his mind, had promised secrecy about this activity where the family was concerned.

Meantime Patrick had made tremendous advances in divining how matters stood between Harry and Carl on the other side, and in instructing Marlene, through Harry, how best to develop her personality.

At the first séance to be held by the newly constructed Circle in Marlene's flat, Patrick had gone under in style with a quivering of the lower lip and chin, upturned eyes and convulsive whinnies. A few threads of ectoplasm, like white tape in the dim light, proceeded from the corners of his mouth. Then, in a voice hugely louder than his own he announced,

"I am now coming in touch with the control. This is control. Henry will speak through Patrick under the control of Carl."

Two or three of the Circle, as they had sat hand in hand round Patrick, shuffled slightly at this mention of Carl and Henry, for that particular combine was, in the experience of the Circle, exclusively interested in the affairs of Marlene and did not seem aware of the claims of the Wider Infinity as a whole.

"Guide Henry speaking: my dear wife, there are two on earth who mean a lot to you. You can depend upon them and especially upon one who will never desert you unto death. Do not be deceived by appearances. I am well and happy. Do you remember the Loebl Pass where we stopped at an inn and ate a marvellous omelette?"

"Oh," Marlene said.

"Control lifting," Patrick said, "Guide Henry is wearing leather shorts and an open-neck shirt."

"Oh, how it takes me back!" said Marlene when the lights had gone up. "Honestly," she said to the newer members of the Circle, "I have a photograph of Harry on that holiday wearing his leather shorts and—"

Later she said to Ewart and Patrick, "I wish they wouldn't concentrate so much on me from the other side. I think some of the less evolved members may feel I'm getting more than my fair share."

Ewart said, "You are the most dominant personality in the room, Marlene. It stands to reason."

"Stands to reason," Patrick said, "Marlene."

"Well, I'll stay outside at our next séance. I definitely felt a hostile aura after Patrick returned to us during our last session. These people feel: you pay your money—pittance that it is—and you take your choice."

"Not everyone feels that way," Ewart said.

"Whom can we trust and respect?"

Ewart mentioned a few of the more docile and regular attenders, Marlene eliminated half of them, and it was thus that the Interior Spiral, their secret group, came to be formed within the Wider Infinity.

"We must keep the ramifications pure," Marlene stated, "we must exert a concealed influence on the less evolved brethren and the crackpots and snobs who keep creeping in."

On the Saturday night before Patrick's appearance before the magistrates was anticipated, when Freda Flower had put down her cup, the company trod reverently into the Sanctuary of Light. Patrick ignored the widow, Freda Flower, exaltedly, as enemies do in church; but she glanced at him nervously. Marlene did not herself join them; this was now her habit on most evenings, since her presence so invariably attracted all the spiritual attentions available to the company.

Tim led the way and acted as usher, placing about twenty people with the conviction of extreme tact, the results of which, however, did not satisfy all. Some who were placed so that they had an imperfect view of the medium's chair were restive, but nothing like a scene occurred in this velvet-hung dark sanctuary of light.

36

This room had previously been a dining room in one wall of which was a service recess opening to the kitchen. The curtains that covered this recess were arranged to part imperceptibly at a point which admitted of Marlene's watching the proceedings from the kitchen, which she felt was only her due. And there she stood, in the dark, watching Tim's arrangements in the dim green-lit séance room.

She was furious when she saw Tim, as it were with the height of aplomb, place Freda Flower, the beastly widow who had gone to the police about Patrick, in the place of honour directly facing the medium.

All were seated except Tim who, before sitting down in the humblest position from the visual point of view, took off his glasses, wiped them, replaced them slowly and, with an elegant lightning sweep of the same handkerchief, dusted the chair on which he was to sit, at the same time replacing his handkerchief in his pocket. He then sat, joining tentative hands with his neighbour, as the others had done. Marlene from her place behind the recess, watched her nephew closely and by an access of intuition despaired of Tim's becoming even teachable as to the seriousness of the Circle, far less a member of the Interior Spiral.

It was then she noticed once more the newcomer, seated in his massive bulk, beside Freda Flower, and in fact he was whispering something to Freda Flower. Marlene realised it was Freda who had brought him to the Circle and felt deeply apprehensive.

All hands were joined. The green light shone dimly. Ewart said, "We will now have two minutes' silent prayer."

Heads were bowed. Before Marlene had taken over the Circle this silence had been followed by a hymn to the tune of "She'll Be Coming 'Round the Mountain" and which went as follows,

> We shall meet them all again by and by,
> By and by.

37

Marlene had found that this hymn was unaccountably not ease-making to the schoolmasters and clergymen and more educated members, and on reflection even herself decided that she did not in fact want to meet the whole of her acquaintance again by and by. And so, after trying several other hymns which, for reasons of association seemed unsuitable to various members, she had eliminated hymn-singing altogether. So they had a silence.

After the silence Ewart said, "Mr. Patrick Seton will now unite the Two Worlds."

Patrick had been bound at the arms and calves of his legs by canvas strips to his chair. He let his head fall forward. He breathed deeply in and out several times. Soon, his body dropped in its bonds. His knees fell apart. His long hands hung, perpendicular, over the arms of the chair. Not only did the green-lit colour but the flesh itself seemed to leave his face, so that it looked like a skin-covered skull up to his thin pale hair.

He breathed deeply in the still dim room, second after second. Then his eyes opened and turned upward in their sockets. Foam began to bubble at his mouth and faintly trickled down his chin. He opened his mouth and a noise like a clang issued from it. The Circle was familiar with this clang: it betokened the presence of the spirit-guide called Gabi. Soon the clang was forming words which became clearer to the listeners in the circle round Patrick and to Marlene behind the hatch.

"A message for one of our sisters present whose name resembles a plant. It comes from a short man in a Harris tweed suit through Guide Gabi who is speaking. The short man appears to be bearing on his back a long tube-like sack of faggots; no, they are golf clubs—"

Freda Flower cried, "That's my husband—!" but was immediately hushed by the rest of the Circle.

"His name is William," clanged the voice. "He appears to be in a most disturbed state of mind. He looks very upset, and is trying to get a message through to our sister whose name is like a plant. He is extremely concerned about her."

"Why is he going for a game of golf if he is so upset?" —This question crashed into the atmosphere, it came from the large newcomer sitting next to Freda Flower.

"Not now, Mike," she said. "Ask the questions later."

The clanging voice had stopped talking through Patrick's lips. Patrick had begun to writhe a little in his bonds. His feet kicked with sharp clicks of the heels on the parquet wooden floor.

Ewart Thornton dropped his neighbours' hands and came over to Mike. He bent over him. He said, "By interrupting the medium you may do him great harm. You may even kill him. If you interrupt again you will have to go outside."

Freda said, "I'm sorry, Ewart, but my friend, Dr. Mike Garland, is a clairvoyant."

"He must not give clairvoyance at this stage."

Dr. Garland smiled and joined hands once more with those on either side of him. Ewart returned to his place. Patrick had stopped writhing and was apparently sunk in a deep sleep. He snored for a while through his open mouth from which presently emerged once more the inarticulate clang of Guide Gabi's voice. For a while it repeated sounds which could not be identified. Eventually it said, "The sister whose name is of a plant is troubled in spirit."

Tears which she could not wipe away, since both her hands were engaged, spurted down Freda's cheeks.

"I see a man," the voice said, "in a Harris tweed suit—"

"What colour?" said Dr. Garland in a persuasive voice.

"A green or a blue," the voice replied, "I can't say exactly."

"That's him!" said Freda, brokenly.

The voice from Patrick's lips said, "His message to the sister with the name like a plant is this: Do not act against another of the brethren. If you do so it will be at your peril."

Several of the group gasped or muttered, for it was known that a court case was pending between Patrick and Mrs. Flower. Many peered forward to scrutinise Patrick's appearance, but not even the most shaken or the most easily prone to doubt, could

39

find evidence that he was faking his trance. His physical characteristics had plainly undergone a change. The skin of his face appeared to cling even closer to the bone than when he had first gone under and the cheek-bones stood out alarmingly; his mouth had widened by about two inches, seeming now to reach almost from ear to ear as the clanging voice continued to proceed from it.

"Let the sister beware of false friends and materialistic advice. The letter killeth but the spirit giveth life. What shall it profit a man if he gain the whole world and loseth his soul?"

"He was so well-read in the Bible," said Mrs. Flower, weeping.

The large pink-faced newcomer announced aloud, "I am going to give clairvoyance."

"No," Freda whispered, though all could hear, "I feel, somehow, this is genuine after all. I'd like to think it all over—"

The newcomer shouted above Patrick's din, "Nevertheless, I am going to give clairvoyance."

Ewart came over to him again and said, "Are you a trained clairvoyant? I've warned you about the danger to the medium of interruption."

"I am a trained and authentic clairvoyant," said Freda's friend.

"Guide Gabi," Patrick clanged on, "is about to give the initials of the spirit in the Harris tweed suit. The initials are W.F."

"William!" said Freda.

"I am a trained clairvoyant," shouted Freda's friend. "And I hereby give notice that I am about to give clairvoyance to the medium in the chair."

"Señor Gabi speaking," Patrick clanged; "I hereby give notice that I reinforce the warnings given by the aforesaid spirit whose initials are W.F. to the sister among our members. These warnings can only be disregarded at the utmost peril to the sister whose name resembles a plant."

40

The man beside Freda had thrown back his head and lifted his hands to his temples.

"No, Mike!" Freda moaned.

"I see," bellowed Mike Garland to the ceiling, "I see the medium in the public court, under a charge of fraud. I see the so-called medium exposed. I see—"

A small rustling hubbub had arisen amongst the audience.

"Señor Gabi speaking," came the voice from Patrick. "There is a hostile spirit among us who may cause infinite harm to—"

"Patrick Seton, you are a fraud," boomed Mike to the ceiling. "And I challenge you, if Señor Gabi is an authentic guide, to give the initials of my name."

The small rustle amongst the audience immediately became a hush.

"Señor Gabi speaking: the first initial of the hostile spirit is M."

"You are a fraud. You heard Mrs. Flower calling me Mike," boomed Mike. "What is the second initial?"

Foam appeared at Patrick's mouth and bubbled for a few seconds.

Ewart murmured, "This is dangerous to him. We must stop it."

"The second initial," Mike shouted.

"The second initial," came the clang, "is G."

"He's right!" said Mrs. Flower. "Oh Mike, I've been mistaken."

"You are a fraud," shouted Mike. "You have heard my name. You heard Mrs. Flower introducing me to a member."

Patrick dribbled from the mouth and his head drooped with exhaustion, and the water from his mouth dripped down his coat. His eyes closed.

Ewart called out, "This disruption must cease. The clairvoyant will kindly leave the séance room."

But Mike, with his hands to his temples and head thrown back began to intone. "There will be weeping and gnashing of

41

teeth. I see the prisoner brought to judgment and cast into outer darkness. There will be a trial. I see a young woman in distress and an older woman justified. I see—"

Patrick cast up his eyes. "Guide Gabi warns the Circle of an evil influence present," he said. He lifted his head high, tossing it like a war horse.

"You'll put him in a frenzy," Ewart shouted, and the audience began also to cry out phrases like "Too bad," "Wicked," "An evil influence," and "Uncivilized."

The room was in turmoil when Marlene flung wide the door. "What is this turmoil?" she said, trembling with the impatience she had been repressing throughout her service-hatch vigil. She then switched on the lights.

The noise ceased except for a sobbing sound from Freda. Patrick drooped once more, and breathed as one in a deep sleep. Mike shook his head, covered as it was with sweat, brought it to a normal level and his eyes into normal focus. Patrick slowly came round and looked at the roomful of people in a dazed way.

Freda then collapsed with a thud on the floor, where she continued her sobbing, her legs moving as in remorseful pain and revealing the curiously obscene sight of her demure knee-length drawers.

"Throw some water over her," ordered Marlene.

"Tim, fetch some water. —Where's Tim? Tim, where are you? Where's that boy?"

But at some point during the dark and troubled séance Tim had slid silently away.

Chapter 3

"NEVER again," said Tim. "It was absolute hell let loose."

"Tell me a bit more," said Ronald Bridges.

Just then Tim's telephone rang.

"Oh, Aunt Marlene," said Tim. "Sorry I keep forgetting—
Marlene. After all, you are my aunt and—yes, Marlene. No,
Mar— Yes, it was just that I was over*whelmed* Marlene. Yes,
I was just going to ring you."

He made a sign to Ronald to fetch over his drink.

"No Aunt—sorry— No Marlene. Yes. No. Of course. Of
course not. Look, I've got a fellow here on official business. Yes,
I do know it's Sunday, but this was urgent and he called—
Tomorrow at eleven. Right, I'll ring you at eleven. Yes, at
eleven. Good-bye Aunt— Yes, at eleven. Yes. No. 'Bye."

Tim took up his drink and subsided on to the sofa. "As I was
saying," he said, then closed his eyes and slowly sipped his
drink.

"I've often been tempted to go to a spiritualist meeting,"
Ronald said, "just to see."

"I nearly died," said Tim opening his eyes behind his glasses.

"I thought you had actually joined the thing," Ronald said.

"Well, yes, I suppose I had. But last night's show was something special."

"How did it end?"

"I left after the second act."

"Finished with it now?" Ronald said.

"Well yes. But it needs caution." Tim nodded over to the telephone as if the spirit of his Aunt Marlene, whose voice had a few moments before come over on it, still lingered there. "She needs handling with tact," said Tim.

"Whatever made you take it up?"

"Well, it was rather exciting to start with. And it's a fairly bleak world when all is said and done." He rose and carelessly slopped more gin and tonic into the glasses, without, however, spilling any. "And, you know," he said then, "there is something in it. This medium, Patrick Seton, isn't altogether a fraud, you know. He's got something."

"Patrick Seton, did you say?" Ronald said.

"Yes. Know him?"

"A meek little thin-faced fellow with white hair?"

"Yes, do you know him?"

"I do remember him," Ronald said, pleased with this functioning of his memory. For now he was able to place in his mind the man he had seen the previous morning in the coffee-bar. "There was a case of forgery about five years ago," Ronald said. "I had to identify the handwriting. He was convicted."

"I believe there's another case coming up against him," Tim said. "I'm not sure if it's forgery. It's the talk of the Circle. What a crowd!"

"Fraudulent conversion," Ronald said.

"You seem to know a lot about him."

"Martin Bowles is prosecuting counsel. He mentioned the case."

"I can't believe he's entirely a fraud as a medium," Tim said. "I've heard him come out with the most terrifying true facts that he couldn't possibly have known about. He once told me during a séance about a personal affair at my office that nobody could

44

have known about except me and another chap. And the other chap hadn't any remote acquaintance with Seton."

"The affair might have been on your mind, and he might have picked it up by telepathy. Do you believe in telepathy?"

"Well, yes, there seems to be evidence for telepathy. But it's odd that Seton keeps picking things from people's minds. He's got *something*."

"I should like to have heard him," Ronald said.

"You can go along if you like. Really, I mean it," Tim said eagerly. "There are meetings on—"

"No thanks," said Ronald. "You'll have to make your escape some other way."

"I only thought, if you wanted to see Seton in his trance—"

Ronald said, "He'll probably be in prison before long."

"Do you think so? What a pity, in a way," said Tim.

"Of course I know nothing about the case. But that type doesn't ever stay out in the open for long."

"I suppose he could be a genuine medium," Tim said, "and a fraud in other respects. It's a widow-woman who's taking action against him. I think he used to sleep with her and he got some money off her, and then he stopped sleeping with her and now she's furious. But she seemed pretty scared of him last night when he started to give out messages from her husband who's dead. She'll probably change her mind and withdraw the action."

"Can she do that?" Ronald said. "It's a police prosecution."

"Oh, I don't know, really."

Tim's telephone rang. "Yes, Marlene. No, Aunt— No. Well, yes, he's still here. No, I can't manage lunch, I'm afraid, I— Don't be upset, Marlene. Listen. Don't. Yes. No. Hang on a minute." Tim covered the receiver with his hand.

"Would you come with me to lunch with her?" he said, mouthing at Ronald. "Not a séance, only lunch."

Ronald nodded.

"Listen Marlene," Tim said, "I think I can come. Can I bring Ronald Bridges? He's the chap that's with me. Yes, of course

45

he'll be interested. No, I don't think so, no he's R.C. Yes, I know I said he was here on business but now we've finished our business chat. But of course he's allowed to lunch with you, at least I think so. We're just going for a drink now. Yes. Quarter past. Yes, thanks. No, yes. 'Bye."

Then he said to Ronald, "She's upset. She thinks I'm going to leave the Circle after what happened last night. She's right."

Ronald said, "Do you mind if I go home first to fetch my pills?"

"I'll come with you. I can't tell you how grateful I am that you're coming for support. I don't particularly want to *fall out* with Marlene."

"I was going to fry bacon and eggs," Ronald said.

"I was going to skip lunch," Tim said. "One can't afford two restaurant meals in one day. And yet one's got to eat, hasn't one?"

"There's something about Sunday," Ronald said, "which is terrible between one and three o'clock if you aren't in someone's house, eating. That's my feeling."

"Same here," said Tim. "Funny how Sunday gets at you if you aren't given a lunch. Preferably by an aunt or a sort of aunt."

"Yes, it's nice to see a woman on a Sunday," Ronald said.

"I sometimes go down to Isobel's with Martin Bowles," Tim said. "She's a difficult woman but still one does like her company."

"On a Sunday," Ronald said.

"I know exactly what you mean," Tim said. "Funny. Now Marlene is difficult, too. But I'm rather fond of her in a way. She thinks I'm after her cash and comforts, the darling. But in fact I'm genuinely fond of her. They don't ever quite realise that."

"What was so distressing," Marlene said, "was hearing all the noise and not being able to *see*."

"There wasn't much to see," Tim said, "it was nearly all noise."

"You shouldn't have gone away," said his aunt. "Why ever did you go away?"

"I was overcome," Tim said.

"Another time" his aunt said, "go and lie down on a bed. Don't just go away."

"Yes, of course."

"I've found out the name of the man who came with Freda Flower. He's a Dr. Garland. Doctor of what, I don't know. He has quite a reputation as a clairvoyant, but of course he's a fraud. So many frauds manage to get themselves good reputations. They prey on gullible women. Is all this boring you, Mr. Bridges?"

"No," Ronald said. "It's very interesting."

"Shall I call you Ronald, Mr. Bridges?"

"Please do, I was going to suggest it."

"I hope you don't mind eating in the kitchen." She pointed to the shuttered hatch. "The dining room is now the Sanctuary. Please call me Marlene. I don't want you to think, Ronald, that what we're discussing is in any way a normal occurrence. It has never happened before at any of our meetings, has it, Tim?"

"Well, things have been working *up* to a row, haven't they?"

"Not at all. The deplorable behaviour of the Circle last night was quite unforeseen."

Tim stretched his long legs and sprawled on the sofa. He took off his glasses and cleaned them with a white handkerchief, then put on his glasses again. He made a rabbit out of his handkerchief.

"Tim!" said his aunt.

Tim sat up, pulled the rabbit back into a handkerchief and said "What?"

"You are not taking this seriously enough. *I* suggest that after lunch we all go into the Sanctuary for fifteen minutes for spiritual repose." She pointed to the hatch to indicate the Sanctuary. "I wish Patrick were here to guide us."

Tim said, "I shouldn't really like to go in there again. At least, not yet."

"What do you mean? There's nothing wrong with the room —what was wrong was the evil spirit of that false clairvoyant among us."

"We can't have spiritual repose while Ronald's here," said Tim, looking desperately at Ronald, "because Ronald is a Roman Catholic and not permitted to have spiritual repose."

"I'm anti-Catholic," said Marlene.

Ronald was used to hearing his hostesses over the years come out with this statement, and had devised various ways of coping with it, according to his mood and to his idea of the hostess's intentions. If the intelligence seemed to be high and Ronald was in a suitable mood, he replied "I'm anti-Protestant"—which he was not; but it sometimes served to shock them into a sense of their indiscretion. On one occasion where the woman was a real bitch, he had walked out. Sometimes he said "Oh, are you? How peculiar." Sometimes, he allowed that the woman was merely trying to start up a religious argument, and he would then attempt to explain where he stood with his religion. Or again, he might say "Then you've received Catholic instruction?" and, on hearing that this was not so, would comment, "Then how can you be anti something you don't know about?" Which annoyed them; so that Ronald felt uncharitable.

There were always women who confronted him with "I'm anti-Catholic," as if inviting a rape. Men didn't do this. Mostly, Ronald coped with the statement as he did on this present occasion, when he said to Marlene, "Oh I'm sure you're not *really*."

"Yes really," Marlene said, as most of them did, "I am."

"Well, well," said Ronald.

"But I don't mean I'm anti *you*," said Marlene. "You're sweet."

"Oh, thanks."

"There's a distinction," Tim pointed out, bright with tact, "between the person and their religion."

48

"I see." Ronald attended closely to his potatoes.

"But you don't like us," said Marlene. "In fact, you detest us."

"Detest you?" said Ronald. "Why, I think you're charming."

"Now, now. You're avoiding the question. The fact is, you're not allowed—"

"Ronald's awfully interested in spiritualism," Tim said.

"He doesn't believe in it," Marlene said. "He thinks it's all baloney. He's one of those—"

"I'm sure it's possible to get in touch with the spirits of the dead," Ronald said.

"Are you?" said Tim. "Now that's interest—"

"Catholics aren't allowed to do it," Marlene said.

"We invoke the saints and so on," Ronald said, "and they are dead."

"A very different thing," Marlene said. "That's idolatry. In Spain, for instance—well, perhaps I shouldn't say. I once had an Irish maid, she was most difficult. But anyhow, you don't *get through* to the saints do you? They don't send you messages. Have you heard the actual voice of any one of your saints?"

"No," said Ronald. "You've got a point there."

"I have indeed," Marlene said. "I've heard my husband's actual voice. Haven't I, Tim? I've heard Harry. His own dynamic voice."

"Uncle Harry was always very dynamic," Tim murmured.

"Have a bit more lamb," Marlene said. "It's got to be eaten up. You boys aren't eating anything."

"Thank you, I will," said Ronald.

"Thanks," said Tim.

"Tim," said Marlene, "fill Ronald's glass and your own, for goodness sake. What do you do for a living, Ronald?"

"I work in a museum devoted to graphology."

"Handwriting," said Tim.

"Throughout the ages," Ronald said.

"Can you read handwriting?"

"I read it all day long."

"Can you judge a person's character from their handwriting?"

"No," Ronald said.

"That's exactly what I expected you to say," Marlene said. "I think you're killing."

"Ronald," said Tim, "is sometimes consulted by the police on questions of forgery."

"No!" said Marlene.

"Yes," said Tim, "he is."

"How thrilling!" said Marlene. "I do love to see a genuine fraud exposed."

"Well now," Tim said, "since you mention it, I did feel that last night—"

"Oh, Patrick completely exposed him," Marlene said, turning to explain to Ronald. "This fraud-clairvoyant Dr. Mike Garland who entered our midst during our séance last night was completely outwitted by our leading medium whose name is Patrick Seton."

"No!" Ronald said.

"Yes," said Marlene. "Garland created a great disturbance, being in the pay of one of our members—one of our *former* members—Mrs. Freda Flower, but Patrick gained the ascendancy. He was unshakable—wasn't he, Tim?"

"I was obliged to leave," said Tim, "before the end."

"Another time you must go and lie down on a bed, Tim. It was too bad of you to leave me with Freda Flower in hysterics. Did you notice the absurd pose that Dr. Garland—doctor so-called—adopted during the séance when he was giving clairvoyance? I *knew* he was a fraud the moment he raised up his head to give utterance. Did you notice, Tim, how he raised his head with*out* relaxing in his chair. He didn't lean back in his chair, you see, he didn't lean back. And I knew right away he was fully conscious of all he was saying. I'm making further investigations about Garland. He ought to be exposed."

Tim's eyes glanced briefly at the hatch. Marlene noticed it and realised she had betrayed her peep-hole. Tim's eyes returned to his soufflé and he said, "This is delicious, Marlene."

50

"I am rather clairvoyant myself," Marlene said specifically to Ronald, with a tiny swing of her earrings, "and this enables me to see through a fraud immediately. They can't get away with anything from me."

"When is Patrick's case coming up?" Tim said.

"Freda will not proceed with the case," Marlene said, "if I know anything of Freda. She has too much faith in Patrick, although she won't admit it, to ignore the warnings which he transmitted to her last night from the other side. However, I have told Freda Flower that she is no longer welcome in our midst." She looked at Tim who was still looking elsewhere. "I feel bound, Tim," she said, "to *keep an eye* on things."

"Oh, quite," Tim said, wiping his glasses with his white handkerchief.

"It's all very well for you to stand in judgment," she said.

"Who, me?" Tim said.

"But you are a comparative newcomer to the Circle. You know nothing of the inner workings. That was evident last night. Your seating arrangements . . ."

She rose and bade them come and see the Sanctuary. Glancing back she noticed Ronald taking his pills and washing them down with water.

"Aren't you feeling well?" she said.

"Ronald suffers from indigestion," Tim said.

"My dear boy, was my cooking so frightful?"

Ronald could not reply. He stood gripping the back of his chair. His eyes were open and, for a moment, quite absent.

But his attack passed and he regained control of himself while Tim and his aunt were still staring at him, Tim fearing the worst and Marlene fascinated.

"Are you psychic?" she said.

"I don't know."

He followed Tim into the Sanctuary, on the threshold of which Marlene took Ronald's arm.

"I do believe," she said, "that you are sensitive to the atmosphere of this flat. For a moment, just now, I thought you were going into a trance. I am psychic, you know. I'm certain you would make an excellent medium, if properly trained."

On the way home, before they parted, Tim said to Ronald, "I adore her, really."

"A good-looking woman," Ronald said.

"She was a beauty in her day. Of course, she's a bit crackers. There is *something*, you know, in her spiritualism, but she hasn't a clue how to cope with it. She cheats like anything herself— thinks it's justified."

"It's a difficult thing to cope with, I should think."

"I can't cope with it," Tim said. "The awkward thing is, how am I going to get out of it?"

"You'll find a way."

"Oh, I'll find a way. Only I don't want to fall out with Marlene, you know. What did you honestly think of her, quite honestly?"

"Rather charming," Ronald said, quite honestly.

Nevertheless, when Martin Bowles rang him up later in the evening and said "Come along to Isobel's for supper: she wants you for supper," Ronald replied that he was engaged. One auntie, he thought, is enough for one Sunday. Enough is always enough.

"God save me" said Matthew Finch, London correspondent of the *Irish Echo*, "and help me in my weakness." He was peeling an onion. Tears still brimmed over his eyelashes when the telephone rang. "Let it not be an occasion of sin," he said to himself or to God as he went over to answer it.

"Hallo," he said, apprehensively, although he knew, really, who would speak.

"Elsie speaking," said Elsie Forrest.

"Oh yes, Elsie. Hallo, Elsie."

"You expecting me, Matthew? You said Sunday, didn't you?"

"Yes, Elsie, I want you to come. Will you find your way? A tube to South Kensington, then a 30 bus, and you get off at

Drayton Gardens. I'll meet you at the bus stop. You'll be there by quarter to six."

"Well I was thinking of getting the Underground to—"

"No, no, the bus from South Kensington is better. I'll wait from quarter to six."

"All right, Matthew."

Elsie had not come to his flat before. He had really preferred the other girl in the coffee-bar, Alice Dawes, but she was tied up to a man. On the whole, he had been glad to discover Elsie. Not that he needed to have taken up with either of them. But, yes, he did want to know a girl again, since his previous girl had gone to America and he felt lonely in London without one. Alice Dawes with her black piled-up hair was the handsomer of the two, but Elsie Forrest was the more accessible.

"God help me with my weakness," said Matthew as he went back to his onion. For he was weak with girls and had a great conscience about sex. It had been easier in Dublin where the bachelors protected their human nature by staying long hours in the public houses. He was not sure what he would do with Elsie. He had to prepare some supper, but she would do the cooking. He was not sure what to do with the onion, and he weighed up what the force of Elsie's attraction was likely to be, and how the evening would turn out. It was for this that he had prepared the onion. For he had found that the smell of onion in the breath invariably put the girls off, and so provided a mighty fortress against the devil and a means of avoiding an occasion of sin. Matthew was not sure, however, that Elsie called for the onion altogether. She was not very pretty. But you never knew when a girl might show the charm she had within her. And again, the onion might be useful for the supper, to mix with the mince-meat. There wasn't another onion left in the box.

Was there not another onion left in the box? Matthew decided that this would be the testing point: if there was a miraculous onion in the vegetable box which could be used in

53

the supper he would, before he went to fetch Elsie from the bus, eat the raw onion he had peeled upon the table; if there was no onion in the box he would risk having Elsie to the flat with a clean breath. He looked in the box. A small shrivelled onion nestled in the earthy corner among the remaining potatoes. He lifted this poor thing, looked at it, pondered whether it was big enough for the supper. He thought perhaps he should peel and eat this little onion and leave the larger one for the cooking.

But then he recalled his previous lapses from grace, and the exact terms of the vow he had made before looking into the box. He thought lustfully of Elsie who would soon be coming back with him to the flat. He seized the peeled onion off the table, ate it rapidly like a man, dabbed his eyes and his brow with his handkerchief, and set off to wait for Elsie at the bus stop.

As if forewarning her, he gave her a breathy kiss when she alighted. She drew back only a little; in fact she took it very well.

He let her go first up the stairs to his flat and was filled with delight as he followed her small hips, which moved at his eye-level.

"Nice room," she said. "Is that your mother over there?"

"Yes, and this is my elder brother and that's my sister with her husband on their honeymoon. I'll put on the light, wait and you'll see them better. My sister's got three children. My younger brother is married, too, but my elder brother isn't." He passed the photographs one by one. "This is the National University of Ireland, Galway, where I was till 1947," said Matthew, and then he poured out the gin. "That's my cousin that was killed in the war, fighting for Great Britain.

"Would you have anything in the gin?" Matthew said. "There's orange juice or water."

"I'll have it neat," Elsie said, "and by God I need it." She placed the photographs aside. "Alice was ill last night and I was on alone at the coffee-bar till twelve. Why didn't you come in?"

"I was on duty," Matthew said. "I'm always on duty on Saturday nights."

"Well, before I left the shop I rang up Alice to see how she felt and she was in such a state I had to go round and see her. Patrick didn't come home."

"What's wrong with her?" Matthew said.

"She's expecting a baby. She's got diabetes. And the man she's living with's no good."

"Can't something be done about the diabetes?" Matthew said.

"She has to take injections every day. The man wants her to get rid of the baby."

"She shouldn't do that."

"She won't do it."

"Yes, she looks a nice girl," Matthew said. "Who's the man?"

"Patrick Seton—he's the medium."

Matthew thought she meant go-between, so he said, "But who's the man?"

"He's the man—Patrick Seton, he's a medium."

"Oh, a spiritualist?"

"Yes, he's a wonderful medium. But he's no good to Alice. Weak as water. He's supposed to be getting a divorce from his wife and then he'll marry Alice. But I don't believe he's getting a divorce. I don't believe there's any wife. And there's a case coming up against him on Tuesday for embezzlement or something like that. He's been up before the magistrates once already, but the police didn't have their evidence ready. Suppose he gets a sentence?"

"What a terrible fellow," Matthew said. "Alice should leave him, a lovely girl like that."

"She's completely under his power. In love with him."

"A terrible thing," Matthew said. "A girl like that taking up with a spiritualist. Aren't they a lot of mad fellows, spiritualists?" He was thinking of Ewart Thornton with whom he frequently had loud arguments on the Irish question. "I know a spiritualist," Matthew said, "who's a schoolmaster, we both belong to a drinking club out at Hampstead. But he won't talk about spiritualism to me because he knows I'm Irish. He talks politics. He's mad."

"Are the Irish against spiritualism?"

"Well, the Catholics, it's the same thing."

"There's a lot in spiritualism," Elsie said. "I'm not a spiritualist myself exactly. At least, I've never joined a Circle. But Alice is a member. And I believe in it."

"Do you really?" Matthew was interested with an eager mental curiosity in direct proportion as he was put off her sexually by the thought of her being a spiritualist. A deep inherited and unarguable urge made him move his chair a little bit away from her, whereas he had previously been moving it nearer; and he reflected, then, that he need not have eaten the onion. A spiritualist girl might dematerialise in the act, if it came to the act. But his mind was alert for knowledge. "How do they summon up the spirits of the dead?" Matthew said. "Would you have some more gin?"

She said, "I need it, after a sleepless night."

"There's some mince-meat and onion and potatoes and there's some custard and fruit. Or you could have bacon and eggs," Matthew said. "You just say when you're hungry. How do they call up the dead from their repose?" He poured the gin and gave it to her while she described the thrilling process of the medium's getting through to the other side.

"I had a friend called Colin that was killed," she said, "and Patrick Seton got through to him and he gave me a message, it was quite incredible because nobody could have known except Colin and me about this thing that he mentioned, it was a secret between Colin and me."

"Can't you tell it to me?" Matthew said.

"Well," she said, "it's rather personal." She looked at Matthew rather meaningly. Matthew felt himself slightly endangered and was grateful, after all, for the strong onion in his breath.

She drank down her gin. Matthew filled her glass, and moved his chair towards her again. "Are you feeling like supper?" he said. "Perhaps we'll just fry a couple of rashers and eggs. Or you'd perhaps prefer to come out, that would be simpler."

She looked at him with quite a glow, and her face, haggard as it was, showed its youth. "I'll just have my drink," she said. "I'm enjoying this rest and opening my heart to somebody."

She came over and sat on the arm of his chair. She began to finger his black curls. He turned and breathed hard upon her.

"You remind me of Colin," she said, "in a certain respect. He used to be fond of onions and I minded at first, but I got used to it. So I don't mind your onion-breath very much."

Matthew clasped her desperately round the waist, and sighed upon her as if to save his soul. But she too sighed and shivered with excitement as she subsided upon him.

At ten o'clock they went out to eat. Elsie then telephoned to see how Alice was getting on and returned to report that Patrick had still not come home and Alice was upset. And so Elsie took Matthew to the room in Ebury Street where Alice sat up in bed with her long black hair let loose, and her beautiful distress; and Matthew fell altogether in love with her.

After he had gone, Alice said, looking at Elsie in a special way,

"You've been to bed this afternoon."

"Yes. He reminds me of Colin in a way. His breath—"

"Have you been foolish tonight, Elsie?"

"Well you know," said Elsie, "that I don't mind a man whose breath smells of onions. Colin's always did."

"Makes me sick, the thought of it."

"Oh well," Elsie said, "I suppose there was something psychological in my childhood. It makes me sick too, in a way."

Chapter 4

PATRICK SETON sat in his room in Paddington, about which nobody except Mr. Fergusson knew anything, and thought. Or rather, he sat and felt his thoughts.

It was the unfortunate occurrence.

Freda Flower: danger.

Tomorrow morning at ten at the Magistrate's Court. Unless Freda Flower had changed her mind again. . . .

Mr. Fergusson would know. Mr. Fergusson had taken his passport away from him.

Patrick brushed his yellow-white hair with an old brush in his trembling hand and went out to see Mr. Fergusson. He walked hastily, keeping well in to the shop side of the streets. He hastened, for something about Mr. Fergusson always brought him peace. Meanwhile, he felt his thoughts, and they began to run on optimistic lines.

A great many witnesses for the defence. They knew he was genuine. Marlene in the box.

Freda Flower: what a gross, what a base, betrayal of all she had held sacred!

You are acquitted, said the judge. After that: Alice.

Alice must be dealt with, and her unbelievable baby. For her own sake. He loved her. And always would. Even unto her passing over. The spirit giveth life.

He had come to the police station. The constable at the desk looked up and nodded. "I'll tell Detective-Inspector Fergusson you're here," he said.

Patrick sat and fidgeted until the policeman came to call him. Patrick dusted the lapel of his dark coat with a moth-like flicker of the fingers and followed the policeman.

Patrick's nerves came to rest on Detective-Inspector Fergusson, who stood sandy-haired, with his fine build, and spoke with his good Scots voice.

"I've come to see if there has been any development, Mr. Fergusson," Patrick said, "in the unfortunate occurrence."

"Mrs. Flower has been here," said Mr. Fergusson. "You must have got at her."

"She's changed her mind, I presume?"

"Yes."

"Oh!"

"But we haven't."

"How do you mean?" Patrick said.

Mr. Fergusson said, "It's a police prosecution, you know. Witnesses can't change their minds."

"Yes, but Mrs. Flower's your chief witness. You'll want the best out of her. You'd want it given willingly."

"You're right there." Mr. Fergusson gave Patrick a cigarette. "The Chief is considering our next course of action. There will probably be a remand tomorrow."

"I won't be sent for trial?"

"The case will merely be postponed," said Mr. Fergusson reassuringly. "We've got your statement."

"I could always deny it," Patrick whispered absent-mindedly. "I was in a dazed condition after a séance when I signed it."

"That didn't get you very far the last time."

"It made an impression on the court." And Patrick waved the subject away as a wife does when reciting to a husband retorts that she has repeated on other weary occasions.

"Keep in touch with me," Mr. Fergusson nodded.

Patrick felt sorry the interview was over. He felt steadied-up when in the company of this policeman. One expected worldliness from Mr. Fergusson. One did not expect it from people with an interior knowledge of the spirit, like Freda Flower.

"It's a very painful occurrence," Patrick said.

"Very," said Mr. Fergusson.

"Is there any chance of the Chief deciding not to proceed?" Patrick said.

"A slight chance. If Mrs. Flower remains reluctant to give evidence against you there's a chance we won't proceed. But Mrs. Flower may change her mind again. We have to see her again and have a talk."

Mr. Fergusson rose and patted Patrick's shoulder, at the same time propelling him gently towards the door. "Ring me every morning," he said, "or call round. I'll keep you informed."

Then Patrick asked his usual question. "If the worst comes to the worst," he said, "how long . . . ?"

The policeman said, as usual, "It depends on the judge. Eighteen months, two years . . ."

"That's a long time."

"They go by the antecedents," said Mr. Fergusson. "Cheer up, you're lucky you're a bachelor. It's worse for a married man. Look on the bright side, Patrick."

At the street entrance Patrick looked out on to the bleak pavements and immediately felt unhappy again. He stood for a moment under the protective porch, then took the plunge up the street. He felt within him a decision to go and see the doctor.

"He can look you in the eyes," said Freda Flower to Mike Garland, "and make you believe it's you that's telling the lie."

"You don't be a fool," Mike said. "You go back to Inspector Fergusson and tell him you're going on with it, as you said in the first place. The whole of your savings gone. Remember that."

"Oh, Mike, I was so good to him. You should have seen how he got round me with his interior decorations and his odd jobs round the house."

Pink-cheeked Mike looked round the walls which were done with a pink wash. "Didn't make much of a job of it."

"He didn't do this room. He did the paint. And he did the kitchen. But I was good to him."

"He's a fraud," Mike said, "and he ought to be exposed. For the sake of the Movement."

"I can't believe it, Mike. I still can't believe, inside me, when I think of him that he's a fraud. He's given me such good advice from the chair, Mike, and last Saturday night—"

"That was a fake-up, clear enough," Mike said. "He wanted to frighten you."

"No, Mike. He was really gone on Saturday night. You could see it."

"Think of your money," Mike said. "What's happened to your two thousand?"

"I still can't believe it, Mike."

"You know what Fergusson told you."

"I don't know what to think, Mike."

"There have been other cases in the past. There are two other women over the last two years."

"I always feel somehow," she said, "that there's some explanation. I was the only woman for Patrick." She saw in her mind's eye the grave thin face and blue eyes of Patrick as it were superimposed on the curtain.

She said, "You don't realise how nicely he could talk. There was something about him lifted you up. He's a poet at heart."

"And he lifted up your cash as well."

"Perhaps there was some mistake."

"He admitted it," Mike said. "And there's your handwriting he's forged."

"Perhaps I did write the letter. I don't know. It could be my

61

own signature, after all, if I didn't know what I was doing. I thought the money was for bonds, but perhaps the bonds were a dream, I don't know—"

"He frightened you by his warnings," Mike said. "Well, let me tell you, there's nothing in them. I'm a clairvoyant and I can *see* he's a fraud."

She looked at Mike's pink face and his large frame. He failed to move her as much as Patrick had done.

"Two thousand," Mike said. "Come, put your hat on and I'll take you back to Inspector Fergusson. You were a fool to part with the cheque."

"I think he said he'd buy the bonds, I don't know." Desperately she looked at the white blossom on the green carpet, and at the curtains, fawn with a touch of pink to match the walls, and her fawn and green suite.

"Two thousand, your life savings," Mike said.

"I've got the rooms all let," she said. "Thanks to you, Mike."

"But nothing in the bank. Come on, let's go. Two thousand, remember. He should get five years' imprisonment."

She said, "It was worth the money."

But she got ready, and accompanied Mike Garland all the way back to Detective-Inspector Fergusson, who had been so severe when she had called previously to withdraw her statement. When he spoke to her on this second occasion he was even more severe, for she was so very full of tears and doubts.

Patrick spoke to the receptionist from the telephone kiosk with a courteous smile, as if she could see him.

"If at all possible," Patrick said.

"His appointment book is very full all day," the receptionist said.

"Perhaps," said Patrick, "you could have a word with him and he'll slip me in. You remember me, don't you? A private patient —Mr. Seton."

"Oh, Mr. Seton." She went away and returned.

"Half-past twelve, Mr. Seton. He can give you some time."

"Thank you," Patrick said. "I am so much obliged."

Patrick was unaware what precisely was the deep secret in Dr. Lyte's career, to which he had given unconscious utterance one night in the séance room, the only occasion on which Dr. Lyte had attended a spiritualist meeting. Patrick, on coming round from his trance, had perceived the shaken stranger and had moved with fluttering obliquity towards him as a moth to the lamp.

The stranger was Dr. Lyte. Patrick rapidly appreciated that he had said something in his trance which had truly got its mark. "How exactly did you know?" Dr. Lyte said in a way which was very different from his nice clothes.

Patrick bashfully screwed his head to the side and smiled.

When Patrick called on him the next day, Dr. Lyte had pulled himself together.

"I only went there as an experiment," he explained.

"By whom recommended?" Patrick said quietly.

"Chap called Ewart Thornton. A friend of—"

"That is correct," Patrick said. "Mr. Thornton recommended you. You are speaking the truth."

"I have no faith in spiritualism," Dr. Lyte said.

Patrick nodded like a man of the world.

"And what you described," Dr. Lyte said, "in your so-called trance, was inaccurate."

"No," Patrick said, "Dr. Lyte, it was not inaccurate."

"Where did you get this information?"

"I don't know what you're talking about," Patrick said with mendacious truth. "I'd rather not discuss the details."

"What do you want with me?"

Patrick closed his eyes reprovingly.

"What can I do for you?" said Dr. Lyte.

And so he never refused Patrick an appointment, or a piece of advice, or a drug to alleviate the effects of a trance. Patrick was not unduly troublesome. Dr. Lyte even went so far as voluntarily to obtain the new drug which had been employed, for experimental purposes, to induce epileptic convulsions in

63

rats, and which, taken in certain minor quantities, greatly improved both the spectacular quality of Patrick's trances and his actual psychic powers.

"What can I do for you, Patrick?" said Dr. Lyte when Patrick was shown in at half-past twelve sharp. Dr. Lyte was untroubled: he had got used to Patrick, as one does get used to things.

"It's about Alice. She won't think of doing away with it. Not by an operation. I mentioned the address—"

"Well, she can get it adopted. Much easier if you don't marry her till afterwards. The State has arrangements for these girls."

"Yes," Patrick said. "Alice," he said, "isn't too well."

"Send her along."

"I think perhaps she isn't taking her injections properly," Patrick said.

"Oh, she's got to take her two injections every morning before breakfast. They need the regular insulin. Tell her she'll die if she doesn't take it."

"How long does it take," Patrick said, "for a diabetic person to die if they deprive themselves of insulin?"

"She's not trying to take her life, is she?"

"I'm not sure," Patrick said, his fingers interlacing each other in agitated jerks. "But don't you think she might try to get rid of the baby by reducing the insulin and making herself really ill?"

"That would be foolish," said Dr. Lyte. "Surely she knows —but why don't you see to the injections yourself until this trouble's over."

"Oh, she won't let me touch them. She won't ever let me use the needle on her."

"Do you watch her taking it?"

"No, you see, she won't let me see her doing it."

"I'll have a talk with her. I'd better come along."

"Well," Patrick said, "I don't think that's necessary. I'll tell her she'll die if she doesn't take her insulin. I'll say you said so. How long would it take?"

"It varies," said the doctor. "My goodness, if Alice really did get negligent she might die within a few days. But she *knows*—"

"Perhaps, on the other hand, she is taking too much insulin," Patrick said. "Would that account for her symptoms?"

"What are the symptoms? Exhausted? Hungry?"

"Yes."

"Really, you know, I'll have to see her. What makes you think she isn't following her proper routine in the mornings?"

"Oh, it's only an idea I had," Patrick said. "I may be quite wrong."

"Is she testing her urine every morning?"

"I don't know," Patrick said. "It's all just a stupid idea in my mind that she may be neglecting her insulin treatment. She's probably just off colour, with the baby and so forth. . . . It's a worry for me. Tell me, if she took *too much* insulin, what might happen?"

"She'd die. I'll look in this afternoon," said the doctor.

"Very well," Patrick said. "Good of you," he said; and the doctor was vaguely disturbed by his docility. Patrick was saying, his voice trailing off, "But my suspicions may be quite unfounded, and how am I to know what she does with the needle and so forth . . . ?"

"Feeling better?" said Patrick.

"Heaps better," she said. "I'm going to work tonight."

"Did you miss me the last two days?" Patrick said.

"You know I did, darling."

"I was worried about you all the time," he said. "I asked Dr. Lyte to come and see you."

"Oh! He hasn't been."

"He's coming this afternoon."

"Well you can put him off. It's too late. I'm better."

"He's anxious in case you've been forgetting to take your insulin."

"I never forget my insulin. But I've missed you giving me the injection." She took his hand. "I've missed that little touch the last two mornings, Patrick."

"Dr. Lyte," Patrick said, "wondered if perhaps you were taking too much."

"I never take too much. Does he think I'm an imbecile? I've been taking injections for six years."

"Well, I'll ring and put him off," Patrick said.

"*I'll* ring and tell him what I think of him," she said. "Suggesting that I'm negligent—"

"Now, Dr. Lyte is a good friend. Better leave him to me. I'll tell him you're all right now."

"And then we'll go out and celebrate," she said, "the collapse of the court case."

"Well, it's only in abeyance. Of course Freda Flower hasn't a leg to stand on. But she's a dangerous woman, and she could change her mind." His voice faded away out of the window where he was looking.

"Hasn't she got a heart?" said Alice. "Hasn't she got a heart?"

"The police want to proceed," Martin Bowles told Ronald in the book-lined barristers' chambers. "But the widow won't stand by her evidence satisfactorily. Seton has scared the pants off her with messages from beyond the grave."

"Is it forgery, then? I thought you said fraudulent conversion," Ronald said.

"Fraudulent conversion on one count. But Seton has now produced a letter by which he hopes to prove that the widow gave him the money. Of course, it's a forgery."

Ronald looked at the letters and the sad second-hand-looking cheque with the bank's mark stamped on it.

"She wants them back," Martin said. "But the police are hanging on to them. We've got photostats."

"I can't work from photostats," Ronald said, locking the documents away in his brief-case. "The widow will have to wait."

"I'll give you a lift home," Martin said. "I'm going along to Isobel's."

They walked through the Temple courtyard to Martin's car.

"What do you think" Martin said, "goes on in a man like

66

Patrick Seton's mind when he looks back on his life?"

People frequently asked this sort of question of Ronald. It was as if they held some ancient superstition about his epilepsy: "the falling sickness," "the sacred disease," "the evil spirit." Ronald felt he was regarded by his friends as a sacred cow or a wise monkey. He was, perhaps, touchy on the point. Sometimes he thought, after all, they would have come to him with their deep troubles, consulted him on the nature of things, listened to his wise old words, even if he wasn't an afflicted man. If he had been a priest, people would have consulted him in the same way.

"What goes on at the back of his mind?" Martin enquired of the oracle. "Tell me."

"I should think," Ronald replied after a meet pause, "that when he considers his past life he suffers from a rush of blood to the head, giddiness and bells in the ears. And therefore he does not consider his life at all." And having thus described his own symptoms when a fit was approaching, Ronald fell silent.

Martin negotiated the traffic all along the Strand to Trafalgar Square. "I think," he said then to Ronald, "that's a terrifically good piece of observation. Do you feel like coming along and cheering Isobel up?"

"All right," Ronald said.

"Got your pills?" said Martin.

"Yes, I've got them on me."

Chapter 5

IF THERE is one thing a bachelor does not like it is another bachelor who has lost his job.

The Honourable Francis Eccles, small, with those very high shoulders that left him almost neckless, leaned over the bar of the Pandaemonium Club at Hampstead, whose members were supposed to be drawn from the arts and sciences. No scientist had yet joined the club in its twelve years' existence, but the members at present in the bar were fairly representative of the arts side: a television actor, a Welsh tenor, a film extra who took peasant-labourer parts when they were available, a ballet-mistress, and a stockbroker who was writing a novel.

It was not only the Hampstead representatives of the arts who frequented this club: many who had left Hampstead occasionally returned to it. Walter Prett for instance, the mammoth art critic of middle age and collar-length white hair, had come from Camden Town; and Matthew Finch, having sent off the last of his week's tidings for the *Irish Echo* had come to meet Walter here on the early autumn evening that tiny Francis Eccles hunched necklessly over the bar so sadly, having lost his job.

"But you don't need a job, Eccie," said Chloe, the young barmaid. "I don't know what you want with a job anyway."

Without exchanging a word or sign and by sheer migratory instinct, Matthew and Walter removed their glasses over to the window-seat where they were separated from the jobless nobleman by a grand piano.

"Tell me," said Walter to Matthew, "do I look any thinner?"

"No," Matthew said, "you look fine."

"I've lost eight pounds," Walter said confidentially, moving his snowy long-haired head close to Matthew's short blue-black curls.

"Don't worry, you look—"

"I've got to lose two stone," Walter said very loudly. "Simply got to. My heart won't stand up to it."

Matthew shied a little. "Were you not on a diet?" he said.

Walter's voice subsided. "I was, but it insisted on no beer, wines or spirits. I'd rather be dead." Walter's eyes bulged redly from the inner circle of his face, for it was surrounded by outer circles of dark blood-pressured flesh. He sipped his wine daintily through his face-wide lips. Matthew thought perhaps the glass would be crushed in Walter's great hand. Walter was liable to sudden outbursts of temper for no reason at all. Matthew looked at him uneasily, his eyes peeping from under his black glossy eyebrows.

Walter, observing this effect, was dissatisfied. He smiled sweetly, and it was indeed a sweet smile, such as wide full mouths only are capable of.

"It's my birthday," Matthew said. "I'm thirty-two today. I come under the sign of Libra, the scales of justice, I'm passionate about justice. Like all the Irish."

"Do they all come under Libra?"

"No. I don't believe in astrology," Matthew said, drinking down his wine in an anxious way.

"Well, well," said Walter. "Many happy returns. I could give you fifteen years."

"Could you?" Matthew said with his mind on something else.

"Forty-eight next year," Walter said, "and what have I done with my life?"

"You've got your column."

"I should have been a painter," Walter said. "I showed promise."

"Did you ever think of getting married?" Matthew said.

"I showed tremendous promise," Walter said, "but my family was indifferent to art. They were interested in horses. My father kept three hunters in the stable and then he couldn't pay the milk bill."

"Yes, you told me that before," Matthew said, looking wistfully at a girl in a large jersey and tight jeans who had just come in and was now sitting up on one of the high chairs at the bar.

Walter stood up and roared, "Well I'm telling you again." For he hated his family stories to be treated indifferently.

"Sit down, now, sit down," Matthew said.

"Vulgar little fellows all over the place," Walter observed, casting his inflamed eyes round the room. "Especially in the art world."

"Sit down," Matthew said. "Would you have a drink?" he said.

Chloe called over from her place behind the bar. "Walter! What's all the noise about?"

Walter sat down broodily while Matthew edged round the room and up to the far end of the bar so that Eccie's hunched back was turned to him. When he had obtained the drinks he did the same detour on his return to their window-seat. On the way, however, he said "Good evening" to the girl in jeans.

"I'm thinking of getting married," Matthew said.

"Oh are you? Who to?"

"I haven't anyone in mind," Matthew said. "Only my brother-in-law thinks I should get married. My sister wants me to get married and so does my uncle. Every time I go home to Ireland my mother's ashamed that I'm not married to a girl."

"I got a young woman into trouble at the age of eighteen," Walter said. "Daughter of one of our footmen. He was an Irish fellow. The butler caught him reading Nietzsche in the pantry. To the detriment of the silver. Of course there was no question of my marrying his daughter. The family made a settlement, and

I went abroad to paint. My hair turned white at the age of nineteen."

Matthew said, "I know a girl who's expecting a baby by an old spiritualist. She's lovely. She's got long black hair." He saddened into silence and gazed upon the girl in jeans dispassionately, recognizing her as Ronald's former girl-friend.

"I went abroad to paint, but my cousin the Marquise—"

"I'll tell you this much," Matthew said, "there's no justification for being a bachelor and that's the truth, let's face it. It's everyone's duty to be fruitful and multiply according to his calling either spiritual or temporal, as the case may be."

"Monet admired my work. Just before he died he visited my studio with his friends, and—"

"These are the figures," Matthew said, and took from inside his coat a bundle of papers from which he selected one which had been folded in four, and which was split and grubby at the folds. He straightened out the sheet, following the typewritten lines with his finger as he read out, "Greater London, the census of 1951. Unmarried males of twenty-one and over: six hundred and fifty-nine thousand, five hundred. That's including divorced and widowed, of course, but the majority are bachelors—"

"I can see him now," said Walter, "as he was when he was assisted into a chair before my easel. Monet was silent for fully ten minutes—the painting was a simple, but rather exquisite rooftop scene—"

"Unmarried males of thirty and over," said Matthew: "three hundred and fifty-eight thousand, one hundred. Since 1951 the bachelor population has increased by—"

"Put that vulgar little bit of paper away," Walter said.

"Tim Raymond gave it to me," Matthew said, putting it away very carefully. "He works in the C.O.I. God help him."

"You'd better get married," Walter said.

"Do you think so? Why?"

"Because you obviously haven't got the courage to get your sex any other way."

"There's more than sex in marriage."

71

"But not in your mind."

"Perhaps that's true. I often wonder if it's only sex when I think of getting married. Still, I feel I should be married and multiply. I feel—"

"Do you really want to get married?" Walter said.

"No."

"I nearly got married," Walter said, "in 1932 when I was out of work and the family had cut me off. The girl had a job. If a girl had a job in those days it was like a dowry. She was anxious to marry me. But I was really more taken up with her father. He was a carpenter, one of the last of the true English craftsmen. But I did not marry his daughter. She was a bourgeois little bitch with her savings in the post office. Her name was Sybil, if you please." The memory of Sybil, though in fact she had never existed, was so fiercely implanted in Walter's mind through frequent elaborations of his imagined affair with her, that he was always thoroughly incensed by her.

"I wished her joy of her savings in the post office and departed," Walter shouted. He rose and set down his empty glass and fastened his black coat on one button across his huge stomach.

"Are you going to go?" Matthew said.

Walter clenched both fists as if to fight with Sybil.

"I'll walk with you to the station," Matthew said.

Walter sat down again and made his lips into a long line.

"I'll have to be going," Matthew said. "My other brother-in-law has just come over and I've got to meet him at my uncle's."

"My boy," said Walter, "you have much to bear."

"Not my uncle at Twickenham. My other uncle at Poplar," Matthew said, with his eyes on the brown bobbed head of Ronald's girl in jeans who was laughing with Chloe.

"I want a drink," Walter said.

"I'm a bit short of cash," Matthew said, "this time of the month."

"Fresh young Chloe will cash me a cheque," Walter shouted.

"Chloe will not cash you a cheque," Chloe called out, "for the simple reason that Chloe is not allowed to cash cheques any more."

Francis Eccles swivelled round in his high chair.

"Why Walter!" he said.

"Why Eccie," said Walter.

"There's a very definite rule about cheques," Chloe said.

Walter ambled over to the bar and said in a tone of dignified reproach, "As it happens I haven't got my cheque book on me. But I'm surprised, Chloe, that you should take up this ridiculous lower-middle-class attitude."

"I have my orders, Walter," Chloe pleaded.

"What will you drink, Walter?" said Eccie.

"You have your orders, Chloe," Walter said. "Very well, you have your orders. But really, my dear, this is dreadfully bourgeois of you."

It worked quicker than usual. Chloe said, "I'm not bourgeois, really I'm not. I'll personally cash you a cheque. It's only that I can't, I mustn't, cash cheques for the club."

"Since when?" said Walter.

"Since last week," she said. "Honestly," she said.

"First I've heard of it," said the girl in jeans.

"I'll cash your cheque," said Eccie, also anxious not to be bourgeois.

"It's of no matter," Walter said. "I only object on principle. As it happens I haven't got my cheque book on me."

Eventually he accepted a loan from Eccie, and when the deal was done Matthew reappeared from the cloakroom. He took a high chair at the bar and helped himself to a pickled onion off a plate.

"Matthew," said Chloe, "meet Hildegarde. Hildegarde, meet Matthew."

Matthew leaned forward and smiled across Walter's bulk at the girl in jeans. "We've met before," he said.

"Where?" she said.

"At Ronald Bridges'. Aren't you a friend of Ronald's?"

"I used to be," she said.

"I know Bridges," mused Eccie. "I wonder if he could help . . . ?"

"No," said Chloe. "I shouldn't think so, Eccie."

"Don't you?"

"No."

"What is this secret conversation?" roared Walter.

"It's something Eccie and I were discussing," Chloe said. "It's private."

"Common little creatures," Walter shouted. "Very bad behaviour."

"I'm not standing for that, Walter," Chloe said. "Are you standing for it, Eccie?"

"Well, no," said Eccie. "I must say, Walter . . ."

"This is too much," said Hildegarde. She swung her long legs off the stool and departed.

"Come on, Walter," Matthew said, "I've got to meet my brother-in-law—"

"I shall not be driven away by a barmaid and a snivelling middle-class younger son of an upstart earl," Walter said.

"You're drunk," said Chloe.

Walter laughed without noise or humour, but with a shaking of his flabby shoulders, chest and stomach.

Eccie said sadly, "Walter, Walter, I don't like this."

"You are deriving a certain pleasure from lumping it," Walter said.

"Walter, I'm out of a job, you know. The Institute is closing down."

"Not before time," Walter said.

"As an art school, I admit it had its weaknesses," said Eccie. "But I flatter myself I was able to contribute something useful with my lectures, especially on the country itinerary which I've been taking for the last two years."

"Nonsense. You contributed nothing. You know nothing of art."

"Oh, Walter, come!" said Eccie, Christianly.

"He's drunk," said Chloe.

74

"I'll have to go and 'phone my sister," Matthew said.

"Drunk," said Chloe, "and this time's the last. He can't come here insulting the members—"

Walter took from his pocket the five pounds that he had borrowed from Francis Eccles. "I'll give you this back," he said, "before I'll admit you know anything about painting, Eccie."

Eccie said "Good night, Chloe. Good night, Matthew," in a tone of gentle reproach, and left.

"That was mean of you, Walter," Chloe said.

"I am an honest man," Walter observed, "when treating of the few existing subjects to which honesty is due."

"I'd better ring my sister," Matthew said. "My cousin will be on the telephone to her as I haven't turned up at my uncle's to meet my brother-in-law."

"It was unkind of you, Walter," said Chloe, leaning over the bar forgivingly. "Poor old Eccie's upset at losing his job."

"He doesn't need a job," Walter said. "He's got his private income and his basement. And he's an Anglo-Catholic. Anglo-Catholics always get jobs."

"He hasn't got much income," Chloe said. "Have you seen the way he lives? That basement is going down and down. No one to look after him."

"He ought to have got married," Matthew said.

"He's not the marrying type," said Chloe.

"He pees in the sink," said Walter, "not that I hold that against him."

"He *doesn't!*" said Chloe.

"True," said Walter. "It's nothing. We bachelors all pee in sinks and wash-basins."

"I don't," said Matthew.

"You're young yet," Walter said.

"Filthy beasts, the lot of you," Chloe said, laughing towards one face and another as she leant over the bar.

Then she straightened up.

"Hallo, hallo," she said, for Mike Garland, accompanied by an elderly man who wore a clerical outfit, had entered.

"Walter, Matthew," she said, "this is Dr. Garland and Father Socket."

"How do you do, Father," said Matthew, jumping off his stool to shake hands.

"Not of our persuasion," Walter informed Matthew, whereupon Matthew drew away his hand nervously and said, "Pleasant evening."

"These two are fraud spiritualists," Walter roared.

"I beg your pardon, sir?" said Father Socket.

"I grant it with a plenary indulgence," said Walter as he pushed Matthew before him out into the high autumnal winds of Hampstead.

"I'd have liked to talk to them a bit," Matthew said. "What was all your hurry? Alice Dawes, that pregnant girl with the long black hair, is a spiritualist."

"These are fraud spiritualists."

"Is there a difference, then?" said Matthew.

Chapter 6

Ronald said, "How long have you known her?"

"Since two weeks," Matthew said. "She's got long black hair. She has it done up on top when she's in the coffee-bar and she lets it go long when she's in bed."

"I should think you've got a chance," Ronald said. "Seton isn't much of a rival, from what I know of him. But are you sure you want to marry this girl?"

Matthew hastily remembered that the last thing he had said might be misconstrued, so he told Ronald, "I saw her in bed because she was ill and her friend Elsie took me along—Elsie's the other girl in the coffee-bar."

"Have some tea," Ronald said. "Help yourself. Pour it out."

"I hope you don't mind me consulting you like this?"

Ronald poured out tea, holding the teapot as high over the cup as possible without making a splash. This had been a habit of his for as long as he had been making tea for himself, and he did not notice now what he was doing as he raised the teapot, by habit, twelve inches above the cup, nor did he remember that the pretty sight of the long stream of golden liquid had once made the process of tea-making less of a bore than if he had poured it from a normal height.

"Be careful," Matthew said, "you don't spill it."

"You will be thirty-three this month," Ronald said, testing his memory.

"My birthday was last week," Matthew said, aimlessly as a boy-seminar answering a tall black frock.

Ronald said, "Everyone consults me about their marriages." Three months ago Tim Raymond, before he had joined his aunt's spiritualist circle, had come to Ronald with the marriage question. He had said, "Do you think everyone will say I'm marrying her for her money and she for my connections?"

"I don't know. I expect so."

"Perhaps that's the truth of the matter."

"Well, you've got good connections. It isn't every set of connections a woman wants to take on. And for your part, it isn't everyone's money you would touch, I daresay. There's an element of mutual respect involved."

"There's something in that. Still, it would be tiresome if people said—"

"Do you love the girl?" Ronald said.

"Funny thing, you know, in a funny sort of way, she's *fun*."

"Well, I don't see why you shouldn't get married. Does she love you?"

"I think so. Of course she says so."

"What does your mother think?"

"Oh, she likes the idea. They all like the idea. And I quite like the idea. But—"

"Do you want to get married at all?" Ronald said.

"No," Tim had said. "I don't know why, but I don't."

Ronald said to Matthew, as he poured tea from a great height, "Do you want really to get married?"

"Well, I'm very much in love with Alice."

"Are you sure you want to get married?"

"I'd like Alice for a wife if I was to marry."

78

"Do you want to marry at all?"

"I can't say I do," Matthew said. He drank down his tea which had become cold through Ronald's method of pouring.

"It's the duty of us all to marry," Matthew said. "Isn't it? There are two callings, Holy Orders and Holy Matrimony, and one must choose."

"Must one?" Ronald said. "It seems evident to me that there's no compulsion to make a choice. You are talking about life. It isn't a play."

"I'm only repeating the teaching of the Church," Matthew said.

"It isn't official doctrine," Ronald said. "There's no moral law against being simply a bachelor. Don't be so excessive."

"One can't go on sleeping with girls and going to confession."

"That's a different question," Ronald said. "That's sex: we were talking of marriage. You want your sex and you don't want to marry. You never get all you want in life."

"I'll have to marry in the end," Matthew said, gazing at the tea-leaves in the bottom of his cup. "The only way I can keep off sex is by going to confession and renewing my resolution every week, and sometimes that doesn't work. It's an unnatural life if one's a Christian."

"Find the right girl, then, and marry her."

"Alice is the right girl.

"Well get her to marry you."

"I don't *want* to get married, you know."

Ronald laughed. He was rather surprised that the conversation was becoming rancorous.

Matthew said, "Do you want to marry?"

"No," Ronald said. "I'm a *confirmed* bachelor."

"Why don't we want to marry? It isn't as if we were homosexuals."

Ronald greatly desired, as he sometimes did, to run his fingers through Matthew's black curls. He thought, well isn't he right? we are not homosexuals. Repressed homosexuality is a meaningless term because no one can prove it.

Matthew said, "I suppose most people would say the confirmed bachelor is a subconscious homosexual."

"Impossible to prove," Ronald said. "You can only deduce homosexuality from facts. Subconscious tendencies, repressions —these ideas are too simple and too tenuous to provide explanations. There are infinite reasons why a man may remain celibate. He may be a scholar. Husbands don't make good scholars, in my opinion."

"I'm only saying," said Matthew, "what people say. They say all bachelors are queers. Hee hee. Or mother-fixated or something."

"Oh, what people say— They always look at what might be, or what should be, never at what is."

"My trouble is this," Matthew said, "I have a mind to consider the lilies of the field. In other words, I'm a lazy Irish lout and I like to feel I can chuck up a job any time, and go off to Bolivia."

"Are you thinking of going to Bolivia?"

"No," said Matthew, "not particularly."

"Your shoes are wet," Ronald observed.

"Yes, can I take them off?"

"You should have taken them off before."

Matthew said, "Are there any women who really don't want to marry?" He let his shoes fall with a plop. Ronald put them straight and at a shrewd drying point near the gas fire.

"Yes, very often, but those are the ones who marry."

"They get married, not actually wanting to?"

"Yes. Like many men."

"Why? Is it sex?"

"Not always I think. It's probably a development in human nature. Something both conforming and unconforming. Otherwise, spinsters and bachelors would all be in religious orders."

"Part of me feels they should be."

"The whole of you should acknowledge that they aren't."

"It's fear of responsibility that puts me off marriage. Responsibility terrifies me. Does it terrify you?"

Ronald considered. "No," he said. "No one offers me much of it." He thought of Hildegarde and her attempt to take him over as a whole burden for herself.

"I've got responsibilities," Matthew said, twiddling his stocking-toes, "I've got to send money home to Ireland to my mother and my aunt. There's only my mother and her sister on the farm and the farm's gone down. They want me to get married, though. I feel immoral as a bachelor. Do you ever feel immoral?"

"Not very often," Ronald said. "I've got my epilepsy as an alibi."

"It used to be called the falling sickness," Matthew said. "Would you come out to the coffee-bar and have a look at Alice?"

Ronald could not forbear to say, "I've seen her."

"Have you? Where?"

"In a café in Kensington. She was with Patrick Seton."

A heap of Ronald's unwashed laundry lay on the carpet. He had started to make a list which bore the words "3 cols." This lay on the top of the pile.

"How did you know it was Patrick Seton? Have you met him?" Matthew said.

Ronald could not forbear to say, "Yes, I gave evidence on his handwriting once. He was convicted of forgery. I have a letter here in my desk," Ronald rattled on, "which will probably convict him again. So your way will be clear," he said, "to marry Alice."

"She told me the case was off."

"That hasn't been decided yet."

"Will you come out and meet Alice?" Matthew said. "She's working at the Oriflamme."

"All right." Ronald kicked the laundry.

"Of course, you know," Matthew said, "she isn't a Catholic. She's a spiritualist."

"I don't suppose she'd let it stand in her way if she wanted to marry you."

"I meant, from my point of view—"

"Yes, I know what you meant."

"Well, as a Catholic how do you feel about—"

Ronald turned on him in a huge attack of irritation. "As a Catholic I loathe all other Catholics."

"I can well understand it. Don't shout, for goodness sake—" Matthew said.

"And I can't bear the Irish."

"I won't stand for that," Matthew said.

"Don't ask me," Ronald shouted, "how I feel about things as a Catholic. To me, being Catholic is part of my human existence. I don't feel one way as a human being and another *as a Catholic*."

"To hell with you, now," Matthew said.

Ronald lifted one of Matthew's shoes, which he had placed so carefully to dry—neither too near the gas fire nor too far from it—and cast it casually at Matthew's head.

Matthew started to hit out, then stopped with his hand in mid air. Ronald's arm, lifted for protection, was arrested for a second before he dropped it, and he realised that Matthew was sparing him on account of his epilepsy.

Matthew stumbled over the laundry, put on his damp shoes, then went off to the lavatory. When he returned Ronald was ready to accompany him to the coffee-bar where Alice was working.

"Her pregnancy doesn't show as yet," Matthew said. "I'd adopt the child as my own if I married her. Do you think, by the way, I ought to try and marry her? She's got long black hair, only you don't see it look so glorious when she piles it up as when she lets it fall."

Time had come round for one of Alice's ten-minute rest periods, and she sat at the table with Ronald and Matthew while they ate tough salty pizza. She delicately picked a speck of tobacco from her tongue and sadly inhaled her cigarette.

"I love the man," she said. "I know he's innocent."

Matthew immediately said, "Ronald here is examining one

of the vital documents in the case. Ronald is a handwriting expert. He is often consulted in criminal cases—aren't you Ronald? He's got this document that's supposed to be a forgery. It's a letter—isn't it a letter, Ronald?"

Ronald smiled as one who had only himself to blame.

Matthew went on, "He puts these documents to all sorts of tests—don't you Ronald? There's a test for the ink, and the paper, and all the folds. The most important thing is the formation of the letters—anyone can do the rest, but Ronald's the best man for detecting the formation of letters. And sometimes the forger has stopped to assess his handiwork and then retraced. That's fatal because there's an interruption in the writing which can be detected under the microscope, at least Ronald can detect it—can't you Ronald?"

Alice was looking at her cigarette, which she was tapping on the edge of the ash-tray.

"I shall never believe he's guilty," she said. "Never."

Ronald thought, How that second, histrionic "never" diminishes her—how it debases this striking girl to a commonplace.

"I'll always believe in his innocence," she said. "Always. No matter what the evidence is."

"I haven't yet looked at the document," Ronald said. "I am sure it will not be incriminating to your friend."

She looked up at him. "Why are you sure?"

"Because he is your friend," Ronald said.

Something in his tone made Matthew collect his senses. "I haven't been indiscreet in talking about the letter, have I?" he said.

"It's perfectly understandable," Ronald said.

"After all, *you* told me about it."

"That's right," Ronald said, "I did."

Matthew kept looking uncomfortably at Ronald. But he chattered on, desperately, in his desire to deprecate the girl's lover.

"Ronald says Patrick Seton has been convicted of forgery before."

"Well, I don't believe it. He's been abroad a lot of his life at famous séances. He was married at one time. His divorce is coming through shortly, and we're getting married. Colonel Scorbin, who's one of the leading spiritualists in Mrs. Marlene Cooper's Circle, and a colonel, said to me, 'Patrick is one of those rare persons who are born to do great things and to suffer injustice and persecution.' I said to him, 'I believe it,' and I do believe it and I always will, always."

She seemed not sure how to look at Ronald, whether to show a predominance of hostility which might frighten him, or of fear which might move him to pity; or whether to affect charm and win him over. She offered all three in a way, by holding her head loftily as she regarded him, by pleading with her eyes under their lashes, and by sitting with the elbow over her chair so that her breasts rose unmistakably towards him.

Matthew realised that he had caused Ronald to be the centre of her attention rather than achieved his desire to discredit Patrick.

Alice's ten-minute rest was up. She sauntered about with her long swing among the tables and the trailing ivy of the Oriflamme taking orders for coffee. Matthew and Ronald stayed for a while and she returned as often as she could to their table, once pausing with her tray, on the way to serve a customer, to say to Ronald what was still on her mind.

"The case may not come off. Have you any idea if the case will be brought?"

"No. It has nothing to do with me."

"It would be easy to frame up a case against Patrick, with that letter."

"Nothing will be framed up," Ronald said. "Please forget about the letter."

Matthew said, "Can I meet you after the shop's closed and take you home?"

"Yes," she said, and she nodded. "Yes."

Matthew had not expected her assent.

84

"Are you sure?" he said, instantly afterwards feeling like a lout.

"Yes, yes, I'm sure." She was looking at Ronald.

"I'll be back here at the Oriflamme at ten to twelve," Matthew said. She was looking at Ronald.

"Good night, Alice," Ronald said.

"Can't you do something for Patrick?" she said to Ronald.

He said, "You should not expect anything of Patrick Seton. Leave him."

Matthew and Ronald walked along the Chelsea embankment. Matthew said, "I didn't expect her to let me fetch her tonight. I'd better 'phone my sister. She's expecting me to stay with her tonight because my brother-in-law's gone over to Dublin with my other uncle, and she doesn't like to be alone in the house with the children. I'd better 'phone and tell her I'll be late. Did you mind me telling Alice about that document you've got to inspect. Was it confidential?"

"It was confidential."

"Oh, you should have made that clear when you told me. But I wanted Alice to know what she's got hold of in this Patrick Seton."

"Yes, she seems to be in love with him."

"Did you think so?"

"Yes."

"Lovely girl, isn't she? And carrying a child inside her."

"Very attractive."

"D'you think I've a chance with her?"

"Chance of what?"

"Well, it would have to be marriage. She's expecting the child, moreover. It makes her more desirable; not many would think so, but I do."

"I think you'll have a chance after Patrick Seton has served a few months of his prison sentence."

"Don't you think she'd be the sort of girl who would wait for him?"

"Not after she had heard his previous convictions read out in court."

"The age of him," Matthew said, "and the look of him! What does she see in him, a girl like that? You would never see such a match in Ireland except in rare cases where the man had a bit of money and the girl was homeless."

"She is obviously a soul-lover," Ronald said.

"She's in love with his spiritualism, that's what it is. He must know a few tricks."

"I think he's a genuine medium, from what I've heard."

"I hope he doesn't get his divorce. It might not come off. Then Alice—"

"From what I recall," Ronald said, "he isn't a married man at all. At least, it wasn't declared the last time he was in court."

"He's supposed to have been married for twenty-five years; so Alice says."

"Well, perhaps he lied to the court. But there's usually a question of maintenance orders. I distinctly recall his being described as a bachelor."

"What a good memory you've got," Matthew said.

"Thanks," said Ronald, and smiled at himself in the glass window of a shop.

"Why should he talk about a divorce if he isn't married, though?" Matthew said. "Do you think he intends to marry Alice at all?"

"I'll find out what I can from Martin Bowles. He's prosecuting counsel."

Matthew stopped walking and was looking out over the full-flowing river at the lights on the opposite bank.

"Have you been eating lots of onions?" Ronald said.

"No, not since yesterday. Can you smell them in my breath?"

"Yes."

"Come on, let's have a drink to take it away before I pick up Alice. They don't like the smell of onions in your breath. Do you really think Patrick Seton is a bachelor?"

They sat in the public house and debated the question of

Patrick's being a bachelor, and if so, why he had told Alice the story of a divorce.

"Perhaps he's putting her off from day to day," Matthew said. "You could understand it; her wanting to be married for the child, and him not wanting to marry at all. He may be a bachelor like us in that respect."

Ronald silently contemplated the no-betting notice on the wall.

"He has no intention of marrying her at all," Matthew said, becoming fierily convinced of it. "What do you expect of a spiritualist? His mind's attuned to the ghouls of the air all day long. How can he be expected to consider the moral obligations of the flesh? The man's a dualist. No sacramental sense. There have been famous heresies very like spiritualism—they—"

"Have another drink," Ronald said, who was accustomed to long evenings of proof that Matthew had emerged from his Jesuit school well versed in the heresies.

"Take the Albigensians. Or take the Quietists even. The Zoroastrians. Everything spiritual. Down with the body. Against sex—"

"Against marriage," Ronald said. "All bachelors. Like us."

"I think the spiritualists have sex," Matthew looked broodily at his knees. "I'm afraid we are heretics," he said, "or possessed by devils." His curls shone under the lamp. "It shows a dualistic attitude, not to marry if you aren't going to be a priest or a religious. You've got to affirm the oneness of reality in some form or another."

"We're not in fact heretics," Ronald said, "under the correct meaning of the term."

"Well we've got an heretical attitude, in a way."

"Not in fact. But does it worry you?"

"Yes."

"Do you want to marry?"

"No."

"Then you've got a problem," Ronald observed and went to fetch more drinks.

"I suppose an heretical attitude is part of original sin," Matthew said as soon as Ronald returned within hearing. "You can't avoid it."

Ronald said, "The Christian economy seems to me to be so ordered that original sin is necessary to salvation. And so far as remaining single is concerned that applies to a lot of people."

They walked to Battersea where their attention was caught by the sound as of a horse galloping. They looked up a side street in the direction of the sound and found it to come from a man lying on his back outside a pub. His legs were kicking out and his heels clop-clopped on the pavement. A few people had gathered in the roadway and a young policeman circled round the man as if he were a tiger.

"Is he drunk?" Matthew said.

Ronald went over to the young policeman. "Turn his head to one side," he said, "or he might damage his tongue."

"Are you a doctor?" said the policeman.

"No, but I understand fits. The man's an epileptic." Ronald took his own wedge of cork from his pocket and handed it to the policeman. "Stick this between his teeth. Then kneel on his knees and try and get his boots off."

"There's an ambulance coming," said the policeman.

"He could bite his tongue in the meantime," Ronald said. "There could be a lot of damage. I'd shove in the wedge if I were you."

The policeman knelt and grasped the man's head. He tried to thrust the wedge into the frothing mouth, but the man's convulsions kept throwing the policeman off.

The policeman looked up at Ronald. "Would you mind trying to get his boots off, then, sir?"

"I doubt if I can do it," Ronald said. He was greatly agitated, for if there was one thing he did not like to see it was another epileptic. The thought of touching the man horrified him. "Matthew!" he called out. "Come and lend a hand."

Matthew approached and, as Ronald instructed, threw himself upon the man's jerking knees. The policeman jammed the

88

wedge between the teeth. Ronald felt for the shoes as one thrusting his hands into flames. He shut his eyes, and felt for the laces, loosened them, threw the shoes aside so violently that one of them nearly hit an onlooker, and sprang back from the kicking figure.

The man was still jerking when the ambulance arrived, and he was lifted up by two men in hospital uniform and taken away.

"Did it upset you?" Matthew said as they went down to look at the river.

"Yes," Ronald said.

"Will you be all right?"

"Oh yes, I'll be all right."

Matthew went off to telephone to his sister and then to read a novel called *Marie Donadieu* in Lyons' Corner House until it should be time to go and meet Alice, while Ronald walked part of the way home, and then, feeling unsafe, took a taxi the rest of the way. There, he resisted taking his phenobarbitone, shaky though he was, for on occasions of extra stress he rather cherished the feeling of being more alive and conscious than usual, he cherished his tension and liked to see how far he could stand it. This evening he got ready for bed without any intimations of an approaching fit, and although he had his little drugs ready to take, he did not take them, and managed to get a living troubled sleep instead of a dead and peaceful one.

Chapter 7

"What is the size of the chalet?" Patrick breathed indifferently.

Dr. Lyte said, "Oh, large enough for two. There are four or five rooms, but as I say it is very difficult of access. You are only a kilometre and a half from the frontier on the one hand and only three from the bus stop on the other, but that's as the crow flies. If you aren't a fairly good climber you would have to be a crow." He laughed. Patrick did not. "I wouldn't recommend it, really I wouldn't," said Dr. Lyte.

"No, it sounds just our sort of thing," Patrick whispered. "Isolated. Mountains. We'll take it on for three weeks as soon as this wretched case is either squashed or over."

Dr. Lyte reached across his desk, lifted the silver lid of his inkpot and let it drop again. He looked at his short white hands. He lifted his card-index box and placed it down again a quarter of an inch from its previous position. He fidgeted with his blotting paper. He said to Patrick, "Suppose the case does come off?"

"Alice and I will go abroad immediately after the case."

"But if . . ."

Patrick's blue eyes looked out at the sky above the roof. So blue, he thought, so calm. A muscle in his small chin twitched. "I'm quite confident of being acquitted," he said in his murmur. "I may not be sent for trial, even. The police keep asking for time. No evidence. I've been remanded twice."

Dr. Lyte said, "I don't know, really, why you haven't skipped away in the meantime. Why don't you go abroad?"

Patrick coughed. "I feel I must stay and see this unfortunate occurrence through." His shoulders moved resentfully. "Do you think I'm afraid to—to—how shall I put it?—to stand trial?"

"No," said Dr. Lyte.

"We'll take over your chalet then," Patrick said. "Alice and I. One way or another, that will be before the end of the year."

"I don't recommend it in November or December," said Lyte.

"Alice likes the cold weather. Alice doesn't like tourist seasons. Alice likes the snow. Will it be snowing?"

"You'll be cut off. Supposing Alice were to take ill, in her condition? Really, you must wait till the spring. March would be all right, perhaps. April, certainly. But November, December. Have you ever been to a lonely part of Austria in November?"

"We shall be taking your chalet for a month." Patrick smiled a little at Dr. Lyte's protests; and the doctor, who did not like to be smiled at in this way, said, "I've a good mind to refuse you."

"Have you now?" Patrick said. "Have you?"

Dr. Lyte thought of his practice and his wife and his house at Wembley Park, his daughter at Cambridge and his married daughter; he thought, also, inconsequentially, of the field attached to a Kentish Georgian rectory which he had recently acquired; he thought of his professional friends, his cottage in France and his chalet in Austria. There was nothing he could think of that he wanted to lose, and he regretted the evening he ever set foot in Marlene's Sanctuary of Light. ("One hopes it will become a Sanctuary of Lyte in every sense," some man had remarked on hearing his name on that one occasion, but the remark had shocked Marlene.) To say this doctor thought of all he could lose is perhaps to put too blunt a point on it, for he felt these things deeply, and all in a second or two while Patrick smiled a little with melancholy.

"You know," said Dr. Lyte, "that Alice can't stand up to anything strenuous. Ober-Bleilach will be strenuous. The climbing—"

"I'll see she doesn't do too much. I'll see she takes her injection every day."

"You'll have to take a supply of insulin with you," Lyte said.

"Yes."

"A good supply," he said. "You can't depend on local supplies. It's a remote place."

"Yes. She knows how to look after herself."

"Are you sure?"

"Yes."

"You were saying the other day," said the doctor, "that you thought Alice might be negligent about her insulin."

"No, I don't think so now. At least, I'll see that she isn't. If she's going to take too much of the stuff or too little she'll do it whether we go away or not."

So she will, thought Dr. Lyte, and he actively dispersed an uneasy idea that had begun to form in his mind.

"We'll take that chalet," Patrick said as if his mind was on something else.

"Let's discuss the details, then, after the trial. You know, Patrick, I've got a roomful of patients waiting to see me."

Patrick discerned a touch of defiance. He was aware that Dr. Lyte possessed, in relationship to himself, a mixture of emotions, including various shades of fear, and so, to encourage them, Patrick said, "I keep on getting through to that control who is so familiar with the unfortunate occurrence in your past life. I can't help it. I keep on getting—or rather he keeps on getting through to me. He keeps on reminding me—"

"Are you short of ready cash?" said Lyte, and already he had risen from his chair and was walking over to a cupboard in which he kept a black tin cash box.

"The Chief hasn't decided," Inspector Fergusson said. "It depends on a number of factors to do with our evidence."

"But when do you think this unfortunate occurrence will be settled, Mr. Fergusson?" Patrick trailed on.

"A month or two."

"I have some little news for you," Patrick said.

"Now, Patrick, I must warn you, we'll do our best but this time we can't guarantee your protection. The Chief told me to tell you. So news or no news . . ."

"I've been helpful to you," Patrick said, shuffling his feet bashfully and looking down at them. "And I could go on being helpful, Mr. Fergusson."

"What's the news, then?" Fergusson said.

"Well—after what you've just said, Mr. Fergusson, I don't really feel inclined—"

"I'm surprised at you, Patrick!" said Mr. Fergusson. "I really am surprised."

Patrick swallowed and looked frail and ashamed. His knees closed in together and he grasped the seat of his chair like a schoolboy.

Inspector Fergusson offered Patrick a cigarette. Patrick took one; his hand was shaking.

"Well Patrick," said big strong Mr. Fergusson, "you haven't ever let me down yet."

"No," Patrick said. "I thought you were going to bear that in mind with reference to Mrs. Flower, the unfortunate . . ."

"I'm being straight with you," said Fergusson, his square good shoulders blocking the lower half of the window-light, "and I'm telling you that we can't promise to protect you this time. I can't promise anything. You've always had a square deal for any information you've passed on."

"There's a lot that goes on in spiritualism," Patrick observed

93

with timid sociability. "From your point of view," he said.

"Tell me, Patrick," said big Mr. Fergusson, "did you never think of getting married? It might have made a man of you. It might have kept you straight."

"I've always believed in free love. I've never believed in marriage," Patrick murmured. "Why should man-made laws . . ."

Fergusson tilted back his chair and heard him out: man-made laws, suppression of the individual, relics of the Victorian era . . . Patrick's thin voice died out ". . . and all repression of freedom of expression and self-fulfilment. . . ." It sounded good-class reading stuff.

"You've certainly got ideas of your own," stated Fergusson, standing up. "I'm a married man myself," he stated. "Well, Patrick, I've got work here in front of me to do. Keep in touch."

Patrick stroked his hair. He stood up, opened his mouth to speak, and sat down again.

"I'd like to be as helpful as possib . . ." Patrick said.

"Well tell me the tale and get it off your chest." Inspector Fergusson drew a note-pad towards him and poised his pen.

"There isn't actually a tale. Only a name. There was an unfortunate occurrence the other night—"

"What name?"

"Dr. Mike Garland."

"What about him?"

"He poses as a clairvoyant."

"A fraud."

"Oh yes. He attempted to question me while I was under the other night. He's very friendly at the moment with Mrs. Freda Flower."

"Where does he live?"

"I'll find out, Mr. Fergusson."

"What does he do for a living?"

"I'll find out if you're interested, Mr. Ferg . . ."

"Only for the records," said the inspector. "What does he do for a living?"

"I'll find out, Mr. Fergusson. I thought his name might be helpful," Patrick said.

"Thanks." Fergusson was scribbling his notes. "Brief description, Patrick please. You know what we want."

Patrick cast his pale eyes to the ceiling. "Nearly six foot, fairly stout, age about fifty, greying hair, fresh complexion, round face, blue eyes."

"Right," said Fergusson. "What does he do for a living?"

"He goes about with a Father Socket."

"Who's he—a clergyman?"

"I don't know, Mr. Fergusson. I haven't met Father Socket."

"Are you sure?" said Mr. Fergusson.

"Yes, Mr. Fergusson," Patrick said. "But I'll find out about him for you."

"Right. What does Garland do for a living?"

"Mr. Fergusson, I hope you can do something for me with regard to the unfortunate—"

"It's in the Chief's hands, Patrick. Defrauding a widow of her savings is a serious crime on the face of it."

"I was tempted and fell," Patrick said.

"So you said in your statement," said Mr. Fergusson, tapping the heap of files on his desk.

Patrick looked yearningly at the files as if wishing to retrieve the statement that lay in one of them.

"Mrs. Flower still isn't prepared to give evidence, though?" Patrick said.

"She'll have to give evidence."

"Satisfactory evidence?"

"We aren't sure of that, as yet."

Dr. Lyte sat in his consulting room after the last of the evening surgery had departed and his receptionist had locked up and gone home. He was in a panic, and this caused him to lose his head so far as he was writing the letter at all; but it was

95

the panic which, at the same time, prompted the lucidity of what he wrote.

Dear Patrick,

Please do not think I don't want you to borrow my chalet in Austria for your forthcoming holiday with Alice, but I feel bound to repeat that I think it inadvisable, from the medical point of view, that Alice should be exposed to the certain inconvenience of this inaccessible place.

I just want to put a few of the drawbacks on record. In fact, I feel bound to do so.

You said previously that Alice was probably careless about her insulin injections. Although you told me today that your suspicions in this respect were unfounded, I feel bound to say that any carelessness in the administration of the injections (too much or too little) while Alice is in a condition of pregnancy, might prove fatal.

In fact, I should feel bound to obtain an undertaking from Alice on the whole question of her injections, before permitting the use of my chalet.

I should also wish to make certain that you took with you sufficient supplies of insulin, because the nearest town has no druggist.

Alice, I believe, would certainly die within a few days or even sooner, if deprived of her insulin. You know she has two sorts which she administers just before breakfast:

(a) Insulin soluble for immediate effect.

(b) Protamine zinc for more prolonged coverage throughout the evening and the following night. She needs 80 units.

But Alice understands all this. I understand she tests her urine for sugar and acetene first thing in the morning, and she can adjust the dosage accordingly. You must see that this is done.

The last time I saw Alice she told me she was still visiting the diabetic clinic every six months for routine assessment of progress.

If Alice were to take *too much* insulin and then, say, went for a hearty climb or long walk, she might easily die on the mountainside. Most

Dr. Lyte stopped writing. What am I saying, what am I doing? he thought. It came clearly to him, then, that he suspected Patrick of an intention to kill the woman, if you could call it an intention when a man could wander into a crime as if blown like a winged leaf.

What evidence have I got? Lyte thought. None at all. He wrote on, nevertheless.

—Most diabetics carry glucose or even lump sugar in their pockets to be taken at the first onset of the symptoms of hypoglycaemia—a dangerously low blood-sugar content, which the patient can check from the urine-test.

Dr. Lyte put down his pen. If Patrick were to add a little sugar to her urine specimen so that she would take a hefty dose of insulin, and then to make her take a good walk without her little tin of glucose—Patrick might say to Alice "Oh you don't need your handbag"—she would probably pass out on the mountainside. Or suppose he substituted his own urine in the test tube so that she would take an under-dose? Or suppose he himself gave her the injections? Insulin was used in the concentration camps as a method of execution. Insulin, said Dr. Lyte to himself, is a favoured mode of suicide amongst doctors and psychiatrists, it is rapid in effect. He looked round the room which he had furnished so carefully to match the red carpet and to be suitable to himself, and it seemed, in retrospect, that when he had chosen the furnishings of this consulting room, he must have been pretending all the time that the world is not a miserable place. It was sometimes not easy to establish death by insulin. He wrote on:

Therefore I feel bound to warn you of the dangers . . .

Then he stopped. I feel bound. I feel bound to warn you. In what position, he thought, am I to issue warnings to Patrick Seton? It is he who comes with his unspoken warnings to me. Dr. Lyte read through his letter. Clearly if he had any suspicions of Patrick's intentions towards the girl, this letter betrayed it. Such a letter might—it certainly would—provoke a man like Patrick. One never knew where one was with a man like Patrick Seton. Patrick knew a lot about his early career. Patrick was dangerous.

And then, what evidence was there for his suspicions? Patrick had said, "How long would it be before she died if she neglected to take insulin?" That was no ground for suspicion.

Lyte tore the letter up into little bits, placed the little bits, a few at a time, in his ash-tray and set fire to them with his cigarette lighter until they were all burned up.

Then he recalled that Patrick had said, "She won't let me give her the injections. She won't let me see her taking the injections."

Then he recalled quite clearly that Alice had told him, "Patrick does the injection for me every day. Patrick is so good at it, I don't feel a thing."

And then the whole problem was too much. The doctor was indignant at being subjected to it. The one incident in his career which he needed to hush up, Patrick had somehow got hold of. This one mistake had occurred twenty-three years ago when he was still a single man, a different person altogether. You change when you marry and establish yourself, everything that happened previously has nothing to do with you any more. But Patrick sitting in his so-called trance had said plainly that night at the séance, "There is a new visitor to our Circle, a man of the medical profession. Gloria wishes to tell him that she is watching over him, and remembers every detail of the incident in 1932 about which there was a certain amount of mystery at the time. Gloria sends this message to the visitor in our midst who is a member of the medical profession: he should become a spiritualist and attend séances weekly. She is exhausted, now, and has no more to say for the present. Gloria wishes to say she is exhausted. The effort of speaking from the other side is exhausting. Gloria is tired. She feels weak. She is exhausted. . . ."

Gloria had died as the result of an illegal operation in the summer of 1932. There had been enquiries. Nothing came of them. Cyril Lyte, newly qualified, was not even questioned, he was abroad during the questioning. He had been one of many lovers during the previous winter. "I'm tired. I'm exhausted," Gloria had said when the hasty operation was over. He had left her with the two middle-aged women, neither of whom knew his name. The two middle-aged women were lifting Gloria's feet and shoving pillows, cushions, blankets under them, for he had said she must not lose too much blood; be careful, keep her feet up, *up*. "I'm exhausted": Gloria had died next day. He was abroad during the questioning. He became a communist for a space, by way of atonement. Within a year he had mostly forgotten the incident and when he remembered it, assured himself he had done his best for her, and what proof had he that the child was his?

Patrick's message, twenty-seven years later in the dark séance room, nearly led him to a nervous breakdown. Whichever way he looked at it, whether Patrick had spoken in innocence or from hard knowledge, the message was frightening. "Gloria sends this message . . . remembers every detail . . . is exhausted, is tired, is exhausted." It sounds like hard knowledge, Lyte thought.

In the end, Cyril Lyte found it less frightening to believe that Patrick was a common blackmailer, and no medium between this world and the other. Patrick had called at the surgery the day after the séance. When the doctor had tormented him-

99

self for a week he gave way and challenged Patrick on the subject. At first he found Patrick vague as to the details of the message, but very soon asserting his power, and this comforted Dr. Lyte. Patrick was no medium, he told himself. There was no danger from the dim spirit of Gloria, the only danger to be reckoned with was Patrick who was tangible and who must have known the truth all through the years that had passed since he himself had been a single man and so different. As he had sometimes, waking at nights in the weeks following Gloria's death, dreaded, he was convinced now, she must have written a letter before she died, or told someone. Patrick had recognised him at the séance. And so Dr. Lyte settled down to supply Patrick with cash, and sometimes to supply Patrick with drugs which assisted him in his trances—"You're certainly a great medium!" Dr. Lyte would permit himself to remark as he handed the drugs into Patrick's meek hands. He had heard somewhere that even genuine mediums used drugs; but the doctor strengthened his will against the idea and was determined not to believe it. "You're certainly a great medium!"—and Patrick would sometimes wink with his eyelid which in any case drooped. Dr. Lyte supplied cash and drugs. If he should seem to falter or keep Patrick too long in the waiting room, Patrick would say, "When are you coming to another séance? I may have another message for you."

Cash, drugs, and now professional advice. How long would it take for Alice to die if she was deprived of insulin? How long if she took too much? She may be careless with her injections. She won't let me give them to her, she won't let me see her taking them.

"Patrick," Alice had said, "always gives me the injections himself, he's so good."

"Your chalet in Austria," Patrick had said. "We shall be wanting it for a holiday after the unfortunate court case is settled. And I doubt if it will come to court, and if so it will only last half-an-hour; I'm certain of acquittal. How big is the chalet? How high up in the mountain? How far from the nearest town?"

Dr. Lyte looked round his consulting room and saw there was no escape. He tore a page from *The Times* and folded it into the shape of a cone. He scooped the black frail ash of the burnt letter into the cone, rolled it up tight. He decided to go to his club for a drink before going home, and as he left his surgery he dumped the paper containing the ashes of his letter to Patrick in the dustbin among the stained cotton wool and empty sample medicine packages of the day. He went to his club and was warmed by the immediate greetings of two of his oldest, most likable friends.

The cheerful thought occurred to him that Patrick Seton might even be convicted of fraud if it came to a trial.

Chapter 8

RONALD was changing to go to Isobel Billows' cocktail party when the housekeeper from the ground-floor flat came up and rang his bell.

"I let in your secretary this afternoon," said the housekeeper. "Just thought I'd let you know. I suppose it was all right."

"What secretary?" Ronald said.

"The girl. The girl that came for your papers."

"What girl?" Ronald said.

When the housekeeper, resentful and dispirited, had gone, Ronald looked mournfully and in vain in the drawer of his desk where he had left the letter which Patrick Seton was suspected of forging in the name of Mrs. Freda Flower.

"She was I should say about twenty-eight, late twenties," the housekeeper had said. "A fair young woman, well I should say near to fair-coloured hair, very pale. How was I to know? She said she was your secretary, and you wanted the papers in a hurry and you forgot to give her the key. I said, I suppose it's all right and I had my niece downstairs so I said, just let yourself out, you know the way. She looked all right. Remember there was that gentleman that came that morning when I was doing your cleaning, that came for your brief-case. Remember you sent him. How was I to know this wasn't another person that came to save you the trouble, on account of your difficulty?"

"I can't think who she can be," Ronald said.

"Well I don't take responsibility."

"Well, no," said Ronald, "of course. Don't worry," and as soon as she was gone he had opened the drawer, knowing the letter would not be there. He opened all the other drawers and looked through the tidy heaps of papers, but simply as a desperate act of diligence.

Ronald was filled with a great melancholy boredom from which he suffered periodically. It was not merely this affair which seemed to suffocate him, but the whole of life—people, small-time criminals, outraged housekeepers, and all his acquaintance from the beginning of time. When this overtook him Ronald was apt to refuse himself comfortable thoughts: on the contrary he used to tell himself: this sensation, this boredom and disgust, may later seem, in retrospect, to have been one of the happier moods of my life, so appalling may be the experiences to come. It is better, he thought, to be a pessimist in life, it makes life endurable. The slightest optimism invites disappointment.

Isobel Billows' house was in a newly smartened street at World's End which lies at that other end of Chelsea. The walls and ceiling of her drawing room were papered in a dull red and black design. She was giving a cocktail party. Isobel had been three years divorced from her husband and always said to her new friends "I was the innocent party," which they did not doubt, and the very statement of which proved, to some of her friends, that she was so in a sense.

Marlene Cooper's earrings swung with animation as she spoke seriously about spiritualism to Francis Eccles who had now got a job on the British Council. Tim, like a bright young man-servant of good appearance, sinuously slid among the guests with a silver dish of shrimps; these shrimps were curled up as if in sleep on the top of small biscuits. Isobel Billows herself, large, soft-featured, middle-aged and handsome, had given up trying to introduce everyone and was surveying the standing crowd from a corner while Ewart Thornton talked to her, he having had three martinis, in the course of which he had told Isobel that he had mounds of homework, that a grammar-school master had no status these days, that spiritualism was the meeting ground between science and religion, and that he always bought his shirts and flannel trousers from Marks & Spencer's. It was at the point of his fourth martini that Ewart's deepest pride emerged, to enchant Isobel and make her feel she was really in the swing by having him at her party. She listened to him wonderingly as he told her of the real miner's cottage of his birth in Carmarthenshire where his father still lived, and the real crofter's cottage in Perthshire where his grandparents had lived till late. "Latham Street Council School; Traherne Grammar School; Sheffield Red Brick—only the brick isn't red," boasted Ewart. "Three shillings and sixpence a week pocket money all the while I was a student. From the age of ten to the age of thirteen I was employed by a fishmonger to deliver fish after school hours and on Saturday mornings. My earnings were four shillings a week which with the similar earnings of my brothers, went into the family funds. I was given a pair of stout boots every year at Easter. Most of my clothes were homemade. We had outdoor sanitation which we shared with two other families—"

"Were you ever in trouble with the police?" Isobel said, looking round in the hope that someone was listening.

Ewart looked gravely at a vase of flowers, as if searching his memory, but obviously he had lost ground. At last he said, "No, to be quite honest, no. But I recall being chased by a policeman. With some boys in some rough game. Yes, definitely chased down a back street." He took out his snuff box, and looked vexed. "I was definitely underprivileged by birth," he said, "though not delinquent."

Isobel said encouragingly, "What was your accent like?"

"Southern Welsh. You can still hear the trace of it, mind you."

"So you can," said Isobel, who could not.

She loved his hairy tweed suit and his middle-aged largeness, his drooping jowl. She wondered why he had never married. She thought, next, that in some way she ought to feel more grateful for her acquaintance with him than she was, and she wondered why this was so, and found the reason in his being now only a grammar-school master after such likely beginnings; a really dramatic rise in life would have been preferable. But still, he was the real thing, and a great asset to a party.

Ewart took a pinch of snuff and said, "My father was a real miner, a real one. Half the men that claim to have come from mining stock, when you look into it, turn out to be the sons of mine-managers or clerks in the coal offices."

Tim came round with his tray of shrimps.

"Have a shrimp," he said.

Isobel said, "Tim, stay and talk to Ewart. I must have a word with your aunt over there."

Tim took her place with his dish beside Ewart and started eating the shrimps off the tops of the biscuits.

"I daresay," Ewart Thornton said, in a definite man-to-man way, as to a senior prefect, "your aunt has told you that she is trying to get together a number of people willing to give evidence as to the bona fides of Patrick Seton, in case he is brought to court by that absurd widow."

"No, Marlene hasn't said anything," Tim said, eating shrimps.

"She will no doubt be after you," said Ewart. "She will want you to give evidence in court for Patrick Seton. I advise you to do no such thing. I advise you rather to come forward as a witness for Mrs. Freda Flower. Not that I care for Mrs. Flower, a silly woman, but I feel Patrick Seton is an undesirable character who does no credit to the Circle. Of course he's a good medium but—"

"Have a shrimp," Tim said, "before I eat the lot."

"No thanks. He's a competent medium but there are many brilliant mediums by whom he could be replaced. He is not irreplaceable. Your aunt, I'm afraid, is not inclined to listen to reason. I feel we should all do our best to support Mrs. Flower and—"

"Have a drink," Tim said, lifting a small glass of liqueur off a tray as the caterer's man passed them by with his tray.

"Thanks. We should all support Mrs. Flower and not Patrick Seton."

"I shan't support either," Tim said, cheerfully. "I don't know a thing about either of them."

"Oh, come!" Ewart said. "You've attended the séances when both have been present."

"Only as a novice," Tim said. "Really, I'd rather not be involved."

"Be reasonable my boy," Ewart said.

Tim ate a shrimp. "Am being reasonable," he said, and licked his finger tips.

"It's a matter of principle," Ewart said. "Surely you've got principles."

"None whatsoever when you actually look into it," Tim said.

"I thought as much," Ewart said. "You fellows that have had every advantage in life—"

"Was brought up rough, me," said Tim, eating two of the biscuits which were now deprived of shrimps.

"Tim!" shrieked Marlene from not very far away. "Come over here a minute, I've been wanting to speak to you all evening."

"Must see my aunt," Tim said, and putting down the dish, took off his glasses, wiped them, put them on, took up a bowl of olives, and joined Marlene.

A serving table had been set up for the caterers in front of the window; it was spread with a white cloth and was laid out with bottles and glittering glasses. Ronald Bridges and Martin

Bowles stood out of the way between a corner of this table and the wall.

"I could go to Switzerland for Christmas," Martin said, "if I could get in one small fraction of the money that's owing to me. Dozens of briefs but no pay. Solicitors are crooks, they won't part with money."

"What do you look like in your wig?" Ronald said.

"Quite nice."

Ronald thought this probably true, for Martin was going bald and the impression of an increasingly high forehead had, over the past five years, thrown his good features out of balance.

Martin said, "I've been invited to Switzerland for Christmas with a party. All married couples except for me, if I go. It makes one feel young being with married couples."

"Or insignificant," Ronald said.

"Yes, or insignificant. I always feel a bit *less* than a married man. Why is that, do you think. Is it because they've got more money than us?"

"No, married men mostly have less. Obviously."

"Well, they seem to have more money, in a queer sort of way, to be economically stronger than single chaps."

"It's an illusion. The truth is, a married man is psychologically stronger."

"Yes, it's psychological. They make one feel young, even men one was at school with. How are you getting on with that forged letter in the Seton case?"

"It's a question of responsibility, I think—if they have kids," Ronald said, to keep Martin off the subject of the letter.

But "How's the forgery work?" Martin said.

"The letter has been stolen from my flat," Ronald said, "I'm sorry to say."

"Come along," said Isobel Billows, "you bachelors in a huddle, over there." She slid her white arm through Martin's and pressed him into a group which included Marlene with her swinging earrings, Tim with his bowl of olives, a girl wearing a pink dress, and Francis Eccles, who, in the confidence of his new job on the British Council, was exuberantly philosophising to the girl and Marlene.

"You see," he was saying, "we are all fundamentally looking at each other and talking across the street from windows of different buildings which look similar from the outside. You don't know what my building is like inside and I don't know what yours is like. You probably think my house is comfortably furnished with its music room and libraries, like yours. But it isn't. My house is a laboratory with test tubes, capillaries and—what do you call them?—Bunsen burners. My house contains a hospital ward, my house—"

"Do you live in a very splendid house?" Martin said to the girl, for his ears had selected from Eccie's speech only the bit about the music room and libraries.

The girl was mightily irritated. "Eccie is talking in metaphor," she said. "I live in a bedsitter."

"I live in a basement flat," said Eccie, still dazed from his elaboration. He looked from one to the other.

"Oh, I see," Martin said. "Well you see, I've only got a crude legal mind. I—"

"Carry on," said the girl to Eccie.

Isobel slid her white plump arm through the dark blue of Eccie's sleeve. "Eccie, I want you," she said, and bore him off somewhere else.

Martin said to the girl, "I'm afraid I interrupted . . ." but he was now looking for Ronald, anxious to know whether Ronald could possibly have been serious when he said the letter had been stolen, and if so, to tell Ronald how furious he was.

He smiled formally to the girl and withdrew, first backward a few steps, then sideways, then right about, so that he could join Ronald where he was standing with Marlene Cooper and Tim.

"—must do something to justify your existence," Marlene was saying to Tim, "and now is the chance to show your mettle."

"Never did have any mettle," Tim said. "Want an olive, Ronald?"

Ronald looked into his glass at the tiny drop of cocktail left at the bottom of it.

"Have an olive, Martin," Tim said.

"What we want to do," Marlene said, "is to present a body of witnesses to the court. We can all testify in our own words. You, Tim, you've seen Patrick and you've heard him. You know he's a real medium, that's all you've got to say. There's no commitment attached. But we must give Patrick a character. He's being positively framed by Freda Flower and that vile lover of hers. There may be no case, but as I say, on the other hand, there may be a case."

Tim said, "Martin Bowles here is the prosecuting counsel in the case, Marlene."

Marlene tilted her face to Martin's. "Are you?" she said. "Oh, are you?"

"Look," said Martin, "I really can't discuss—"

"I should think you couldn't," Marlene said. "You wouldn't have a leg to stand on. Nor will you have if it comes to court, let me tell you that. We are all behind Patrick. I'm behind him. Tim's behind—"

"I'd rather not be involved," Tim said.

"But you are involved," said his aunt.

"How did it happen?" Martin said as he drove Ronald home.

"A woman came to the house this morning and pretended to be my secretary. The housekeeper let her in. The letter was gone when I looked for it. I think I know who's got it."

"Who?"

"Patrick Seton's girl friend. It wasn't she who actually came to the flat, but I think Matthew Finch knows the girl."

"Who? Which girl?" Martin enquired in his legal voice. "You don't make it clear which is which."

"I'll try and get the letter back."

"We'd better have the police informed right away," Martin said.

"All right," Ronald said.

"Well, I know it won't do your reputation much good," Martin said, "losing an important document like that. But I don't suppose you depend much on your forgery detection work, do you?"

"I like it," Ronald said.

"Do you think you *can* get it back?"

"I don't know," Ronald said, deliberately, as one refusing to be a mouse even while the claws were upon him.

"I'm not trying to make things difficult," Martin said, "but . . ."

"But what?"

"Well, you say you can't work from the photostats. I daresay the photostats would be taken as some sort of evidence. But you can't give any evidence of forgery from a photostat, can you?"

"Not really. I've got to test the ink and study the writing on the folds in the paper. That sort of thing."

"You've got us in a pickle," Martin said.

"Matthew Finch knows the girl. I'll see if he can do something about it."

"He was at the party tonight, wasn't he?"

"Yes."

"Did you speak to him about this?"

"Yes."

"You told him what had happened?"

"Yes. I made the mistake of telling him about the letter in the first place. Then he informed the girl. He thinks the girl who got into my rooms must be the girl he knows who works with Patrick Seton's girl in a coffee-bar. This girl is the friend of the other girl, and—"

"Who? Which girl is which? What are their names?"

"Alice and Elsie," Ronald said. "I think we'd better get the police to handle it, as you suggested."

Martin had stopped for the traffic of South Kensington. He sat back from the wheel and pondered. Then, as he started up the car again, he said, "Let's leave it that you get the letter back by tomorrow night or we'll get the police to find it. If it hasn't been destroyed by then."

"It has probably been destroyed by now," Ronald said in a louder voice than usual. "And actually I think we must inform the police in any case."

"They might ask you awkward questions," Martin said.

"How do you mean?"

"Well, it's obvious you've been careless."

"That can't be helped now."

His melancholy and boredom returned with such force when he was alone again in his flat that he recited to himself as an exercise against it, a passage from the Epistle to the Philippians, which was at present meaningless to his numb mind, in the sense that a coat of paint is meaningless to a window-frame, and yet both colours and preserves it: "All that rings true, all that commands reverence, and all that makes for right; all that is pure, all that is lovely, all that is gracious in the telling; virtue and merit, wherever virtue and merit are found—let this be the argument of your thoughts."

For Ronald was suddenly obsessed by the party, and by the figures who had moved under Isobel's chandelier, and who, in Ronald's present mind, seemed to gesticulate like automatic animals; they had made sociable noises which struck him as hysterical. Isobel's party stormed upon him like a play in which the actors had begun to jump off the stage, so that he was no longer simply the witness of a comfortable satire, but was suddenly surrounded by a company of ridiculous demons.

This passage from Philippians was a mental, not a spiritual exercise; a mere charm to ward off the disgust, despair and brain-burning.

This was the beginning of November. It is the month, Ronald told himself in passing, when the dead rise up and come piling upon you to warm themselves. One is affected as if by a depressive drug, one shivers. It is only the time of year, that's the trouble.

III

With desperate method he began to abstract his acquaintance, in his mind's eye, from the party, and examined them deliberately to see the worst he could find in them. One must define, he thought: that is essential.

Isobel Billows, with her hungry lusts, her generosity wherever she thought generosity was a good investment, smiled up at him in the glaring eye of his mind.

"What's wrong with me?" she said.

"Nothing," he said, "but yourself."

"Oh, Ronald, you always see the worst side of everything, there's a diabolical side to your nature."

"What do you mean, diabolical?"

"Well, possessed by a devil, that's the reason for your epilepsy."

"Adulterous bitch."

"Oh Ronald, you don't know how basely men treat me. Men have always treated me very badly."

"A woman of your class shouldn't talk like that."

"But they come and sponge on me, Ronald, and then they go away and say, 'Oh her. You don't want to have anything to do with her. Don't listen to her.'"

Martin Bowles was her lover, and was also her financial adviser, and, in his legal capacity, handled her property. ". . . and you see," Martin said—he was sitting at his desk in chambers, in the bright eye of Ronald's imagination, leaning one hand on his high bald forehead—"I haven't much freedom, what with my old ma and the housekeeper, and then there's Isobel, I'm fairly tied to Isobel."

"Will you marry Isobel?"

"No, oh no. It's a question of business interests."

"Have you misappropriated Isobel's money?"

"No, oh no. I'm on the right side of the law."

"Yes, the right side of the law."

"Don't be vulgar, Ronald."

"It was you who employed the phrase."

"Isobel's very well off although she pretends to be poor. She doesn't live up to her money, you know."

"Fraudulent conversion, it's revolting."

"Not at all. There's nothing fraudulent about it, I'm perfectly safe in the law. There's a large sum involved, Ronald, but I'm perfectly safe."

"Forty thousand?"

"How do you come to know all this, Ronald?"

"From piecing together what I hear and see in one direction and another."

"My old ma's a tyrant, quite a drag upon my life."

"You shouldn't be living with your mother, at your age. It makes a mess of a man. It makes for a mean spirit, living with mama after the age of thirty."

"You know, Ronald, you should have been more careful with that letter."

"Yes."

"And now you've gone and lost it. Shall we inform the police? Shall we ruin your little reputation as a reliable expert? You shouldn't have talked."

"Please yourself. I don't particularly want to get the letter back. Why should I hound Patrick Seton? He has offended in the same way as you, on a smaller scale than you, but less cleverly than you."

"This is rather absurd," said Martin Bowles in the mind's ear of Ronald. "I won't have it."

"I won't have it," Marlene Cooper said, brushing her earrings past Ronald's mouth as if he were not there. "I won't have Tim remaining on friendly terms with that revolting bald barrister."

"I like Martin Bowles," Tim said.

"If Patrick's case comes to court your friend will be prosecuting counsel."

"Someone's got to be prosecuting counsel," Tim said.

"Well you must give up your association with him."

"I haven't got any particular association with him. Martin is just a friend," Tim said.

"But Tim, dear, I saw you with him at Isobel's party, laughing away as if nothing had happened. Do you realize that when you give evidence for Patrick, the man is sure to cross-examine you."

"I don't want to be involved," Tim said. "I'm not giving any evidence. We treat your conspiracy as a joke."

"You are weak," Marlene said, "like your father and his father before him."

And so he is, Ronald thought, viciously, for he was especially fond of Tim. He doesn't want to be involved at all; except, of course, with Hildegarde.

"I did everything for Ronald that a woman possibly could do," Hildegarde said. "I washed his shirts, mended his clothes, I bought the theatre tickets and I set the alarm clock for him. I made every possible allowance for his disability. I even helped him in his job. I made a study of handwriting and even ancient manuscripts. What more could I have done?"

"Nothing at all," said Tim in the bemused ear of Ronald's imagination, as he sat there in his flat in the small hours of the morning. "Nothing at all," said Tim. "Move over, darling, and don't kick."

"It makes me kick," Hildegarde said, "to think of Ronald. If only he had given me some excuse when he broke with me. . . ."

"Shut up about Ronald," Tim said. "It's jolly off-putting."

"Does he know about us?" Hildegarde said.

"No, of course not."

"He mustn't know about us," she said. "It would upset him and he would never forgive you. I don't want to break up your friendship with Ronald."

"You're sweet," Tim said, snuggling down. "Lovely to think tomorrow's Sunday," he said, "and a long lie in."

"Let me put your pillow straight, sweet boy," said Hildegarde. "You are all crumpled up."

Matthew had told Ronald: "I saw Hildegarde Krall the other evening in the Pandaemonium Club at Hampstead. She was wearing jeans, looked very nice."

"Was she alone?"

"Yes, alone."

"Did you speak to her?"

"Only briefly. She left early. Walter Prett was with me. She left when he started making a nuisance of himself and insulted Francis Eccles."

Tim, Hildegarde, Matthew Finch, Francis Eccles, Walter Prett. Ronald got through the list by half-past three in the morning. Who are they, he thought, in any case, to me? Why be oppressed by a great disgust? "We must go to court," Ewart Thornton says, "we must oppose Patrick Seton at all costs. Let us give evidence for a Mrs. Freda Flower, about whose wrongs none of us cares." But why does he induce in me a condition near to madness?

Because one is formed in that way, and at times of utter disenchantment no distraction whatsoever avails, even the small advertisements in the newspapers are vile, in the same way that I, in my epilepsy, am repulsive. He recited over to himself the passage from Philippians: ". . . all that is gracious in the telling; virtue and merit, wherever virtue and merit are found —let this be the argument of your thoughts." By a violent wrench of the mind Ronald was capable of applying this exhortation in a feelingless way, to the company of demons which had been passing through his thoughts. He forced upon their characters what attributes of vulnerable grace he could bring to mind. He felt sick. Isobel is brave simply to go on breathing; another woman might have committed suicide ten years ago; she knows how to decorate her house and how to dress. Marlene is handsome, Tim is lovable, Ewart Thornton is intelligent, has gone far in the world considering his initial disadvantages, and moreover he is a schoolmaster, and, moreover, one who respects his career and so finds difficulty in the practice of it. Martin Bowles is considerate to his mother. Matthew Finch is afflicted by sex and is blessed with a simple love of the old laws. Walter Prett is beset by neglect and foolish fantasies and he loves art and is honest in his profession. Hildegarde has a tremendous character. Eccie has a job on the British Council. . . .

By four o'clock he was in bed. At five o'clock he rose and vomited. Next morning he had an epileptic seizure lasting half an hour; it was a type of fit in which his drugs were useless. This often happened to Ronald after he had made some effort of will towards graciousness, as if a devil in his body was taking its revenge.

He resolved to go to confession, less to rid himself of the past night's thoughts—since his priest made a distinction between sins of thought and these convulsive dances and dialogues of the mind—than to receive, in absolution, a friendly gesture of recognition from the maker of heaven and earth, vigilant manipulator of the falling sickness.

Chapter 9

"I can't help feeling sorry for little Patrick Seton," said Matthew Finch. "That widow and her friends seem to be ganging up on him in a most unpleasant way."

"I'm sorry for him too, in a way," Ronald said.

"He's half Irish," said Matthew.

"The thing is: about this letter."

"It sounds like Alice's friend Elsie," Matthew said. "I'll see Elsie this afternoon."

"It may be destroyed by now."

"I doubt that," Matthew said. "Alice is a sentimental girl."

"It's hardly a sentimental letter."

"What does it say?"

"Get the letter back and you'll find out."

"I know I'm to blame for this, I shouldn't have told Alice you had it," Matthew said. "I'm a foolish fellow, you know."

"Where will you see Elsie?"

"I'll go round to the coffee-bar. She's always on duty on Saturday afternoons. I've got to see my cousin later, but—"

Ronald's telephone rang. Martin Bowles said, "I say Ronald.

I thought it best to have Fergusson told that the letter had been stolen. I hope you—"

"Who's Fergusson?" Ronald said.

"The detective-inspector who keeps his eye on Patrick Seton. He says he'll be seeing Seton about it and doesn't seem to be worried about getting it back, that is, if Seton has it. I hope you agree that was the best course. If it comes out in court—"

"Yes, it was quite the most sensible thing to do," Ronald said. "I'm much relieved."

"Sure you don't mind? If it comes out in court that you—"

"No, I don't mind a bit. In fact I'm glad. I ought to have done something of the kind straight away. The police should be informed of a theft of this kind. Only, in these particular circumstances, I doubt if Seton actually has the letter. His girl's got it, we think."

"Who's *we*?"

"I've just been discussing it with Matthew Finch. As you know he's a friend of the two girls in question."

"*Which* two girls?"

"Seton's girl and the other girl, her friend, the one we think stole the letter for Seton's girl."

"I really can't make out who these girls are, Ronald. What has Matthew Finch to do with this?"

"Well you know I was indiscreet enough in the first place to tell him I was working on the letter. And he was indiscreet enough to tell Elsie, and—"

"Who's Elsie?"

"She's the other girl who's a friend of Seton's girl. I told you—"

"Yes, but I didn't make notes. Look, Ronald, you can't conduct a case like this."

"I'm not conducting the case."

"If it comes out in court that you've committed these indiscretions, you won't blame me, will you?"

"No," Ronald said.

"I expect Fergusson will want to see you," Martin said. "A

nice chap. Straight with you if you're straight with him."

"What the hell are you talking about?"

"Now, Ronald, don't be—"

Ronald hung up. "Some detective-inspector is going to find the letter," he said. "So let's forget it."

"I've got you into trouble," Matthew said. "My sister thought probably this would happen when I told her about the letter—"

"Where are you lunching? I haven't done my shopping yet, what with one thing and another."

"I've got you into trouble with my talk," Matthew said. "Would you like me to see Elsie in any case? It wouldn't do any harm, would it?"

"You'd better see Elsie," Ronald said. "Because I doubt if the detective-inspector will find the letter."

"You said just now he was going to find it."

"I know I did," said Ronald. "And I'll end up in the bin, I daresay. Come on, let's go out."

The telephone rang again just as they were leaving. Ronald returned to answer it.

"Oh, Ronald," said Martin.

"Yes."

"Are you all right?"

"Yes."

"Look, Ronald, I don't want you to misunderstand me. It's just that I'm bound by certain rules, you know. One has to observe certain—"

"Of course," Ronald said. "Obviously."

"You'll help Fergusson all you can? I've told him you will."

"Of course. But look, I don't really think Patrick Seton has the letter. I think it's something the girls have cooked up."

"Which girls?"

"Polly and Molly," Ronald said.

"Who?"

"Cassandra and Clytemnestra," Ronald said.

"Look Ronald. This is awkward for me. You know me, you like me, don't you?"

Here it comes, Ronald thought.

"Of course," he said.

"Well, put yourself in my place. I've got my old ma on my hands. She's going blind. Can't see the television. The housekeeper's going blind. They fight like cat and dog, they were pulling each other's hair the other day. Can't get a new housekeeper, and anyway my old ma won't have anyone new. The housekeeper—"

"Hold on a minute," Ronald said, and placing his hand over the receiver, murmured to Matthew, who was hovering at the door, to make himself comfortable on the sofa for at least five minutes. Have a drink. Cigarette— "Yes, hallo," he said, returning to Martin on the telephone.

"The housekeeper," Martin said, "was my old nurse and my old ma won't get rid of her, she's got nowhere to go and we can't afford a pension. Then I do the shopping for the week-end. Not on weekdays, I draw the line there. Then Isobel's affairs take a bit of looking after, you know. I give her my professional services, she doesn't realise what I save her. Still, Isobel's a good sort, as you know, and very attractive. I say, Ronald, would you say Isobel was an attractive woman?"

"Oh, yes," Ronald said.

"Doesn't show her years," Martin said. "Of course she's got the money and the leisure. She depends on me a lot, you know. She's had a lot of bad luck with men, and I think she appreciates me in a way. Wouldn't you think so?"

"Oh, I think she does."

"Look Ronald, come along to my club for lunch. You see—"

"Sorry, I'm not free."

"You see, there's a personal problem I'd like to consult you about. Could you make it one-thirty?"

"Sorry, really I'm not free."

"I can't make it tomorrow," Martin said, "because the housekeeper goes off in the afternoon and I've promised to read *Jane Eyre* to my old ma. She says she was forbidden *Jane Eyre* as a girl. I don't see why, do you? You see she can't see well and the television isn't much use to her. Then tomorrow night I've simply got to collect Isobel off a train. When can we meet?"

"I'll come and see you in your chambers one day next week. I've got to go now, Martin."

"I'll ring you on Monday, then. Sure you're not worried about Fergusson looking into this theft?"

"No, but I doubt—"

"It's breaking and entering, and stealing, to be precise. They'll be sending a couple of fellows round to ask questions."

"I see."

"You should have been more careful, Ronald. You can't conduct a case . . ."

When they were seated in the pub Ronald said, "You can tell Elsie that the cops will be looking for her."

"Now, she's a nice poor girl," Matthew said.

"Well, give the poor girl a fright. Tell her the cops will be after her fingerprints or something."

Elsie Forrest climbed the stairs to an attic flat in Shepherd's Bush, and pressed the bell on a door marked The Rev. Father T. W. Socket, M.A. The door was opened by Mike Garland, wearing a green and white striped dressing gown over his suit, and looking, with his pink cheeks, like a lump of sticky bright confectionery. He blocked the door.

"Father Socket is expecting me," Elsie said, "to do some typing."

"Oh, I don't know whether it's convenient, now. But come in."

"I like that!" Elsie said as she walked into the large front sitting room. "I've taken the afternoon off from the coffee-bar especially to help Father Socket. So I should hope it is convenient."

"I daresay it will be," Mike Garland said. "Take a seat."

Elsie was irritated when he said "Take a seat," for on all the chairs in the room were cushions that she herself had made for Father Socket, and this obviously gave her rights which rose above formalities. She had not expected to see this strange man with his peculiar garb in Father Socket's flat. She usually walked straight in to the kitchen and put the kettle on the gas.

Elsie heard voices from Father Socket's bedroom. She wondered if the Master was ill, but did not like to investigate in the presence of the stranger.

The room was hung with Chinese scrolls which reached to the low bookcases. These contained the books of which Elsie had made a list, and for each of which, under the Master's instructions, she had made an index card. The Master was learned. He was a real priest, he told her, ordained by no man-made bishop but by Fire and the Holy Ghost; and a range of brightly woven vestments was hung in a cupboard in his bedroom to prove it.

Elsie had never before been to Father Socket's on a Saturday afternoon. Thursday afternoon was her usual time, and it was then she typed his manuscripts, over and over again—for he was always revising them, never satisfied, like the true Master of writing that he was.

"He ought to pay you for all that work," Alice had said. But, to Elsie, it was a labour of love typing out his papers on the subjects of the Cabala, Theosophy, witchcraft, spiritualism, and Bacon wrote Shakespeare, besides many other topics.

"It's a labour of love," Elsie said to Alice. After all, Alice had Patrick; and it was nice for a girl to have someone on the spiritual side of life. Men like Father Socket lifted one up whereas young men so often pulled one down.

"You've got queer tastes," Alice had said the day before, sitting in the window with Elsie, at dusk.

"There isn't any sex between Father Socket and me," Elsie said.

"That's a detail," Alice said.

"He smells of a perfume, like musk or incense," Elsie said.

"You always smell things," Alice said.

"Patrick smells of goat, like a real bachelor."

"Go on with you. Patrick's a man of the world. He's been married."

"That boy Matthew Finch who'd been eating onions that time . . . It's terrible, the smell of onions. Because I used to sleep beside my uncle, we were all in the one room, in Sheffield where I was born. My uncle was the only one of them that didn't drink, drink, drink. So I went with Matthew and yet afterwards I didn't like myself for it. It's all explained in psychology."

"Disgusting," Alice whispered. "Onions."

They laughed as they sat in the darkening room, in a down-scale trill, one following the other.

"It wasn't funny at the time," Elsie whispered. "He didn't go right on to the end in case I got a baby, I suppose. That's what makes me really upset; when they go so far and no farther."

"You don't want a baby without a man to marry you," Alice said.

"It makes you feel there's not much of a man in them when they only go so far."

"If Patrick wasn't the man he is," Alice said, "he wouldn't be much of a *man*."

"I always said he wasn't much of a man to look at. Thin about the thighs. You can't disguise it."

"But he's so different to other men. Patrick treats you with a difference."

"Oh yes, he's all talk. Still, talk makes a difference. Father Socket talks beautifully. That's what gets me, Alice. The boys are after one thing and one thing only, but a man who's a bit older and can talk, and if he's got a beautiful voice . . ."

They sat hand-in-hand on the window-seat and looked down on the lights of long Ebury Street.

"Yes," Alice said, "I suppose the main thing about Patrick is the talk."

"Do you think he's going to marry you?"

"Of course. As soon as the divorce comes through."

123

"I can't believe in that divorce, you know."

"What d'you mean?"

"Are you sure he's got a wife?"

"He says so."

"You don't look well, Alice."

"No, it's difficult for a diabetic in pregnancy. I've got a craving for parsnips, too. I'd like a whole plate of parsnips."

"Aren't you afraid of Patrick?"

"Afraid? What is there to be afraid of?"

"Well, nothing that you know about. It's all those things you don't know about him. They say, about his forgeries—"

"Yes," said Alice's voice in the dark, "I'm afraid of the things I don't know. I don't want to know."

"I feel the same," Elsie said as she sat, almost invisible, "about the Master."

"You're not tied to him," Alice said, "like I am to Patrick."

"But there's a bond between the Master and me."

"He's got a hold on you," Alice said. "Shall we put the light on?"

"Not yet," Elsie said. "I go on Thursdays and I do a bit of typing and then I stop. And he talks and reads poetry. Then I do a bit more typing. Then he reads me a bit of what he's just written of his spiritual autobiography."

"Patrick recites poetry," Alice said.

"Father Socket's voice is beautiful. He was brought up in a big rectory and he broke away from the Church of England. It's true you don't have to go to church to believe in God. I agree with that. Father Socket knows psychology."

"Put on the light," Alice said, and when Elsie had switched on the light she jumped from her seat, and now they spoke aloud.

"He ought to pay you for all that work. We're both of us far too soft," Alice said.

"It's a labour of love," Elsie said, "I'm going to his flat tomorrow afternoon. He asked me specially to come, so I've put off the coffee-bar."

"That's money down the drain," Alice said. "At least Patrick gives me a bit of money."

"So he ought, in your condition. But where does he get the money?"

"I don't know," Alice said.

"He's hiding something from you," Elsie said.

"There's always something hidden," Alice said, in such a way that Elsie was startled, uncertain whether Alice knew about the letter concealed in her handbag. She looked at Alice, to make sure, but Alice was holding her stomach and pulling her face with indigestion.

The gilt sunlight which sometimes happens in November poured through the window of Father Socket's flat on Saturday afternoon. Elsie waited, withering, in the sitting room, listening to the voices coming now from the spare bedroom where apparently the stranger was lodged. Father Socket must have put him up for the night, and here he was staying on to the afternoon and keeping him back from his work.

Then she knew, of course, with a kind of exasperation, that the stranger was one of the Master's friends, and that they were all perverts, and she had really known it all along.

The voices rose to the pitch of a quarrel of which Elsie could not make out all the words. She went and stood by the door, the better to hear. ". . . where to draw the line, Mike . . . appearance's sake . . . the girl is . . ." and then a door closed, muting the voices to a querulous rise and fall. This filled her with irritation and impatience. She was inclined to leave the flat with a banging of doors, or at least to bang one door as a token. But then she thought of the letter in her handbag, and what palpitations she had gone through to obtain it, what risks taken. She had looked forward all the previous day and part of the night to her triumphant casual opening of her handbag and the producing of the letter before the astonished eyes of the Master.

Last week he had said, "Do you know the man well?"

"I've seen him in the coffee-bar. He's quite nice. He works in a handwriting museum."

"Ah yes," said Father Socket, "in the City."

"He isn't very strong. He takes fits. He's quite nice-looking, but a bit odd, you know, fussy in his ways. You can tell from the way they put their sugar in the coffee, and stir it, and place the spoon back in the saucer. And his paper neatly folded with his umbrella and all that. A confirmed bachelor. Not that I mean anything by that. He's a friend of a friend of mine, an Irish fellow called Matthew Finch."

"And this man's name?"

"Ronald somebody. Well, Matthew was in the Oriflamme with him the other night, and talking to Alice. He was talking about this letter that Patrick Seton wrote. Ronald is to test it for forgery. The police gave it to him and—"

"Not the police, surely. It would be in the hands of the police solicitor. Unless the case is in abeyance, in which case, possibly the police . . ."

"One or the other. So Ronald's got this letter that Patrick forged. Alice was upset and I saw her next day. She wants to try to get the letter back through Matthew. Matthew is keen on Alice."

Father Socket had thought this unwise. So, when she came to talk it over with him, had Elsie.

"Alice may even go a long way with Matthew," she said, "to get that letter."

"Do you know where this Ronald lives?" Father Socket had said.

"I could find out."

"I should like to have a look at that letter myself," he said.

"Would you?" she said.

Here, then, she was with the letter in her handbag, and Father Socket quarrelling in the spare bedroom with the big man in the green and white striped dressing gown, and she sitting like a fool, having lost an afternoon's work at the coffee-bar.

She opened the door of the sitting room and bumped into Father Socket just as he was about to enter. His small face looked puffy and red. He looked suspicious at finding her so near to the door and seemed convinced she had been listening to the quarrel.

"I've been waiting a long time, Father," she said.

"Oh, poor creature! Oh, poor creature! I am so very sorry. Come and sit down."

He wore his best cassock and his broad hips swung under it as he put to rights a deep pink chrysanthemum which had fallen from its vase.

He turned and jerked his thumb over his shoulder to indicate the stranger in the other room. The gesture startled Elsie, for she had never seen the Master anything but utterly dignified. He mouthed and breathed a message to her, contorting his face as if she were a lip-reader. "My—friend's—up—set. Won't—remove—dressing gown."

"Who is he, Father?" Elsie said in a normal voice.

He hunched his shoulders and flapped his hands to hush her. She whispered. "Who is he?"

The Master jerked his thumb once more over his shoulder and was about to convey a reply when Mike Garland walked in. He still wore his bright dressing gown.

"Ah, Mike," said Father Socket, pulling himself straight, "come and meet my amanuensis Miss Elsie Forrest. Dr. Garland, Miss Forrest."

"We've already met, at the door," Elsie said.

"How do you do," Mike said. He sat down defiantly.

"Something unforeseen has arisen," Father Socket said to Elsie, "and so I'm afraid I've brought you here on a wild goose chase, my dear, this afternoon. However, I will make some tea and I must read you my new translation of Horace, where did I put it?"

"I'll make tea," Elsie said.

"I shall prepare some tea," Mike said. Elsie noticed as he left the room, that he wore lipstick.

"Have you received any information from young Matthew?" Father Socket said to her softly when Mike had left the room.

"Matthew?"

"Or young Ronald? —The letter I mean. I don't of course, want Mike to know anything about this— But you haven't had time to investigate the possibility of obtaining it. . . ."

Elsie clutched her handbag, indignant and very put out, especially by Mike's lipstick. "No, I haven't any news," she said. "I expect the letter is locked away somewhere safely."

Father Socket sighed and looked at the carpet.

"Poor Patrick Seton!" he said. "He does need taking care of. I feel if I could get matters in hand I could do something for Patrick."

"He isn't any good to Alice. I don't mind if he gets sent for trial!"

"Hush," said Father Socket, looking at the door.

"I'd like to see Alice rid of him," she said, sitting down in a hard high chair, "good medium though he is, he's—"

"Ah," said Father Socket, "Patrick has many enemies." Again he jerked his thumb over his shoulder and mouthed, "He's—one of—them." He pulled his spine straight in his chair and said, "But I am not an enemy. What Patrick needs is *control*. Someone ought to control him. Find out about that letter, my dear, find out. If once we know where it is—where young Ronald keeps it, I daresay we should be able to obtain it. I am thinking in dear Patrick's best interests. I have no wish to impede the course of the law of the kingdom but the laws of the spirit come first, we ought to serve God rather than man, we must— Ah —tea!" He rose to admit the tinkling tea-tray with Mike rosily proceeding behind it.

During tea, Elsie ate a slice of walnut cake very quickly because she was so very upset inside at the sight of Mike in his highly sexual attire. She clutched her handbag all the closer, and was damned if she would part with the letter now that Father Socket had let her down so badly. Be damned to his paternal solicitude for dear Patrick. She should have known before, indeed she had really, inside, known all along that the Master was homosexual as Alice had said. She could have put up with it, even preferred it, if he had no sex at all, was above sex, but if there was one thing she detested . . .

Father Socket, meanwhile, said, "Let me read you my little translation of the much-translated Horace, one, nine. Mine pays special attention to alliterative quantities. . . ."

The impudence of it, Elsie thought, talking round me all these months, and reading his poetry, and there I've been typing out his papers, page after page, Thursday after Thursday. . . .

"Mount Soracte's dazzling snow," boomed Father Socket in his reading voice, "piling upon the branches . . ."

Stroking my hair and saying, "There, my child," week after week, and putting on, thought Elsie, the holiness and spiritual life and all that.

"So, Thaliarch . . ." said Father Socket.

Elsie swallowed the last of her cake and washed it down with the last of her tea. She gathered together her gloves and clutched her handbag. Father Socket, without interrupting his reading, moved one hand to bid her sit still. In her distress she had swallowed a whole walnut off the top of the cake, and it went down in a lump, causing her face to go red. Mike Garland looked at her and smiled with one half of his mouth.

Father Socket read on,

> All else trust to the gods by whose command
> Contending winds and seething seas desist,
>   Until the sacred cypress tree
>   And ancient ash no longer quake.

Father Socket interrupted himself to tap the paper with his forefinger. "Now the cypress tree *was* sacred," he said, "and although Horace . . ."

Elsie rose and sped to the door.

"*Elsie!*" said Father Socket, in a kind of wail, letting his paper drop.

"Elsie!" he called after her as she opened the outside door and ran down the stairs. "What's wrong with the girl? Elsie, this is quite a proper decent poem, I assure you. It is Horace, it is merely—"

"I've got the letter that Patrick Seton forged," Elsie shouted up at him. "But I intend keeping it. It's here in my bag, but I'm keeping it."

Matthew sat at a table in the Oriflamme watching Alice who had told him, "Elsie won't be here this afternoon."

"I thought she always worked on Saturday afternoons."

"Well, she's not coming today, I don't think."

"Any idea where she is?"

"No idea. She may come in later, of course."

"I'll wait," Matthew said. "I'm on duty tonight from six, but I'll wait till five."

"You're very keen," said Alice.

"No I'm not," he said. "I like sitting here watching you."

"While waiting for Elsie."

"I've got to see Elsie on some business. Can you guess what it is?"

"No." Alice said, "and I wouldn't care to try."

"She's a very nice girl, of course. A beautiful girl," Matthew said.

"Oh, is she beautiful? —Not that I'm saying—"

"Well now," Matthew said, "I believe in original sin, and that all the utterances of man are inevitably deep in error. Therefore I speak so as to err on the happy side."

"She has a beautiful nature, Elsie has, I'll say that," said Alice anxiously. "I'm sorry she's not here for you. But I'll give her a message for you. You can't sit here drinking coffee all afternoon."

"I'll take a cup of tea," Matthew said. "Do you serve teas?"

"No." Alice hung around him, as if waiting for more information. It was early yet for the afternoon trade and only two other tables were occupied. "Elsie may not come," she said.

"Sit down a minute," Matthew said, "and rest yourself." Her

small stomach showed a slight pear-shaped swelling which appealed considerably to Matthew.

She sat down, resting her wrists on the table and drooping her long neck. Her shoulder-blades curved gracefully.

"Has Elsie got the letter?" Matthew said.

"What letter?" Alice said.

"Has she mentioned anything to you about the letter in Patrick's case? The one he forged—"

—"The widow wrote it. Patrick did not forge it. That's a lie. It will be proved when—"

"Has Elsie seen the letter?"

"Elsie? Why should Elsie see the letter? Ask your posh friend Ronald with his rolled umbrella about the letter. He's working on it, isn't he? I bet he's being paid to say it's a forgery. He hasn't got anything to do with Elsie if that's what's in your mind."

"Ronald's all right."

"Well, so's Patrick."

"He isn't, you know."

"A lot of people are jealous of Patrick. It's the price he has to pay. Why are you waiting for Elsie?"

"You're jealous of Elsie," he said.

She jumped up and went to the bar where she ordered coffee for him. When it was ready she brought it over to his table and placed it before him with a gesture which was as near to throwing it at him as was compatible with not spilling a single drop of the coffee. Meanwhile, he admired her pear-shaped stomach.

"I said tea," Matthew said. "However, this will do, Alice my dear."

"I said we don't do teas. Patrick is a poet beneath the skin," she said.

"I'm a poet in the marrow of my bones," he said.

She stroked her head, drawing her hand up and over the high piled hair, and looking up at the blue and starry ceiling, disappeared into the back quarters.

Matthew wrote a secret poem to Alice to while away the afternoon. As he wrote she served him with three more cups of coffee and a slice of walnut cake.

There was still no sign of Elsie at half-past five, so he paid his bill and left the secret poem on the table where she later found it.

To Alice, Carrying Her Tray

O punk me a mims my joyble prime
And never be blay to me.
The wist may reeve and the bly go dim
But I'll gim flate by thee.

And all agone and all to come,
The sumper limm beware.
I'll meet thee ever away away
At Wanhope-by-the-Pear.

Chapter 10

NEXT DAY, Sunday morning, Sunday afternoon and the long jaded evening—the very clocks seeming to yawn—occurred all over London and especially in Kensington, Chelsea and Hampstead, where there were newspapers, bells, talk, sleep, fate.

Some bachelors went to church. Some kept open bed all morning and padded to and from it, with trays of eggs and coffee; these men wriggled their toes when they had got back to bed and, however hard they tried, could not prevent some irritating crumbs of toast from falling on the sheets; they smoked a cigarette, slept, then rose at twelve.

Those who were conducting love affairs in service flatlets found it convenient that the maids did not come in with their vacuum cleaners on Sundays. They made coffee and toast on the little grill in the alcove behind the curtain.

Tim Raymond had a large front furnished room on the first floor of a house in Gloucester Road, Kensington. The carpet was green, the walls a paler green, the sofa and easy chairs were covered with deep brown plush. He had hung on the walls of this furnished room some seascape water colours executed by a deceased uncle; he had placed on the lower shelves of a bookcase, behind the glass, three pieces of Georgian silver—a coffee pot, a fruit dish and a salt, relics of a great-aunt; on the upper shelves were some fat light-brown calf-bound racing calendars dating from 1909, which Tim rightly thought looked nice.

There was a divan bed, in which Hildegarde Krall still lay half-asleep, and in the opposite wall an alcove containing a small electric grill and a wash-basin where Tim was brushing his teeth.

Hildegarde's head was turned away from Tim, and at this angle of profile he thought she looked masculine. She turned round and propped up on her elbow to watch him. She said, "It's twenty to eleven."

Tim brushed his teeth at her, turning his head towards her. She said, "Is it raining?"

The telephone rang. Tim spat out his tooth water into the basin and went to answer it. "I suppose it's my Aunt Marlene," he said.

"Hallo," he said. "Yes, Marlene. No, I've been up for hours. Yes. No, I'm afraid not today. No, not, I'm afraid. I'm afraid not. All day today, no. Well, yes I do see, Marlene, but I don't want to be involved, really. One doesn't want . . . Well, Aunt Marlene, I hardly ever really saw him in action, I mean. I mean, I know he's a good medium, but really don't you think the law should take its course? Yes the law, but I mean it should take— They cross-examine all witnesses, you know. I can't possibly manage today, Marlene. Tomorrow, yes at six." Tim tucked the receiver under his chin and wiped his glasses on a handkerchief. "At six, yes. Yes," he said, "tomorrow. Oh, I'm lovely, how are you? Good-bye, darling. Yes, ye—six."

He flopped into the brown plush chair and lit a cigarette. "I'm too young for all this," he said. The telephone rang again.

"Hallo— Marlene! No, not at all. Yes, Marlene— Well, can't we discuss it tomorrow? Yes, of course, do tell me now— Yes. Yes. Oh, but Ronald's probably away. Away for the week-end. In fact, I'm sure he is, I think so. I haven't got his number, Marlene, isn't he in the book? He wouldn't discuss it with you, any-

way, he's awfully strict about confidential— Oh, no, I'm sure
he couldn't have lost anything. He never loses— No, you've
been misinformed, really. No, I'm sorry, I haven't got Ronald's
number. I'll ring him at his office in the morning. Yes, don't
worry. The morning. I'll ring— No, not at all. I say, I must go,
I'll be late for— Yes. Bye-bye."

"What has Ronald lost?" said Hildegarde.

"A letter connected with a criminal investigation."

"Ronald has lost it? He needs someone to look after him. I
used to do everything for him. I used to—"

"Yes, you told me."

"Well, so I did. What does your aunt want with Ronald?"

"I don't know. I don't want to be involved, quite frankly."

"I used to mend all Ronald's clothes. I used to buy the theatre
tickets. I used to rush to his flat after my work and—"

"I know," said Tim, "you told me." And he plugged in his
electric razor, the noise of which drowned her voice.

Ronald came out of church after the eleven o'clock Mass and
noticed that the youngest priest was standing in the porch saying appropriate things to the homegoing faithful. Ronald did not
like seeing this very young priest, not because he disliked the
priest but because the priest was young, and of a physical type
similar to himself, and reminded Ronald of his own blighted
vocation. This very young priest prided himself on knowing the
majority of the parish by name.

"Well, Eileen," he said, as they emerged. "Well, Patsy. Well,
Mrs. Mills. Well, John, and what can I do you for?"

"Oh, good *morning*, Father." . . . "How's yourself, Father."
. . . "Oh, Father, when are you coming to see us?" . . . "The
bingo drive was nice, Father." ". . . delightful sermon, Father."

"Well, Tom," said the priest. "Well, Mary, and how's your
mother?"

"A bit better, thank you, Father."

"Well, Ronald," said this very young priest as Ronald came
out.

"Well, Sonny," Ronald said.

The young priest stared after Ronald as he rapidly walked his way, then remembered Ronald Bridges was an epileptic, and turned to the next comer.

"Well, Matthew," he said, "and how's life with you?"

"All right, thank you, Father," said Matthew Finch. "Father, if you'll excuse me I can't stop. I've got to catch up with Ronald Bridges, Father, before he gets on the bus. But I'll be seeing you, Father."

Matthew caught up with Ronald at the bus stop.

"I managed to see Elsie early this morning," he said. "She's got the letter but she won't part with it unless I sleep with her again."

Ronald said, "Tell me later," for a number of the church people in the bus queue had turned to take note of this talk.

"I told her she'd be arrested," Matthew rattled on, "for entering your flat on false pretences and for robbery. I told her—"

"Come back with me and then tell me all," Ronald said.

"Well, she wants me to sleep with her again, and I'm not going to. She's a pervert, I can tell you that much, and I don't like perverted girls. If she isn't a pervert she's a nymphomaniac, it's just the same."

The bus drew up. Ronald and Matthew followed the queue on to it. Those who had formed the most interested audience for Matthew followed them upstairs. Two girls sat behind them, giggling.

"Don't say any more now," Ronald murmured. "People can hear you."

"Two to South Kensington please. I don't want," Matthew said, "to sleep with Elsie, I want to sleep with Alice. If I was to sleep with Elsie again I'd have to pretend it was Alice. And anyway, I'm not sleeping with girls any more, it's a mortal sin and you can't deny it," and he took his change from the conductor. "Elsie," he said, "is—"

"Shut up."

"Elsie," Matthew whispered, "is a bit jealous of Alice and her beauty. She hasn't a man of her own, and she was after some spiritualist clergyman but she found out he was homosexual, and she couldn't stand for it. Homosexuals send her raving mad. She was going to give him the letter yesterday, and didn't she find out yesterday—"

"What did this clergyman want with the letter?"

"He's in the spiritualist group. They all want to plot against Patrick Seton or plot for him, there's a great schism going on in the Circle just now."

They got off at South Kensington and walked to Ronald's flat.

"Elsie is going to use that letter to get a man and it isn't going to be me," Matthew said. "She's got some passionate ways in sex. Not that I'm narrow-minded, only she's not beautiful like Alice, and you can't allow for funny passions in a girl that isn't beautiful."

In the flat, Ronald said, "I'd better see Elsie. Will she be at the Oriflamme today?"

"Yes, at six tonight."

"What's her address?"

"Ten Vesey Street near Victoria, first floor flat."

Ronald wrote it down. Matthew said, "But don't go there. She's a dangerous woman. She—"

The telephone rang. "Marlene Cooper here," said the voice. "Ronald, you'll remember coming to lunch with me. I'm Tim's aunt." She articulated the vowels as if addressing a mental defective.

"Yes, how are you?" Ronald said.

"Listen carefully," she said. "You have lost a document, haven't you?"

"A document?" Ronald said.

"I'm sorry if you're going to take up that attitude," she said.

"Attitude?" Ronald said.

"Yes, because there might be a chance of my helping you."

"Helping me?"

"Yes, helping you. I think I might be able to give you the name of the person who holds the document, and this would save you a lot of embarrassment, if only—"

"Embarrassment?"

"It is not a forgery," Marlene said. "And if you would come along here and discuss the matter, I think you would find it to your advantage. Can you manage six o'clock? It isn't a forgery, that must be made plain. Patrick Seton must be cleared of this slander. I will explain everything. Sherry at six o'clock or six-thirty and stay for supper, Ronald—"

"Forgery?" Ronald said.

"It is not a forgery," Marlene said. "On that I insist. And if you will agree simply to say so to your superiors I can give you the name and address of a certain young woman."

"Thanks," Ronald said, "but really I don't like young women."

"Can you manage today, six o'clock?" Marlene said.

"I'm afraid not. I've got to see a young woman."

He said to Matthew after he had hung up, "Tim's auntie is a woman of few scruples when she's after something."

"Would you come across the road for a drink?" Matthew said. "All women are unscrupulous under the sun if there's something they want."

"She was prepared to sell me Elsie's name and address," Ronald said. "But as I've got it from you for free, I'll purchase a drink for you."

"But isn't it a great mistake to be bitter about the female sex!" Matthew said. "We owe them everything."

On Sunday afternoon Isobel Billows stoked up the fire and sent Martin Bowles to fetch in some more coal. He put the brief he was reading down on the floor beside his chair and went to do her bidding. As he could not hear the front door bell from the back of the house where he was filling the scuttle with coal, he was surprised on his return, to find Walter Prett, the art critic, plumply occupying his chair. Walter had one foot on Martin's brief.

138

"You are trampling on my brief," Martin said, bending to extricate it from under Walter's heel. He smoothed out the squashed manila cover of the file which held his brief. "There's a hundred and eighty pounds' worth of business in here," Martin said fretfully.

"Don't be vulgar," said Walter.

"Now bachelors," said Isobel, "don't quarrel."

"I deny there's anything particularly vulgar about money," Martin said.

"Did you put on the kettle as you came through the kitchen?" Isobel said.

"No, you didn't ask me to," said Martin.

"Well go and do it now," Walter said.

"Walter!" said Isobel, and she pushed the Sunday papers off her lap and got up, setting her fair hair straight. "We'll have some tea," she said and departed.

Walter said, "I wonder if you'd let me have—"

"No," said Martin.

"Vulgar little fellow," Walter said, tossing his snow-white locks. His dark face turned a shade more towards purple. He took a cigarette from a packet which was lying on the arm of his chair. They were Martin's cigarettes. Martin lifted the deprived packet and put it in his pocket.

Walter tore a strip of newspaper and lit his cigarette from the fire.

"I didn't see you here at the party," Martin said.

"Which party?"

"Oh, sorry. I suppose you weren't invited."

"I believe Isobel *did* mention something," Walter said. "But I was busy."

Martin began reading his brief.

"Too busy," said Walter, "to mix with those common little people that hang round Isobel at her parties. Pimps and tarts and Jews."

Martin read on.

"Spongers and soaks. Third-rate lower-middle class . . ."

Isobel pushed open the door with her tray.

"Walter is describing the people who come to your parties," Martin said, "Isobel dear."

"What people?" said Isobel, settling the tray.

"The sort of people who were at your cocktail party the other night."

"Oh Walter," Isobel said. "My party— I tried to get you on the 'phone, but you were always out. And I meant to send you a card but completely forgot, hoping to get you on the 'phone, you see—"

"I wouldn't have come," Walter shouted. "A vulgar third-rate set. Journalists. British Council lecturers. Schoolmasters. A typical divorcée's salon." And so saying he rose, lifted the tray of tea-things, smashed it down into the fireplace, wormed his bulk into the ancient camel's-hair coat which he had thrown on a chair, and left, banging both doors.

"You must have upset him," Isobel said to Martin.

"A good thing too. He only came here to sponge on you. He tried to touch me—you weren't five seconds out of the room."

"Oh, what a creature. And he can be so interesting when he likes, it's my favourite china." She started to cry.

"Send him a bill."

"Don't be silly."

"You must be protected," Martin said, with his arm around her, "from spongers."

He was hoping the fuss would not now make it difficult for him to get away after tea, for he had promised his old mother to be home for Sunday supper.

"I am not a possessive woman," his mother always said to him. "You are perfectly free. Just use the house as a lodging and come and go as you please. Or take a flat, live elsewhere, do anything you like. Don't think of me, I've *had* my life. I am not a possessive woman."

"She is not a possessive woman," he told his friends. "My old ma says, 'Take a flat if you like, go and live somewhere else, I don't want you tied to my apron-strings.' She isn't a possessive mother. But," Martin told his friends, "I've got to stay with her. You can't let your old widowed mother stew in Kensington when she's got arthritis. All her cronies have got arthritis. And she fights with Carrie, she literally fights with Carrie. Literally, they pull each other's hair."

Carrie was Martin's old nurse, now, by courtesy, the house-keeper. When Martin was first called to the bar, and was short of money, old Carrie would wander off to the post office and draw out three pounds at a time of her savings; these three pounds she would privately slip to Martin. Several times Martin told his mother of this, intending it as a rebuke to her for her meanness. Mrs. Bowles then wrote a cheque for Martin and, when he was out of the way, went and had a row with Carrie.

These latter days Carrie lived with Mrs. Bowles as an equal. Sometimes they quarrelled and had a real fight, pulling each other's hair and, with feeble veined hands, pushing each other's faces, pushing spectacles awry and knocking at each other's jaws with their helpless knuckles. Carrie had left all her life's savings to Martin, and she had saved since she was a girl of four-teen. Mrs. Bowles suspected that Carrie's fortune now sur-passed her own dwindling funds, and therefore Carrie was a real rival.

"I'm not a possessive woman," said Mrs. Bowles.

"You should of pushed him out the nest long ago," said Carrie. "You should take a lesson off the birds. You got to push them out. When my brother was a boy thirteen my mother said to him, 'There's five shillings, now go.' That's pushing them out the nest. My brother had a good position in a club before he died."

"This is a different case. A barrister has a struggle. I'm not a possessive woman. Let him marry, let him go."

"You got to *put* them out," Carrie said.

"Are you telling me to turn my own son out of doors?" said his mother and her eyes, which bulged naturally, shone with a bevelled light.

"Yes," said Carrie. "It would make a man of him."

"Then why do you give him money?"

"Me give him money? —Catch me."

"Martin told me. Last week you gave him money. Twice the week before that. Last month you—"

"Well, you keep him short, don't you?"

So Martin could never bring himself to leave Carrie and his mother, even although he no longer needed Carrie's little offerings. He lost his hair. He worried about his old mother if he went away to the country with Isobel for the week-end. He tried to entertain them and to be a good son. They bored him, but when they went away from home he missed the boredom, and the feud between them which sometimes broke into it.

"Carrie will have to go away to a home," said his old mother, "if her arthritis gets bad."

"No," said Martin. "Carrie stays here."

"You're after that money of hers. You may be disappointed," his mother said. He hated her fiercely for her continual robbing him of any better motive.

"I'm fond of Carrie," he said. But now his mother had left him wondering if he really meant it.

"Your mother will be bedridden before long," Carrie said. "What's to happen then?"

"We'll get a daily nurse," Martin said. "We'll manage."

"They won't stop," Carrie said. "Not with your mother. Look at Millie."

"Oh, nurses are different from maids. Maids always come and go."

"Millie was a good girl. She would of stopped if your mother hadn't made her life a misery."

He took them both to the country to his mother's younger sister on occasions. Then he went shopping for small supplies of groceries, pined for the boredom, and cooked whatever meals he did not have with Isobel. He missed the two old women pottering about and blaming each other.

"I've lost a vest, Carrie."

"I haven't got your vest."

142

"I have not said you've taken my vest. I think Millie must have taken it."

"What would Millie of wanted with a vest down to her knees?" said Carrie.

"It was a good warm vest," said Mrs. Bowles.

"You've put it away in the wrong place," said Carrie, "that's what you've done. Look among the table linen."

This was what Martin missed when they went away to the country and then, even on his comfortable week-ends with Isobel he thought of the empty house and the time when he was due to drive down to fetch them home and plonk them in their chairs in front of the television.

"It isn't clear."

"Be quiet, Carrie."

"I'm going to turn it up."

"Sit still, Carrie."

Carrie's niece had once offered to take her off their hands.

"Let her go," said Mrs. Bowles, and in her anger strained a muscle in her shoulder while heaving Carrie's trunk from the box room out on to the landing.

Carrie surveyed the box. "I'll go when it suits me," she said, "and it won't be to my relations I'll go. I could make myself a home tomorrow if it suited me."

Martin had heaved the trunk back into its old place, for it had left a clear oblong shape on the dusty floor. Martin brushed his trousers and washed his hands.

"Fetch me the liniment for my shoulder," said his mother, "there's a good boy."

He had bought them the television, and now, comforting Isobel for her broken china, he was wondering how he could get home in time for supper, as he had promised them he would.

He picked up the broken pieces and said, "You mustn't allow Walter Prett into the house again."

"He's never done this before," she said.

"Does he come often?" Martin stood up in his alarm, with half

143

the sugar basin in his hand, so that a little shower of sugar fell to the carpet.

"No, Martin," she said.

He was suspicious because of the "No, Martin," instead of merely "No."

"He's disreputable," Martin said. "A sponger and a drunk."

"Yes, Martin, I know."

He was frantic with curiosity. "What could any woman see in him?"

"He can be interesting when—"

"When he's not drunk."

"Well, he's got something about him, he's different from anybody else."

She got down and picked up all the china. "Pour me a drink," she said.

Martin looked at his watch and at her plump behind as she knelt over the broken pieces, and wanted to kick it. For he felt suddenly that he was to her only the man who handled her property and shares, and that she slept with him only to ensure his loyalty and save herself the trouble of investigating the property deals.

"I can't stay very long. My old ma's expecting me for supper," he said.

"Let's have a drink." She sniffed away the last of her tears and carried off the tray of broken china.

He had poured their drinks when she returned with new make-up on her face. He had often felt the only safe course would be to marry her, and he felt this now, with fear, because she did not always attract him, and he was not sure she would accept him. At the times when she stood out for her rights, not crudely, but with all the implicit assumptions, he thought her face too fat and found her thick neck and shoulders repulsive. At this moment, when she leaned against the mantelpiece with her drink in her hand, he finding himself without the right to question her about the frequency of Walter Prett's visits, he thought her jaw was too square and masculine. He saw it would be safer to marry her. Often, when she had said, "Martin, what should I do without you? I should never be able to manage my affairs without you," he had recognized her strong-boned beauty and thought how a sculptor might do something about it. Even at these moments, when he had found the idea of marrying Isobel a soothing one, the panic returned that she might refuse. The thought was not to be borne. He recalled the two old women and thought, after all, it would not be the decent thing to leave them alone.

"Carrie, you have wiped the oven with the floor cloth."

"How could I of wiped the oven with the floor cloth, when the floor cloth's looking you in the face over there? . . ."

He left at seven, and on the way home pulled up at a telephone kiosk. He wanted to talk secretly to Ronald Bridges and tell Ronald a little bit about Walter Prett's offensive behavior, and to put himself right with Ronald, feeling now as if Ronald's eye had been invisibly upon him all the afternoon. He was never comfortable when he did not feel all right with Ronald.

But there was no answer from Ronald's number. Soon Martin was eating cold lamb and beetroot opposite Carrie and next to his mother.

He laid his bald head on his hands and said, "Oh stop nagging each other you two women." And they stopped their quarrel for a little space.

Towards half-past seven on Sunday evening, Ewart Thornton was seated in Marlene Cooper's flat in Bayswater. He said, "I've got a pile of homework to do. Maths papers."

"Never mind that now," she said. "Come and have supper."

He had been smoking a pipe. He tapped it out and worked himself stiffly and hugely out of the deep upholstered chair.

"Maths papers," he said. "Preliminary tests."

"Ewart," she said at supper, "the Interior Spiral will be meeting on Tuesday at eight-thirty to discuss our evidence with regard to Patrick Seton. We must present a united front if it comes to a court case as I suspect it will. Now, whom can we trust?"

"Well you can trust me, for one," said Ewart, "but I must say I won't be able to give any evidence in court."

"What!" said Marlene, holding the cold peas in the serving-spoon suspended.

"I can't come to court."

She tipped the peas on to his plate and still stared at him. "You must," she said. "I'm counting on you."

"It will be too near the end of term," he said.

"Why," she said, "have we got to quarrel every time we meet, Ewart?" She started to eat.

"There is no quarrel," he said, sprinkling pepper on his salad.

"You can't let me down," she said, "after all this preparation. Patrick's future may depend upon it."

"I'm not convinced of Patrick's innocence. As you know, I'm a man of principle. I'm not sure that Mrs. Flower isn't in the right."

"But all you need to say is that Patrick is a genuine medium, and that Freda Flower ran after him unmercifully, as you know she did. As you know."

"Marlene," he said, "I advise you to keep out of the case alto-gether. You are talking wildly. No one would be interested in my evidence."

"Well, this is sudden," she said.

"I have told you my views. I've advised—"

"Yes, but I thought, as a member of the Interior Spiral, when it came to the point, Ewart, you would stand by me and . . ."

She was crying, and it satisfied him to see her cry and to think that he had brought about this drooping of her stately neck, the leaning of her head on her hand, the tremor of her jade earrings, the resigned dabbing of her eyes with her handkerchief, and the final offended sniff.

He introduced his fork into his mouth judiciously and chewed

146

like a wise man until she should be delivered of her distress.

"I don't see why you are so surprised. I've told you all along that I consider it absurd to go into the witness box on Patrick Seton's behalf. It would do him far more harm than—"

"Oh Ewart," she said. "No, you were never definite. I can't believe it."

It was true he had never been quite definite on the subject before tonight, but he had said enough, from time to time, to allow him now to extricate himself from any charge of sudden betrayal. He recalled that some time previous he had said to Marlene, "I can see Mrs. Flower's point of view. Of course, she was foolish to hand him over the money, even allowing it was a gift—"

"Oh, it was a gift. Patrick says so. He can prove it. There's a letter."

"It's a large sum for her to give."

On another occasion he had said, "My sympathies are not entirely with Patrick. He may be a good medium, but as a citizen—"

"It is time spiritualism was recognized as a mark of good citizenship," Marlene said.

More recently, at a meeting of the Interior Spiral—the secret group within the Group—Ewart Thornton had said, "There is bound to be a certain amount of prejudice against spiritualists if the case is brought up. My advice is to keep out of it and let the law take its course. Mud sticks."

"We must fight prejudice," Marlene had said. "And we all intend to support Patrick in every way. We must decide what we are going to say. We can't carry on the Group without Patrick." On that occasion Patrick had arrived, frail as a sapling birch with rain on its silver head. "We are just discussing," Marlene said, "our combined witness on your behalf, in the event of its being called for."

"Ah-ah," Patrick sighed, hunching his shoulders together, "the unfortunate occurrence."

"And what is more," Marlene said, "we want your assistance in settling what we are to say about Freda Flower. You will have to give us the relevant dates so that—"

"We do not all know Mrs. Flower," Ewart had said.

"Oh, don't we?" said Marlene.

Ewart had thus feebly worked towards this moment on Sunday evening when, sitting at Marlene's supper table he said, "I've told you all along that I consider it absurd to go into the witness box."

"Oh Ewart. No, you were never definite. I can't believe it."

"Think back," he said. "I've told you all along what my position is."

He leaned both arms confidently on the table, and felt a great awkwardness inside him, and looked at Marlene with an overpowering stare until he perceived her submission: she thought him altogether sure of his rectitude.

Then he experienced a sense of this rectitude, and was satisfied. He would have liked to have disappointed her more than this, because he was greatly attracted by her and greatly disapproved of her. He disapproved of, and was attracted by what she took for granted in life—by her freedom to indulge her spirit, and buy the acquiescence of her followers, and run up debts without worry, and cultivate spiritualists and mediums, and have no need of lovers. He was attracted by and disapproved the departed Harry who had bought earrings to dangle against this tall lady's neck, and who had died and been buried and dug up again by her, and cremated, and who was now being trafficked with beyond the grave. He had feasted on anecdotes of her past life, and wanted more, and was avid, in an old woman's way, for her downfall.

"I have counted on you," Marlene was saying, "to witness for Patrick because it would be such good publicity for the Infinity. People would know we are not cranks. No one would take you for a crank, Ewart."

This did not move him. He liked very much to see Marlene with her private means trying to win him over; and he knew already he was not a crank. He set his face squarely at her, and felt glad he had conferred with Freda Flower and had canvassed witnesses for Freda.

"Ronald Bridges," she said, "has also let me down rather badly today."

"He isn't one of us, surely?"

"Oh, he's not a spiritualist. But he has let me down, all the same. One thing about Patrick," she said, "he has never let me down."

He was anxious to go, for he wanted to telephone to Freda Flower from the cosy seclusion of his own study at Campden Hill. He loved a gossip with a homely woman like Freda Flower, and it had been most pleasant, recently, to settle in to telling her how things were going in the Wider Infinity group, and what was being said. For, like a Christian convert of the jungle who secretly returns by night to the fetish tree, or like one who openly supports a political party and then, at last, marks his vote for the opposite party, he felt justified in Freda Flower to the extent of these telephone conversations even although she was an unsuitable person to meet.

"Freda, I was at a party last night at Isobel Billows'. You won't know her—she's not a member of the Circle. But a lot of us were there. I did my very best, Freda, to persuade members to come forward in your favour. After all, where did all the money go? The members know that Patrick has had far too much handling of the funds, in any case. I tried to impress it on young Tim Raymond, but I'm afraid he is too young and irresponsible. And, my dear, I'm not saying anything against Marlene, but she . . ."

"Patrick Seton could look you in the eye," she would say, "and tell a lie so that you would believe you were telling the lie, not him."

"I can well believe you, my dear," he would say time and again, into the telephone receiver, lolling back largely in his chair and pulling his waistcoat over his stomach. "And I can't think why you hesitate to give your evidence in full force."

Marlene was piling the supper things on to a tray. She looked at Ewart several times as she did so, to see if he appeared as if he could still be persuaded. He stood up like a righteous husband, and contemptuously added the pepper pot to the tray.

"I won't keep you, then, Ewart, if you are in a hurry to get back to your work," she said.

But he was anxious to help Marlene wash the dishes before returning to gossip with Freda Flower. He liked putting an apron round his large body and he liked holding the cloth in his hands to dry the dishes one by one. Sometimes at the end of term, after the examinations, he invited three of his best boys to dinner on Saturday at his rooms, and he liked that very much—planning the menu, buying in the food, preparing it, cooking it for them, fussing over the stove for them, seeing they had enough to eat, like a solicitous mother.

He wiped Marlene's dishes and put them away carefully and proudly. He was encouraged by her dejection and satisfied, now, he had taken the only course.

His hips were wide for a man. He smoothed the apron while waiting, cloth in hand, for the next plate. Marlene did a vexed scouring of a saucepan. Ewart made neat the bow which tied the apron strings behind him.

"Is that the lot?" he said.

"Will you be here tomorrow night?" she said, "for the Interior Spiral."

"I'm afraid not, my dear." He was prepared to be charming.

"I can't understand you," she said. She took off her apron. He untied his and held it out to her. She cast the aprons, with graceful carelessness, over the back of a chair.

He touched her arm consolingly as a man of integrity a woman who could not be expected to understand integrity.

"You will come to the séance on Wednesday?"

He looked reproachful. "Oh, yes," he said. Marlene must be made to understand that simply because he refused to support her favourite he was not therefore a lapsed spiritualist.

"Good," she said sadly, "I'm glad, Ewart. I'm grateful for that."

She went over to that serving-aperture in the wall which divided the kitchen from the séance room and flicked a straying fold in the short curtain.

"Patrick will take the chair on Wednesday," she said.

"It may be his last appearance," Ewart said.

"Not if I know it," she said and moved past him out of the kitchen.

He put on his hat, scarf and coat in the hall.

"Thank you for a pleasant evening," he said.

"I am disappointed, Ewart."

"You will be grateful one day, Marlene."

He kissed her on both cheeks and departed to his rooms at Campden Hill where, from the depths of his leather arm-chair, he telephoned to Freda Flower.

"I have definitely made a stand, Freda, as regards Patrick Seton. It had to come, Freda. Now, Freda, don't be silly. That is sheer superstition. Patrick can do you no further harm. I believe you've still got a weak spot for Patrick, Freda, but believe me . . . And if I were you, my dear, I'd keep away from Mike Garland. Yes, keep him away from you. Yes, keep away from . . . We'll clean up the whole organization between us, you and I together. And Marlene will come to heel. . . ."

His hips expanded in the chair, and his chin went into extra folds as his face sank into the skull. A smile of comfortable womanliness spread far into the cheeks as he spoke and his eyes were avid, as if they had never moved dispassionately over an examination paper. "Yes, Freda my dear, I made no bones about it and I just said to her, I said . . ."

Meanwhile the Reverend T. W. Socket said to Mike Garland who had at that moment arrived at his flat, "Mrs. Flower is resolved to go ahead with the case."

"She has no alternative. It's in the hands of the police."

"But will she be a willing witness? That's what they need."

"I've done my best with her," said Mike Garland.

"I hope you didn't have to de-Flower her," said the Reverend Socket who then closed his eyes and shook with mirth.

Mike Garland smiled unpleasantly.

"I don't trust Mrs. Flower," he said. "I don't know for certain, but I think she may have been discussing me with the police. A plain-clothes man called last night. Somebody's been talking to the police."

"What did he want? What did he ask?"

"About my clairvoyant activities. Where did I operate? What did I charge for a horoscope? I told him. I showed him the card index. All postal commissions, I said."

"I'm glad I suggested that card index," said Socket. "There is nothing like having a card index in the house. You can always produce a card index. It puts them off their stroke."

"I invited the man to look through it, but he didn't trouble."

"Who has tipped them off, I wonder?"

"He mentioned Freda Flower."

"Really, in what connection?"

"He asked me if I knew her. I said yes, she was a friend."

"How many girls have you got staying with Freda Flower at the moment?"

"Only three."

"Transfer them to Ramsgate right away," said Father Socket. "I blame Marlene Cooper for this. You made an enemy of her the other night, I'm afraid. It was ill-considered of you to challenge Patrick Seton at an open séance."

"I can't transfer the girls to Ramsgate right away."

"Why not?"

"Because Freda Flower will be suspicious if they all leave at once. She thinks they work in the all-night kitchen at Lyons' Corner House. I can't trust Freda Flower."

"Whom can we trust?" said Father Socket.

"Someone has tipped the police," said Mike Garland.

"Could it be Elsie? Surely it couldn't be Elsie."

"She stole that letter—she's capable of anything."

"I told you, didn't I?" said Father Socket, "that you should have been more discreet when Elsie called yesterday."

"Having stolen a letter which was Crown property I doubt if she would go to the police. Besides, what could she say? That I was wearing my green striped dressing gown?" Mike Garland smiled with full lips pressed together.

"This is grave," said Father Socket. He was inserting a roll of tape into a recording machine. He switched it on. It was his own voice rending Shelley's "Ode to the West Wind." He stood listening to it, with critical attention, while Mike leant back with eyes closed.

When it was finished Father Socket said, "I should have taken 'Drive my dead thoughts . . .' more slowly. They are all mono-syllabic words, each word should be spoken with equal stress. Drive—my—dead—thoughts . . . like that."

"It gives one a frisson," said Mike.

"All troubles are passing," said Father Socket. "My son, the fever of life will soon be over and gone. We will take this police enquiry in our stride. Do not be disturbed, Mike. Patrick Seton will be brought to trial, the Wider Infinity will be brought to disrepute, the Temple will be cleansed and we shall then take over the affairs of the Circle ourselves."

"We'll take over the whole shooting-match," said Mike. "How you soothe me, Father."

"Some will have to go," said the Reverend Socket. "Marlene, of course, will no longer be in control. We shall not meet at Marlene's flat, we shall meet here. Ewart Thornton will have to go. Freda Flower—she is suspect, and to say the least, has been a troublemaker—she will have to go. It makes one's eyes narrow. We may retain Tim Raymond, a biddable youth. We shall—"

"But I didn't like that plain-clothes policeman calling on me last night," Mike whispered. "I didn't like it at all."

"Do nothing for two weeks," said Father Socket. "My son, go nowhere, do nothing."

"But the girls—"

"I shall myself convey the girls to Ramsgate," said Father Socket, "one by one."

Mike Garland took comfort from his elder partner whom he had revered for eight years, since that summer evening at Ramsgate when he had just heard Father Socket preach. This was in a private house, before the séance had commenced. Mike newly released from Maidstone prison, where he had served a sentence for soliciting, was deeply moved when he heard Father Socket say, "There are those amongst us who are not of the human race, but are aliens, and nevertheless must walk in the midst of mankind disguised as members of the human race. He who hath ears let him hear." Mike told Father Socket after the séance, "I was deeply moved by what you said tonight." Father Socket adopted him. Mike was then forty. He had a job as a waiter in a huge hotel. For the winter he had intended to return to London and take up private service as a manservant, for he had made a good butler in his time, with many profitable sidelines. Father Socket had changed all that. He had bestowed larger thoughts on Mike, who began to experience a late flowering in his soul. Father Socket cited the classics and André Gide, and although Mike did not actually read them, he understood, for the first time in his life, that the world contained scriptures to support his homosexuality which, till now, has been shifty and creedless. Mike gave up his job as a waiter and went into training as a clairvoyant. His appearance assisted him, he flowered. Father Socket instructed him in the theory and practice of clairvoyance, and Mike's late overflowing of the soul actually did evoke pronounced psychic talents. Father Socket's villa at Ramsgate was filled twice weekly with residential widows and retired military men—for it was widows and retired colonels who were the chief clients—come to receive clairvoyance from Mike.

"There are certain aids to perception which it is unwise—nay lacking in humility—for the clairvoyant to ignore," Father Socket told Mike, and he taught him how to observe his subjects and how, in the daylight hours, to gain useful information as to their private lives. Mike's previous career in the catering and domestic worlds assisted him, for he knew his way about the back stairs of hotels and boarding houses, he knew a friendly waiter when he saw one.

"But we must not neglect the little things of life," said Father Socket. "The gas bill must be paid." Mike knew a street photographer. He knew which wealthy men were taking the air on the front with their friends during illicit week-ends. The couples were photographed, the man handed a ticket, and the ticket was thrown away. Mike acquired these photographs at a higher price than the nominal three for seven-and-sixpence. But he did not lose on the deal and, even though certain members of hotel staffs had to be paid out of his earnings, still Father Socket's gas bills were paid.

"Never touch a woman," said Father Socket, "for a woman cannot enter the Kingdom. Have dealings with a woman and the virtue departs from you. You should read the Ancients on the subject."

Mike felt secure with Father Socket in all his summer and all his winter activities. He was no longer an aimless chancer sliding in and out of illegal avenues, feeling resentful all the while. Mike now was at rights with the world, he was somebody. He had a religion and a Way of Life, set forth by Father Socket. Mike, tall, straight, with his pink and white cheeks, did not appear to be an adoring type; nevertheless he adored Father Socket and was jealous of any other potential acolytes who might put in a tentative appearance, and would not stand for them.

Now, after eight prosperous years, Mike could not believe that a mere visit from a plain-clothes policeman could shake the benign rock which translated Horace, recited Shelley, knew the writings of the Early Fathers, and studied the Cabala. This winter's venture, a continuation of last summer's venture, was a private cinema show lasting half an hour. It comprised two films, entitled, respectively, *The Truth about Nudism* and *Nature's Way*. The three girls, who appeared on the stage in person afterwards, were more or less thrown in with the price of the ticket. Mike had thought the employment of these girls unnecessary. "Suppose the place is raided, it is easier to destroy the film than to conceal the girls."

"The show would lose its attraction," said Father Socket, "without a peppering of real flesh and blood. I prefer, myself, the more artistic exclusiveness of the film, but we must allow for the cruder tastes of the Many."

They lodged the girls with unsuspecting Freda Flower, who was known to Father Socket as a spiritualist and a widow and who touchingly gave him fifty cigarettes every Christmas and a spray of carnations on the birthday of the late Sir Oliver Lodge.

"Freda will take the girls," said Father Socket. "Now that Patrick Seton has let her down so badly over her savings, the good woman will need the money."

Mike had not been happy about Freda taking the girls to lodge. "Never have to do with a woman . . . they draw the virtue out of you."

A slight disturbance in Mike's mind had recently occurred to make him wonder if perhaps Father Socket was not more interested in women as such than he claimed to be. There was a certain Elsie, who did his typing. He was furiously jealous of Elsie. And these girls. But Mike, shivering as from a flash of clairvoyance, cast the thought from him.

But when Father Socket said, "I shall myself convey the girls to Ramsgate. One by one. You must lie low. I confess I don't like the sound of this policeman who visited you. Are you sure he was a policeman? Did you ask for his credentials? You should always demand their credentials." —When Father Socket spoke like this, Mike recalled his first hesitation in dealing with Freda Flower, he remembered his flash of doubt, whether Father Socket was reaching an age—sixty-two—when he might become weak. In a fever of clairvoyance and apprehension he looked at his patron and everlasting lean-upon, and said, "Never have dealings with women, Father. They are denied the Kingdom. They suck the virtue—"

"Well, my son," said Father Socket, "don't be fearful." He patted Mike's shoulder. "After all, you are now forty-eight and you must endure whatever may betide."

"Things look unlucky," said Mike, rising tall above Father Socket. "We had bad luck with Elsie Forrest yesterday, and that was a start. We should have got that letter out of her. Perhaps our good luck is turning."

"I told you not to put in an appearance in that dressing gown with that stuff on your face," Father Socket said. "I told you she was not a true spirit. What ever must the girl have thought?"

Alice Dawes sat up in bed combing her long black hair on that Sunday evening. A syringe lay on the table beside her.

"Some time next week, I imagine," said Patrick, in his murmur.

"And the divorce—now how about the divorce case?"

"Oh yes, I meant to tell you. The divorce has been held up. Something technical—but never mind that, I've got our honeymoon all arranged."

"Held up? How can we have a honeymoon if we can't get married?"

"A holiday, dear. We shall be married eventually."

"I wish you'd tell me more about your divorce."

"You trust me," said Patrick softly, "don't you?" He put out his hand and stroked her arm.

"Of course," she said, and after a space she said, "Are you sure the case will come up next month?"

"The divorce will—"

"No, not the divorce. The case, the charge of fraud."

"It may not come to anything after all. The police may decide they haven't good enough evidence."

"I should like to give that Freda Flower a piece of my mind. Saying you forged the letter. Have you seen anything of Elsie?"

"No, I wish she hadn't touched the letter. It puts me in an awkward position. The police think I'm behind the theft." He placed his head on one side with pathos.

"Do they know? Who told them?"

"The man who lost it, I suppose."

"That's Ronald Bridges," Alice said. "He takes fits. What's in the letter?"

"Not very much. It came with the cheque Freda sent me and it says, 'Please use this money to further your psychic and spiritualistic work. I leave it entirely in your hands'—something like that. An unprincipled woman. I should never have taken the money."

Alice moved in a desperate access of temper against Freda Flower and her own doubts; she sat up violently and began to throw back the covers and reach for her clothes at the same time. "I'll go and see that woman right away. I'll frighten the wits out of her—"

"No, no," Patrick said.

"I'll tell her it won't be you who's going to gaol, it will be her that's going to Holloway if she stands up before the magistrate and says you forged that letter. I'll tell her, and she can see for herself, that I'm pregnant, and I'll say, 'What right have you,' I'll say, 'to come between me and the man I love with a court case. You should have thought it over,' I'll say, 'before you sent him that cheque—'"

"No, no, keep calm," Patrick said.

"I'll say, 'You should have thought it over, and no doubt you thought he would marry you when he got his divorce, you ridiculous old bag' I'll say, 'now he's devoted the money to a cause and distributed it among the spiritualist students, now you say you didn't give it to him' I'll say. And I'll say, 'Mrs. Flower,' I'll say, 'you know the police are prejudiced and everyone's prejudiced against spiritualism and, they will swear it's a forgery and pay their men to swear to it. Now, Mrs. Flower,' I'll say, 'where will that get you, Mrs. Flower? It will get you to Holloway, that's where. You think you're going to come between Patrick and me? No, Mrs. Flower,' I'll say. 'Oh no, Mrs. Flower.'" Alice curled up and wept noisily.

Patrick sat in his calm, watching her, and he experienced that murmuring of his mind which was his memory. He could not recall where he had seen a similar sight before, but he felt he had. His memory was impressionistic, formed of a few distinguishable sensations among a mass of cloudy matter generally forming his past. He remembered most of all his childhood, and could possibly have brought to mind the latent image of being taken with his class round an art gallery by his art teacher, a woman. She is endeavouring to explain impressionist art by bidding them look at the palm of their hands for a moment, and nowhere else. "All round your hand you are aware of objects—you see them, but not distinctly. What you see round the palm of your hand is an *impression*." Patrick's memory had become this type of impression and if he focused his attention for long upon the things of the past it was mainly of his childhood that he thought, a happy childhood, and his lifelong justification for all his subsequent actions. It had bewildered him when the prison psychoanalysts had put it to him as a matter of course that something had been wrong with his childhood. That is not the case at all: something has been wrong, from time to time, ever since. Life has been full of unfortunate occurrences, and the dream of childhood still remains in his mind as that from which everything else deviates. He is a dreamy child: a dreamer of dreams, they say with pride, as he wanders back from walks in the botanical gardens, or looks up from his book. *Mary Rose* by J. M. Barrie is Patrick's favourite, and he is taken to the theatre to see it acted, and is sharply shocked by the sight of the real actresses and actors with painted faces performing outwardly on the open platform this tender romance about the girl who was stolen by the fairies on a Hebridean Island. As a young man he memorises the early poems of W. B. Yeats and will never forget them. Now, on his first enchanted visit to the Western Isles he first encounters an unfortunate occurrence, having sat up reciting to an American lady far into the night and the next morning being accused of having taken money from her purse. He is thinking of her, in his poetic innocence, as a kindred soul to whom money does not matter, but now she carries on as if money mattered. A little while, and he learns from a man that the early Christians shared all their worldly possessions one with the other, and Patrick memorises this lesson and repeats it to all. Another little while, and he has sex relations with a woman, and is upset by all the disgusting details and is eventually carried away into transports. There is a lot of nasty stuff in life which comes breaking up our ecstasy, our inheritance. I think, said Patrick, people should read more poetry and dream their dreams, and I do not recognize man-made laws and dogmas. There is always a fuss about some petty cash, or punctuality. "Tread softly," he recites to the young girls he meets, "because you tread on my dreams." The girls are usually enchanted. "I have spread my dreams under your feet," he says, "tread softly. . . ." Even older ladies are enchanted. His wispy father fully accepts the position of Patrick, and dies. The widowed mother cannot understand how he is not getting on in life, with such fine stuff in him. She protests, at last, that she is penniless, and when she dies, and turns out not to have been quite penniless, Patrick is amazed. He had not thought her to be a materialist at heart. There is a girl at the time going to have a baby, and that is her business. He removes to London, then, away from these unfortunate occurrences and finds his feet as a spiritualist and becomes a remarkable medium, which he always was, without knowing it, all along. There are ups and downs and he always does his best to help Mr. Fergusson with information. Patrick trembles with fear and relief when he thinks of Mr. Fergusson who first put him on a charge; and that was the first meeting.

Patrick has tried to explain how let down he always feels by people who trust him and enter into an agreement to trust him, as it were against their better judgment, blinding themselves, and then suddenly no longer trust him, and turn upon him. Mr. Fergusson perhaps understands this.

There is another charge, and the unfortunate sentence, but afterwards Mr. Fergusson, with his strong-looking chest and reliable uniform, is still sitting at the police station, and they make another arrangement about information so that Patrick feels much better and feels he has a real friend in Mr. Fergusson with his few words, even though Mr. Fergusson cannot help putting him on a charge sometimes; and he is afraid of Mr. Fergusson.

Patrick contemplates Alice curled up in distress. It is so much easier to get away from a girl in any other part of the country than in London. In the provinces one only has to go to London and disappear. But once you have a girl in your life in London she knows all your associates, you have established yourself, she knows some of your affairs; she knows where to find you; and it is impossible to disappear from Alice without disappearing from the centre of things, the spiritualist movement—Marlene— his Circle—"My bread and butter." Patrick is indignant. He has loved Alice.

He has not taken any money from her. He has given her money, has supported her for nearly a year. She has agreed to trust him, it is a pact. She is mine, he is thinking. The others were not mine but this one is mine. I have loved her, I still love her. I don't take anything from Alice. I give. And I will release her spirit from the gross body. He looks with justification at the syringe by her bedside, and is perfectly convinced about how things will go in Austria (all being well), since a man has to protect his bread and butter, and Alice has agreed to die, though not in so many words.

Patrick watched her calmly and reflected that he had been weak with Alice. She had talked and talked about marriage, as if he was a materialist with a belief in empty forms. He had told her frequently he was not a person of conventions: "I live by the life of the spirit." She had only replied "I'm not conventional, either." And when she had conceived this disgusting baby she had been frantic for marriage. It was absurd that she refused to have the baby done away with and was frantic for marriage.

It was her love for him and his spiritual values that made her so like the other women, crumpled up on the bed after their fury. A little dread entered in among his bones: it was about the chances of the Flower case coming up, and the possibility of a conviction. He absented himself from this idea and gave himself up to spiritual reflection again. Before Alice had recovered herself, he, watching from his chair, was surprised by a sensation which he had never experienced before. This was an acute throb of anticipatory pleasure at the mental vision of Alice, crumpled up—in the same position as she now was on the bed—on the mountainside in Austria. She is mine, I haven't taken a penny from this one, I have given to this one. I can do what pleases me. I love this one. She has agreed to trust. Crumpled up on the mountainside in Austria, Alice, overloaded with insulin, far from help, beyond the reach of a doctor, beyond help—far from the intrusive knowledge of his friends and enemies in London, outside the scope of his bread and butter, free from her heavy body, beyond good and evil. She has agreed to it, not in so many words, but . . .

She looked up from the bed, and was startled. But the fear left her face. There is a pact, he thought. She has agreed to believe in me.

It was still Sunday night and Ronald had gone up the stairs to Elsie Forrest's room at 10 Vesey Street near Victoria and had sat on the stairs awaiting her return at half-past eleven, when, as she approached her door, he stood up.

"Christ!" she said when she saw him.

"I hope I didn't give you a fright?"

"What d'you want?"

"To come inside and talk to you," Ronald said.

"You threaten me, I'll wake up the house."

Ronald sat down on the top stair. "I'm not threatening you. I'm only asking if I may talk to you. If you don't want me to talk to you, would you mind talking to me?"

She opened the door. "Come on in," she said, and stood and looked at him as he walked into her bed-sitting room.

"I've got nothing in the place to drink," she said.

"Not even tea?" said Ronald.

She said, "Take your things off and sit down."

She took off her own coat and hung it in the cupboard, from which she brought a coat-hanger and carefully set Ronald's coat upon it and set it up on a hook behind the door. Ronald sat on the divan and stretched out his legs.

As she put the kettle on the little electric grill stove behind a curtain she said,

"What was it you wanted to talk about?" She looked at him from the sides of her eyes as she set out the tea-cups.

"Anything you like."

She was looking at him, not to size up what he had come to talk about, but in an evaluating way which made Ronald feel like something in the sales.

"You're Ronald Bridges," she said.

"You're Elsie Forrest," he said.

"You want the letter," she said. She went over to the window and drew the limp short makeshift curtains.

He said, "Have the police been to see you?"

"No," she said. "And you know they haven't. You wouldn't be fool enough to tell the cops until you had tried to get it back yourself. It would tell against your reputation, losing a confidential document, wouldn't it? Why didn't you keep it confidential if it was confidential?"

"I don't know," he said.

"You wouldn't be foolish enough to tell the cops," she said.

"No," he said. "But a friend of mine has done so."

"I don't believe it," she said. "No detectives have called here."

"I've told them to leave it to me for the time being."

"I don't believe it," she said.

"All right," he said. "The kettle's boiling over," he said.

She made the tea, and Ronald watched her. She looked very neurotic, moving in a jerky way, her body giving little twitches of habitual umbrage. Her blond greasy hair hung over her face as she poured out the tea.

"Your friend Matthew Finch came to see me," she said.

"Yes, I know," Ronald said.

"He was after the letter."

"Yes, I know."

"He didn't get it," she said.

163

"I know."

"And that's why you've come after it."

"I didn't need to come after it," he said.

"All right," she said, "send the police. I'll face all that." She sat down beside him on the sofa and folding her hands in her lap, looked straight ahead of her. "I've faced it already," she said with tragic intensity, such as Alice employed when talking to a man and the stress of the occasion demanded it.

All at once, Ronald quite liked her.

"I have died," she said, "many deaths."

"Tell me," he said, "how that has happened."

She pushed back her hair from her bumpy forehead. She had a warped young face.

"I have loved too much and trusted too much," she said, perceiving the success of her style, "I have given and I haven't received."

"Have you had a lot of sex relations?" Ronald said.

"I have had sex without any relationships. I don't know why I'm telling you this the first five minutes."

"You've met the wrong chaps," Ronald said.

"All the chaps are wrong ones. If they aren't married they are queer, if they aren't queer they are hard, if they aren't hard they are soft. I can't get anywhere with men, somehow. Why am I telling you all this?"

"I'm the uncle type," Ronald said.

"Why d'you say that? Are you interested in psychology? — I'm very interested in psychology. Why are you the uncle type?"

"Because everyone tells me their troubles," Ronald said.

"And don't you tell people your troubles?"

"No," Ronald said, "my troubles are largely self-evident and I'm not the filial type. To be able to tell people your troubles you have to be a born son. Or daughter, as the case may be."

"I must be a born daughter," Elsie said, "according to psychology."

"At the moment you're being a niece if I'm being an uncle. Let's keep our terms of reference in order."

"Well, I know a Father Socket," Elsie said. "He's just let me down badly. I looked on him as a father, and now I've found out he's a homosexual."

"You can overlook that," Ronald said, "if you think of him as second cousin."

"I can't overlook it. I hate queers. I want to conceive a child."

"Fond of babies?"

"Not particularly. It's not a question of having a child so much as conceiving a child by a man I love."

"You'd better get a husband," Ronald said. "That would be the obvious course."

"There aren't any husbands that I know of. My own brother's unfaithful to his wife, it makes me sick. And he expects me to encourage him. 'Lend us your room for the afternoon, Elsie,' he says. And when I won't lend the room he says, 'You're not much of a sister.' I said, 'I object to the type of woman you pick up with.' So I do. I couldn't have them coming here. That's what my brother's like. I always knew he would make a rotten husband."

"You'd better find a husband that isn't like your brother."

"There aren't any husbands so far as I've met. All the men I know want to lean on me or take it out on me. I did all Father Socket's typing. That friend of yours, Matthew Finch, he only wanted to commit a sin with me and he ate a lot of onions and breathed on my face so I shouldn't enjoy it. If he's your friend, I can only say—"

"Oh, if he's my friend, we might leave him out of the discussion."

"Now, there's another thing—the way you men stick together against us."

"Haven't you any friends?"

"Well, there's Alice."

"We'll leave her out of the discussion, then."

"No we won't. Alice is a case. She's mad in love with that little weed Patrick Seton. I'll admit he's a brilliant medium. But what else is there to him? Now she's getting a child by him. And what's he done about it? Wanted her to have it taken away. She thinks he's going to marry her, and she's mistaken. I've told her. I've told Alice. I've told her he'll never marry her. He says he's getting a divorce, and the divorce never happens. And she believes him. Any awkwardness, and he recites poetry to her to explain everything away. I'll bet he hasn't got a wife. He was never the husband type from the start. He won't marry Alice. She refuses to see that."

"Then why are you defending him, like a sister?"

"I'm not defending him at all, I'm—"

"You're concealing the evidence of his forgery."

"Oh the letter—I'm hanging on to that. I know that's what you've come for. But I'm keeping it and I'll take the consequences. I've already faced the consequences. So you can go."

Ronald got up and went to take his coat off the hanger.

"Stay the night," she said, "and I'll give you the letter in the morning."

Ronald sat down again. "No," he said.

"Why? Don't you want to sleep with me?"

"No," Ronald said.

"Why, tell me why? Is there something wrong with me?"

"Uncles don't sleep with nieces," Ronald said.

"Isn't that carrying the idea a bit far?"

"Yes," Ronald said, "it is. I'm not an uncle, I'm a stranger. That's why I can't sleep with you."

"Am I a stranger?"

"Yes," Ronald said.

"You're only playing for time," she said. "I'm well aware you're trying to handle me. It's the letter you're after. Take all and give nothing."

"I thought we were having an interesting conversation, mutually appreciated as between strangers," Ronald said.

"Yes, and when you go away you'll feel 'Well, I haven't got the letter but at least I cheered up the poor girl for an hour.' And what d'you suppose *I'll* feel? It's much better for men not to come at all if they're always going to go away and leave me alone. I'm not lonely before they come. I'm only lonely when they go away."

"There's a whole philosophy attached to that," Ronald said. "It turns on the question whether it's best not to be born in the first place."

"That's a silly question," she said, "because if you weren't born you couldn't ask it."

"Yes, it is silly. But, since one has been born, it's one of the mad questions one has been born to ask."

"I think it's better to be born. At least you know where you are," Elsie said.

"Aren't you contradicting yourself?" Ronald said.

"I don't care if I am. There's a big difference between feeling lonely after a man's gone away and not being born at all. Being born is basic. You don't need to have company in the same way as you need to be born."

"There's a lot in what you say," Ronald said.

"I say it's a mistake to have company, I wish I could stop it."

"You only need stick a note on your door saying 'Away for a few weeks' and leave it there."

"I haven't the guts," she said. "And I don't get much companionship out of the men I know. All they want is sex, and perhaps we have an evening out with sex in view, but they're anxious to get back to their mums and aunties or their wives."

"You should make them entertain you without sex," Ronald said, "—an intelligent girl like you."

"They don't want intelligence. They don't come if there's no sex. I'm a sexy type, I get excited about it. And that's what they like. But it only leaves me lonely."

"Don't you enjoy it at the time?"

"No. But I can't do without it, and these men know it. They fumble about with their french letters or they tear open their horrible little packets of contraceptives like kids with sweets, or they expect me to have a rubber stop-gap all ready fitted. All the time I want to be in love with the man and conceive his child, but I keep thinking of the birth-control and something inside me turns in its grave. You can't enjoy sex in that frame of mind."

"I know the feeling," Ronald said, "it's like contemplating suicide."

"Have you thought of committing suicide?"

"Yes," he said, "but something inside me turns in its grave."

"I've thought of suicide, but in the end I always decide to wait in case another possibility turns up. I might meet a man that wants to live with me and not keep slamming the door in my face with birth-control. There were plenty wanted to live with Alice before she took up with Patrick Seton. And now *she's* in for a let-down, though she won't admit it. But at least she's had her sex with a baby coming up."

"You can't have babies all over the place," Ronald said. "It isn't practical."

"I know," she said.

"Will you give me back the letter?" Ronald said.

"Why should I?"

"Because you took it," Ronald said.

"It's the first time I've taken anything worth having off a man. And I want to keep it."

"What for?"

"It may come in useful. It may help Alice. If Patrick gets convicted she'll be in the cart. I'd like to see him in gaol, but still he's Alice's man, and I don't see why I shouldn't destroy the evidence against him. I'm quite sure it's a forgery."

"You won't destroy the letter," Ronald said.

"How do you know?"

"It has too many possibilities of exploitation. You could form a blood-brotherhood with several persons out of that letter. You have already offered to give it to me if I slept with you."

"Well, how do you know I would have given it to you in the end?"

"You're mistaken if you think it's going to make any difference to the evidence against Patrick whether you keep it or not," Ronald said. "There are photo-copies which will be accepted in court together with evidence of the loss of the original."

"Why do you want it, then?"

"To save my own reputation. I get jobs from the police in the detection of forgeries. I shouldn't have told anyone about this document—that was my mistake. And it's obviously my responsibility that it was stolen. But if I can produce the letter after all, the matter will be forgotten."

"If I give you the letter will you promise to come and talk to me again?"

"No," Ronald said.

"I don't see why I should give you the letter. You've been talking as a friend and getting round me, and all you want is the letter."

"I'm not a friend, I'm a stranger," Ronald said. "I've quite liked talking to you."

"Well I'm a stranger too. And I'm keeping the letter. There's a price on it."

"Give it to me for love."

"What love do I get out of it?"

"That's not the point."

"Well, you've got a nerve, I'll say that. But you all come for what you can get."

"Give it to me for love," Ronald said. "The best type of love to give is sacrificial. It's an embarrassing type of love to receive, if that's any consolation to you. The best type of love you can receive is to be taken for granted as a dependable person and otherwise ignored—that's more comfortable."

"It's all talk," she said. "I'm tired. I've been doing a late shift at the Oriflamme."

"Well, think about it in the morning." He took down his coat and shouldered his way into it.

"If I give you the letter now," she said, "will you come back again some time?"

"It's unlikely," he said. "You go to bed. Thank you for talking."

"If I don't give you the letter what will you do?"

"I'll come back and try again."

"Christ!" she said, "you're driving me mad." She went over to the window and thrusting her arm far into the deep makeshift hem, drew out a four-folded paper. "Take it and run quickly," she said. "Run now before I change my mind." She came and pushed it into the pocket of Ronald's coat. "Go away," she said, "get out of my sight."

He sat down in his coat and smoothed out the paper. "You've crumpled it but let's hear what it sounds like," he said and read aloud,

Dear Patrick,

I would like you to accept the enclosed cheque for two thousand pounds. Please use the money to further your psychic and spiritualistic work. I leave the details of its disposal entirely to you.

May I say how greatly I admire and have been inspired by your great work. I shall never be able to thank you enough.

Yours sincerely,
Freda Flower

"You've crumpled it," Ronald said, "but at least you haven't folded it. In forgery detection you have to watch out for the folds."

"Why's that?"

"Sometimes a line has been inked over after the fold has been made. The forger very often has second thoughts about the job after the paper has been folded, and to make everything perfect he unfolds the paper again and he touches something up; let's say the stroke of an 'f.' It's possible to see under the microscope if that sort of thing has been done."

"Is that what Patrick's done, do you think?" She peered over at the letter. "It looks like a woman's writing to me."

"So it does to me. He's a clever forger. He's done it before. He's been convicted, served a sentence."

"Well, Alice doesn't know that. Well, she does know it in a

way, but she won't face it. The baby makes her believe in Patrick."

"She'll know sooner or later."

"Will he be sent to prison?"

"Oh, one can't guess," Ronald said, "it's not such an easy thing to prove. This may be a difficult document. Experts often disagree. Seton's side would have their own expert. And then, everything depends largely on the witnesses. If Mrs. Flower's evidence should break down, for instance—"

"But if they know he's a forger from the past, surely—"

"The court isn't told till after the verdict."

"Alice thinks the case won't come off."

"No, perhaps it won't come off. Perhaps he won't be sent for trial."

"Is it confidential that Patrick has been to prison?"

"No, it's common property." He was examining the letter upside-down.

"Perhaps I won't tell Alice. She thinks they're going to get married, some hope. Anyway, he's taking her away to Austria as soon as the charge is settled one way or another."

Ronald folded the letter and put it far away into his inner pocket. "I must go," he said.

"Will you come again, Ronald?"

"It's unlikely," he said.

"You've got your letter," she said.

"Thank you," he said.

"You need someone to look after you," she said.

"I was once engaged to a girl who wanted to be a mother to me. It didn't work."

"You think I'm not good enough for you," she said. "Not your class."

"I'm an epileptic," he said. "It rather puts one out of the reach of class."

"I know you're an epileptic," she said. "I was told."

"Well good night, Elsie." He went down the stairs and out into the dark streets of Monday morning.

Chapter 11

"IT'S TREACHERY," Alice said, quite loud in the empty café.

"Now look, Alice," Elsie said, "I've never signed any blood-pact with you. We're friends. And being friends doesn't mean being blood-sisters. For goodness sake let's keep our relationships straight. Treachery is not the word."

"Where did you get all this kind of talk?" Alice said.

"Now don't you turn cat, Alice. You need a friend just at this moment."

"To think that you actually handed over that letter without even letting me see it," Alice said, "and now the case is coming up and the letter will be used against Patrick."

"To begin with," said Elsie, "I didn't know whether he was going to go for trial or not when I gave him the letter. Secondly, it wouldn't have made any difference to the case because they photo'd the letter and that would have been good enough. Third, I gave it to Ronald for his own sake and I'd do it again—"

"What you wouldn't do for a night with a man . . ."

"He didn't so much as shake hands with me. Fourthly, it was more his letter than mine, and—"

"It's Patrick's letter," Alice said, "by law."

"No, it's Crown property, excuse me. But it's his forgery, all right. Five, if you don't believe Patrick forged the letter I don't see what you're worried about. They can't prove a forgery if there isn't a forgery. It goes by folds in the paper and pauses in the writing. They see it under the microscope. Ronald—"

"Oh shut up," said Alice, "with your one, two, three, four, five. You're such a clever cookie since you saw that man, a pity you don't stop to think he's in the pay of the police."

"Well, it's his job."

"Yes, to fake up the evidence. He'll say whatever they want him to say."

"You don't know Ronald," said Elsie.

"Now he's got the letter, you won't be seeing *him* again," Alice said. "You wait and see."

"I know," Elsie said.

"God," said Alice, "it's kicking again. I feel faint when it does that."

Elsie leaned over the café table and looked at Alice's stomach as she clutched it. "Take your hand away," Elsie said, "and let me see."

Alice took her hand away.

"I can't see anything," Elsie said.

"Don't stare like that. Someone might come in the shop."

"No one will come in, it's too early. I can't see it move."

"You have to look close. It only looks like a butterfly, but it feels like a footballer inside me."

Elsie slid around to the seat beside Alice and put her hand on Alice's round stomach. "I can feel it!" she said. "Kick, kick. I can feel it."

"It makes me giddy," Alice said.

"I'll go and draw you another espresso."

"All right," Alice said.

"I wish I had something alive and kicking inside me," Elsie said.

Tim Raymond sat in his club, looking as lonely as possible in the hope that someone married would take him home to supper, but prepared, if not, to dine alone at eight o'clock. Hildegarde had just written from Gloucestershire, after a long silence, to say she was entering a convent. On hearing this news Tim had telephoned to Ronald. "Have you heard from Hildegarde?"

"That's the second girl you've driven to religion," Ronald said.

"*I've* driven?"

"Well, yes, in a way."

"Hildegarde told you about our affair?"

"Well, not directly. Anyway, of course I knew about it and now that's the second girl—"

"I know," Tim said. Two years ago his first real girl friend had entered an Anglican Sisterhood.

"What about that other one you were thinking of marrying?" Ronald said.

"Oh, that's all off. *She* hasn't taken to religion."

"Well, two's plenty."

"I wonder why they take to religion?"

"There must be something wrong with you," Ronald said.

"So there must. Do you know, I always felt Hildegarde was still keen on you, Ronald."

"Well she must have got over it. What Order has she entered?"

"Some Canoness affair. I feel rather shattered. Not that I felt all that strongly about Hildegarde, it's just that a loss is a loss. And I didn't know she was R.C. When did she go Roman?"

"Two years ago," Ronald said, "and two months. I forget the odd days."

"What a good memory you've got. Did she join under your influence?"

"Yes. I rather regretted it later."

"Why?"

"Because she lapsed."

"Well, she's gone back. There's definitely something odd about Hildegarde. She was a spiritualist for a time, not long ago."

"Under your influence?"

174

"Well, it gave us something to talk about. One has to have something to talk about. Hildegarde was a difficult girl to find something to talk about with. Anyway she gave up spiritualism when I got out of it and she must have gone bang back to Rome. Funny going from spiritualism back to Catholicism, don't you think, all prejudices apart? A bit extreme. There are other religions she could have tried if she had to have a religion."

"There are only two religions, the spiritualist and the Catholic," Ronald said.

"I say, that's going a bit far. There's the Greek Orthodox and the Quakers and of course the C. of E. and some people are Buddhists, and—"

"You must take it in a figurative sense," Ronald said, "or leave it, because I need a drink."

"Well, that's the news. I thought I'd let you know. Come and drink with me."

"I'm going out. I'm late, actually," Ronald said.

"I've got nothing to do tonight," Tim said. "What would you do?"

"See a film."

"Don't want to, somehow."

"Sit in your club and look as lonely and miserable as possible. Someone will turn up and take you home."

Tim was doing this when the porter came to announce that his Aunt Marlene was enquiring for him downstairs.

"I'm not here," Tim said, and moved to another chair. The chair he had been occupying was placed in the window and the curtains had been left undrawn. He suspected that Marlene had seen him from the street. He took off his glasses, polished them with his handkerchief, and put them on again.

An almost telepathic communication from the entrance hall —for nothing could be heard from that direction—told him that an argument was going on between Marlene and the porter at the desk. Tim tiptoed attentively to the door, tripping over the legs of someone whose face was hidden by a newspaper, so that Tim's hand came to rest on the man's lap.

"Oh," Tim said, "it's you, Eccie." He straightened up, by which time the porter had appeared again.

"The lady said she is convinced you are in the building. I've told her I would have another look."

"I'm going along to the bar," Tim said. "Tell her you've had another look."

"I'm not sure," said Eccie, "that the British Council is going to suit me. Their notions of art—"

"Come along to the bar," Tim said, urgently. "My aunt's downstairs."

"Well she won't come up here."

"Oh, won't she?" said Tim.

Eccie puckered his face in puzzlement and followed Tim, who, looking over the banister, perceived a corner of his aunt in the hall as she argued with the porter.

They slipped into the bar.

"I have a series of twelve lectures," Eccie declared over his drink. "They have gone down well for twelve years. They are old and tried and have stood the test of time at the old Institute. They cover the Renaissance to Kandinsky. They were the nucleus of the Art course at the Institute. Thousands of people passed through our hands south of the Humber. I travelled the length and breadth, to W.V.S. centres, National Service units, prisons, summer schools—all over the place. And everywhere I went those lectures got a tremendous reception. They were highly appreciated. From the Renaissance to Kandinsky, with a set of colour reproductions, tested and tried. And now, when I'm all fixed for my injections for Malta, the chap at the British Council says—and mind you it's we who pay them, it's the taxpayer, you and I, whose money goes into their pockets—he calls me in and he says—"

"Tim, oh there you are!"

Marlene stood by the other door leading from the back stairs.

Tim put down his drink and disappeared out of the opposite door. Marlene did not pursue him, as he expected, through the bar. She retreated down the back stairs to the first landing, walked along a passage, and came out on to the big oak-panelled first-floor landing where she again encountered Tim.

She said, "The trial is on, and it is settled that you are to be a witness. We have decided, on Patrick's own advice, not to give evidence for his character as he prefers his character to speak for itself. But there is a question of a statement that Patrick made to the police under duress, while still in a state of trance after a séance. We must testify about this séance. I have the date and the time. Eleven-thirty on the morning of August the twelfth. Patrick made his statement at twelve noon. He was not properly out of his trance. You are to give evidence that you saw him in a trance at eleven-thirty, but we must decide exactly what you are to say because you are inclined to be hesitant and vague. I am calling a meeting—"

"Marlene, you shouldn't be here."

"Get your coat immediately," she said, "and come with me."

"I'm just going to the lavatory," Tim said and disappeared with his long legs up the main staircase like an anxious spider. He did not, however, go into the lavatory, but into the library where an aged member and a young man were bending over an architectural-looking plan spread out on the table. They looked up at Tim. The aged member said "Who?" and they both looked down again at their plan. Tim wandered over to the window and there slipped behind the curtains. Marlene waited outside the lavatory. A man emerged with eyebrows which were by nature fixed in slight astonishment, and which when he saw Marlene, seemed to try to rise. "Is my nephew in there?" Marlene said.

The man moved off, assuming her to be one of the maids gone mad in her private life.

Marlene waited. In ten minutes' time she knocked loudly on the door.

"Tim!" she said.

"Tim," she said.

"Listen, Tim," she said. "I will take you across to Prunier's. We can discuss everything there. You *know* you like Prunier's."

"Timothy!" she said.

A very young man came round the corner. "Oh!" he said at Marlene's back.

"Would you mind going in there and telling my nephew, Tim Raymond, that he's wanted urgently? A matter of life and death. Hurry."

The young man went in as one accustomed to military training, leaving the door open. Marlene stood in the doorway and watched while he politely looked round.

"There's nobody here," said the young man.

The aged member from the library approached the door, followed by his young companion.

Marlene was saying, "Nonsense. He is hiding from me. Have a good look."

"Who?" said the aged member behind her.

"Let *me* look," said Marlene, entering this tiled enclosure.

"Who?" said the old man.

He was ushered away by his fellows.

Marlene continued her simple but fruitless search. When she came out she caught sight of the porter as he came up the stairs with the look of one who had been sent.

Marlene tripped along the passage and into the library. The room appeared to be unoccupied. A thin and feeble little cloud of cigarette smoke proceeded from the join of the window curtains. Marlene observed the bulge where Tim had pulled a chair behind the curtain to console his vigil, and made straight for it.

"Tim, you are wasting my time."

Footsteps approached outside and the door-handle was turned. Marlene got behind the curtain with Tim just before the porter put his head round the door. As soon as he had withdrawn Tim moved out to the far side of the big table.

"It is a matter of life and death," Marlene said.

"I've got to go to the lavatory," Tim said. This was genuine, and he departed.

Marlene found a place of concealment at the end of the passage. Tim came out of the lavatory and, looking to right and left, darted upstairs. Marlene followed, in time to catch him as he attempted to close a door behind him. She pushed her way in against him and confronted him in a bleak vacant bedroom. She locked the door.

"Now, Tim," she said, "what's all this fuss about?"

"I don't want to give evidence in Seton's case," he said. "It's got nothing to do with me, Marlene."

"It isn't a matter of what you want. It's a question of what is necessary."

"No," said Tim, "really."

"What?" she said.

"Nothing doing," Tim said.

"You are out of your mind," she said.

Tim made a dash for the door, unlocked it, fled downstairs, grabbed his coat and dashed into the street where he turned several corners and then caught a taxi.

Marlene walked solemnly downstairs and demanded some scrap paper from the hall porter.

"Mr. Raymond has left, Madam."

"I wish to leave a note."

She folded it in four when she had written it and wrote Tim's name on the outside. She gave it to the porter who, when she had gone, read the message: "I shall see my solicitor tomorrow with a view to altering the legacy arrangements. Marlene Cooper."

Ewart Thornton sat with his elbow resting on the arm of his wide chair, and in his hand the telephone receiver.

"There is a meeting tonight. Of course I shall not be present. Freda my dear, there is something you should know about the Wider Infinity. There is a group within the Group. A secret group within the Group. Now you didn't know that, Freda dear, did you? Doesn't it surprise you?"

Freda Flower sat in her chair by the telephone, looking up at a cobweb in the corner of the ceiling which she dared not sweep away for fear of bad luck, and spoke into the telephone.

"You amaze me, Ewart," she said.

"I thought that would surprise you," he said. "My dear, this secret group within the Group is called the Interior Spiral."

"That's a make of mattress, isn't it?" she said.

"It may be, it may be. I say, my dear Freda, you are taking this seriously, aren't you?"

"I think it's a very serious matter indeed, Ewart. After all, it was my money that was—"

"Yes, quite. Well, as I was saying, there is this secret group, and I admit I was a member. There was some good in it Freda, we did a lot of good. But an evil spirit got abroad amongst us. I have resigned. There is a conspiracy amongst them to support Patrick Seton at the trial. Of course, this is illegal and they won't have a leg to stand on, but—"

"Oh Ewart, oh Ewart. I do wish I had never gone to the police about that money. They will make me say more things against Patrick, and with him standing there in the dock, with his eyes on me. I don't know how I managed the other day in the Magistrate's Court. I came home to bed, and—"

"You only have to speak the truth, Freda. It is the truth, isn't it? You did give him that money to buy bonds?"

"Oh yes, but—"

"And he used it for his own purposes?"

"Yes, but—"

"And forged a letter to cover himself?"

"Yes, it's true, but . . . Oh, Ewart, I somehow knew all the time he was deceiving me and I let it go. It makes—"

"You knew?"

"Well I knew and I didn't know. I wouldn't admit it to myself. And now to get up in the criminal court with his eyes on me again and stick to the facts as Mr. Fergusson says, it will be such a sort of let-down, a betrayal, and poor little Patrick, he's so thin."

"Tell me, Freda dear—I'm a man of the world—was there any—were there any *relations* between you and Patrick Seton? In confidence, my dear?"

"Well, Ewart, I don't want to talk about it, naturally I've got my pride. But he got round me, you know, Ewart, and I let myself go. He—"

"My dear, if this is mentioned in court, deny it. Simply flatly deny it. It is irrelevant to the case. I doubt very much if Patrick would bring it up in court—it would go against him, if anything. You were foolish, Freda my dear."

"I know I'm a foolish woman. It's not just the disgrace of it coming up that's worrying me. But it was terrible the other day to stand up in front of Patrick and denounce him to the magistrate after being together like that. He looked at me. It—"

"That's just his trick, my dear. Don't you see? He counts on women being weak. He—"

"Oh, I do believe he meant everything in his heart at the time when we were together, really. And he can see through everything, Ewart. You don't know how psychic he is. He's in touch with my poor husband. He's in touch with the Beyond. He—"

"Are you afraid of him?" Ewart said.

"Yes."

"What are you afraid of?"

"His looking at me. He used to recite 'Season of mists and mellow fruitfulness,' it was a deepening experience, Ewart."

"You must definitely speak to Father Socket, Freda. If you feel an evil eye upon you, Father Socket will exorcise it for you—"

"Father Socket has gone away. Dr. Garland can't find him anywhere. He isn't at Ramsgate and he's left the flat. Dr. Garland's upset. Dr. Garland's sent those girls away—and between you and me, good riddance. You don't tell *me* they were waitresses. No fear."

"There must have been a break between Socket and Mike Garland," Ewart said. "*My* dear. Tell me more."

"Oh, definitely a break. I don't know what about."

"Have you seen Mike Garland recently?"

"No. There's rent owing for the girls."

"Freda my dear, you simply must keep clear of these cranks."

"Ewart, I feel I can count on you. If only I didn't have to go to court and stand up. The case might go on for a whole day or more. Will you be at the trial?"

"Oh no. Exams."

"I should like to see you. Won't you come over?"

"Sorry. Loads of homework." The comfort went out of his face at the notion of his telephone-relationship getting out of hand.

"Suppose Patrick gets off?" she said.

"He won't get off if you stick to the facts."

"But this Interior Spiral. They might get up and say anything. Suppose Patrick gets off?—He'll do me damage, Ewart, and I'll only have myself to blame."

"The Interior Spiral, as I was about to tell you, Freda my dear, is dwindling fast. Marlene will find herself with very few friends when it comes to a court case."

"Suppose Patrick *doesn't* get off?—He'll do me damage."

Ewart Thornton suddenly desired to ring off. The act of gossiping with her over the telephone was a need, but the need was fulfilled in the act. He did not like it when the conversation seemed to be getting somewhere. "Patrick will do me harm." She upset him by going on like this. What if Patrick did her harm? Ewart felt uneasy about Patrick. He might well do harm. It was best to keep out of Patrick's reach. Patrick was definitely in touch with things out there in the Unseen.

"Patrick," said Freda, "has the *power* to do—"

"Freda my dear, I must go. Mounds of homework."

He sulked for a moment after he had put down the receiver, then he rose fatly, and presently stood up tall so that his hips lost their broadness. He tidied his room for the night. He put this away and that in its place, and sighed for his superannuation.

Marlene sat in her indignation, awaiting the meeting of the Interior Spiral. Everyone was late. It was a quarter to nine and the meeting had been called for half-past eight. The six coffee cups and the plate of biscuits stood on the tray like messages of regret for inability to attend. Ewart Thornton had said he would not come. Still, one had hoped. . . . Tim, to whom had been offered this unique opportunity of becoming acquainted with the Interior Spiral, was *out*. Out—she had seen her solicitor that morning and Tim was out of her Will. Five others had promised, were expected, might still come, would surely . . . Patrick himself, why was he late? The two retired spinsters, the Cottons from round the corner, where were they? Disloyally attending those life classes they had recently taken up, Marlene had no doubt. She had told them of the urgency. Billy Raines, the photographer? Osbert Jacob? Jacynthe— The door bell rang.

It was Patrick.

"I'm sorry to be late," he uttered in his half-voice, "but Alice, I've had trouble with Alice. Keeps talking of suicide . . . one day . . . suicide. It's sure to happen."

"That girl should be in a home," Marlene said. "You are too good to her, Patrick. She is only after what she can get. You are too good."

She placed her arm round his shoulders and he rested his head upon her bosom of bones.

"Well," she said, "take your coat off, Patrick. It is nine o'clock and no one has come. I fear we are deserted, but we are not a sinking ship. Not yet. I told everyone of the urgency, and what was to be discussed. After all I have done for the Infinity. My own nephew, my own flesh and blood, has—" The door bell rang.

At first she thought it was the Rector of Dees coming up the stairs. She had not expected the Rector of Dees, since he was getting on in years and the trains were so irregular. But she had written to him. And now he had come. "In my hour of need," she called down the stairs. "Dear Rector."

He looked up from his wide-brimmed hat. It was not the Rector of Dees, it was Father Socket of the enemy faction, protector of Dr. Garland so-called.

183

"Well," said Marlene, blocking the doorway.

Father Socket removed his hat and looked humble. "May I come and break bread with you?" he said.

"Come this way," Marlene said.

She took him into her sitting room where Patrick stood by the fire. Father Socket held out his hand to Patrick.

"I have come to make my peace," he said.

Patrick placed his effortless hand in the strong white-hairy one of Father Socket. White hairs bristled on Father Socket's face. He had not shaved.

"Dear lady," he said to Marlene. "I have been through the deep waters."

"Did you say you were hungry?" said she, perceiving he had come as an ally.

"It was a manner of speaking," he said. "I have come to ask you to accept what assistance I can offer in your courageous efforts to—"

"You want to witness for Patrick at the trial?"

"I do. I have been greatly deceived in my clairvoyant protégé, Dr. Garland. The serpent's—"

"He is no clairvoyant," said Marlene, "and he is no doctor."

"You are right," said Father Socket. "And would that I had known it earlier. He is tonight under arrest for activities the nature of which I will not sully my lips by describing. I myself have just come from the police station where I was given to understand that attempts had been made to implicate myself in these activities. Fortunately—"

"What were the activities?"

"Young women were involved. I say no more," said Father Socket. "Fortunately there is no shred of evidence against me. I have been away for some days, and I find on my return this afternoon that my flat has been searched in my absence. Needless to say, nothing of the least incriminating nature was found. My name is clear. I have come straight to you to offer my services in atonement for the harm done to Mr. Seton by Dr. Garland."

"Doctor so-called," said Marlene.

"A very wise move," Patrick said meekly to Father Socket. Father Socket looked at him, opened his mouth and closed it again.

"We must have our refreshments," said Marlene. "The Interior Spiral goes on!" She went to heat the coffee.

"A very wise move," Patrick said to Father Socket.

"The police have no evidence against me," Socket said.

"Not unless I lay it before them," Patrick said meekly, "because I have proof of the facts."

"I have come to offer my services, my son," said Socket. "I cannot do more. Under the influence of my cloth, my evidence—"

"Come now," Marlene said, bearing in the coffee pot, "we shall refresh ourselves while we discuss the details. How glad I am, after all, that the members of our little Interior have defected! They were not worth their salt. All things work together for good. Do you take sugar, Father?"

"No, nor coffee at this hour, if I may be excused."

"Details," said Marlene. "Now, it is a question, before we see Patrick's counsel, of what you were doing on the morning of the twelfth of August. You were at Patrick's rooms on that morning, receiving a private séance. Patrick was in a trance. . . . You saw a police car pull up outside just as you were leaving the premises . . . his statement . . . in a trance."

By midnight they were rehearsed.

"Before you leave," Marlene said, "shall we go into the Sanctuary for a few moments' spiritual repose?"

In the Sanctuary a dim green light was burning. Patrick automatically took the carved-oak séance chair while Marlene and Socket sat facing him.

They breathed deeply. Suddenly Patrick's head jerked backwards. Marlene whispered to Socket, "Take my hand. He is going into a trance. He may prophesy."

Patrick gurgled. His eyes rolled upward. Water began to run from the sides of his mouth which at last he opened wide. In a voice not his, he pronounced,

"I creep."

Marlene's arm went rigid. Socket tried to release his hand but could not.

Patrick's mouth was foaming. His head drooped and his eyes closed. He breathed loudly. His fingers twitched on the end of the chair-arm. Presently he lifted up his head again and his eyes opened into slits.

Marlene said, "He's coming round."

They left the Sanctuary of Light, Marlene assisting Patrick.

"Did I give utterance?" Patrick said. "What did I say?"

Walter Prett leaned his bulk over the bar of the wine club in Hampstead. It had just opened and he was the first customer. He said to the barmaid, "I say, Chloe, you know everyone, don't you?"

"Just about," she said.

"Do you know Isobel Billows?"

"Now who is she?" Chloe said, concentrating her sharp young face on the subject.

"She was married to Carr Billows of Billows Flour."

"Oh, Flourbags?"

"Yes, his first wife."

"I don't know of her," Chloe said. "What about her?"

"She's got lots of money. I broke her china the other day."

"Whatever do you mean, you naughty boy?"

"I'll have another," Walter said.

"You broke her china?"

"Yes, all her china tea-cups. They were on a tray. I smashed the lot."

"Why d'you do that?" Chloe said, polishing the glasses on the counter so that her time should not be altogether wasted.

"Why? That's what I ask myself between opening times. I love that woman, Chloe. And yet I go and behave like a hog."

"Just a minute," said Chloe, drawing inspiration from the embossed cornice. "Just a minute. Haven't I heard that she's got a barrister friend?"

"She has indeed. Martin Bowles. Do you know him?"

"No, I don't think—"

"No, you wouldn't know him. He's nobody. Only he hangs round Isobel for her money. He's the financial wizard, you see. And lines his own pocket on the right side of the law. A common little, vulgar little—"

"Now don't start that," Chloe said, "Walter please. Not at this hour of the evening. Hallo Eccie," she said as Francis Eccles came in.

"And he's bald," said Walter. "At least I've got a good head of hair." He shook his white mane.

"You could do with a trim," said Chloe.

"I've resigned from the British Council," said Eccie.

Walter hugged him like a bear and embraced him on both cheeks. He drew from his pocket three five-pound notes and gave one to Eccie. "What's this for?" Eccie said.

"A congratulatory gift."

"The return of a loan," said Chloe. "I remember the last time you were here—"

"Vulgar little lower-middle-class ideas you have, Chloe. I do not borrow and return. I take. I give."

"You can give me sixteen-and-six and clear out," Chloe said. "I won't be talked to like that."

Walter beamed at her.

"Yes, it's all right when you're in the right mood," Chloe said, "but you turn about like the weather."

"My lectures," said Eccie, "were designed to reveal the essence of art from Botticelli to Kandinsky, with reference to the lives of the artists themselves, supported by coloured plates, excellent reproductions. Those lectures have stood the test—"

"I should leave out the lives of the artists," Walter said. "They don't bear looking into."

"Oh come, I wouldn't say that."

"They break up ladies' china cups," Walter said mournfully.

"Since when were you an artist?" Chloe said.

Walter looked dangerous.

187

"Walter, now Walter," said Eccie, "don't *do* anything."

"I have spent a long time not doing anything," Walter said. "The sins of the artist are sins of omission. You should do a lecture on that, Eccie, with reference to the lives of the art critics."

"Well, as I was saying," Eccie said, "this chap called me in, and he said . . ."

"I pray," said Alice, "day and night. I go into churches and pray if the doors are open, and I pray that Patrick will be saved from prison."

"I wouldn't build on it," Elsie said.

"I am building on it. I pray for Patrick, and that's the test. If Patrick doesn't get off, I don't believe in God."

"Patrick hasn't much chance, with the statement he made to the police against him."

"He was half in a trance when he made that statement. There's a police officer that's got an influence on Patrick, and he talked him into it. Patrick was just out of a trance."

"The jury won't know what a trance is."

"They'll learn."

"There's a prejudice against spiritualism," Elsie said.

"Oh can't you look on the bright side, Elsie?"

"I don't know what's bright about you having Patrick wearing you down for the rest of your life."

"Well, he's my choice, Elsie."

"I know that. I'm afraid for you."

"Don't be afraid for me. And you needn't be afraid for Patrick either, now that Father Socket's come forward to speak for him. There's no denying the impression Father Socket makes on people."

"Father Socket?" Elsie said. "He's against Patrick. He was in with Mike Garland. A couple of *those*."

"There's been a rift. Garland is in trouble with the police and let Father Socket down. So Father Socket has come in with Patrick now. It's going to be all right, I feel it. Father Socket was with Patrick on the morning of the twelfth of August, and he saw Patrick in a trance just before the police came—"

"Twelfth of August was my birthday," Elsie said.

"So it was. Well, that was the day that Patrick made the statement. But everything's all right now."

"I don't see you need to pray for Patrick if you're so sure of that."

"It's a test of God," said Alice.

Elsie telephoned from Victoria Station to Ronald. "I've got to see you. It's about the evidence for Patrick Seton. Father Socket is going to give false evidence. I've got to see you."

"Father who?"

"That Father I told you about, that let me down."

"Oh, yes."

"Well, he's going to say that on the morning of twelfth of August—which was my birthday and I had the day off—he's going to swear—"

"Look," said Ronald, "I'm not the police."

"Can't I tell you? I'd rather give you the story."

"It's not my business. Go straight to the police station. Ask for Detective-Inspector Fergusson. Have you any evidence?"

"No, only my word."

"Well it's as good as Socket's. Go and see Mr. Fergusson."

"I'll ring and tell you what he says."

"No need to," Ronald said. "It's not my business."

"Then I don't know if I shall bother," Elsie said. "It's not my business either."

Marlene was on the night train to Scotland.

"I'm very sorry, Patrick," she had said, standing at the door of her flat, her baggage packed and visible in the hall behind her, keeping him out. "Very sorry indeed. But on consideration I simply must safeguard my reputation for the sake of the Circle. Nothing has changed, my feelings are the same, but on consideration I can't give evidence. And as it happens I've been

189

called away urgently. You have Father Socket. I am no loss."

She thought, now, perhaps she had been hard on Tim. It had been well-meaning of him to telephone to her.

"I say, Marlene, do keep out of the Seton case. You'll be charged with suborning, Marlene dear. The police may be on the alert for suborners, Ronald Bridges gave me the tip."

"What is suborning?"

"Conspiracy. Cooking up evidence in a law case beforehand."

"There has been no cooking up on my part. There is no contrary proof whatsoever. There—"

"It's a criminal offence, Marlene dear, you might go to Holloway prison. I should hate—"

"You beastly little fellow. You snivelling . . ."

She had hung up the receiver in the middle of his protests. All the same, on consideration . . .

The train to Dundee was a rocky one. She stood up in her bunk and tried to adjust the air-conditioning equipment of the sleeping compartment, but failed. She pressed the bell. No one came. She wondered if Patrick might have some spiritual power over her, even in Scotland. She could not sleep.

"The key," said Dr. Lyte miserably, handing Patrick the key.

"A month's supply of insulin," he said, handing Patrick the prescription. "When will you be going?"

"The day after the trial. Alice is upset, you know. Very depressed. She needs the holiday."

"I'll be seeing you in court then tomorrow, Mr. Fergusson."

"Yes, Patrick. Be there at quarter past ten."

"If I get off, Mr. Fergusson, I may have some news for you."

"Let's have your information now, then, Patrick."

"I'd rather wait and see if I get off."

"Your news wouldn't be about Socket, would it?"

"I'd rather not say, Mr. Fergusson."

"We need information about Socket. I don't mind admitting it," said Fergusson.

"That statement I signed in August—you'll be using it in court?" Patrick said.

"Yes, Patrick. We can't let you get away with that, I'm afraid. You've been useful to us, but a statement's a statement. It's filed."

"You got me in a weak moment when I gave you that statement," Patrick whispered. "I was upset, you remember, Mr. Fergusson—" He looked at the broad shoulders and did not want ever to have to leave the chair in which he sat contemplating them, and go out into the streets again.

"I have no recollection," said Fergusson, "that you were upset."

"Don't you remember, I was all shaken up that morning?"

"Yes Patrick, I know that. But as far as the law is concerned I have no recollection."

"There's the question of the letter," Patrick said.

"It was foolish of you to go and forge that letter. Another couple of years on your sentence at least."

"Our expert is convinced the letter's genuine," Patrick mumbled.

"Our expert isn't," said Fergusson.

Patrick wrenched himself away. But when he had plunged out into the street again, he felt better, and considering the chances, was confident of his release, so that he did not give thought to the matter again that day, but thought of Alice.

Chapter 12

FROM TIME to time throughout the trial, Patrick Seton sat in the dock visualizing, with fretful eagerness, Alice as she should lie on the mountainside, crumpled up, overdosed with insulin; the liberation of Alice's spirit was so imminent, it was like a sunny radiance to distract his understanding from the proceedings of the court.

When the time came for him to speak, he was lucid and calm and clear-voiced. Alice had never heard him speak so clearly, she was astonished.

"His voice has changed, hasn't it?" she whispered to Matthew, up in the public gallery.

"I don't know," Matthew said. "How should I know what his voice is like?"

"I think he must be making a special effort," Alice whispered. "He feels a strong clear voice is called for."

"Don't talk. I want to listen," Matthew said, "to this bit."

"He's doing well, isn't he?" said Alice. "After the mess they made of the Prosecution case this morning—"

"Don't talk," Matthew said, leaning over the rail of the gallery. "I want to listen."

"I do think," Alice said, "that Elsie might have come."

Ronald walked through the late night streets, recovering his strength. He had spent the day in court. He had been the third witness for the Prosecution.

"Have you ever in your life made a mistake?" said the Defence counsel in his cross-examination.

"Yes," said Ronald.

"This couldn't be one of them?"

"I have never, so far as I know, made a mistake in a case of forgery."

"So far as you know. Thank you, Mr. Bridges— Oh, oh . . ."

"Oh!" said the whole world at once, "what's happened? He's falling, fainting."

Ronald had put on his best dark suit for the occasion. He had arrived at the Criminal Court at ten minutes past ten. He had never before seen Martin Bowles in his wig and gown in court; it was an amazing sight. Martin had become instantly wise, unimpeachable. Once, at Isobel Billows', she having found Martin's wig at the back of his car and brought it into the house, Ronald had seen her try it on and, watching herself in the rather dim gilt-framed looking glass, recite,

"The quality of mercy is not strained . . ."

"They always say that," said Martin. "Women, when they try on a lawyer's wig, always do that."

The case opened at half-past ten. Hugh Farmer, counsel for the Defence, lolled back against the bench, sometimes whispering to his pupil behind him while the indictment was read for the second time. He was thinking of his elder daughter, at that moment taking her most important examination in music.

"Fraudulent conversion . . . forgery . . . Mrs. Freda Flower."

Martin Bowles got up to open the case for the Prosecution. Hugh Farmer watched him respectfully as Martin gave small reasonable waves of his hand, with upturned palm, towards the jury.

"Detective-Inspector Fergusson will read you a statement made and signed by the accused . . .

"Mrs. Freda Flower will tell you . . .

"I will call an expert in the detection of forgery who will give evidence on the count of . . ."

Now Fergusson was in the witness box, not in uniform. He took his oath. He read Patrick's statement: ". . . I was tempted, and fell. The cheque was for premium and defence bonds. Mrs. Flower asked me to obtain them for her. She felt they were safer with me. I did not buy the bonds. I do not know where the money has gone. I have read this over . . ."

Hugh Farmer got up to cross-examine.

"Mr. Fergusson, when you saw Mr. Seton on the afternoon of twelfth August, the day on which you say he made this statement, did you notice anything peculiar about him?"

"Nothing whatsoever," said Fergusson.

"Are you sure?"

"Absolutely certain," said Fergusson.

"Nothing about the eyes? No slight foaming at the mouth?"

The judge said, "Mr. Farmer, what is the—"

"It is relevant, my lord. My client is a spiritualistic medium and I shall show that he was in a trance when he signed that statement at the police station." He resumed his cross-examination.

"You said just now you were unaware, when you obtained this statement from Mr. Seton, that he had received a letter from Mrs. Flower asking him to use the money for his own purposes?"

"He said nothing about a letter on that occasion."

"Then Mr. Seton called on you the following week and told you he had made his statement while in a dazed condition, and wished to withdraw it?"

"I have no recollection of that."

"He told you he had in his possession a letter from Mrs. Flower in which she made it plain that the cheque was freely given for his use in his profession?"

"I have no recollection of him saying that."

"When you say you have no recollection you mean that in fact you do not remember whether he said it or whether he did not? He might in fact have stated his desire to withdraw his statement or to make a further statement, but it has slipped your recollection."

"He didn't ask to withdraw his statement or make a further one. He said nothing about a letter on that occasion."

"You have said you did not know about the existence of a letter from Mrs. Flower until some weeks later."

"That is correct."

"You said . . ."

Alice whispered to Matthew, "You can see the power he's got over Patrick. Just look at poor Patrick."

Patrick was sitting in the dock between two policemen, looking at tall square Fergusson with his head slightly to one side and tears shining in his pale eyes.

Next came Freda Flower. She began to swear on the Bible, glanced towards Patrick, and ended on a faltering note.

"You are a widow?" said Martin Bowles. ". . . You let rooms for a living? . . . Do you know the accused? . . . How long have you known the accused? . . . Did he offer to do a little decorating and painting in your house? . . . When did you become interested in the spiritualist movement? . . . Did you attend séances with the accused?"

"Yes," said Freda Flower. ". . . Yes . . . Yes . . . That's right . . . I started going to spiritualist meetings with Mr. Seton, that would be about three months after he came to my house."

"He was in charge of these meetings?"

"Oh no, he was the medium."

"Can you describe to the court in your own words what took place when Mr. Seton acted as a medium?"

"Well, he went under and I must say he always gave every satisfaction as a medium, I must say that. He—"

"When you say he went under, Mrs. Flower, what does that mean? He sat in a chair, did he not?"

"Yes, he was bound to the chair hands and feet."

"And this was in the dark."

"Well there was always a small light burning in the Sanctuary."

"There was a dim light in the séance room where the meetings were held— Am I right? . . ."

"Yes, that's right . . . bound hand and foot to a chair. . . ."

"Could you describe the trance, please. You must remember that most people present in this court have not attended a spiritualist meeting."

"He closed his eyes and went under."

"He appeared to lose consciousness?" said Martin.

"No, because he spoke as a medium after that. The control took over, you see."

"He appeared to be unaware of what was going on around him?"

"Oh, yes."

"Will you describe his appearance?"

"Well, you see, he's a medium. His eyes rolled upward and he foamed a bit at the mouth and his legs and arms twitched as far as was possible because they were bound to the chair."

"Did he obtain messages purporting to come from an invisible world?"

"Yes, he got through to the other side. He—"

"Were any of these messages directed specifically to you?"

"Yes, he got through to my late husband." She looked at Patrick and looked away. Patrick was accusing her. "His messages were often a great comfort," she said.

"These messages from your late husband through the mediumship of Seton contained practical advice?"

"Yes, sometimes. Well, not exactly practical, but—"

"Will you give an example?"

"Well, only advice to keep happy and cheerful," she said, on the verge of tears.

"Anything else?"

"Well, it's difficult . . ."

"On one occasion there was something about money?"

The Defence counsel was allowed his objection.

Martin said, "Were you advised as to your friends, the company you kept?"

"Yes," said Freda, "my late husband wanted me to be friends with Mr. Seton."

"Was this according to what the accused said while in his trance?"

"Yes."

"Now," said Martin, "about this cheque for two thousand pounds . . ."

Up in the gallery Matthew said to Alice, "She's giving very bad evidence."

"What other sort of evidence could she give?" said Alice.

"Will you look at this cheque for two thousand pounds made out to Patrick Seton and say if that is your signature?" Martin was saying.

"Yes," she said, "it's mine."

"Martin Bowles is a clot," Matthew said.

"He hasn't got much of a case," said Alice.

Martin was referring to Freda Flower's statement.

"Yes," she said. ". . . Yes, I told him to buy them for me." . . . "No, it was his suggestion." . . . "I thought he had bought the bonds." . . . "Well I thought the bonds would be safer with him. . . ."

"What do you mean by safer?" said the judge.

"I thought he would keep them safer than me," she said.

Patrick looked up at Alice. She smiled at him. Her pregnancy, he thought, is hidden by the railings of the balcony. I'm winning. She won't live.

"I did in a way promise him a little help with his spiritual research. I said he should ask me for money."

197

Some of the jury were making notes.

"And did he ask you?"

"No, he never asked . . ."

Martin read out the letter to the court. "I should add," he said, "that the letter is undated."

"Will you look at this letter," he said, "and tell the court whether you wrote it or not?"

"No, I never wrote it."

"Is that handwriting similar to your own?"

"It looks very like my writing. But I couldn't have written it unless I was in a trance or something."

"Have you ever been in a trance?" said the judge.

"I don't think so, my lord."

"Don't you know? Have you ever foamed at the mouth and rolled up your eyes, and twitched?"

"No, my lord."

Matthew said, as the cross-examination began, "Now we're for it."

"Serve her right," Alice said. "She's just showing herself up for what she is."

"You have said that Mr. Seton gave every satisfaction as a medium?" said Patrick's counsel.

"Yes, he was always a good medium."

"You had every faith in his powers?"

"Yes."

"And still have?"

"Oh, yes."

"You had every reason to believe that he was genuine, whatever may be the opinions of others on spiritualism in general?"

"Oh, he was genuine, I admit."

"And you say he brought you comfort, and did repairs and decorations to your house?"

"Oh, yes, he—"

"Did you pay him for those repairs and decorations?"

"Well, not exactly. I let the rent go. We were very friendly, you see, after I got to know him."

"And, finding him trustworthy as a medium, you had confidence in his practical advice and judgment."

"Yes, I told him everything."

"His lordship has asked you whether you have ever been in a trance. I am going to repeat that question."

"I don't think so, sir."

"Think carefully. Because you said"—he consulted his notes —"you told the court, when you looked at the letter, 'It looks very like my writing. I couldn't have written it unless I was in a trance or something.'" His voice rose with nasal emphasis on the words "or something," and he repeated her words again: "unless I was in a trance or something." He put down his notes and breathed deeply. "Now, Mrs. Flower," he said, "I am going to put it to you that you have, in fact, had the experience of trances."

"I couldn't say," she said. "It only looks funny that my handwriting should be on the letter and I don't remember writing it."

"And it may have been written while you were in a trance?"

The judge said, "Has anyone ever seen you in a state of trance? Has anyone ever told you or suggested to you that you have been in a trance?"

"No, sir. But I could have been in a trance on my own."

"Were you in anything like a trance last April when it is suggested that the letter was written?" said the judge.

"I couldn't really say. I was poorly in April."

The Defence counsel continued: "You admit the possibility that one day when you were alone you wrote that letter while in a state of trance."

"It *is* possible. If you'd seen as much as I have of spiritualism, you would know that the gift can descend on anyone, even an untrained person."

"By 'gift,'" said the judge, "do you mean a state of trance?"

"Yes, and then becoming a medium and getting in touch," she said.

"Let us get this clear," said the judge. "A person in a state of trance as you call it, rolls up his or her eyes, foams at the mouth and twitches. Then he or she begins to speak?"

"Sometimes they say nothing."

"What happens," said the judge, "when they come out of their trance? Describe it."

"They look very exhausted, sir, and don't know where they are for some minutes."

"Have you ever experienced a sensation, while alone, of exhaustion and not knowing where you are, by which you could assume you had just come out of a trance?"

"Sometimes I've dropped off and felt a bit strange, my lord, for a few minutes."

"Have there been any other signs of a trance such as saliva from foaming at the mouth?"

"Oh no, sir."

"Do you yourself think you have been in a state of unconsciousness," said the judge, very slow and clear, "and at the same time able to write that letter? Try to be explicit."

"I don't know, sir, I'm sure."

Martin got up to re-examine her. "He'll make matters worse," Matthew said, and he was right.

Martin's tones became menacing as she muddled on. "Mrs. Flower, I am going to call an expert," Martin said nastily to his witness, "who will swear that this letter is a forgery. Are you suggesting that he is mistaken?"

"No, I'll abide by what he says," said Freda.

"Here comes Ronald," said Matthew, "in his new dark chalk-stripe. He should have been a civil servant."

"Detestable man," said Alice.

"Not a bit of it," said Matthew. "You don't know him at all."

"The jury are whispering together. Are they allowed to do that?" Alice said.

"Yes," said Matthew. "It's their court, really. Everything depends on them."

"I don't like that blond woman," Alice said. "With her dyed hair she shouldn't be on a jury."

Ronald, as he walked up the steps to the witness box, caught a flash-like impression of the jury, as they leaned across and consulted each other, head to head, and this reminded him of some fresco of the Last Supper. The jury righted itself when Ronald reached his post.

Ronald's evidence, as he compared the precise points at which the handwriting of the letter departed from examples of Freda Flower's handwriting and coincided with examples of Patrick Seton's, provided a perceptible rest-cure for the bewigged minds. The barristers stopped fidgeting with their papers. The judge stopped resting his head on his left hand.

"I have found," said Ronald, "from microscopic examination that certain letters have been formed from a starting-point different from those of Mrs. Flower's handwriting. The letter 'o' for example—although to the naked eye it is completely closed both in Exhibits B and D—has apparently been formed by different hands. In Exhibit B the 'o' has been started from the top. In Exhibit D the 'o' has been started from the right-hand curve."

"Exhibit B," said the judge to the jury, "is the letter which it is alleged has been forged. Exhibit D is the example of Mrs. Flower's handwriting."

"The effect of trembling in some of the upward strokes of the signature in Exhibit B," said Ronald, "is visible under the microscope. This trembling in some of the upward strokes is not present in the body of the letter and suggests that the signature has been traced. The formation of the letter 'l' in Exhibits B, C and D—"

"Just a moment," said the judge. "The jury must be clear. Exhibit B is the alleged forgery. Exhibit D is the example of Mrs. Flower's handwriting. Exhibit C is the example of the accused's writing."

"The formation of the letter 'l' in Exhibits—"

"He's marvellous," said Matthew. "I didn't know Ronald had it in him."

Ronald was fumbling in his inner pocket.

"Too damned smart," said Alice. "You just wait till he's cross-examined. We've got a first-rate barrister in Farmer."

"What is your conclusion, Mr. Bridges?" said Martin.

"That the letter, Exhibit B, is a forgery and that it has been forged by the accused."

Ronald was fumbling in his outer pockets.

"Now here's our man," said Alice, as the Defence counsel heaved himself to his feet.

But Farmer was content to await the conflicting evidence of his expert, he was content to say to Ronald,

"Mr. Bridges, have you ever made a mistake?"

"Yes," said Ronald.

"This opinion of yours couldn't be one of them?"

"I have never, so far as I know, made a mistake in a case of forgery."

"So far as you know. Thank you, Mr. Bridges— Oh, oh, watch out . . ."

Ronald swayed. He fumbled in his pockets for his pills. They were in his other suit, at home. He gave up. He stumbled down the steps and fell two steps before he got to the bottom. There he foamed at the mouth. His eyes turned upward, and the drum-like kicking of his heels began on the polished wooden floor.

"Is this man a medium?" said the judge.

The clerk approached Ronald. Two male members of the jury came out of their places, looking suddenly deprived of any excuse for their presence in the court. It was difficult to get near Ronald. "Put something between his teeth," said Martin Bowles, in the tones of a zoophobic veterinary practitioner. "He's an epileptic."

The judge rested his head in his left hand. Patrick looked solemnly up at Alice. She was peering over the balcony, looking down at Ronald. Patrick was filled with solace at the sight. I will look down on her, he thought, when she is lying on the mountainside, and the twitching will cease.

"Do you believe in prayer?" said Alice to Matthew when they

went down, after the fuss was over, to lunch in the public canteen.

"He's putting up a marvellous fight," Alice whispered. "I've never seen Patrick in such good form. I've never heard him speak up like this. It's as if he was fighting for his life."

Once or twice Patrick glanced at her from the witness box for he could get a better view of her from there. The thought of Alice kept him going.

"I know," whispered Alice, "he's making the effort for me. It's as if he was fighting for my life. He's not an outspoken man as a rule. It shows what's in Patrick."

The answers came without hesitation, clear and strong. It might have been the voice of one of those army men who know exactly what they think, and say it. He took courage from his desire to be acquitted, rather than timidity from his fear of being convicted and the practised members of the jury noticed this. Ronald, sitting defiantly in his exhaustion among the witnesses, managed to recall the last time he had heard Patrick speak. That had been at the Maidstone Assizes. Then, Patrick had mumbled.

Freda Flower sat horrified at Patrick's manner.

"I am, in spite of my calling, a man of the world, a practical man. . . .

"There was never any question of my buying defence bonds. . . .

"Mrs. Flower frequently went into a trance. She is herself an excellent medium with extraordinary psychic powers. . . .

"It is impossible that she does not know that she possesses this gift. . . .

"I suggest, without wishing to implicate Mrs. Flower further than necessary, that she became incensed when I left her, and dreamed up this story. . . .

"I prefer to say no more about my private relationship with Mrs. Flower, if that is permissible. . . .

"I made the statement at the police station while still in a state of semi-trance. In such a condition the subject is highly suggestible. . . . I signed this statement at the suggestion of the officer in charge. I have no recollection of doing so. . . .

"I would describe the statement as a forced confession. . . ."

Patrick kept his eyes off Fergusson. He looked from time to time at Alice.

"You would think he'd been saving it up," Alice breathed. "Like an athlete that spares himself till the time comes."

"I deny it," Patrick said, when asked if he had forged the letter.

His counsel sat down. Martin Bowles coughed and stood up and adjusted his robes.

"Do you really expect the court to believe, Mr. Seton, that a widow in Mrs. Flower's position would hand you over her life savings of two thousand pounds to use for your own purposes?"

"If you will refer to her letter you will see that she requested me to use the money to further my psychic and spiritual work. She did not ask me to use it for my own purposes. I have used the money to further my psychic and spiritual work as she requested."

"You have heard the evidence of the Crown's graphologist. I suggest that Mrs. Flower did not write that letter, but that you forged it after you had made the statement to the police, in order to discredit the statement."

"I deny it; and I deny that I made a statement to the police in any circumstances which could be described as free."

Matthew whispered, "I wish my sister-in-law could have seen all this."

"What's it got to do with her?" said Alice.

"Hush," said Matthew, "don't talk."

The judge said, "In what manner have you used this money to further your psychic and spiritual work?"

"I have spent it on the scientific training of mediums, the purchase of books on psychical research, and in travelling abroad to exchange views on the subject with foreign mediums, and on travelling in this country to extend my knowledge and impart it.

Spiritualism is a science, and a science requires financial support."

"In what does the training of mediums consist?" said the judge.

"A scientific course comprising various exercises of mind and body. An untrained medium is proved by experience to be a menace to society. Properly trained, the medium is a useful and practical vehicle of human aspirations."

The blond member of the jury was leaning forward attentively. Seton has got a new customer, Ronald thought, if he gets out of this.

The judge's pen scratched on. The typist in the corner listlessly pounded her silent machine. Martin continued:

"Do you consider it a reputable action to accept money from a widow in Mrs. Flower's circumstances to use for your professional advancement?"

The moron, Ronald thought, why doesn't he pin him down on the questions of the forgery and the bonds.

"I was acting under Mrs. Flower's instructions. I do not need professional advancement. I employed the money for the professional advancement of others."

"I suggest that if you spent two thousand pounds between April and August you spent it somewhat rapidly."

"Mrs. Flower said in her letter that she left the details of the disposal of the money entirely to me."

Why does he go on about the spending?—Ronald sat with the demonic aftermath of his fit working within him. Why doesn't he plug away at the forgery, he has my evidence? Then it occurred to Ronald: He doesn't believe in my evidence, he doubts its validity, and this barrister can't argue a case he doesn't believe in.

"You admit," said Martin, "that you accepted two thousand pounds from a woman of middle age?"

And you deny, thought Ronald, that you are swindling Isobel Billows?

"You have said," said Martin, "in reply to a question, 'I prefer to say no more about my private relationship with Mrs. Flower.' "

"That is correct," said Patrick.

"May I ask why you are so reticent?"

"My lord," said Patrick, addressing the judge, "if it is not relevant to the case, I would prefer—"

"I can't see why you need go further into that question, Mr. Bowles," said the judge.

"I submit that it is a relevant question," Martin said, "since the jury will wish to know the extent of the influence exerted by the accused upon Mrs. Flower."

"Very well," said the judge and rested his head on his hand.

"I suggest that your relations with Mrs. Flower were of an intimate nature," said Martin.

"I deny it," said Patrick with an elaborate air of gallantry.

"And that you used these intimate relations to gain an influence over Mrs. Flower?"

And, thought Ronald, on the strength of these intimate relations you obtained control of Isobel Billows' money.

"I deny it," said Patrick. "Mrs. Flower herself has said nothing of our intimate relations."

"And," said Martin, "you employed this influence to obtain Mrs. Flower's savings."

"I deny it."

"In your statement to the police of the twelfth August you said—" Martin shuffled and found his document—"you said 'Early in April Mrs. Flower handed me a cheque for two thousand pounds for the purpose of purchasing premium bonds and defence bonds. I was tempted and fell. I did not purchase the bonds. I do not know where the money has gone.' Now, Mr. Seton," said Martin, "I put it to you that this is the true and accurate story."

"I deny it. I was incapable of making a statement. I was in a state of semi-trance, and was in a condition of high susceptibility to any suggestion whatsoever."

"Do you mean that Detective-Inspector Fergusson hypnotized you?"

206

For a moment Patrick seemed to sag. His lower jaw receded.

"Are you suggesting that Detective-Inspector Fergusson invented this story?"

"He put the words in my mouth."

"I did not hear," said the judge, for Patrick's voice had suddenly failed.

Patrick looked at Alice and revived. "He put the words in my mouth," he said out loud.

"How did you get to the police station if you were in a state of partial insensibility?"

"I was taken there in a police car. Two policemen called at my rooms immediately after I had completed a séance."

"On the morning of twelfth August?"

"Yes."

"Do you usually conduct séances in the morning?"

"This was a private séance."

Patrick was allowed to go. The judge looked at his watch. "Is medical evidence to be called as to the effects of a trance?" he said.

Patrick's counsel said, "No my lord, there appears to be no useful source of medical opinion devoted to the nature and effects of the spiritualistic trance specifically."

Martin Bowles looked confused. Ronald thought, he has slipped up properly. He should have brought in a cataleptist to refute them.

The door from the witness's room opened and Ronald looked round to see a fellow-graphologist, sweet old Fairley, emerging. Fairley climbed the steps to the witness stand, took off his glasses and exchanged them for another pair. He read the oath slowly, and took his usual leisure throughout.

"So that, in your opinion," said Patrick's counsel, "mere inconsistencies in the formation of characters which can only be observed under the microscope do not imply that the characters have been formed by separate hands."

"I do not say so," drawled Fairley. "That would be too large a generalization. I say only that in my opinion, the inconsistencies between the formation of characters on the document marked Exhibit B and those on the document marked Exhibit C, taken together with peculiarities common to Exhibits B and D, do not necessarily lead to the conclusion that Exhibit B is a forgery."

The jury fidgeted.

"You are saying," said the barrister, "that the letter which the Crown alleges to be a forged document, need not necessarily be so merely on the evidence afforded by the microscope?"

"Yes," said Fairley.

"What is the length of your experience in this field, Mr. Fairley?"

"Forty-six years," said Fairley.

Martin got up.

"The methods of forgery detection have changed in forty-six years, have they not?" Martin said.

"There have been developments," said Fairley.

"You changed your spectacles when you came into the witness box. Do you suffer from any weakness of eyesight?" Martin said.

It's a dirty world, thought Ronald.

"Yes," said Fairley courteously. "But I have an excellent optician who provides me with two pairs of spectacles. One pair is for normal use and the other is for reading."

"And you changed into your reading glasses in order to stand and give evidence in court?"

"I changed into my reading spectacles in order to read the oath, which I take seriously."

"Oh, quite," said Martin. "Did you," he said, "when you were examining the documents, notice any peculiarities in the formation of the letter 'o'?"

"Yes," said Fairley. "In Exhibit B the 'o' has been started from the top. In Exhibit D the 'o' has been started from the right-hand curve."

"Does that not suggest to you that these letters have been formed by different hands?"

"Not necessarily. There is always the possibility that the writer was at one moment in a disposition to start from the top, and at another time disposed to begin elsewhere."

"Do you agree that there are other inconsistencies similar to those which relate to the letter 'o'?"

"Yes."

"Do you agree that the peculiar formation of many letters in Exhibit B—the document which is alleged to be a forgery—coincide with peculiarities of formation in Exhibit C—the example of the accused's handwriting?"

"There are many similarities but not enough, in my opinion, to permit the inference that B and C are the work of the same hand."

"Did you observe in the course of your examination of the signature the effect of trembling in some of the upward strokes?"

"No," said Fairley.

"You did not find anything to suggest that the signature had been traced?"

"No," said Fairley.

"You are aware that an eminent graphologist, Mr. Ronald Bridges, has submitted that the effect of trembling in the upward strokes is an indication of tracing."

"I was not present at Mr. Bridges' evidence. But I agree that an effect of trembling in handwriting is sometimes due to a process of tracing. Sometimes it is due to sickness, fear, or old age."

"You agree that forgers commonly trace the signatures on false documents?"

"Oh, yes."

"You did not notice an effect of trembling in some of the upward strokes of the signature on the document alleged to be forged?"

"No, I did not observe any effect of trembling."

"Did you look for it?"

"Oh, yes, it is part of the routine."

"How does the scientific equipment available to Mr. Bridges compare with that available to yourself?"

"We use the same laboratories and stuff."

Ronald saw how vexed Martin was. He had told Martin that Fairley used private equipment, believing this to be so.

"But you did not notice this trembling effect, while Mr. Bridges did?" Martin said crossly.

Oh shut up, Ronald thought.

"There is room for varying opinion as to what is an effect of trembling," said Fairley.

"It couldn't be a question of eyesight?"

"The documents are greatly enlarged by the microscope," Fairley drawled wearily.

"Thank you," said Martin.

Fairley smirked slightly at Ronald as he left. Ronald winked. A member of the jury noticed this and whispered to his neighbor. They are saying, Ronald thought, that we are in our racket together, regardless of the law. But perhaps that's not what they are whispering.

The door through which Fairley had passed now admitted Father Socket in black suit and clerical collar, the last witness for the Defence. As he was shown up to the witness box, the main door on Ronald's right opened, and Elsie came in. She moved in beside Ronald and started to whisper to him. The attendant policeman placed a finger to his lips. Ronald pushed his note pad and pencil towards her. On it she wrote, "I've come to give evidence against Father Socket." Ronald wrote, "You're too late," and pushed it back.

"Isn't Father Socket marvellous?" whispered Alice.

"Father my eye," said Matthew.

Father Socket described himself as a clergyman.

"Of what religion?" said the judge.

"Of the spiritualist religion and allied faiths."

"Spiritualism has already this afternoon been described as a science. Is it a science or a religion?"

"It is a scientific religion, my lord, and has been recognized as such by countless eminent citizens including—"

"Yes, quite," said the judge, "I only want to get our definitions clear so that the jury can see what it is dealing with. There has been a great deal of mystification in this case."

Elsie was scribbling away on the note pad.

Socket's eye was on the jury.

"You remember the morning of twelfth August?" said his counsel. "Where were you . . . What were you doing . . . ?"

"At Mr. Seton's rooms . . . a private séance . . . he was in a trance, a deep trance. I am, if I may say so, something of an authority on the conditions of a spiritualistic trance. . . . I left Mr. Seton at ten minutes to twelve, he was in a state of complete exhaustion and insensibility to external surroundings."

Alice looked over from the gallery.

"Elsie's going to make trouble," she said. "What is she writing, down there? She wouldn't come and keep me company as a friend, but she's come to make trouble."

"She should have come up here with you," Matthew said, "but never mind, you've got me."

Elsie folded her note and gave it to the policeman, indicating Martin Bowles.

Father Socket kept his eye on the jury. The blond woman looked impressed.

"As I left the building after the séance I noticed a police car containing two police officers draw up outside the front door. This was just after ten minutes to twelve. . . ." Socket said.

"In your opinion, Mr. Socket," said Patrick's counsel, "was it likely that by twelve noon, less than ten minutes later, Mr. Seton would be in a reasonable and clear state of mind?"

"Certainly not. It is impossible. He would be in a state of semi-trance, perhaps not discernible at a casual glance, but certainly apparent to anyone attempting to question him. He would be in a suggestible condition. . . ."

"We've won the day!" said Alice.

Martin was looking at Elsie's two scribbled pages torn from the note pad.

The blond jurywoman spoke to her neighbour.

Patrick's barrister sat down. Martin got up.

"I suggest," said Martin to Socket, "that your evidence is a pack of lies from start to finish."

The jury seemed offended. Socket's white collar gleamed round his throat. It seemed a tasteless attack.

"It is nothing but the truth," said Socket, with a look of ministerial reproach.

"I have a witness in court," said Martin, "who is prepared to swear that you were not with the accused between the hours of ten a.m. and twelve noon on August the twelfth."

"Mr. Bowles," said the judge, "are you wanting to put in additional evidence at this stage?"

"I was about to ask . . ."

The judge looked at his watch. Then he looked hard at Socket.

"Yes, I'm quite sure it was the twelfth of August because it was my birthday, and that's why I took the day off," Elsie said.

"What time did you arrive at Mr. Socket's flat?" Martin said.

"Ten o'clock in the morning."

"What time did you leave?"

"One o'clock."

"Mr. Socket was present all morning?"

"Yes, he gave me dictation, and he read some poetry."

She started to leave the witness box immediately she had answered all Martin's questions. It was indicated to her that she had to remain for cross-examination. Patrick's counsel was conferring with Socket in whispers. Presently he straightened up.

"You say you took the day off from your work because it was your birthday?" Patrick's counsel hammered out.

"Yes."

"Was it not an odd way in which to spend your day off—going to work as a typist in a voluntary capacity?"

"Well, I was taken in by Father Socket. I thought he was doing good work and I thought he was a fine person."

"On what date did Mr. Socket dismiss you from his service?"

"He didn't dismiss me. I never went back after I sensed something wrong."

"I suggest that Mr. Socket dismissed you on or about the twentieth of July, and asked you not to come again."

"No, I left two weeks ago because I sensed something wrong."

"I suggest he dismissed you, and that you are embittered."

"Yes, I was embittered all right after I sensed something wrong," said Elsie like a needle.

The barrister became irritated. "You keep saying you sensed something wrong. What do you mean? —Let's have it. Did you sense something wrong with your sight, hearing, smell, touch, taste—which sense did you sense something wrong with?"

"I sensed it with my common sense," said Elsie, "when I went there and found a man with lipstick and a dressing gown that looked like—"

"Miss Forrest, you are an impulsive girl, aren't you?" said this counsel of Patrick's who now roused himself for work.

"Yes, fairly," she said, rather put out by his new intimacy of tone.

"You did not come forward with this evidence at the proper time. And yet you have seen fit to dash in at the last minute with accusations against a man whom up to two weeks ago, according to your own evidence, you thought to be a fine person. Why is that?"

"Well, I thought about it, and I decided it wasn't my business. Then this afternoon I decided to come along."

"On an impulse of malice?"

"Yes, if you want to put it like that," said Elsie.

"You admit to malice against Father Socket."

"I don't see why he should get away with his sin."

"You realize, Miss Forrest, that you have not brought a scrap of evidence to this court to support your story—apart from malice?"

"Well, you can take it or leave it," Elsie said. "I was with him all morning on August the twelfth."

"And you have no evidence to support your statement?"

"No," said Elsie, "there's only my word."

Alice said, "That girl's treacherous. Why did she have to mention the man with lipstick?"

Patrick's counsel told the jury that there could be no end to the calling of one witness to discredit another. He asked them to ignore the extraordinary and, on the face of it, wild accusations of Father Socket's former and, on her own admission, embittered typist, Miss Elsie Forrest. She had admitted to malice.

The extremely dubious evidence of Mrs. Freda Flower . . . Everything to show that she was in the habit of trances. . . .

The clear evidence of the accused . . . his insistence that the statement was not made while he was in a responsible condition. . . . Reflecting, as it did on our ancient liberties . . .

The case of forgery was wiped out by the evidence of Mr. Fairley. Particularly to be noted was Mr. Fairley's insistence on the effects of variable human moods on handwriting. . . .

The jury must rid itself of prejudice against spiritualism.

Patrick's counsel then listed a number of prominent persons, dead and alive, who had adorned the spiritualist movement. He looked at his watch and sat down.

Martin Bowles rose to recite the discredit of all witnesses except his own. "The letter is undated," said Martin. "Why? —Because when he forged that letter he forgot the exact date of the cheque which Mrs. Flower had given him, and which he now claims accompanied the letter." He repeated Elsie's story. He reminded the jury that Fairley was getting on in years, and though much to be respected, could hardly compete with a younger mind. He started to ridicule all references to the mediumistic trances which had cropped up in the case—"foaming mouths, upturned eyes, twitching limbs and so forth"—but seemed suddenly to be visited by a deterrent thought, which Ronald assumed to be a mental image of himself lying kicking and foaming only a few hours ago under the witness box. Martin switched away from trances and weighed into Patrick and his influence on Mrs. Flower.

"You will recall that this man affected a certain delicacy in revealing his intimate relations with Mrs. Flower. Yet he did not hesitate to defraud her. . . ."

Ronald, heavy with the effects of his fit, sat with his eyes on Martin.

"He did not hesitate to rob her, he did not hesitate to exert his influence by means of those intimate relations with Mrs. Flower."

With Isobel Billows, thought Ronald.

"And yet he stands here and poses as her protector. You observe the irony, ladies and gentlemen of the jury."

The irony, ladies and gentlemen, thought Ronald.

It was a very disreputable case, said the judge in his summing up, and in some respects a nauseating one. It was his duty to direct the jury to rid their minds of all prejudice against spiritualism as such. . . . It was his duty to define both fraudulent conversion and forgery. . . . Forgery was . . . Fraudulent conversion was . . .

This was a case which, if there were any substance in it, could have grave and serious implications. Detective-Inspector Fergusson had sworn on oath that the accused had made a certain statement while in a lucid condition of mind. That statement had been produced in court. It contained an admission of the charge of fraudulent conversion. It bore the signature of the accused.

Moreover, Detective-Inspector Fergusson had denied that the accused had at any subsequent time applied to withdraw the statement. The jury should give these facts their weightiest consideration.

"They always stand by the police," Alice whispered, "but the jury knows different."

The judge looked at his watch. Much, however, he was saying, hinged on the question of forgery.

The evidence of the two graphologists tended to cancel each other out and if he might say so, was less than useless. No prejudice should obtain in the case of Mr. Ronald Bridges whose unfortunate collapse in court, he understood, had been due to an inherent disease and was in no way connected with the dis-edifying trances described by various witnesses.

Mrs. Flower appeared to be a very foolish woman. It must be taken into account that she had strongly indicated in her evidence the possibility of having written the letter while in a state of insensibility. The jury would have the opportunity of examining the letter and forming their own conclusions on this point. But while such a doubt was present in Mrs. Flower's mind it must certainly receive every consideration. . . . The letter was undated. It had been suggested that the accused forgot the date of the cheque. . . .

A man was innocent until he was proved guilty. While there was reasonable doubt that the accused was the author of the letter he could not be found guilty.

The jury must be clear that if they brought in a verdict of Not Guilty for forgery they could not logically bring a verdict of Guilty for fraudulent conversion. Everything hung on the question of forgery. . . .

The evidence of Mr. Socket must be weighed against the evidence of Miss Elsie Forrest, and vice versa. The fact that Miss Forrest had offered evidence at the last moment must not be allowed to weigh against that evidence. She was, on her own admission, impulsive by nature. On the other hand she admitted to a motive of malice against Socket, and this, whether justified or not, must be taken into account.

"Whatever your sympathies in this case," he said, "it is the evidence that counts. I will run over the evidence once more. . . ."

The jury withdrew at twenty minutes to five. "We'll have time for tea," said Matthew. "They'll be out for at least an hour."

"The judge was against us," Alice said, "but the jury can't find him guilty if there's a reasonable doubt about the forgery. The judge said so himself."

"Come on," said Matthew.

She was looking at Patrick and he at her before he turned

through the dock door. His face was radiant. The bags packed, the insulin.

"Our bags are all ready packed," said Alice. "We can leave in the morning."

"The blond woman was looking pretty nasty about Socket after Elsie had finished."

"I'll never speak to Elsie again. The whole court was with us after Father Socket's evidence. The whole court. No matter what they say about evidence."

They sat over their hot canteen tea. "It's kicking," said Alice. "Oh, God, I wish this was over."

Patrick looked up at Alice. It was the only thing, to look and look at Alice. Imprisonment was not the end of the world, he had always found a niche in prisons. But now, this thirst for Alice. She is mine, I have paid. . . . She would probably twitch before she died. She had agreed by acquiescence.

The jury was filing in. It was twenty past five.

To make Alice into something spiritual. It was godlike, to conquer that body, to return it to the earth. . . .

"On the charge of forgery."

"Guilty."

"On the charge of fraudulent conversion."

"Guilty."

"I don't believe in God," said Alice. "There will have to be an appeal."

"Quiet, now," said Matthew.

"It was Elsie mentioning the man with lipstick," Alice said. "That did it. I knew!"

"It was a help," said Matthew.

Fergusson was up in the witness box again. He was reading out a list. At Canterbury in May 1923 . . . three months for larceny. At Surrey Quarter Sessions in 1930, six months for obtaining on false pretences . . . in 1932, six months . . . in 1942, eighteen months and six months to run consecutively for

217

fraudulent conversion . . . Maidstone Assizes, in 1948 three years for forgery and fraudulent conversion. He is described as a spiritualistic medium, unmarried, resident at . . ."

"What's this all about?" said Alice.

"They call it the antecedents. It's Patrick's criminal record."

"I don't believe it," she said. "There's got to be an appeal."

"He can't appeal with that record."

"The bags are packed," she said. "And he's a genuine medium."

"Just keep still," Matthew said. "Nothing matters."

"A most disreputable case," said the judge. "A widow . . . her savings. The distasteful proceedings—I may say without prejudice to any more respectable manifestations of the cult as might exist—the distasteful proceedings of the séance room and the scope it offers for the intimidation of weak people . . . The evidence given by Mr. Socket must be looked into: these courts must be kept clean of . . . Mrs. Flower has been a very foolish woman." He glanced towards Patrick. "Have you anything to say?"

Patrick looked at Fergusson and then at the judge.

"Only," he said, "to ask—"

"Speak up, please."

"Only to say that the lady I am living with is expecting a baby and needs me by her side, and—"

The judge did not look up. "I cannot sentence you to less than five years."

"I don't believe in God," said Alice, clutching her stomach.

Ronald went home to bed. He slept heavily and woke at midnight, and went out to walk off his demons.

Martin Bowles, Patrick Seton, Socket.

And the others as well, rousing him up: fruitless souls, crumbling tinder, like his own self which did not bear thinking of. But it is all demonology, he thought, and he brought them all to witness, in his old style, one by one before the courts of his mind. Tim Raymond, Ewart Thornton, Walter Prett, Matthew Finch

—will I, won't I marry her?—Eccie, and himself kicking under the witness box, himself, now, incensed; and all the rest of them. He sent these figures away like demons of the air until he could think of them again with indifference or amusement or wonder.

How long will it take, he wondered to distract his mind, for Matthew to marry Alice? Not knowing at the time that it would take four months—a week before the baby was born—Ronald laid a bet with himself for three months.

It is all demonology and to do with creatures of the air, and there are others besides ourselves, he thought, who lie in their beds like happy countries that have no history. Others ferment in prison; some rot, maimed; some lean over the banisters of presbyteries to see if anyone is going to answer the telephone.

He walked round the houses, calculating, to test his memory, the numbers of the bachelors—thirty-eight thousand five hundred streets, and seventeen point one bachelors to a street—lying awake, twisting and murmuring, or agitated with their bedfellows, or breathing in deep repose between their sheets, all over London, the metropolitan city.

"we can make a book about crocodiles!"

Amelie P

Protagonists

Adam 3 years, 11 months
Aidan 3 years, 4 months
Amelia 4 years, 10 months
Amelie C. 4 years, 3 months
Amelie P. 4 years, 8 months
Angus 4 years, 2 months
Aoife 4 years, 7 months
Arden 4 years, 0 months
Ashlei 3 years, 8 months
Ben 4 years, 5 months
Charlie 3 years, 11 months
Cordelia 3 years, 6 months
Decland 4 years, 3 months
Ela 3 years, 1 month
Elinor 4 years, 6 months
Ella 3 years, 6 months
Elliot 3 years, 0 months
Emily 3 years, 8 months
Erin 3 years, 1 month
Finn 4 years, 3 months
Frankie 3 years, 1 month
Gabrielle A. 3 years, 11 months
Gabrielle P. 3 years, 1 month
Georgius 3 years, 1 month
Harry 3 years, 5 months
James 3 years, 0 months

Kai 4 years, 6 months
Katie 4 years, 3 months
Kyran 3 years, 0 months
Lachlan 3 years, 6 months
Lucas 4 years, 9 months
Maddie 4 years, 6 months
Madison 3 years, 6 months
Maia 3 years, 6 months
Maisy 4 years, 3 months
Marlin 4 years, 5 months
Mischa 3 years, 8 months
Olivia 2 years, 10 months
Ollie 4 years, 5 months
Phoebe 4 years, 1 month
Quinn 4 years, 6 months
Rohana 4 years, 8 months
Rory 4 years, 10 months
Ryan 4 years, 3 months
Saffy 3 years, 10 months
Scarlett 4 years, 10 months
Stanley 3 years, 2 months
Tawny 4 years, 6 months
Thomas 4 years, 2 months
Zach 3 years, 7 months
Zachary 3 years, 6 months
Zara 3 years, 10 months

A *huge* thank you to all the children, parents and staff at Reflections Nursery

Crocodiles!

A pre-school project at Reflections Nursery, Worthing.

Context

Reflections Nursery in Worthing, West Sussex draws its inspiration from the infant-toddler centres and pre-schools of Reggio Emilia in Northern Italy. The nursery employs two full-time indoor Atelieristas (or artists) and a part-time outdoor Atelierista. The Senior Atelierista, Angela Chick visited Reggio Emilia on study tour in 2010 and senior management at the nursery have attended many such study tours. Children at Reflections have the opportunity to regularly engage in long-term project work, usually inspired by their own interests.

The 'crocodile' project in the Pre-school Atelier (or art studio) covered the period from July to September 2010.

At Reflections long-term project work often involves a number of children dipping in and out of the project owing to the high proportion of part-time attendance. During the summer the four year old children in the pre-school section were preparing to go to school whilst the three year old children were moving into the section from a younger section of the nursery; these transitions affected the trajectory of the project.

The work on crocodiles directly involved about fifty children; twenty-five of whom were present for the first six weeks and twenty for the second half of the project, with three children present throughout the entire three months. This change in protagonists created two phases to the work.

The project began, when in the summer of 2010, the children's role-play conversations in the pre-school rooms tended to include a crocodile as the ultimate 'baddie'. At this time, Angela had the opportunity to inherit a taxidermy crocodile skull and brought it into the Atelier as a 'provocation'.

"snap! snap! snap! snap! snap! snap! snap! snap! snap! snap! snap!" Harry

Investigating the Crocodile

The skull frequently featured in small group discussion and the children began observational drawing of the crocodile head in July. For the next three months the children would revisit drawing the head, learning observational skills and ways of working with different media.

At first they observed by simply looking at the crocodile skull. Children drew the skull with pencil, ink, charcoal, pastel, fine liner pens, felt tips and crayon. At each stage the children talked about the different properties of the medium they were using and children shared their learning with each other.

Angela chose to provide further provocations to support the children's interest and projected documentaries featuring crocodiles onto the wall in the Atelier. Children could see how the crocodile walked, swam and fed as well as where it lived and who shared its habitat. We used the overhead projector to cast images of crocodiles and swamps onto the Atelier wall each day - the room oozed 'crocodileness'. The documentaries provided new information which gave the children a deeper understanding of crocodile life and prompted role-play with children enacting the life of the crocodile.

We provided photographic images so children could observe certain details such as the eyes, teeth and scales. Using microscopic images the children made close observations comparing crocodile scales with their own skin and with snakeskin (which hangs from the Atelier ceiling). In their drawing children took great care to include detail of the eyes and eyelids, making conscious decisions about each line. They were sharing their thoughts and advice with each other about how to observe closely.

Following further close observational drawing we chose to introduce clay as a medium. Children enjoyed modelling the crocodile skull and making clay teeth and scales in three dimensions.

"did you buy it at the shop?" Aidan

"you're not allowed to shoot animals are you? and maybe someone shooted the crocodile, and that's how he's dead" Amelie P

After some time, the children expressed interest in depicting the crocodile using paint but realised we didn't have the appropriate colours. They set about mixing powder paints to create their own palette. The children spent days creating beautiful hues and became adept at making a very specific 'crocodile green', which they chose for the front cover of this project book.

The children were beginning to ask questions about what was inside a crocodile, so Angela sourced a crocodile model showing a cross-section of the skeleton and organs. The children constructed the model together, naming each piece. Elliot and Angela shared a conversation about the crocodile's lungs, which was extended by other practitioners in the pre-school section by introducing books on anatomy and how our bodies work. Having realised that a crocodile shared some of the same internal organs as humans, the children began to make a deeper personal connection that later became apparent in their role play.

One of the parents from the setting brought in a tortoise egg. Angela introduced this to the children without saying where it had come from and they immediately decided it must be a crocodile's egg. Even Thomas, whose mother had brought in the egg, believed it to have come from a crocodile. They each had the chance to hold the egg and then chose to draw it.

The crocodile documentaries projected onto the Atelier wall gave the children an understanding that crocodiles aren't always the 'baddies' and that they too have enemies to watch out for. When the physical image of animals was projected directly onto the children they took on the personality of whichever animal was projected. They noted the contradiction between tough and tender, as they observed crocodiles carrying their babies in their mouths and the 'naughty' lizard who would sneak in and steal the crocodile eggs.

Discussion of crocodile enemies developed into storytelling and the children created drawings to support their stories. The storytelling was incorporated into their role play and they would tell each other the stories whilst some would act them out, becoming the different animals and different characters.

"maybe a fire dragon breathed on it and killed it"
Aoife about why the crocodile is dead

Becoming the Crocodile

During one of their rhythm & movement sessions, the children focused on how to walk and turn like a crocodile, making careful and considered movements. The Atelier soon became a crocodile swamp and children chose fabrics such as green silks and satins, dark green velvets, brown cotton and organza, to create an imaginary world for their amphibious friends. Children became the crocodiles themselves, draped in swamp coloured fabrics and inhabiting dens they had constructed. They would move around the Atelier keeping a watchful eye on the documentary as they carefully stalked their prey.

In August a group of younger children joined the pre-school section as the older children left for school. Noticing the dens and role play of the older children they immediately adopted a more physical approach to the project. The younger children didn't want to sit down and draw the crocodile they wanted to *become* the crocodile.

Further Crocodile Observation

Working in groups, the older children had some time to share with the younger ones and they took this time to impart their wisdom of crocodiles and the observational skills they had acquired. We noted that they had also acquired the tools to teach each other.

The project took a different turn when Arden & Charlie, who had spent a full three months on the project began to introduce torchlight into the crocodile dens and used the overhead projector to illuminate the wall with crocodile shadows. This led onto a new project proposal to examine the properties of light.

A RETROSPECTIVE TIMELINE NOTES BY ANGELA CHICK

PROVOCATION
· Angela brings in a crocodile head as a provocation

OBSERVATIONAL DRAWING
group work; Maisy draws her crocodile; Aoife uses ink; drawing from a projected image; the documentary is introduced

child-initiated ROLE PLAY
children observe animals in the documentary + mimic their actions

further OBSERVATIONAL DRAWING
younger children join us and begin to draw; Lachlan draws his first crocodile; children draw the eyes, mouth + teeth

CLAY
children use clay to create teeth and scales of crocodiles

OBSERVATIONAL DRAWING continues
clay work leads on to drawing scales; Cordelia's scales; Amelie's scales

COLOUR MIXING + PAINTING
children realise they need to make their own crocodile green and begin to mix colours

ANATOMY
after looking at outside of croc. children begin to ask whats inside; Arden + Elliot have 2 fascinating interactions with croc. model

FRIENDS + FAMILY
children continue talking about friends and family; Thomas' mum brings in tortoise egg

STORYTELLING
children tell stories, I record them, they illustrate them; Aoife's story

MOVEMENT
children move from physical movement in role play to capturing movement with a drawn line

HOMES + DENS
children create homes for the crocodile using sticks, natural resources + fabrics - CHILDREN BEGIN TALKING ABOUT LIGHT

COLLABORATIVE DRAWING
children draw crocodile homes together, combining their perceptions

NEW PROJECT PROPOSAL?
children begin investigating light (obs. of Arden making shadows with overhead projector and crocodile head)

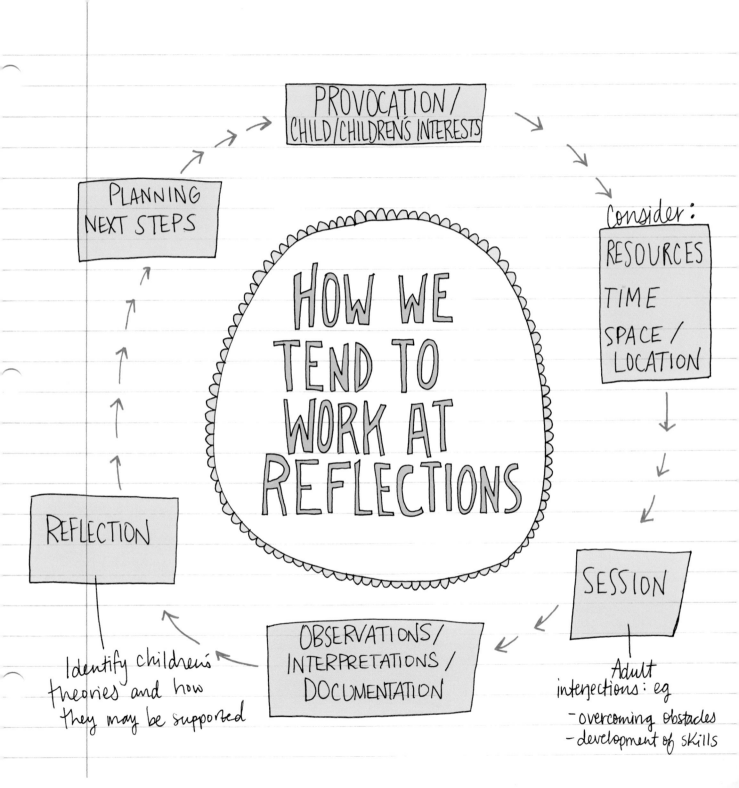

"once children are helped to perceive themselves as authors and inventors, once they are helped to discover the pleasures of inquiry, their motivation and interest explode."

Loris Malaguzzi, Reggio Emilia

"crocodiles look like this..."
Gabrielle snapping her hands together and giggling

+ + + +

"snap! snap! snap! snap! snap! snap! snap! snap! snap! snap! snap! snap! snap! snap! snap! snap! snap! snap! snap! snap!"

Katie running around snapping her crocodile jaw, clapping her hands

provocation

"he feels rough" Mischa
"verrrrry rough" Aoife

"can i *draw* the crocodile?" Cordelia

"i saw a crocodile at Drusillas!" Zach

"i'm doing teeth at the bottom and at the top" Ryan

"it's teeth are jaggy" Arden

Rohana 4 years, 8 months

observational drawing

"i'm looking at him and drawing his pointy teeth" Aoife
"i'm gonna draw all of it, 'cos i see all of it" Tawny

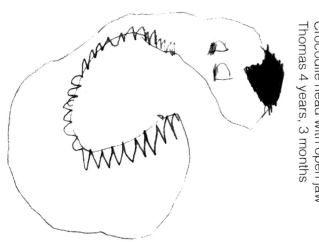

Crocodile head with open jaw
Thomas 4 years, 3 months

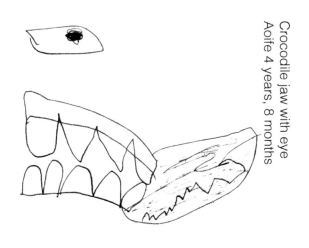

Crocodile jaw with eye
Aoife 4 years, 8 months

"that crocodile looks a bit funny to me,
he's not got any body, it's just his head" Phoebe

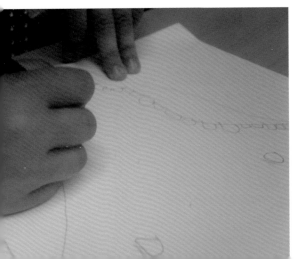

"**we're** deciding about nostrils. Ryan says there's 2 nostrils and 2 nostrils. I don't know if those ones are nostrils as well" **Finn**

group work

Crocodile with eye and four nostrils
Finn 4 years, 3 months

"i can do that!" Lachlan
"can you help?" Harry

Crocodile in four different ways
Rohana 4 years, 9 months

Cordelia came into the Atelier on one of her first visits to the pre-school section. She sat down and began to observe the other children drawing the crocodile head. She started to draw and an older child, Rohana said, "You need to look when you draw, you can't just make it up."

Weeks later, Cordelia was drawing the crocodile's head again, when a younger child, James joined the group. Cordelia observed James drawing and not looking closely at the crocodile's head and said to James, "You have to look at it, don't make it up."

"are you looking Ashlei? find the spots on the picture"
Katie encouraging a younger child to observe what she is drawing

"we don't want to scribble with them, just little lines"
Tawny explaining to the younger children how to use a fine liner pen

"you don't smash it down, you draw gently with it"
Thomas explaining to Zach how to use a fine liner pen

Crocodile head with open jaw
Tawny 4 years, 6 months

"i've done a *brilliant* picture of the crocodile!" Thomas

Crocodile head with open jaw
Katie 4 years, 4 months

Crocodile head with open jaw
Thomas 4 years, 2 months

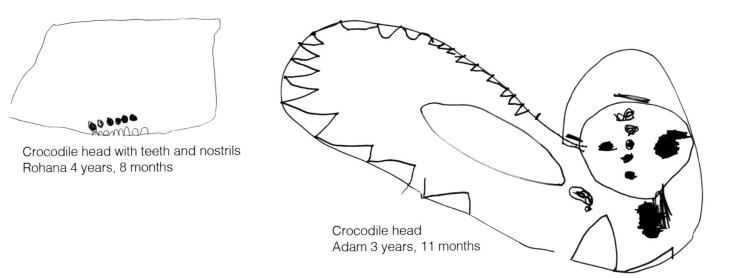

Crocodile head with teeth and nostrils
Rohana 4 years, 8 months

Crocodile head
Adam 3 years, 11 months

"how do i do it?" Kyran asking an older child how to draw a crocodile

"i know it doesn't look like a crocodile but that's how Maddie drawed it"
Katie explaining Maddie's drawing to another child

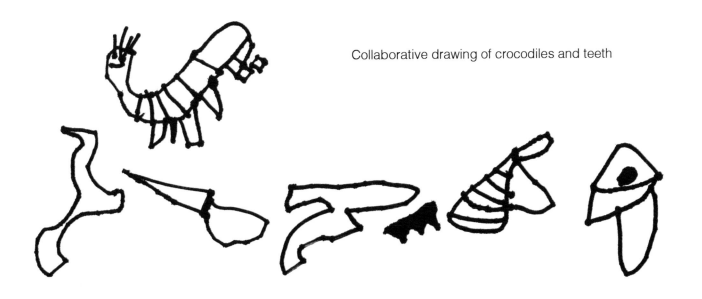

Collaborative drawing of crocodiles and teeth

Maisy's crocodile

Maisy came into the Atelier and began drawing the crocodile's head using a fine liner pen. She then observed the crocodile documentary as she drew the body, watching as the crocodile hunted.

Quinn observed as she drew and commented on her drawing. When she finished her line drawing, she selected some green ink and carefully filled it in with a fine brush. This was Maisy's first interpretation of the crocodile.

"now the body.
some legs. some more legs.
and now for the feet. sharpy sharp toes."
Quinn

Crocodile with legs
Cordelia 3 years, 6 months

Crocodile with friends
Cordelia 3 years, 8 months

Crocodile head
Elinor 4 years, 7 months

Crocodile head
Elinor 4 years, 6 months

"snap! snap! snappy snap!
that's how they talk!" Quinn

"Do you see what he has under his eye? Come look! It's all red!" Finn
"That's because it's a marble!" Katie
"It's not, it's an eye" Finn
"No, it's a marble" Katie
"I have to draw it now" Finn

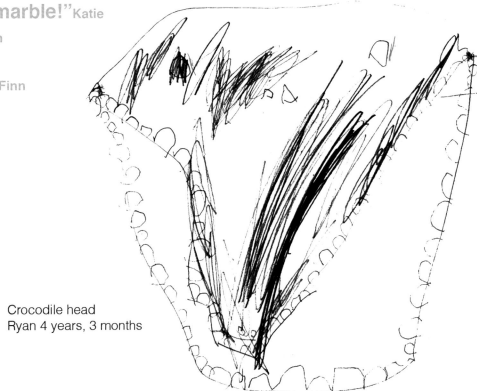

Crocodile head
Ryan 4 years, 3 months

Aoife's drawings

'Inky crocodile'
drawn with fine liner pen
and ink from imagination
Aoife 4 years, 8 months

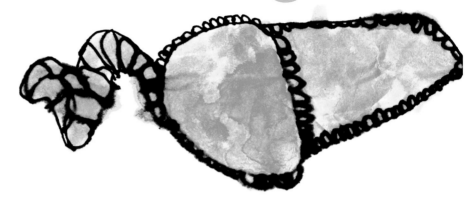

Throughout the project Aoife completed a variety of drawings of crocodiles, both from observation and imagination. She began with human-like crocodiles, standing upright. These wore bows in their hair, and had few details. As her observation increased she began to include details such as scale patterns, more teeth, and finally she began to consider perspective. It was interesting to see how her drawing developed and changed through the project, each crocodile interpretation looking completely different to the one she had drawn previously.

Crocodile mouth from the front, drawn from observation
Aoife 4 years, 9 months

Crocodile head from the side from observation
Aoife 4 years, 9 months

Crocodile head drawn from observation Aoife 4 years, 7 months

'Crocodile Princess' drawn from imagination
Aoife 4 years, 7 months

'A crocodile and a baby' drawn from imagination
Aoife 4 years, 9 months

Crocodile head drawn from observation
Aoife 4 years, 8 months

Large scale collaborative drawing of a crocodile from a projected image

drawing from a projected image

As the observational drawing continued, Angela noticed the children were choosing to work on a small scale. To introduce drawing on a larger scale the overhead projector was used to first project images of crocodiles onto the wall for the children to draw, and then to project images of the children's drawings onto the wall. They worked together to trace the lines of the pictures.

watching the documentary

Ela seeing a pelican on the screen. "A seagull!"
Kyran: "no, i think it's a bird!"
Ela: "no! it's a seagull"
Ela: "a chicken! 'cos he's got that on there" Ela strokes her throat referring to the Pelican's beak pouch

"crocodiles!!!" Georgius

"they kick dirt! stop kicking dirt in my eye!" Quinn
"why is the baby lizard under the dirt?" Lachlan

"i saw the crocodile's big spiky back" Lachlan
"crocodiles! there's the crocodile!" Kyran

"it's a crocodile. they don't have crocodiles at Drusillas.
that's like your crocodile!" Gabrielle (looking at the documentary)

"i like these crocodiles i do" Zachary

Lachlan was in the Atelier watching the documentary about crocodiles. He would often move toward the screen, and watch the film projection move across the front of his body.

One day his attention was captured by the birds on the screen. He moved closer and began to move his arms to stretch across the projection screen. As the birds flew, he flapped his arms moving back and forth across the screen. He mimicked the slow flapping movement, and would speed up when he saw a crocodile come onto the screen.

"i'm a birdy!"

"flap flap flappy"

"you crocodiles can't get me"

"crocodiles can't get birdies"

"oh no look! it's a crocodile!"

Lachlan
and the projector

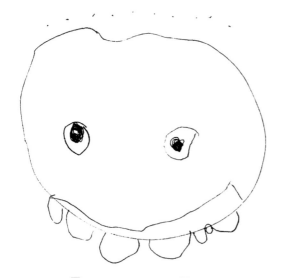
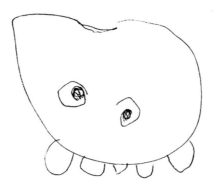
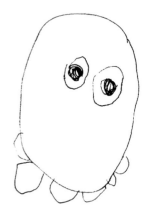

Three crocodile heads
Lucas 4 years, 9 months

role play

When the younger children joined the group the role-play developed further as they got more involved in the physical aspects of the project. Whether this meant they were becoming animals they saw on the documentary, or making families of crocodiles. They were extremely observant of the crocodile's behaviour in its habitat, and mixed reality with fantasy often including crocodiles and mermaids in their role-plays.

"i'm a crocodile i can be snapping you and eating you" Ela
"i'm a crocodile and i can eat the mermaids all up" Ela

"i'm making crocodile pie for Angela" Arden
"i want to make crocodile pie as well" Charlie
"i'm making crocodile pasta" Arden
"peppers? green peppers. broccoli!" Arden
"Arden, we could have some carrots" Charlie
"sausages and bacon" Arden
"aah, i love bacon" Charlie

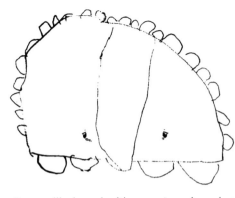

Crocodile head with snout and scales
Lucas 4 years, 10 months

"I'm being quick because the hippo is so much to get me" **Ela**
"I'm going to eat you because I have a big mouth" **James**
"I'm going to eat YOU!" **Ela**
"You're not a scary crocodile" **Gabrielle**
"No, I'm a hippo" **James**
"Chomp chomp" **Ela**
"A lizard!" **James (seeing a lizard on the projector screen)**
"Let's eat some eggs then" **Ela (as the lizard on screen eats the crocodile eggs)**
"Let's!" **James**
"Let's eat Angela then, because we are nasty hippos" **Ela**
"Hippo! Hippo!" **Ela**
"Hippo is just here washing his hands for snack" **James**
"Have a crocodile snack hippo" **Ela**
"Hippo is back. I'm gonna be a hippo now" **James (re-entering)**
"I'm like the crocodile in Peter Pan!" **Gabrielle**
"We're eating the crocodiles!" **Ela**
"Eat! Eat! Eat! Snap!" **James**

further
observational drawing...

The children role playing as they mimicked the animals they watched on a crocodile documentary projected in the room.

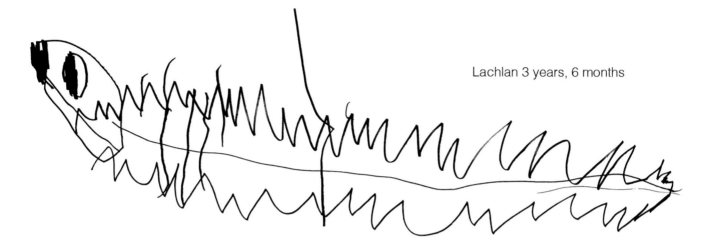

Lachlan 3 years, 6 months

"these are the snappy snappy snap you teeth"Lachlan

'Crocodile teeth' by Lachlan 3 years, 7 months

Lachlan

When Lachlan entered the Atelier, he sat down and said, "I can't draw a crocodile". I asked him if we could try. We looked at the crocodile head together, and talked about which bits he wanted to concentrate on. He was keen on the crocodile's "snappy" mouth, as he called it. He began by drawing a long line across the bottom of the page. As he finished the line he began drawing zig zags across the top and bottom of the line. "These are the snappy snappy snap you teeth!"

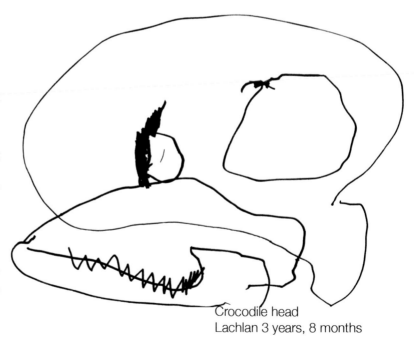

Crocodile head
Lachlan 3 years, 8 months

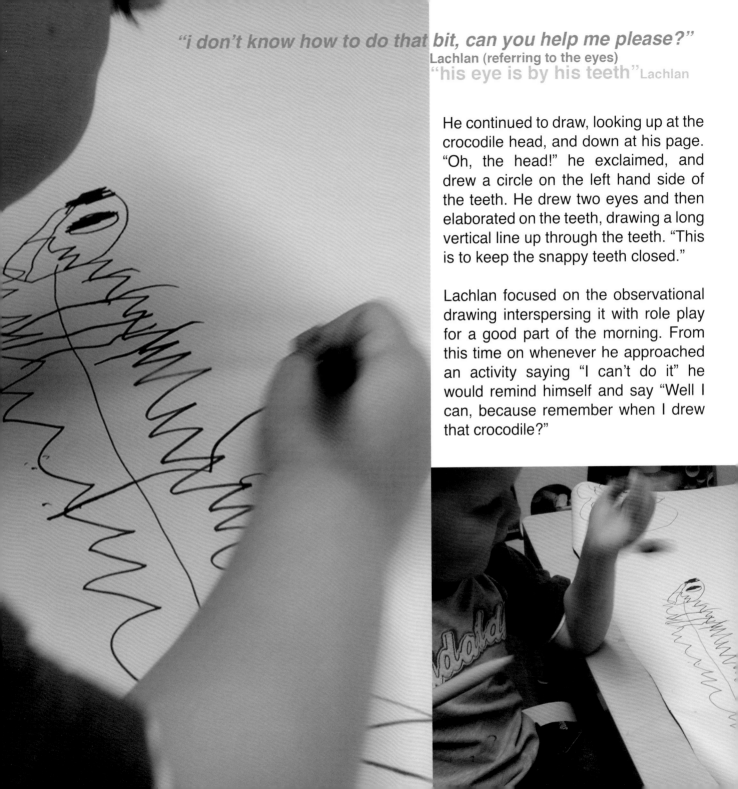

"i don't know how to do that bit, can you help me please?"
Lachlan (referring to the eyes)
"his eye is by his teeth" Lachlan

He continued to draw, looking up at the crocodile head, and down at his page. "Oh, the head!" he exclaimed, and drew a circle on the left hand side of the teeth. He drew two eyes and then elaborated on the teeth, drawing a long vertical line up through the teeth. "This is to keep the snappy teeth closed."

Lachlan focused on the observational drawing interspersing it with role play for a good part of the morning. From this time on whenever he approached an activity saying "I can't do it" he would remind himself and say "Well I can, because remember when I drew that crocodile?"

eyes

Aoife 4 years, 8 months

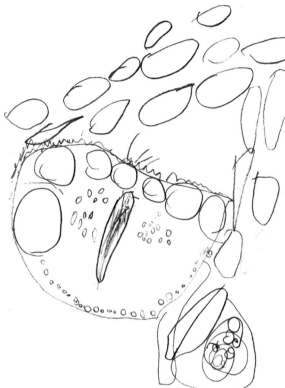

"he's got fierce eyes" Katie

"i'm trying to do the eye bumps"
Rohana looks closely and concentrates

"i want to do his eyeball first" Adam

"i'm doing the bottom. is that a diamond in his eye?" Ashlei

"he has one red eye and one black" Amelie C.
"no he hasn't" Aoife
"turn him 'round and you can see it" Amelie C.
"it changes when you turn it" Aoife
"yeah, it does" Amelie C.

Leading on from Lachlan's comment about the eyes of the crocodile, Angela decided to further develop observational drawing by providing close up photographs of crocodile eyes for the children to observe and draw.

"i'm doing the pupil" Scarlett

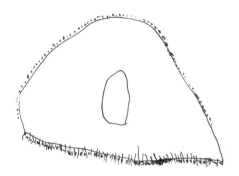
Rohana 4 years, 8 months

Marlin 4 years, 5 months

Elinor 4 years, 6 months

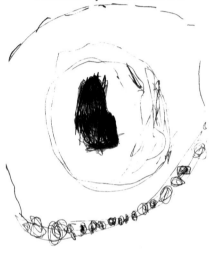
Scarlett 4 years, 10 months

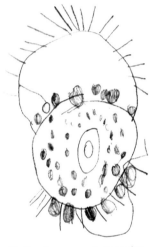
Katie 4 years, 4 months

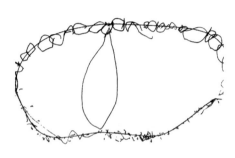
Madison 3 years, 6 months

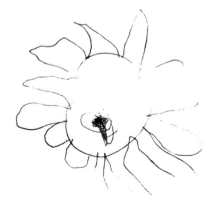
Thomas 4 years, 3 months

Katie 4 years, 3 months

Maia 3 years, 6 months

mouth and teeth

The ongoing fascination with the crocodile's mouth and teeth led us to examine a series of crocodile and alligator teeth as well as shark, sheep and human teeth.

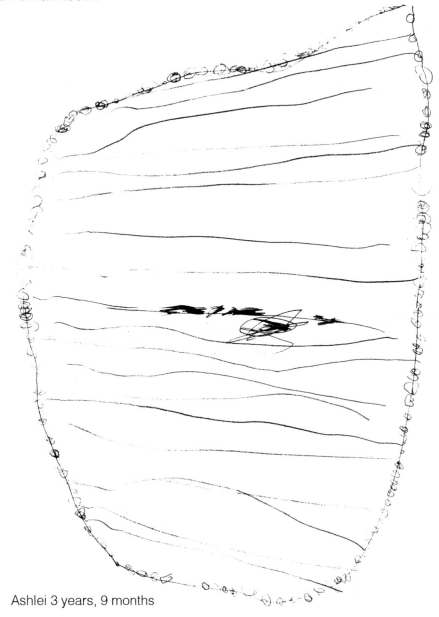

Ashlei 3 years, 9 months

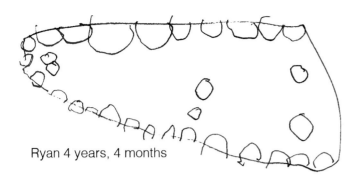

Ryan 4 years, 4 months

Cordelia 3 years, 7 months

"i can see his spiky teeth" Cordelia

"Angela, look at my big teeth" Arden

Ollie 4 years, 6 months

"i spent a long time on the teeth" Ben

Elinor 4 years, 7 months

"do his teeth!" Emily

Frankie 3 years, 1 month

"my crocodile with his snappy, snappy teeth" Elliot

Finn 4 years, 3 months

Quinn 4 years, 7 months

"i'm making crocodile teeth" Arden

"i'm making lots of teeth. i need a knife to cut these teeth up" Madison

"cut it into little bits" Charlie

After drawing the teeth, we chose to explore three-dimensional work with clay.

The children created their own impression of crocodile teeth from clay. At the same time we introduced various clay tools.

making teeth from clay

clay scales

The children made comparisons between crocodile scales, the snakeskin on the Atelier ceiling, and our own skin. They then experimented with clay to achieve similar textures.

Crocodile scales:
"it's a bit light"**Emily**

"it's soft and it's nearly turning black"**Harry**

"it's rough, it's dark"**Amelia**

"it's soft"**Elinor**

"it's black and white"**Cordelia**

"a snail skin because it has the same colour"**Aoife**

"it looks like different lines"**Amelie**

Snake skin:
"bubble wrap"**Elinor**

"a big circle"**Harry**

"I can't tell you"**Emily**

"it's got shapes like rectangles"**Maddie**

"it's spotty"**Maddie**

"it's different"**Cordelia**

"scales, circle shapes, they get bigger, then smaller and smaller"**Katie**

"circles, some big big, then little"**Rory**

Our skin:
"yellow"**Thomas**

"soft"**Quinn**

"it's like grey"**Arden**

"brown"**Ashlei**

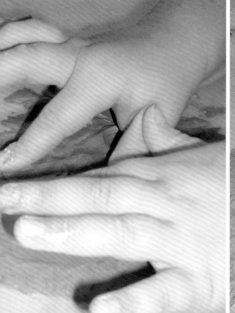

'Crocodile man' by Katie 4 years, 3 months

"do you know what i like about animal's scales? all the little bits." Aidan

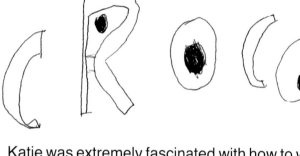

Katie was extremely fascinated with how to write the word 'crocodile' during the project. She observed Angela's writing on a display board and asked for help to copy it. These were her interpretations.

She also began to draw patterns of scales and, after the clay work, this led us back to observational drawing once again, this time looking at scales.

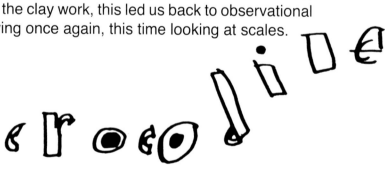

'Scales' by Katie 4 years, 4 months

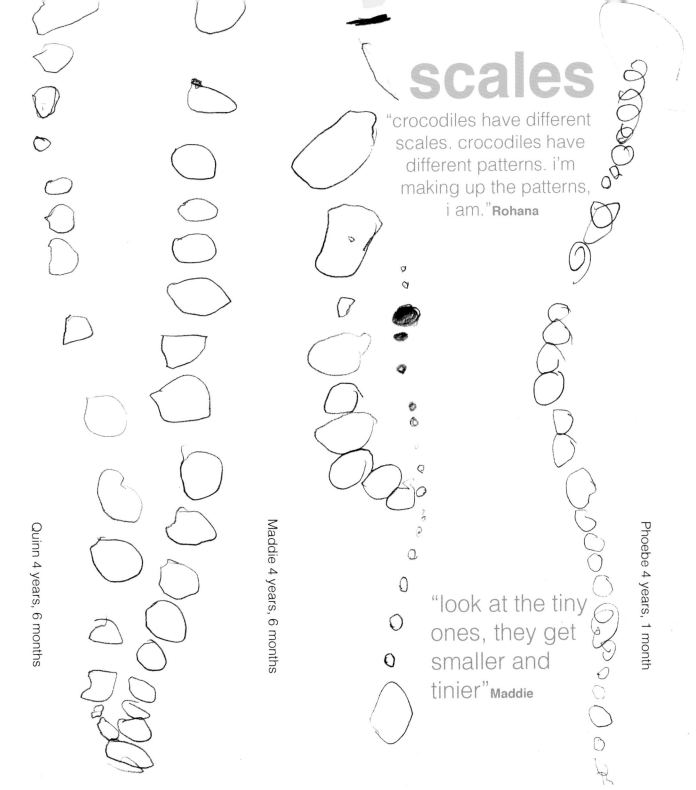

scales

"crocodiles have different scales. crocodiles have different patterns. i'm making up the patterns, i am." **Rohana**

"look at the tiny ones, they get smaller and tinier" **Maddie**

Quinn 4 years, 6 months

Maddie 4 years, 6 months

Phoebe 4 years, 1 month

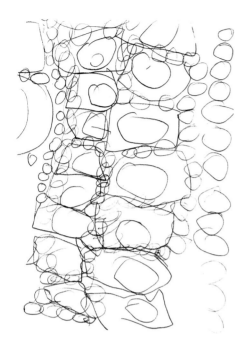

Gabrielle 3 years, 11 months

Maddie 4 years, 6 months

Aoife 4 years, 8 months

"he's scaley"
Frankie

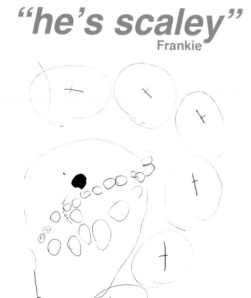

Ashlei 3 years, 8 months

Amelie 4 years, 8 months

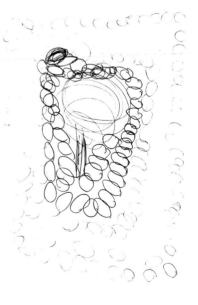

Cordelia 3 years, 7 months

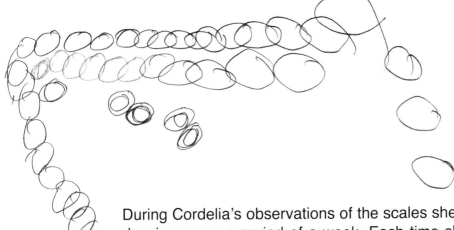

During Cordelia's observations of the scales she created a series of drawings over a period of a week. Each time she drew the scales, she depicted them completely differently. She observed the older children as they drew, which influenced the variety of styles in her drawing. She experimented with different weights of line and various shapes. She created one drawing which resembled a web of linked, small shapes. On another drawing, she used quick shading to fill in the shapes of the scales. She combined this with small round spots. She also experimented with fine line circles, and a small amount of colour, petering out into pencil lines.

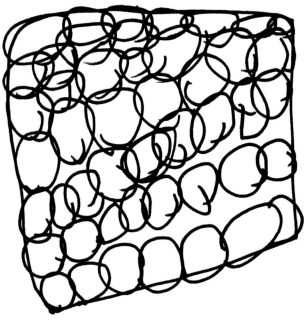

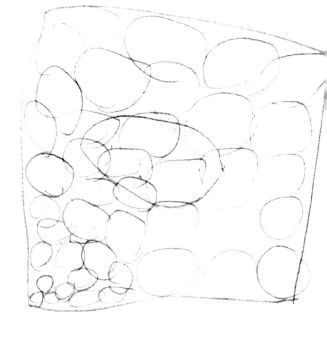

An interesting contrast can be seen between Cordelia's (previous page) and Amelie P.'s drawings of scales. Amelie P. made a series of three drawings, exploring a similar shape and quality. Each time, she worked alone, unlike Cordelia, and it was rare that she would share her drawings with other children. Amelie P. experimented with encasing the scales in a box shape. She used pencil, and fine liner pens to create her drawings. In two of her drawings a larger shape featured in the middle, which closely resembled the magnified pattern on the scale plate of a crocodile.

We saw Cordelia exploring different styles, whilst Amelie refined her own style.

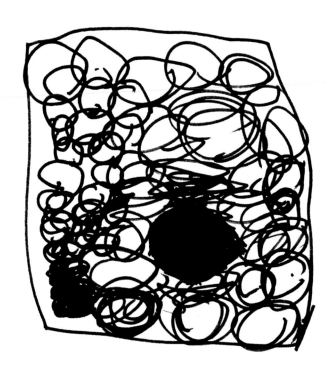

painting + colour mixing

After observing scales, the children talked a lot about the colour of a crocodile. They explored the Atelier for the perfect shade of green but were unable to find it. This led them to set about making their own 'crocodile green' by colour mixing with paints. Different green paint swatches were brought in for provocation and to help the children find their perfect colour. The children explored this many times over, each time demonstrating new knowledge and understanding of colour theory. They worked on large sheets of paper and did collaborative paintings to show off their colours. They applied colour theory to other areas of the project such as the crocodile fabrics.

first experiments + further experiments

"i put more blue and it goes darker"

Emily sharing her colour mixing observations with her friends

"blue and yellow for green i think"

Ella choosing her colours

In the first investigation of colour mixing the children were given free rein of the colours, and chose to use blue, yellow, red and white powder paints to create green. Angela thought it was important for them to use powder paints rather than ready-mixed as this offered measurement and calculation opportunities and allowed them to achieve truer colours. Not only did they have to consider the amount of powder paint they used, but also how much water was needed for their colours. After some quick experimenting, they were able to ascertain that the red was not needed. Many of the children chose to experiment with blue and white. Few of them used yellow in this stage.

When we returned to colour mixing the children remembered their earlier experiments using blue and yellow, and this time created an array of beautiful hues. They mixed some lovely dark, swampy greens all the way up the palette to very delicate pastel greens and pale yellows that reflected the crocodile's scales in the sunshine.

"mix it! mix it! mix it!" Quinn

"crocodiles aren't *blue*, they're *green!*"
Aoife looking around the table at all the blue paint

"some yellow on the end of his nose" Scarlett

"mine's green for the scaley crocodile" Zach

"do you remember when we mixed yellow and blue and white together?"Kai

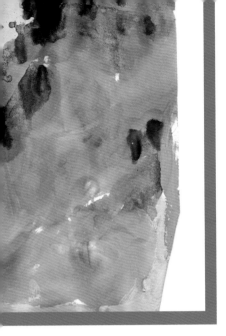

Arden's crocodile colours

Arden was working in the Atelier colour mixing. He began by scooping a large amount of yellow powder paint into his pot. He added water then made a mark on the page comparing it with the colour swatches that were out for provocation. He then added in a small amount of blue, mixed it up, and made a second mark on the page. He carried on mixing like this until he had a dark blue-green in his pot then said, "there's no more green." He began adding yellow back into the dark green, each time he said "I'm adding yellow and it's going lighter". As he mixed, he carried on making different marks on the page. He smiled each time he made a new colour. He continued with this activity for nearly 30 minutes staying completely focused. Once he put down the colour mixing, he looked up and saw some fabrics which had just arrived. He asked to have the "black one" when he was told there was no black, he said "the dark greeny." An adult asked him how he could make the "dark greeny" into a lighter green. He said "you need to put yellow." He picked up a lighter green fabric and put it against the dark green. "You can't mix them" he said, and then pretended to be a crocodile as he draped himself in the dark green fabric, creeping around the room.

"crocodile colours!" Arden

"i'm adding more yellow and mine's light"

Arden says as he mixes the colour that becomes the front cover

"i wonder what's inside its tummy" **Quinn**

"how can we find out?" **Angela**

"ermmm, i don't know"**Quinn**

anatomy

"**what's that?**"Elliot

"**those are the lungs**"Angela

"**what for?**"Elliot

"**take a deep breath, see your chest go out?**"Angela

"**we have those?!**"Elliot

"**here in our bellies? for breathing!**"Elliot

"a skeleton! we have skeletons too but you can't see them. this is where he eats it and it goes all the way through down to his tail. he's not eating it, it's stuck. snap! snap!"**Arden**

Throughout the explorations of the exterior of the crocodile the children asked questions about what was inside. Angela was able to source an x-ray crocodile model and the children worked together to put the small parts together using photographic instructions. The children found this model really exciting as they could finally see what a crocodile looked like inside. Some of the children reacted to the crocodile in different ways.

"we've got our head together with our neck so where is the crocodile's neck?"**Tawny**

Arden:

Arden was in the Atelier exploring the new crocodile model. He put his hand in its mouth, touched the different textures on the model and then when he saw through into its stomach, he put a pencil in and looked to see if it had gone through to the belly.

Arden was looking at the crocodile model on another occasion when he picked up a torch, and shone it on the outside of the crocodile. He looked closely to see the inside light up. He then shone the torch inside the mouth of the model and repositioned it over and over until he found what he believed to be the optimum angle. He then turned the model to see the side of it, and checked to see if it had lit up. He spent a long time trying to get the light in the right position to see into the crocodile's stomach.

Elliot:

Elliot explored the model for a few minutes before placing a sheep's jaw along the tail. He then picked up the taxidermy crocodile head and put it in place of the model's head saying, "Don't chomp me!" He carried on playing with his created crocodile moving it around the table and rearranging the different pieces to make new creations.

friends + + +

After exploring the crocodile model some children asked where crocodile babies came from. They continued to observe the documentary and showed continued interest in the crocodile's friends and crocodile eggs.

These are the friends of the crocodile the children had invented. These friends help take care of the crocodiles.

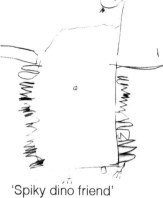

'Spiky dino friend'
by Ryan 4 years, 4 months

"in an egg" **Rohana**

'Dinosaur man' by Katie 4 years, 5 months

'Angry naughty man who
looks after the crocodile' Amelie 4 years, 9 months

"oh lizard! don't eat my baby eggs!" **Aoife**

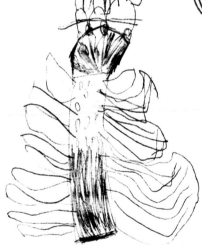

'His buggy-bug friend' by Rohana 4 years, 8 months

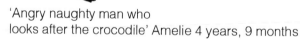

"hello baby, come with mummy" **Cordelia**

"*baby crocodiles! be careful!*
the mummy has it in her mouth!" **Aoife**

'This is the crocodile and that is his egg"
Saffy 3 years, 11 months

family

Thomas' mum brought in a tortoise egg to share. All the children, including Thomas, were convinced it must be a crocodile's egg. They looked closely at it and drew what they saw.

"you see, this is a baby crocodile coming out of the egg" **Angus**

"got to wait 'til it cracks" **Adam**

"the baby is in that and then it cracks and the baby comes out"
Saffy carefully holding the egg

"the little crocodiles come out of eggs! it's so cute! it's so cute!"
Kyran explaining to his friend

"the egg is all dirty" **Amelia**

"now i've got to draw the dirty bits on this egg"
Quinn drawing spots on his egg

"you need to be *so* careful with it" **Aoife**

"the eggs crack and then they walk into the sea and in the cave to see their mummy and daddies" **Maddie**

Amelia 4 years, 10 months

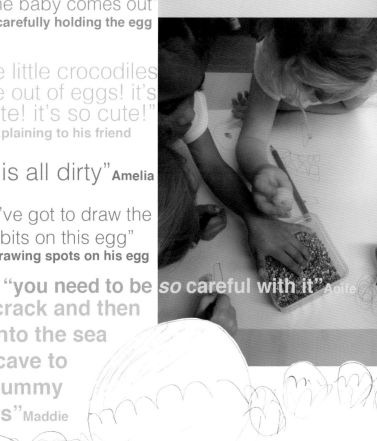

Amelie 4 years, 4 months

Storytelling

After continued interest in the friends, family and enemies of the crocodile, the children decided to tell their own stories, which Angela recorded and the children illustrated. These stories featured 'baddies' and 'tricksters' who were not very kind to the crocodile.

Finn's story:
"Once there was a mummy crocodile and she went to fly her kite. And do you know what her kite was? It was a teddy bear kite and then it was stuck. She flew it into the tree and she was very sad and crying and then she saw a man and the man was stretching. He had stretchy legs and he got her kite and she was happy again. But there was a big, big, big scary crocodile that scared her and she ran but she was too slow, and he ate her up because she was too slow. Then she jumped on the crocodile's tongue and jumped back out and then she had a gun and killed him and that's all of my story. That's the end."

Drawing to accompany story by Aoife 4 years, 9 months

Aoife's story:
"My story is about the crocodile. One day the crocodiles were looking outside their river and the crocodiles were so happy because she saw a human thing, but it actually wasn't a human it was a big giant whale. And the big giant whale was so cross because the crocodile put his tail around and it squeezed him. And he was so cross that the whale squeezed him and the crocodile put out his snappy jaws that were so big and huge and big. A hunter was hiding behind the tree. And he put out his gun and killed the crocodile. The crocodile he wasn't killed. It wasn't a gun it was actually a special camera. The crocodile still had his snappy jaws out and he SNAPPED all of the pieces of the man and swallowed him. Because the hunter wasn't a hunter, he was a little boy. Then a real hunter went through the village and saw the pond that the crocodile lived in, and then put out his big gun and killed that crocodile's body off, except his head and that's why it's here. That's the end of my story because he ate the crocodile."

Maddie's story:
"They saw the crocodile and then they saw the cave and went into the cave 'cos they were scared, but the crocodile wasn't in it. They had to go back home but the crocodile was in it again so they went to another one but had to run and so the crocodile went into his home instead."

Further drawing to accompany story by Aoife 4 years, 9 months

"we're looking at the film to see how crocodiles move" Cordelia

"reeeeeeeeealllllllllllly slowly. i'll show you!" Decland
"it's a line of movement" Decland

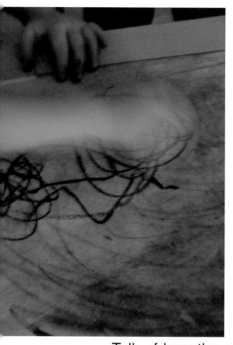

Talk of how the crocodile moved featured quite heavily throughout the entire project. Children chose to represent the movement using pastels, charcoal and pencil.

movement

drawing movement

Ashlei and Cordelia sat together watching the documentary. They both experimented with how to represent movement on paper. Cordelia was open-minded to try this.

"crocodiles don't move on the paper" Cordelia

"we can *make* them!...
this one is moving FAST!" Ashlei drawing spirals

"this crocodile is going reeeeallllllyyyy slloooooowwwww"
Ashlei slows the speed of how she draws and draws a curved line

"mine's going really slow.
reeeeaaalllly sloooooow then really fast!"
Cordelia shouts excitedly as her and Ashlei draw spirals quickly on their pages

Arden 3 years, 11 months finding special sticks the crocodile will like

Katie 4 years, 5 months sprinkling leaves over her crocodile drawing to keep him safe

Ella 3 years, 7 months sprinkling leaves

"bigger like my house" Gabrielle

"mind out, 'cos i'm gonna do a big drill" Arden

"i'm gonna do a big hammer"
Charlie working with Arden to build a house

"all done! crocodile's house!" Olivia

"we're making a special home for crocodiles"
Stanley

making a home

dens

"will you come to the crocodile home with me?" Charlie
"my crocodile eyes can't see" Arden
"we need lights" Ashlei

"maybe we could make a hippo home.
we can put these on here and then...
green first...and.."
Lachlan places fabric onto the table
"these can be the windows"
Noa holding up a bicycle tyre
"this could be the key"
Lachlan holding up a plastic stick

The children continued with their drawings, even while making dens. Quinn (4 years, 7 months) drew this before he began to make a crocodile den and said, "I forgot to do the dirt" as he watched the documentary.

"i'm just making a crocodile swamp" Aoife

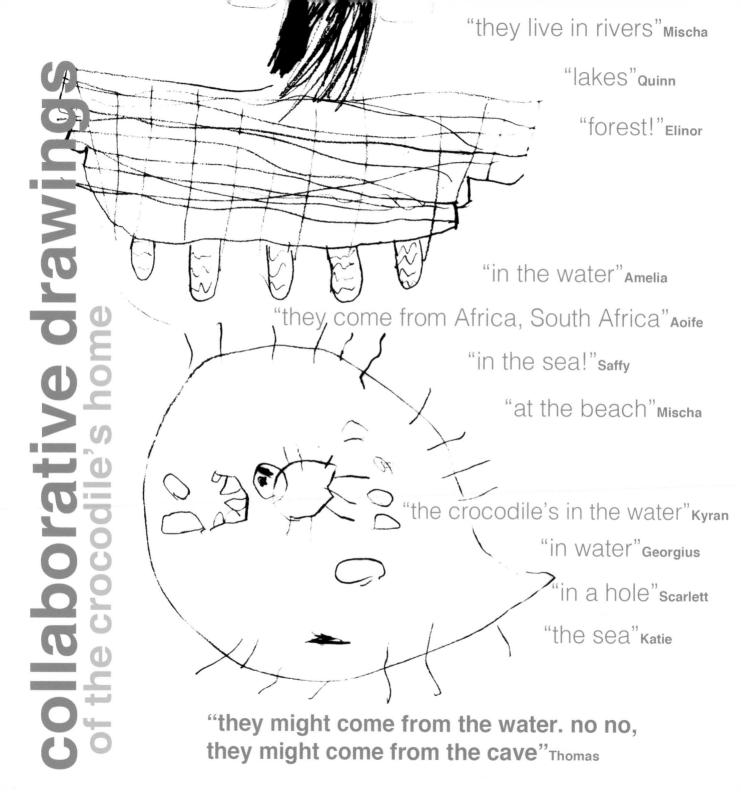

collaborative drawings
of the crocodile's home

"they live in rivers" **Mischa**

"lakes" **Quinn**

"forest!" **Elinor**

"in the water" **Amelia**

"they come from Africa, South Africa" **Aoife**

"in the sea!" **Saffy**

"at the beach" **Mischa**

"the crocodile's in the water" **Kyran**

"in water" **Georgius**

"in a hole" **Scarlett**

"the sea" **Katie**

"they might come from the water. no no, they might come from the cave" Thomas

"crocodile city" Elinor

Elinor's 4 years, 8 months
crocodile city where everything would be green

"crocodiles live in the sea and in a cave and in a forest and in a water"
Lachlan

Angela's reflections

"As a relatively new practitioner working with children, it was through this project that I found more confidence to take time to explore a subject in-depth alongside the children. I believe that the long-term nature of this project generated deep learning opportunities because it was driven by the children's motivation and interest. My role became a facilitator in overcoming obstacles.

Time is always a consideration in determining the course of a project. There were times when I felt that the project wasn't moving quickly enough but I stepped back from intervening. In fact, had we taken the time to experience things at an even slower pace I now believe it would have provided a deeper and more valuable experience for the children.

As we have noted from our project work in the past, by following the children's motivation each aspect of the project could have developed into a new strand. From the children's questions about the crocodile model we could have developed a project entirely about anatomy. When looking at each of the features (eyes, teeth, scales, etc.) we could have considered many more features and in more depth. The children particularly noted the patterns in the scales of the crocodile, drawing on their experience of an earlier project involving patterns, and we could have revisited this topic again and again.

Some children learned drawing skills and gained great confidence, such as Lachlan who originally doubted himself and his drawing capabilities but then learned that if he observes an object as he draws, he can create a wonderful likeness (which he still talks about, months after the event).

Other rooms in the section were involved in the project. By sharing my observations with team members each day these would feed into the section's weekly planning; however we reflected later on how we could have pursued different strands of the project by creating a different crocodile experience in each room. For instance, if we had been concentrating on drawing from observation in the Atelier, perhaps in the Construction Room they could have focused on building dens. In the Communication Room they could have told story after story and recorded them (as we later did in the Atelier), and made them available to share with their friends.

At the outset of the project I felt as though I could predict where things were going. Although guided by the child, I had an idea of where I wanted it to go or questions I wanted to ask. However, as the group made the transition from the older to the younger children, things became more surprising.

I noticed a new project developing when the younger children didn't get involved in the crocodile project in the same way as the older children. They would interact with each other in front of the overhead projector, noticing their shadows. Influenced by the older children they also used torches when they were in their swamp dens. This developed into another project about 'Light'."